For a m...
Lady Gord...

It was both a blessing and a curse, he thought, as she turned on the sofa to face him and a stray beam of weak sunlight caught her glorious hair again.

"Thank you for acting so promptly, Lord Edward," she said. "I had to wait four days to see Mr. Fowler the first time."

"I wouldn't have dreamed of delay." What would her hair look like down? He pictured a waterfall of coppery waves spilling over her bare shoulders, down her bare back . . . God Almighty, he had to stop doing this.

She smiled rather wryly. "Of course," she murmured. "I'm sure not."

Edward supposed there was more than one way to interpret that, but he hoped she had chosen an innocuous reason rather than the truth: that he was looking forward to the end of their association because he was far too attracted to her for his own good. In a matter of days—even hours—it would be over and she would never walk through his door again. And he would never admit to thinking about her again. Ever.

By Caroline Linden

ONE NIGHT IN LONDON
YOU ONLY LOVE ONCE
FOR YOUR ARMS ONLY
A VIEW TO A KISS

Coming Soon

BLAME IT ON BATH

CAROLINE LINDEN

One Night in London

London

The Truth About the Duke

AVON

An Imprint of HarperCollinsPublishers

AVON BOOKS
An Imprint of HarperCollins*Publishers*
10 East 53rd Street
New York, New York 10022-5299

Copyright © 2011 by P. F. Belsley
ISBN 978-0-06-202532-6
K.I.S.S. and Teal is a trademark of the Ovarian Cancer National Alliance
www.avonromance.com

First Avon Books mass market printing: September 2011

Avon Trademark Reg. U.S. Pat. Off. and in Other Countries, Marca Registrada, Hecho en U.S.A.
HarperCollins® is a registered trademark of HarperCollins Publishers.

Printed in the U.S.A.

10 9 8 7 6 5 4 3

For Rebecca
(for free)

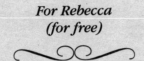

Chapter 1

The Duke of Durham was dying.

It wasn't spoken of openly, but everyone knew. With quiet steps and whispered instructions the servants were already preparing for the mourning. The solicitor had been sent for. Letters had been urgently dispatched to the duke's sons, one in the army and one in London, summoning them home. Durham himself knew his death was nigh, and until a sudden attack of heart pains the previous evening, he had been approving the funeral arrangements personally.

Edward de Lacey watched his father doze, the gaunt, stooped figure propped up on pillows in the bed as he struggled to breathe. The doctor had assured him there was no hope, and that the end was swiftly approaching. Edward would be very sorry to lose his father, but there was no question that the duke's time on earth was spent.

Durham stirred. "Charles?" he said faintly. "Is that you?"

Edward moved forward. "No, sir," he said quietly. "Not yet."

"I must . . . speak . . . to Charles," his father gasped.

"Need . . . to—" He raised one hand and clutched weakly at Edward's sleeve. "Get Charles . . . you must."

"He's on his way," promised Edward, although he wasn't sure of any such thing. He'd filled the letter to his brother with the direst language possible, but that could only have any effect after the letter found its way into Charlie's hands, and even then he might be too drunk to understand that he must come home immediately, let alone actually make the journey. Edward clasped his father's hand between his own and expressed his hope, rather than his expectation. "He will surely be here at any moment."

"I have to tell him . . ." Durham mumbled fretfully. "All of you . . ."

Edward waited, but his father just closed his eyes, looking anguished. Unwillingly, Edward felt a flicker of petty annoyance; always Charlie, the firstborn, even though he was the son who was always there when the duke wanted him. He shoved it aside. It was unworthy to think such a thought as his father sank closer and closer to mortality. "Tell me, sir," he whispered. "I will tell Charlie in the event . . ." *In the event he doesn't arrive in time.* "I will make sure he knows as soon as he arrives, if you should be asleep then."

"Yes . . ." came the duke's soft, slurred voice. "Sleep. Soon. But not . . . without . . . telling Charles . . ." He sighed, and went so still Edward feared the worst for a moment, until the faint rise of his father's chest proved him still alive.

In the utter quiet of the room a distant drumming sounded. Hooves pounding hard up the gravel drive, Edward realized, at the same moment his father bolted upright in bed. "Charles," croaked the duke, his face ashen. "Charles—is it he, Edward?"

Edward rushed to the window in time to see the rider's scarlet coat before he flashed out of sight beneath the portico in front of the house. "It's Gerard, Father."

"Ah," said Durham, slumping once more into his pillows. "A good boy, Gerard."

Edward smiled wryly at his father's masked disappointment. He was glad his younger brother, at least, was home. "I'll go fetch him right up."

"Do that," murmured Durham. "I will be glad to see him. And Charles . . . Charles will be here soon?"

"At any moment," Edward said again as he slipped through the door, then held it for the doctor to take his place in the room. He reached the top of the stairs just as his brother came running up.

"Am I too late?" demanded Gerard.

Edward shook his head.

Gerard exhaled and ran one hand over his head. His dark hair was damp with sweat, and dust covered him from head to toe. "Thank God. I've been riding all day; probably damn near killed the poor horse." He glanced at Edward. "Charlie?"

"No sign of him, as usual," muttered Edward as they walked down the hall. "Father's been calling for him for two days now."

"Well, some things never change." Gerard sighed and pulled loose a few buttons of his coat. "I should wash."

Edward nodded. "I had all the rooms prepared. But Gerard—hurry."

His brother paused on the threshold of his bedchamber. "He's really dying, then?"

It did seem incredible, even to Edward. Durham had been a vital person, every bit as robust and daring as his sons. Since the death of the duchess over twenty years ago, the household had been a preserve of male pursuits, and no one pursued them harder than Durham himself. Edward was almost eighteen before any of the brothers could outshoot their father, and they outrode him only when the doctor flatly ordered His Grace out of the saddle at the age of seventy after a bad fall injured his back.

But now Durham was eighty. He was an old man, and had been dying for the better part of a year. Gerard just hadn't seen the decline. "Yes, he's really dying," he said in answer to his brother's question. "I would be surprised if he lasts the night."

When his younger brother slipped into the sickroom a few minutes later, Edward had already returned to his post by the window. Durham had told him to wait there, to announce Charlie the moment he arrived. He wondered what his father wanted so desperately to tell Charlie; God knew Charlie hadn't cared much for anything the duke had to say for the last ten years or so, and apparently still didn't. But whatever final words Durham had for his heir, they were obviously of tremendous importance. When the duke heard the creak of the door at Gerard's entrance, he lurched up again and cried out, "Charles?"

"No, Father, 'tis Gerard." Not a trace of offense or upset marred Gerard's soft tone. He crossed to the bed and took his father's hand. "Edward wrote me some nonsense that you were ill," he said. "I came to thrash some sense into him."

"But why did you not bring *Charles*?" whispered the

duke in anguish. "Ah, lads. I have to tell Charles . . . ask his forgiveness . . ."

That was new. Edward abandoned his window post as Gerard shot him a curious look. "Forgiveness, Father?"

A tear leaked from the duke's eye, tracing a glistening path down his sunken cheek. "I must beg pardon of you all. I didn't know . . . If only I had known, in time . . . You, Gerard, will come out well enough—you always do—and Edward will have Lady Louisa . . . But Charles—Charles will not know what to do . . ."

"What do you mean?" Edward had to admire his brother's calm, even tone. The duke's demeanor was raising the hair on the back of his neck.

"Edward . . ." Durham reached feebly for him, and Edward stepped forward. He knelt beside the bed, leaning closer to hear the duke's quavering voice. "I know you would forgive me, and even know what to do . . . Forgive me, I should have told you earlier . . . before it was too late . . ."

"Told me what, Father? What is too late?" Edward fought down a surge of apprehension. Behind his back, Gerard hissed quietly at the doctor to leave.

"Tell Charles . . ." rasped the duke. An ominous rattle echoed in his breath. "Tell Charles . . . I am sorry."

"You will tell him yourself when he arrives," Edward said. Gerard crossed the room in two strides, but shook his head as he gazed out the window facing the road from London. Edward turned back to his father. "Rest yourself, sir."

"Rest!" Durham coughed, his entire body convulsing. "Not until you grant me forgiveness . . ." His blue eyes were almost wild as he stared at Edward.

"I—" Edward stared. "Yes. Whatever it is, Father, I forgive you."

"Gerard!" cried the duke.

"You know I will forgive you, sir." Gerard had come back to the bed. "But for what sin?" Even he couldn't joke now. "I tried . . ." The duke's voice faded. "The solicitor . . . will tell . . . Sorry . . ." Durham never spoke with any clarity again. He slipped in and out of consciousness the rest of the day and into the evening, and finally breathed his last in the darkest hour of the night. Edward slumped in the chair next to the bed and listened to the silence when the tortured breathing finally stopped. Gerard had been sitting with him until a few hours ago, when he finally went to bed, exhausted from his hard ride. The doctor had long since dozed off, and Edward saw no reason to wake him, either. Durham had lived a long and full life, and suffered the last several months of it in pain. It was a kindness that he was at peace now.

Slowly, he levered himself upright in the chair and leaned forward to take his father's hand. It was still warm; it felt just as it had for the last year or so, when the wasting illness had taken hold of the duke and shriveled his flesh. But there was no strength in it, and never would be again. "Fare thee well, Father," he said quietly, and laid the limp hand back on his father's chest.

The duke's solicitor, Mr. Pierce, arrived the following day. He had handled the Durham affairs for twenty years, as his father and grandfather had done before him. Edward was waiting in the front hall when his carriage pulled up to the steps.

"I see I should begin with condolences," Pierce said, glancing at the black crepe already on the door. "I am very sorry for your loss, my lord."

"Thank you." Edward bowed his head.

"His Grace sent full instructions, as always. I was delayed a day, gathering everything he wished me to provide you." Pierce paused. "I will be available as soon as you are ready."

"My brother, Lord Gresham, is not yet here. Captain de Lacey and I are in no hurry to proceed without him."

Pierce nodded. "As you wish, sir."

"There is just one thing." Edward raised one hand. "My father was quite agitated near the end, begging us to forgive him, but he wouldn't say for what sin. He said you would explain."

Pierce looked startled. "He didn't—he didn't tell you?"

"Tell us what?" Gerard was coming down the stairs, buttoning his scarlet jacket.

"Welcome home, Captain. My deepest sympathies," said the solicitor with a quick bow.

"Thank you, Mr. Pierce." Gerard turned to Edward. "The mysterious sin?" Edward nodded once, and Gerard fixed his penetrating gaze on Mr. Pierce again. "Do you know what Durham meant by that?" he asked in his usual direct way.

Mr. Pierce's eyes darted between the two of them. "Yes," he said. "I believe I do. I have a letter, as well as many other documents from His Grace, which will explain everything—as much as can be explained. But I think we should await Lord Gresham so that you might hear it, and the contents of His Grace's will, together."

"God only knows when Gresham will find his way out to Sussex," said Gerard. "My brother and I would like to know now."

"Yes," Edward said when the solicitor shot him a questioning look. He and Gerard had been unable to guess what Durham meant, and it was bothering Gerard as much as it was him. Over breakfast they agreed that since Durham had pushed the task onto the solicitor, it was undoubtedly some matter of inheritance. Perhaps their father had imposed some onerous conditions in his will or made some unexpected bequests—but that, of all things, was something completely in Durham's power to change, and had no need of forgiveness. They were both at a complete loss, and very impatient to know the answer.

Mr. Pierce drew in a deep breath. "His Grace wished you to hear it at once—all three of you, since it affects you all."

"Now, Mr. Pierce," snapped Gerard.

"If you please," Edward added more politely. "On this we do not wish to wait."

"Your father—"

"Is dead," said Edward. "I believe you are in my brother's employ now—at the moment."

Everyone knew Edward ran Durham, right down to which flowers were planted in the gardens. Everyone knew Charles, the new duke, wouldn't give a damn which solicitor handled his affairs. If Edward wanted to sack Pierce, Charles wouldn't lift a finger in protest. And Mr. Pierce knew just how profitable it was to handle Durham's legal affairs. He hesitated only a moment, glancing from Edward to Gerard and back.

"The trouble is," the solicitor began in a lowered voice, "it is not a well-defined problem; it stems from events many, many years ago, and unwinding the knot after so long has proven very difficult."

"What knot?" growled Gerard.

"There is a chance," said Mr. Pierce, as though choosing each word with care, "a very small, *remote* possibility, although it is impossible to ignore, that . . ."

"What?" prompted Edward sharply when the man hesitated again. This was doing nothing to ease his bad feeling about anything.

"That you—all of you, I mean—may . . . not be . . . able to receive your . . . full inheritances."

"What?"

"Explain." Edward held up one hand to quell Gerard's outburst. "Why not?"

Mr. Pierce winced at his cold tone. "His Grace was married before he wed your late mother, the duchess," he said, almost whispering. "Long ago." He paused. "He and the young lady both decided the marriage had been a rash, youthful mistake and they parted ways." Another pause. "But . . . there was no divorce."

He didn't need to say more. The implications came at Edward in a blinding rush. He looked at his brother, whose expression reflected his own dawning horror. Holy God. If Durham had been married . . . If his first wife had still survived when he married again . . . when he married *their mother* . . .

The solicitor was still speaking. "Unfortunately, recent letters received by the duke made clear this marriage was not as forgotten as His Grace had believed, and implied the woman might still be alive. His Grace expended a great deal of effort and expense trying to locate her—"

"Are you saying," said Gerard in an ominous voice, "our father was a *bigamist*?"

A fine flush of perspiration broke out on Mr. Pierce's forehead. "That has not been proved."

"But it is a distinct possibility." Gerard stabbed one finger at the man. "And you didn't tell us!"

"I was expressly ordered not to, sir!"

"What do the letters say?" demanded Edward. He felt struck numb. It was one thing for Gerard not to have known; Gerard had been on the Iberian Peninsula until two months ago, and then with his regiment at Dover. It was even understandable that Durham would have kept it from Charlie, even though he was the heir apparent. Charlie wouldn't have taken it well, or been much help in getting to the root of the problem. But his father had kept this dreadful secret from *him*, from the son who stayed at his side and managed his estates and dined with him every evening and cared for him in his final illness. Of all the people Durham might have trusted enough to confide in, Edward thought he would have been the one.

Apparently, he was wrong.

"I have brought them, as His Grace instructed." Mr. Pierce indicated his bulging satchel apologetically. "I believe he wished to take care of the problem himself and spare all three of you any uneasiness, my lord."

Great lot of good that did, thought Edward bitterly. "We'll look at them later," he said, masking his emotions with effort. The butler stepped forward at his wave.

"Thank you, my lord," said Pierce with a bow. He

followed the butler up the stairs, his relief evident in his quick step. Edward strode after his brother, who had turned and left the hall. Gerard was already pouring a drink when Edward stepped into the drawing room.

"The bloody scoundrel," muttered Gerard.

"Father, or the solicitor?" He closed the doors behind him. No need to titillate the servants further.

"Both." Gerard swallowed his brandy in one gulp and poured another. He raised one eyebrow at Edward, who shook his head. "But mostly Father, I suppose. What the bloody hell was he thinking?"

"I have no idea, and I was right here all the time."

His brother glanced at him, apology flickering in his eyes. "I didn't mean that. Just . . . What kind of fool keeps that secret?"

"A fool who doesn't want to look like one," said Edward. "Or an old fool who still thinks he can control everything."

"Bastards," Gerard said, and Edward flinched at the word spoken aloud. "We'll be bastards if this woman turns up alive. All this"—he swept one hand around to indicate the room, the house, the estate—"will go to someone else." He paused. "To whom would it go? I can't even recall."

Edward sighed, not wanting to think about that. Durham was supposed to go to Charlie. "Some distant cousin. Augustus, I suppose."

"Perhaps he's the one who sent those letters," said Gerard.

"Perhaps. Perhaps it's the woman herself. Perhaps her children. Good God," he said as the thought struck him. "You don't suppose Father had other children?"

"Wouldn't that cause a stir?" His brother gave a harsh crack of laughter. "Rather odd they haven't come forward in all this time."

"Rather odd our own father never mentioned the possibility of their existence." Edward walked to the tall windows that overlooked the lush gardens his mother had designed and planted, and he himself had maintained. He felt at home in those gardens, at peace—usually. A hot fury burned in his chest that all this might be yanked out from beneath him and given to another. He had spent his life here, doing everything that was required. He was needed here. Without Durham, what would he be, where would he go? How could he face his fiancée, Lady Louisa Halston, and tell her he was no longer Lord Edward de Lacey, brother of the Duke of Durham, but just some bastard son with no property? The scandal over his father's bigamy would be enormous. How could he ask Louisa to endure that gossip? It simply staggered the mind that Durham had kept a prior marriage secret, knowing it could have come to light at any time and upended everything in their lives. In that moment he was almost glad the duke was dead, because he would have surely doomed himself to hell for what he would say to his father now.

Gerard came up beside him. He tossed back the remainder of his drink with a flick of his wrist. "We've got to find Charlie."

"So that he might offer his sage counsel and guidance, and exert himself to deal with the problem?" Edward muttered.

Gerard gave a snort. "Hardly. But it's his problem, too—he's got even more to lose than you and I do."

"When has that mattered?" But he knew his brother was right. Of course they had to tell Charlie, and since Charlie couldn't be bothered to come to Sussex, even for his father's death, it appeared they would have to go to him. And perhaps this would actually spur their brother into some action that didn't involve personal pleasure. Perhaps that was why Durham had been so desperate to beg Charlie's pardon; he knew very well how terribly his eldest son's life would change if he were to lose his name, his title, and his fortune.

Unfortunately, for all that their father seemed to think them better equipped to cope, he and Gerard would suffer much the same fate.

Because if they couldn't disprove this shadow on their claim to Durham, they would all lose everything.

Chapter 2

They found Charlie, not in a gaming hell or a brothel, but quietly asleep in his own bed. Of course, from the number of empty wine bottles in the room and the items of female clothing that had obviously been left behind, Edward guessed it was mere chance that they'd found him alone. But still, it was convenient to have him where he ought to be.

"Get up, Charlie." Gerard strode around the bedroom, throwing open the drapes and making a great racket. Edward had stopped to soothe the worried butler and was a few steps behind. Having assured the poor man that he wouldn't be sacked for letting them disturb Lord Gresham, Edward sent the butler for some hot tea and followed, every bit as set on rousing his elder brother as Gerard was.

Charlie grunted and rolled over. "Go away," he moaned. "I'm ill."

"We can tell." Gerard picked up something from the chaise and held it up: a lady's silk stocking. "On death's doorstep, obviously."

Charlie squinted at the stocking, then closed his eyes again. "Agatha's. Only she wears violet."

"And I suppose Agatha gave you the pox or the consumption or whatever ails you."

"I have a headache, you damned idiot."

Gerard snorted. Edward gave him a quelling look. He had located a chair by now, and pulled it up beside the bed. "You'd better get well soon, Charlie. We've got a much bigger problem."

"What? Oh yes, I got your note about Father." Charlie blinked open his eyes again. "I suppose I'm too late to pay my final respects."

"Indeed," Edward said dryly. "By several days."

"I assumed as much. Well, the old man will rest in greater peace for not having had to deal with me one last time."

"On the contrary," Edward replied. "He called for you desperately in his last hours."

For a second Charlie's face went still, and not for the first time Edward wondered just what had gone on between his father and brother. But Charlie just shrugged, his expression relaxing again. He stuffed another pillow behind his back and pushed himself up a little. "Then I'll be on watch for his ghost, come to haunt me throughout eternity for denying him the pleasure of one last lecture."

"You would deserve it," said Gerard. "We had to tell him you were on your way."

"No one asked you to lie for me." Charlie shot him an insolent look. "It's just one more sin for my collection: disappointing Durham on his deathbed."

Gerard shot him a disbelieving look. "Have you lost every shred of care for our father?"

"Obviously," said Charlie with a twist to his mouth.

"But if he's dead and buried already, and long past any groveling for forgiveness on my part, why must you rouse me from my sickbed?"

"You don't look terribly ill to me," muttered Gerard.

"Stop it," Edward snapped. There was a feverish brightness to Charlie's eyes, and when a footman slipped in with the tea tray, Charlie sat up to pour a cup, and sipped with alacrity. Unless the tea in the pot was really brandy, it wasn't his usual behavior. Edward got up and closed the door securely behind the servant. "Charlie, I would be glad to leave you to your suffering, but you haven't got time to be ill now. We—all three of us—have a serious problem, and time and secrecy are vital."

Charlie leaned back against his pillows, looking tired again. "What is it? I'm sure I'll be no help at all in solving it."

"It turns out Father had a bit of a secret," Edward said grimly, ignoring his brother's attempt to dodge all responsibility. "A clandestine marriage some sixty years ago. He and the woman decided it had been a mistake and went their separate ways."

"Really?" Charlie smiled in a vaguely bitter way. "Who knew the old dog had it in him?"

"He never divorced her."

Charlie just looked at him, eyebrows raised.

"And he had no proof she died."

It took a moment, then Charlie's eyes closed. "Ever?"

"Ever," Edward confirmed. "Let alone before April of 1774." When Durham had wed his duchess, their mother.

For a long moment everyone was silent. "Well," said

Charlie quietly. "That is a bit of a problem, isn't it?"

"Not for you, clearly," exclaimed Gerard. "You've lost a dukedom, and all you can say is, 'that's a bit of a problem'? Are you mad? Don't you understand what's at stake here?"

"Gerard," said Edward in warning. Charlie was still sprawled across his pillows as before, one arm draped over his forehead, but his hand had curled into a fist. Whether it was anger at Durham, or at their new circumstances, or at Gerard for baiting him, Edward didn't know, but they didn't have time for an argument. "No one knows just how deep the trouble is. Some months ago, Father began receiving letters from someone who hinted that the secret marriage wasn't so secret after all, and that more trouble was waiting if Father didn't pay."

"Someone blackmailed Durham? How very ironic," murmured Charlie.

"There was no proof of anything," Edward went on sharply, glaring at Gerard to keep quiet. His younger brother snorted and stalked away to the window. They had agreed Charlie must be told, but Gerard was straining at the bit to *do* something, not keep talking. Perhaps he should have told Gerard to go ahead and charge off while he took care of telling Charlie . . . Well, it was too late now. He plowed on with his explanation. "The letters arrived sporadically, beginning almost a year ago, and Father took extensive measures to discover the author, but could not. He also tried to discover if his first wife lived or died, but couldn't find a trace of her, either. But still the letters came, four in all. Pierce handed them over, along with a letter from Father detailing his efforts. And now that Father's dead, this person—or the woman, if she's still alive—may announce this publicly. I'm sure you can guess what would follow."

Charlie was silent for a moment. "Not everything was entailed."

"No, the estate in Lincolnshire is clear, left outright to you. We each have a modest sum of money. But everything else . . ."

"Yes," repeated Charlie. "Everything else."

"That's quite a lot," said Gerard from across the room. Arms folded over his chest, he leaned against the window frame and fixed a hard look on both of them. "The name, for one thing. Legitimacy, for another. I don't fancy being a bastard, let alone a bastard with only a thousand pounds a year. We've got to do something, and the sooner the better."

"You could go shoot this woman and solve all our problems."

"Charlie!" Edward scowled at him as Gerard bristled. "Do take this seriously. We could lose everything—*everything*, do you hear me?"

"Of course I heard you," muttered Charlie. "But what do you suggest we do?"

"Engage the best solicitors in London at once. We don't wish to challenge the will—right now it leaves everything to us, as expected, and a challenge will only tie up the estate. But if another claim is filed, we need to have our case prepared to counter immediately."

Charlie lay back and stared at the ceiling. "That sounds reasonable."

"It sounds slow." Gerard came back across the room and sat on the edge of the bed, ignoring Charlie's hissed curse as the mattress shifted under his weight. "What

shall *we* do? Engaging a pack of solicitors is all very
good, but then what—shall we three go on as if nothing
is wrong? What if word of this leaks out?"

"Unless this woman comes forward, there is no
problem."

"This woman, or her heirs, or the blackmailer,"
Gerard retorted. "You're thinking too tamely. We could
still end up decimated by gossip."

"Gossip about what, Gerard?" Edward said testily.
"Something that might never happen and hasn't been
uncovered in sixty years?"

"Gossip that we're about to lose everything. You
know as well as I do that the appearance of ruin is
almost the same as ruin itself."

"Then what do *you* propose we do?"

Gerard leaned back against the bedpost and propped
one fist on his knee. "Find the blackmailer. That will
put an end to it."

"How do you plan to do it? Father searched for
months and hadn't a clue who it was."

"It's better than sitting around waiting for a sniveling
lawyer to tell me what my fate is!"

Edward pinched the bridge of his nose and reined in
his temper. It did no good to argue with his brother. He
wished he could be a bit more like Charlie, who simply
poured another cup of tea and leaned back into his pillows, watching with detached interest. "If you think you
can find the blackmailer, Gerard, I will be the last to
stand in your way," he said. "In fact, I wish you the
best of luck. But I cannot, in good conscience, leave us
legally unprepared. If this woman—or her heirs, as you
say—should come forward, I want to be ready. We'll

have to contest the validity of her marriage, and that will take time to prepare, no matter that she hasn't lived as Durham's wife in over half a century. Even if her heirs have no credible claim on Durham, we could still lose it to Father's cousin Augustus if he files a rival petition to be granted the dukedom. In fact, even if you find the blackmailer and throttle him with your bare hands, if the man has solid proof his charges are true—and provides it to Augustus—we're still in trouble."

"Not if he never gets the chance to present it," muttered Gerard grimly.

Edward clenched his jaw and turned to Charlie. "What do you think?"

His brother lifted one shoulder. "Both plans sound excellent to me. Gerard will go kill the blackmailer and you'll raise an army of lawyers. Fine ideas both. I agree wholeheartedly."

"And what do you plan to do?"

Charlie gave Gerard a smirk, and raised his teacup as if in salute. "Stay out of the way, of course."

Gerard stared at him in astonishment. Even Edward was surprised. Charlie was acting as if he didn't care at all whether he was the next Duke of Durham or an illegitimate son with only a single Lincolnshire estate. Deep inside his head, a little voice whispered that Charlie didn't really deserve Durham, and it would serve him right if he lost it all. He certainly hadn't valued it much to date. Part of Edward took some malicious glee in the thought of Charlie left with nothing but a small country estate whose income wouldn't cover his tailoring bills. He could just picture his brother moldering away in Lincolnshire—lovely country, really, hundreds of miles away from the glittering splendor of London.

But of course, surrendering Charlie's birthright would also have the unfortunate effect of surrendering his own. No matter how ungrateful or disinterested his brother was, Edward knew he still had to do everything in his power to keep Durham. It was the only life he had ever known, and he wasn't giving it up just because his brother was a lazy sot. It would merely be one more time Charlie coasted along on the fruits of his efforts.

"Very well then," he said in truce. "Gerard shall pursue the blackmailer. I'll see to the solicitor. Charlie . . . carry on as you were."

"Always planned to," murmured Charlie, pouring more tea.

Gerard held up one hand as Edward started to rise. "And we must all pledge absolute secrecy. It would unleash a storm of gossip unparalleled in London's history. Not a word of this unpleasant business to anyone— excepting of course whatever you must tell the solicitor. Agreed?"

Charlie shrugged. "Of course."

Edward nodded. "Agreed, except . . . I must tell Louisa."

"Louisa!" Gerard frowned. "Must you?"

"How can I not?" Edward frowned back. "She deserves to know."

His brother looked unconvinced. "I know you care for her, but I suggest you reconsider. You'll have to put the wedding off because of Father's death, but there's no need to tell her of . . . this."

"Gerard, she is my fiancée," Edward replied, each

word coated in ice. "I cannot keep something like this from her."

Gerard hesitated. "Perhaps you should, if you want to keep her as your fiancée."

Edward stilled. "I will pretend I didn't hear that," he said quietly. "Louisa is a woman of understanding and discretion. Moreover, she is the woman I love, and the woman who loves me. I wouldn't dream of keeping such a terrible secret from her."

A dull flush burned his brother's face. "Right," he muttered. "I apologize. Do what you think is best."

He nodded stiffly. "Accepted." An awkward silence filled the room. Edward didn't feel like breaking it. How dare Gerard imply Louisa wouldn't stand by him? Theirs wasn't an arranged marriage, but a love match. He hated to tell her, but it was inconceivable that he could keep such a secret from her. He would be distracted and busy, and she would notice that at the very least—and that was if the scandal didn't burst over London like the fireworks at Vauxhall. Somehow it seemed incredible Charlie wouldn't let it slip to someone. It would probably be a comfort, in fact, if Louisa knew; Edward wasn't about to tell another soul, and he knew it would be a relief to confide in someone. And if the news did get out, she deserved to hear it from him.

Gerard cleared his throat and got to his feet. "Well, good. Glad we're agreed. I'll look over the blackmail letters again and get started."

"Godspeed, and good luck," said Charlie gravely.

Gerard growled something rude under his breath.

Edward glared at his older brother. "Thank you for sparing us a few moments of your time." If Charlie heard the sarcasm in his voice, he didn't respond to it. Edward followed Gerard from the room, closing the door behind him.

"I know he didn't get on well with Father, but this is too much," said Gerard, quietly seething, as they went down the stairs. "Is he too stupid to realize what this could mean, or is he just unspeakably indolent?"

"I don't know, but it doesn't matter." Edward repressed any hint of the sympathy he felt with Gerard's frustration. "We would press on no matter what Charlie's attitude. And I cannot believe he doesn't care at all."

"What, then?" said Gerard in a sharp, low voice. They had reached the hall, and Edward motioned to the footman waiting nearby to bring their coats and hats. "Why can't he even express the slightest dismay or outrage?"

"Because that's not how Charlie is." Edward raised his eyebrows. "Charles de Lacey, scoundrel and rake extraordinaire, show any concern? Don't you remember when he lost his favorite horse in a wager to old Garston? Came home whistling as if he hadn't a care in the world, but late that night I caught him staring at the portrait of himself astride that horse."

Gerard sighed, some of his flush of anger fading. "Lord, I'd forgotten. And Garston made sure to ride the damned horse every time he called, didn't he, just to rub it in Charlie's face. He did love that beast."

Edward nodded in agreement. He'd almost forgotten that story, too, but the look on Charlie's face when they broke the news had summoned up the memory. His brother cared about things—some things—but for some reason laughed off everything.

Still, this was far more important than a lost horse. This was Durham itself. Whether Charlie cared or not, whether he exerted himself in any way or not, this wasn't something either Edward or Gerard was willing to just let him suffer through and laugh off. "I don't expect Charlie to do anything," he said to Gerard. "In fact, it may be easier if he stays out of the way, as he said."

"You're probably right." Gerard took his coat from the footman. "Not that it wouldn't give me a fair bit of pleasure to see him suffer the pains of his own short-comings once. Can you imagine him consigned to the wilds of Lincolnshire, without a curricle race or an opera dancer in sight?"

Edward smiled and shook his head, and stayed the footman with his coat. "I'll be along shortly."

"You aren't going to apologize, are you?" exclaimed his brother as Edward turned back toward the stairs. "For what?"

"For cutting up so rough at him. He's ill."

Gerard stared after him in disbelief for a moment, but put on his hat and left without another word. Edward went back upstairs, shaking his own head at himself. He hadn't done anything wrong, really; one day he would get out of the habit of caring so much for his brothers' peace. He tapped twice at the door and opened it. Then he stopped short in surprise.

Charlie was sitting on the side of his bed as if in the process of rising, arms braced on the mattress and feet on the floor. But one of his legs was out straight in front of him, bound in bandages and splints that didn't quite conceal the reddened, swollen flesh. Charlie's valet Barnes, kneeling beside him to support the leg, glanced up at Edward's entrance and froze in apprehension.

"Bugger all, don't you knock?" Charlie shot an annoyed glance at Edward through the rumpled waves of hair that had fallen over his eyes.

Now Edward realized the sheen of perspiration on his brother's forehead wasn't just from a headache. That was a badly broken leg. He stepped into the room and closed the door. "I beg your pardon."

"No, you don't, not really, but never mind." Charlie settled his injured foot on the floor, flexing his arms. His valet hurried to his side, and with a heave Charlie was on his feet. The valet snatched up a green silk dressing gown and held it up as Charlie shoved his arms into it, balancing precariously on one foot.

"It doesn't look as though you should be walking about," Edward observed.

His brother took the cane his valet offered him and hobbled to the table, where a tray with breakfast dishes and a fresh pot of tea sat. Leaning heavily on the cane, Charlie poured a cup and sipped deeply. "Not even I can spend my entire life in bed—not alone, at any rate."

"I came to apologize," Edward said to his brother's back. Charlie didn't turn, but his shoulders tensed, visible even through his dressing gown. "Gerard was out of bounds, and I was impatient as well. This problem has consumed us for several days now, and you seemed oddly unmoved by it."

Charlie said nothing. Listing on his cane, teacup

clutched close to his chest, he stared out the window, a strangely pensive figure. Edward crossed the room to stand beside him. "I didn't realize you were in no state to travel," he said.

"Damn it, Edward, I wouldn't have come to Sussex anyway," Charlie muttered. He seemed fascinated by something outside the window, although Edward couldn't see anything worthy of note. "We all know that. Durham certainly knew it."

"He called for you," Edward reminded him. "I was there. He wanted to see you again. Perhaps he knew you didn't want to see him, but he was dying, and he wanted to see you."

"And what did he want to say to me?" A heavy, brooding expression had settled over Charlie's face.

Edward hesitated. "He wanted to beg your pardon," he said reluctantly, knowing how it would sound to his brother. "For this terrible mess, I believe. He worried for you."

A dark smile curled Charlie's mouth. "Ah. No wonder. I suppose he knew you and Gerard would get on just fine, but poor Charles wouldn't know what to do."

Edward said nothing.

"And you think he was right," Charlie went on. "You came to tell me what you planned to do, but only out of obligation."

"You must admit," said Edward dryly, "your response did not overturn our expectations."

"The bloody bounder," Charlie said, bitterness seeping into his voice. "How dare he do such a thing?"

"I expect it was shame, and age, and outraged pride." Somehow Charlie's belated anger at Durham made

Edward want to defend their father, even though he agreed with every word his brother said.

"That damned Durham pride," Charlie muttered.

Edward sighed. "He tried to apologize."

"And now he's left us all to be humiliated and dispossessed."

"It certainly wasn't what he intended; it left him heartsick at the end. And he left us everything he had so we can solve what he could not."

Charlie just gulped some more tea. This time Edward caught a whiff of brandy, and almost shook his head. He should have known . . . But perhaps this once Charlie deserved a little nip. "Dare I ask what happened?" he asked, looking at his brother's leg.

"Ah." Something of the usual gleam returned to Charlie's eyes. "It was quite a fight. Three of them, all monstrous brutes. I battled back two, but in the end had to flee on horseback. The horse cleared the first fence, but not the second. And as I was lying there in a daze, the last villain caught up to me and finished what he had started." He extended his injured leg, regarding it almost proudly. "I'm quite an invalid now. I shall have a terrible scar."

Edward didn't believe a word of that story. He could tell when Charlie was telling a tale. "I hope she was worth it," he said with a straight face.

His brother flashed a lazy grin. "Absolutely."

This time when Edward left, he beckoned to the valet, who slipped out of the room behind him. "How long has his leg been like this?"

"Just over a week, my lord," replied Barnes. "The doctor thinks it will heal well."

Edward nodded. "How?" Barnes hesitated, and Edward added, "I know it wasn't a fight, nor a runaway horse. I want to know if there is any danger of a similar fate awaiting his other leg."

"A slip on the stairs," murmured Barnes, glancing guiltily over his shoulder. "After a late evening out."

So there wasn't a jealous husband or an angry card-sharp contemplating breaking Charlie's other leg. Edward let out his breath in relief. "Thank you, Barnes. Do your best to keep him under a doctor's care."

"Yes, my lord." Barnes bowed and then hurried off at Edward's wave of dismissal.

So Charlie was truly out of the way, though not due to disinterest. Gerard had effectively removed himself from the scene, taking off on some quixotic pursuit of the blackmailer. If Durham, with all his money and steely determination, hadn't found the villain, Edward didn't see how Gerard could, charging off alone with only the same information that had led Durham's investigator into a blind end. But this plan suited him rather well; Charlie was inclined to do too little, Gerard too much. Now he could deal with the solicitor unimpeded. He would be free to act as he saw fit, without having to persuade his brothers to his prudent way of thinking.

After all, he was used to being responsible for everything, and he was quite content with that.

Chapter 3

Francesca, Lady Gordon, arrived early, which was very much against habit for her.

She did take her usual care in dressing. First impressions were terribly important, and Francesca was keenly aware of the need to strike just the right tone this morning. She wore her gray silk with black velvet trim, a smart, sharp ensemble that played up her coloring but also signified status and position. It might have suggested a bit more wealth and dignity than she actually possessed, but that could only help. The man she needed to impress today wasn't a politician or a lord, nor one of the society darlings she found so amusing. James Wittiers was something far more important to Francesca today: he was widely considered the best solicitor in London, fearless, tenacious, crafty, and cleverer than half the King's Bench put together. According to his very satisfied clients, Wittiers danced right to the edge of legality in pressing their interests, and sometimes succeeded in moving the boundaries of that legality. All this suited her perfectly. She needed a lawyer, and she needed a damned good one.

Wittiers's success had made him selective. It had

taken almost a fortnight for Francesca to secure an appointment to see the man. She hated to waste that time, but every other solicitor and investigator she interviewed had been lacking in some way. She didn't want to hear the reasons why her case might fail; she was already well aware of them. She wanted to hear someone assure her she had a chance, and that he would pursue that chance to the very end of the earth. That was all she asked—that, and success.

A clerk showed her into a small office to wait, and offered to bring tea. Francesca declined. She didn't need anything to distract her from her interview. She had prepared for it intensely, knowing how much depended on winning his interest, and asked a variety of acquaintances for advice. Sir Phillip Blake, her neighbor, told her to engage the solicitor's love of a challenge. Mr. Ludlow, husband of her dear friend Sally, suggested she stress the urgency of her situation, to pique Wittiers's urge to champion someone in need. Lord Alconbury, a longtime friend, told her to avoid dramatics, especially tears. And Mr. Heatherington, incorrigible rogue and flirt, advised her to look beautiful, because Wittiers was just as much a man as he was a solicitor. Francesca wanted to leave nothing to chance. She was determined to meet every point, no matter how minor.

She perched now on the edge of the small settee and mentally ran over her rehearsed speech. Other solicitors had told her the case was a wretched tangle, as if she couldn't have guessed that herself, but she was counting on Wittiers to find the thread that would unravel it. A stickier point might be the fee; from his reputation alone, Wittiers must charge a small fortune. Francesca lived a comfortable life and had some money, but she wasn't enthusiastic about the prospect of beggaring herself. She had fretted a bit over it, but then thought again of her niece, and hardened herself against worries about money. To save darling Georgina from her vapid and venal stepmother, Francesca was willing to risk everything. Somehow she would come to an agreement with Wittiers about his fee.

After a while the door opened. She rose, feeling composed and measured, and turned to greet Mr. Wittiers, who was younger than she had expected. Fair and barrel-chested, he was just the same height as she was, and he met her gaze levelly, with no trace of condescension or scorn. There was a vital, snapping intelligence in his eyes that reassured her even more. After a brief polite greeting, he got right down to business.

"My clerk, Mr. Napier, tells me you have a highly complex situation," he said, seating himself in the chair near her. He propped one elbow on the armrest and focused his intense gaze upon her. "Would you be so kind as to explain, from the beginning?"

"Of course." Francesca folded her hands in her lap. She didn't want to lose herself and become excited. "The story is more complex than the situation. To be concise, I wish to have the care of my late sister's daughter bestowed upon me. My niece, Georgina, is currently living with her stepmother, and I fear the woman is taking advantage of Georgina's inheritance and using it to support her own family."

His dry smile was gone almost before she registered it. "I presume you have proof of that charge, Lady Gordon."

"Hard proof, in the form of confessional letters or receipts, no," she said carefully. "Proof that the woman, Mrs. Haywood, inherited a very small portion from her late husband, yes. Proof that she lost her home soon after his death, yes. Proof that her brother, Mr. Watts, has influenced her to keep me from seeing my niece since I offered to raise her, yes."

"Suggestive," he said, "but not proof."

She raised her eyebrow, still calm and cool. "I understood you were willing to act as investigator as well as solicitor for your clients."

"It has been done," he agreed.

Francesca smiled. "Then I am sure we will be able to deal very well together."

Wittiers stared at her for a moment, a thoughtful set to his lips. Then he sat forward in his chair. "Explain to me the family situation in detail. How did your niece come to be in the care of this woman?"

She had his interest. Francesca breathed deeply to control her leaping pulse. "Several years ago my half sister, Giuliana, came to visit me from Italy. She had grown up there with our mother, while I was reared in England by my father's sister. My mother," she added quickly as a thin line creased his brow, "was Marcella Rescati, the Italian soprano. She married my father while in England, but after his death returned to Italy, where she married again, to Giuliana's father."

"Ah," he said, his expression turning keen. "I heard her sing in Florence, some years ago. *Armida*, I believe."

Francesca smiled in real pleasure. "One of her particular favorites!"

"So," he said briskly, returning to the main point, "you and your sister have different fathers."

She nodded. "Yes. Her life was quite different from mine, but I was very content here in England. I married and settled in London, and soon after, my sister came to visit. She was just seventeen, beautiful and vivacious. Within a month she had received several marriage proposals, and to my surprise she accepted one from Mr. John Haywood."

"Surprise?"

"Because she was so new to England; her grasp of English was not complete, and although Mr. Haywood was an eligible match, he was several years older than she," Francesca explained. "But she was determined, and Giuliana asked for and received her parents' blessing. She married Mr. Haywood and had a child, her daughter Georgina, a year later."

"Haywood had money?" Wittiers queried.

Francesca shook her head. "No, quite the contrary. He had connections, but little fortune of his own. Giuliana's father was a very wealthy man, though, and had no other children; on her marriage he granted her a large allowance. At Georgina's birth, he changed his will so that all the funds were settled on Georgina, with the income to Giuliana during her lifetime."

"No marriage settlement?"

"There was one, of course, but I do not know the size. I suspect Giuseppe—Giuliana's father—was wary of Mr. Haywood's management. Mr. Haywood did not have a head for money." That was putting it mildly, and Francesca had proof of her brother-in-law's inability to account for his spending. Her sister had mentioned it often in letters. "Fortunately, Giuliana did," she went on. "They lived a happy, comfortable life for some years. Georgina grew into a beautiful, unspoiled child. I was named godmother to her and visited often."

"Excellent," he murmured.

"Unfortunately their happiness was short-lived." She had to steady her voice for this part of the story, a litany of deaths. "Giuliana died two years ago in childbed. I did my best to provide a maternal influence on Georgina, but my own husband died unexpectedly at the same time. Within a few months of my sister's death, Mr. Haywood had married again, to a woman named Ellen Watts, so Georgina would have a mother. I was welcome in their home, and still visited as often as I could."

"Was this woman unkind to the girl?" Wittiers queried. "Was she cold?"

Francesca hesitated. "Not that I could see," she admitted. "Georgina did not seem neglected or unhappy. But then her father was killed in a riding accident last summer, and suddenly things changed."

"Not surprising, given the death of the father," Wittiers pointed out. "How did his will leave the girl's custody?"

"He had not changed his will since my sister's death. Giuliana was still named as the caretaker of their daughter, and Mr. Haywood's brother as guardian—but he had also passed away. The Haywoods, it seems, have a tendency toward mortality. The court has not appointed anyone else yet. I believe, if there had been more money left to her, Mrs. Haywood would have gladly allowed me to take Georgina and raise her, as she was expecting a child at the time of Mr. Haywood's tragic death. But Mr. Haywood had no money of his own, only what he received when he married my sister. I know the amount had dwindled to a very small sum after Giuliana's death. There was little left for his widow."

"And the child's inheritance?"

"Giuliana's father died a year before she did. He named as executor Mr. William Kendall, a barrister in Dover whom he knew through business dealings, to oversee the fortune he left Georgina. Mr. Kendall takes no interest in Georgina except to pay out her quarterly maintenance. I've already approached him for assistance, only to be told he has gone abroad and isn't expected back before the winter."

"I begin to see your difficulty." Wittiers leaned back, a faraway look on his face. "He pays the maintenance to whomever has custody of the girl. The stepmother has little money of her own, I presume? From her family, perhaps?" At Francesca's shake of her head, he smiled, a vaguely dangerous look that sent her hopes soaring. "Venality," he said softly. "She has lived with the girl for a year?"

"Yes. Almost a year and a half now."

"Ah. And you have seen the girl in that time?"

Francesca nodded.

"Was she mistreated? Unhappy? Ill or otherwise uncared for?" He fired each question without waiting for a response.

"Initially, she was brokenhearted over her father's death." Francesca struggled with her answer. She didn't want to mislead the solicitor and damage her credibility, but neither did she want him to dismiss her concerns. "She did ask me to take her away from home, which reminded her so strongly of her parents. I offered then to take her and raise her, since I'm related by blood and her stepmother isn't. I have a good home and could easily afford to raise Georgina, as well as love her like my own child. But Mrs. Haywood said no, saying she had grown attached to Georgina. I agreed, reluctantly, but my sense that things weren't right grew over the next months. Mrs. Haywood bore twin boys three months after her husband died, and that threw the household into greater turmoil. And now . . . I don't know, sir. I haven't been allowed to see Georgina in several months."

Wittiers glanced sharply at her. "She has denied you access?"

"We had a disagreement." Francesca held her head high, even though she knew this was her great weakness. "A heated one. I implied she wasn't able to take care of Georgina properly, as the mother of two infants, and asked again to take Georgina home with me. Her brother ordered me out of the house and threatened to call the watch if I did not go."

"Her brother?"

"Mr. Percival Watts moved in with the family after Mr. Haywood's death. I believe he is the main force behind Ellen's desire to keep Georgina. He certainly isn't supporting them with his own funds." She tried hard to keep her loathing of Percival Watts from her voice.

Wittiers nodded, clasping his hands together and resting them against his chin. For several minutes he sat deep in thought. "Lady Gordon," he said suddenly, "I believe you have a fair case. We must gather evidence of the stepmother's lack of other funds, of the necessity to her household of your niece's maintenance funds, and of her lack of nurturing attitude toward the girl. You must provide evidence of your role in the child's life, with anything that will demonstrate you have been present and involved with her parents' blessing and at their invitation. It will not be easy, but I believe it is possible."

"And you'll take the case?" She could barely breathe. This was such an important step . . .

Mr. Wittiers rose, extending his hand to her. Francesca placed her hand in his and got to her own feet. "Yes, madam, I am inclined to do just that."

Emotion almost choked her. "Thank you," she said fervently, pressing his hand. "Thank you, sir."

"If you'll excuse me, I'll take a moment to consult a few resources, to check my memory of certain laws and precedents before we proceed. Would you care for tea?"

She shook her head, almost giddy with success. "Thank you, no."

Wittiers nodded and left. Trembling, Francesca sank back into her seat. He hadn't definitely agreed, but he said her case had merit; he was inclined to take it on. That meant he believed he could win. *She* could win.

The wait dragged on for some time. After a while Francesca got up and paced about the room, wishing Wittiers would come back soon. Something seemed to be going on in the outer offices; she could hear the rapid tread of feet, back and forth, and the rushed murmur of voices. It went on for such an extended period of time she finally grew too curious. She went to the door and opened it just a little.

The clerk, Mr. Napier, stood across the room, his back to her, and was scribbling furiously in the notebook he held as Wittiers spoke rapidly to him, raising his finger to interrupt with a question from time to time. Another clerk was flipping through a large file, pulling out pages. Her heart leaped at the sight of such purposeful activity. She couldn't make out what Wittiers or his clerk was saying, but Wittiers had the look of a general ordering his troops into battle, and the confidence emanating from him was hard to mistake. Francesca eased the door closed, not wanting to be caught spying, and returned to her seat feeling positively joyful.

It was over a quarter of an hour before the door opened again. She looked up to see Mr. Napier. "I beg your pardon, madam," he said. "Mr. Wittiers has been called away on an urgent matter. He bade me express his deepest regret, but he won't be able to take your case after all."

"O-Oh," she stammered, completely thrown. "But— no, we just spoke and he was quite intrigued by it. Will the emergency pass? Shall I return tomorrow? I can afford to wait a day or so . . ."

The clerk wet his lips. "Mr. Wittiers is most apologetic, Lady Gordon, but it appears very likely he won't be able to take any new cases for some time." She gaped at him, and he gently added, "He must recommend you seek other counsel."

"Other counsel?" she echoed numbly. No. No. She *had* sought other counsel, and found it all wanting. Mr. Wittiers was the best—and he had agreed her cause had merit. To have that hope, that confidence, stripped away now was unthinkable. "I don't understand," she said, her fingernails biting into her palms even through her gloves as she clung hard to her poise. "Why did he lead me to believe he would accept if he is now unable even to consider taking my case?"

"An urgent matter arose," he replied. "Unexpectedly."

"For another client?"

"I cannot say, madam. Mr. Wittiers is truly sorry he cannot help you." The clerk's face creased in polite sympathy. "May I bring you a cup of tea? I am dreadfully sorry, Lady Gordon."

Francesca felt the door slam shut in her face—again. "No," she said faintly. "No, thank you. If I could just have a moment . . ."

He nodded. "Of course." Quietly, he left, drawing the door closed behind him.

Francesca pressed a hand to her forehead. What was she to do now? Which other solicitors had been recommended to her? A spark of bitterness flared in her chest that she had waited so long to see Wittiers, that she had been so sure of his abilities, that he had *agreed*, the blighter, and then refused. Perhaps she was well-shot of him if he couldn't even keep his word for half an hour, but went rushing off on a moment's notice. She tried to calm herself, reasoning that if she *had* become his client, she would have wished for just this sort of immediate response from him in her time of need. But it stung, to be summarily rejected mere minutes after being accepted, after he had allowed hope to sprout and surge forth within her. And now she would probably have to return to one of the other solicitors who had been doubtful or downright pessimistic about her case. Her chances of rescuing Georgina suddenly looked rather grim, and for a moment a film of tears blurred her vision. She dashed them away at once. There was no time to waste on tears.

She put on her bonnet and gathered up her reticule and shawl, then left the room. The outer office was a flurry of activity, as Wittiers's clerks rushed back and forth in response to the directives being called from the office at the end of the hall. As Francesca made her way out, two clerks were bent down searching a tall bookcase.

"Make sure you find my treatise on the Commissary Court," called Wittiers from his office. "And hurry!"

"What the bloody hell is this case?" one clerk asked the other. "Parish records, parliamentary procedure, now commissary law?"

"I don't know," muttered the other clerk, taking down a large box of documents and rifling through them. "I never even heard the name. But it must be the case of the decade, to set Wittiers off like this."

Francesca's steps slowed. She fumbled in her reticule for her handkerchief, then dropped the reticule as she dabbed the handkerchief first to one eye, then the other, eavesdropping shamelessly. Unaware, the clerks continued speaking behind her.

"I haven't seen this much fuss since the Cowley case, and there was a barony at stake then."

"There was a crest on the seal," the other clerk said. "I wouldn't doubt we've an even more important client now. Wittiers is to wait on him in an hour."

The first clerk rose with a stack of books in his arms, and noticed Francesca lingering just inside the door. He gave his companion a look, then set down his books and came toward her. "May I help you, Lady Gordon? You look rather pale."

"I— Yes," she said, stooping to pick up her reticule to hide her expression. It wasn't illness but anger that had sent the blood rushing from her head. Wittiers had thrown her over for another, more prestigious, new client. An emergency, indeed—only if one considered power and wealth a cause for urgent action. "I do feel a trifle unwell all of a sudden. Would you be so kind as to summon my carriage?"

"Of course, madam." He went out and returned a few moments later, saying her driver was waiting. Francesca gave him a look of wan gratitude, and he helped her into the carriage with great solicitude.

But as soon as he had gone back into the offices, Francesca told her coachman to circle around and wait. She wanted to see who this very important client was, who could compel Wittiers to drop everything—especially her—and rush to serve him. A crest, one of the clerks had said; that meant nobility. Her husband had been a mere baronet, but she'd met a number of lords. Insufferable conceit was a common flaw in the nobility, the sort of arrogance that would summon a prominent solicitor to attend him on a moment's notice. Wittiers, of course, had jumped like a trained dog, which did not reflect well on him, either. She twisted her handkerchief into a knot, fuming in impotent frustration.

Almost three-quarters of an hour later James Wittiers emerged from his offices. He was followed by Mr. Napier, now wearing his coat neatly buttoned up. They climbed into a hackney cab the clerk hailed in the busy street and set off at a quick pace. Francesca told her coachman to follow, sitting with her head almost out the window to watch where they went.

True to her expectation, they drove through nicer and nicer streets. Francesca's eyes narrowed as the solicitor's carriage drew up in front of an imposing stone mansion facing a fenced green square in the most elegant part of Mayfair. The house was enormous, taking up most of an entire side of the square. Nobility, probably; but wealth most certainly, in great abundance. Perhaps the prospect of a large fee, more than any prestige, had lured Wittiers away from her case. Mr. Wittiers and his clerk were admitted at once, indicating they had been expected.

She sat back in a dark mood. The rational, sensible side of her knew it was pointless, now that Wittiers had turned her away and taken this other case. Her best hope was to find another solicitor, and quickly, before Georgina's stepmother could make any progress in lodging her own case. But the other side of her, the hot-blooded Italian side of her, wanted to march into that towering mansion and demand recompense from the owner. Or at least give him a scathing set-down.

With a word to her driver to wait, she gathered up her skirt and stepped down. Wittiers had dismissed his hired carriage, meaning he expected to be some time inside. Settling her shawl around her shoulders, Francesca set off down the street.

At the corner she stopped a woman with two young children in tow, heading for the lush green park in the center of the square. "I beg your pardon, is this the residence of Lord Alconbury?" she asked, indicating the stone edifice. She knew very well it was not, but Alconbury would enjoy a great laugh at the thought of living in such a place. when she told him the tale.

"No, ma'am, 'tis the Duke of Durham's mansion," replied the nursemaid.

"Indeed," exclaimed Francesca, only half in pretense. Good Lord; a *duke*. "What a blunder I almost made!"

The nursemaid gave her a sympathetic smile. No doubt in this neighborhood she looked like someone applying for a companion's post in her simple, severe gray dress. "I'd say so! But take heart; the butler, Mr. Blackbridge, is a kindly sort. He'd not blister your ears for ringing the bell in error. He never complains when the little ones throw the ball on the steps."

"That is good to hear," said Francesca, pressing one hand to her bosom as if in relief. "A duke!"

The maid sobered. "His Grace was a decent man, but he's dead, God rest his soul." Belatedly Francesca noticed the black-ribboned wreath on the door. She had been so fixed on watching Wittiers, it had escaped her.

The children began quarreling between themselves then, and the nursemaid murmured a quick apology to Francesca before hurrying them off to the square. Francesca resumed her stroll, watching the maid and her charges. A *duke*—no wonder Wittiers had jumped at the summons. Of course, it also reinforced her belief that Wittiers was the best solicitor in London, and made her furious all over again that he had been whisked away from her.

But that was neither here nor there, not anymore. Wittiers's services were lost to her now. There was nothing to be gained by lurking in the square like some hysterical female, nursing her disappointment. She drew

a deep, calming breath and told herself it was not the
end of her hopes. If Wittiers could see merit, someone
else could as well. She just had to find that man, and
pray no other dukes wanted his counsel as well. She
sent one more black look at the imposing mansion as
she returned to her carriage, and directed her coachman
to Cheapside.

Ellen Haywood had taken a small, narrow house in
a small, narrow street. It wasn't the nicest neighborhood, and Francesca held her skirts carefully high as
she stepped down from her carriage and walked to
the door. Ellen hadn't let her in the last four times she
called, claiming every excuse from illness in the house
to excessive cleaning that made it impossible to receive
guests. All Francesca had wanted to see was Georgina,
but by some suspicious chance, Georgina never seemed
to be home when she called. On more than one occasion
Francesca had to admit she'd lost her temper and raised
her voice at the woman, which probably had not helped.

Today, though, she desperately wanted to see Georgina, no matter how she had to apologize and grovel
to Ellen. The drive to Cheapside from Mayfair had
been long enough for most of her anger over Wittiers
to drain away, leaving weariness and a tinge of despair.
She had never thought it would be this difficult. She
had expected Ellen to be relieved by her offer to take
Georgina; the girl was no relation to her, and Ellen
must have her hands full with two small infants. She
had been puzzled, then frustrated by Ellen's stiff refusal, and then incensed when she realized Georgina's
maintenance must be providing vital funds to Ellen's
household. Flinging the accusation in the woman's face

probably hadn't been the best course, but Ellen's reaction had been ample confirmation. Her face had gone pale, and then Percival Watts had ordered Francesca out with the parting promise that she would never be allowed to see Georgina again for saying such a thing. And she hadn't been.

Even then Francesca hadn't thought she faced such long odds. After Giuliana's death, John had promised to name her custodian of Georgina in his will, but he met his unfortunate end before he made the change. Surely the court would at least consider her petition. The reluctance of nearly a dozen solicitors to embrace her case had infuriated and frustrated Francesca, but today she felt the first real chill of despair. The last thing she wanted to do was start a battle with poor Georgina stuck in the middle. And at this rate, Georgina would be grown and married before she even saw her again.

She rapped the knocker and waited, and waited, and waited. She rapped again, feeling her shoulders tense in grim anticipation. An apology was certainly going to be required, and she would duly make it, even to Percival Watts's face if necessary, but she would not enjoy a moment of it. Just standing here on the stoop was making it loom ever more galling in her mind. Just as she was reaching to knock a third time, a neighbor came out of the house next door, a large basket on her arm.

"Are you wanting Mrs. Haywood?" the woman asked, squinting at Francesca.

"Yes. But I fear they are not in."

"Not at all, ma'am, not anymore!" The woman juggled her market basket and closed her door, then hurried down her steps. Francesca slowly followed suit. The woman met her beside the street. "I'm Mrs. Jenkins; we were neighbors, you see. They've moved house," she said. "Left . . . oh my, it must be three or four days now."

"Oh." Francesca could feel the blood draining from her face. "I had no idea . . . Where have they gone?"

The neighbor's plump, pink face creased as she shook her head. "I cannot tell you, for I don't know. We'd no idea they were thinking of leaving! Although Mr. Jenkins wasn't sorry to see the twins go; such a racket those two could make."

"The little girl," Francesca asked urgently. "Have you see the little girl recently? Georgina?"

"Of course," replied Mrs. Jenkins with a smile. "Such a sweet girl, and so helpful. I've seen her sweeping the steps ever so often, and so polite she always is. Much too thin, to my mind, but pretty all the same."

She closed her eyes in relief, but just for a moment. Georgina looked thin? She was always out sweeping the steps, like a servant child? Francesca struggled to keep her voice even. "But surely they left some word of how they can be reached."

"Not that I know of." The woman's expression melted into pity. "I've seen you call on them before. On the outs with Mrs. Haywood, are you?"

"In a way," Francesca murmured. "The little girl, Georgina, is my niece. I just wanted to see her . . ."

The woman cleared her throat, and sidled a step nearer. "It's not my concern, o' course, but I think the family might have fallen on some difficulties. You weren't the only one Mrs. Haywood turned away."

"Oh? Who else?" Francesca asked in surprise.

Mrs. Jenkins lowered her voice even more. Gossiping

had brought a glow to her round face. "Tradesmen," she said with relish. "Some of them more than once. Mr. Watts threatened one with his cane, and Mr. Jenkins swears he heard quarreling just last week."

"Quarreling? Between whom?" Francesca eyed the woman with a mixture of intense curiosity and apprehension.

"Mr. Watts and Mrs. Haywood!" exclaimed Mrs. Jenkins in indignant glee. "Going at it like furies, they were. And those two babies howling right along with them."

Francesca was speechless. Ellen was quarreling with her brother? They had moved away without notice to anyone? Tradesmen had been threatened with violence? Georgina was being treated like a servant? "But where have they gone?" she asked again with forced patience. "Surely they couldn't have decided overnight to leave. Someone must know . . ."

"No one here." Mrs. Jenkins gazed at her with pity. "Mr. Brown at the end of the street is the landlord's agent for most of us here, and he didn't know, either. They were three weeks behind on the rent, and when Mr. Brown came to collect it, the rooms had been quite cleared out."

"Mr. Brown." Francesca latched onto the name. "At the end of the street?"

"Number two," said Mrs. Jenkins. "He'll tell you just what I've done. Mr. Jenkins and I had him 'round to tea just Wednesday, and he related every detail."

"Thank you," she murmured. "Thank you very much."

Mrs. Jenkins's gossip was sound. Mr. Brown confirmed that the Haywood family had left without word, and owing several weeks' rent. He hadn't wanted to tell her, until she told him she was Georgina's aunt—and then had to grit her teeth when Brown referred to Georgina as Ellen's daughter—but once he realized she might be able to find his wayward tenants, he readily told her how late Ellen always was with her rent payment, how he'd had to threaten to turn them all out, how she'd wept so pitifully and begged him to have mercy for her babies' sake, while Mr. Watts stood sullenly at the side doing nothing. By the time he finished, Francesca was shaking with anger. She thanked Mr. Brown, marched back to her carriage, and looked at her coachman.

"Back to Berkeley Square, Mr. Hotchkiss," she told him. "Posthaste."

She had changed her mind about confronting the dreadful duke.

Chapter 4

James Wittiers responded with gratifying alacrity to his inquiry. Edward had chosen him carefully, after a discreet investigation of several solicitors. Wittiers was reputed to have a keen, quick mind, a thorough understanding of the law, and was something of a specialist in probate cases. He had won the infamous Cowley case just last year, claiming for his client a barony that had been in abeyance for nearly a century. It was quite a surprise that anyone succeeded, for the Cowley family had been a large one. One newspaper had reported there were at least five people with legitimate claims to the barony. But Wittiers had directed the case and won it, and that made him very appealing to Edward.

The man himself was modest in appearance, except for the intelligence that all but crackled off him. He listened intently as Edward explained his needs, then asked several pointed questions. His clerk sat beside him, scribbling notes as fast as Wittiers could speak. The solicitor understood was what needed and what must be avoided. He had a plan, and an alternate plan. His mind seemed to work much faster than normal; twice he realized Edward's point before the conversation had reached it. He broached the subject of the fees very frankly, but Edward waved it off. Whatever the man charged to secure Durham to him and his brothers would be well-earned. He was demanding a great deal of the solicitor, and was happy to pay for it. By the end of the interview Edward was well pleased with the arrangement, and from the expression on Wittiers's face, so was he.

"I'll send word to Mr. Pierce that he should expect you." Edward rose. He'd already told the Durham solicitor that he would be engaging another attorney on this most delicate matter, and Mr. Pierce had been very relieved to hear it. Pierce was good at what he did, but he had no experience in this sort of matter. "He should be able to provide any additional information you need."

"I will see him first thing tomorrow." Wittiers bowed. "You shall have my first report as soon as I have reviewed the will."

"Very good, sir." Edward inclined his head, and the solicitor and his clerk left.

He walked to the window and looked out over the green at the heart of Berkeley Square. Two young children were rolling a hoop under the watchful gaze of a nurse, just as he and his brothers used to do on their infrequent visits to London. Durham had believed boys needed country air to grow, and rarely brought them to town with him. Even now Edward had little affection for London. He would have preferred to stay in Sussex.

But it was far more convenient to be here at the moment. It would save considerable time, as just proved by the fact that he had sent for Wittiers late in the morning and already spoken to the man well before dinner.

He could keep an eye on Charlie far better here than from Sussex. And he could see Louisa, whose family had already come to London for the Season.

As he began to turn from the window, a small carriage dashed down the street and pulled up right at the steps of the house with a jangle of harness he could hear all the way from where he stood. Edward spared a glance at the arrival in idle curiosity. He wasn't expecting anyone and had no wish to receive guests. Still, it was rare to see a carriage speeding through Berkeley Square, let alone to his own house.

A woman emerged from the carriage. She wore a dark gray dress, rather stark and staid, but her hair gleamed like a new copper penny under her hat, and from his angle high above her, he could see that she had a spectacular bosom. She twitched her skirts smooth, then raised her eyes and cast a look of such loathing at the house, he blinked. Even from this distance he recognized a woman enraged. She straightened her shoulders and marched up the steps and out of his view.

Charlie, he supposed, must be to blame for this somehow. There was surely more to the story of his broken leg than Barnes had admitted.

The clang of the knocker echoed through the house, several loud, emphatic bangs. Edward wondered what his brother had done to set the woman off so violently, and why she'd come here instead of to Charlie's own house. He was in no mood to pacify a jilted lover or an outraged mistress. Charlie would have to deal with this problem himself, since he was doing his brother quite a considerable service already, looking out for his inheritance and title.

He stalked toward his own rooms to change. Now seemed like a fine time to call on Louisa. The butler tapped at his door several minutes later. "There is some-one to see you, sir: a Lady Gordon."

"I am not in." Edward slid his arms into the fresh jacket his valet held out. "In fact, I am going out. Have the carriage brought around."

"Yes, sir. But she is most insistent that she speak with you."

"With *me*?" he said sharply, swinging around to glare at the man. "She mentioned my name?" And not Charlie's?

"She did not mention your name, my lord," said Blackbridge, unflappably calm. "She said she had an important matter to discuss with the person who had summoned James Wittiers, and that she would not leave without doing so."

Edward paused in the act of tugging his sleeves into place. That was unexpected. "Did she?" he murmured. "What did she say about Wittiers?"

"Nothing specific, my lord, just that she wished to discuss him with you."

"Indeed." Edward stood still and thought as he let his valet finish ministering to the proper set of his coat. "Very well. Show her into the blue salon and I will see her presently."

Perhaps there was some shady aspect of Wittiers he hadn't uncovered. He had made discreet inquiries and heard nothing but praise and admiration for the man's ability, but that was not conclusive. If this woman, Lady Gordon, had dealings with Wittiers, she might know something he didn't. It was certainly possible Wittiers's reputation wasn't entirely supported. By the time he made his way to the blue salon, Edward was more than a little curious—and wary. He hadn't forgotten the look of hostility on the woman's face when she stepped out of her carriage.

A footman swept open the door of the salon before him. His guest didn't appear to notice. She was standing by the fireplace, gazing down at something cupped in the palm of her hand. Her expression was pensive and still, but something in her pose hinted at anguish. Indoors her hair appeared to be light brown, without the coppery sheen he'd noticed before. Her figure, though, was every bit as luscious as it had looked from the upstairs window.

Edward closed the door behind him with a loud click. Her head jerked up, and her hand squeezed into a fist about whatever she was studying. "Lady Gordon," he said, bowing politely. "I am Edward de Lacey. You wished to see me about James Wittiers?"

A flush rose in her cheeks. She shoved the object in her hand into her reticule and pulled the strings tight. "Yes," she said in a warm, husky voice that stroked across his senses like a siren's lure. "I do."

Francesca had almost begun to regret her impulsive action. After some small wait, the butler had shown her into an elegant room done up in icy blue, a cold but beautiful room that looked more like a museum than anything else. She eyed one of the exquisite marble tables flanking the tall windows, and would have bet a month's housekeeping that the only thing that touched their surfaces was a maid's dust cloth.

Perhaps she had better just go. The owner of this mansion wouldn't be impressed, let alone deterred, by her cause or her outrage. She had been consumed by fury when she realized that Ellen had stolen away with Georgina and not left a word where she could be found, and in the absence of any pertinent party, she had searched for someone on whom to vent that fury. *This won't do any good,* whispered a little voice in her head. It was the voice of reason, finally breaking through the shrieking storm of emotion. Francesca straightened her shoulders and dug out her tiny miniature of Georgina. It had been done right before Giuliana's death, as a gift for Giuliana's parents. But no one had sent it when Giuliana died in childbed, and then John had given it to her.

A round, cherubic face stared up from the golden frame, the dark eyes serious, the mouth a dainty little pink bow. She was a beautiful child, and as dear to Francesca as her own child could be. The portrait was two years old; Georgina had grown since it was done. Mrs. Jenkins said she was thin now, and Francesca's heart constricted that she didn't know what her own niece looked like anymore.

The door opened as she was sunk in maudlin thought, and she looked up. Not the butler again, nor any other servant. From the cut of his clothing, this was the man she had come to see, the man who could summon James Wittiers with a snap of his fingers. She took in her nemesis with one critical glance. He was tall and on the lean side, although with a nice breadth in his shoulders. Dark hair, cut neither long nor short; well dressed, but in singularly dull, dark colors; a face that was neither arrestingly handsome nor unremarkably plain. Even his eyes were ordinary, a colorless gray, with all the warmth of the steel they resembled. All in all, he was the most uninteresting man she had met in a long time. And he had stolen her solicitor, the one she had maneuvered for weeks to hire, which was simply intolerable. She closed her fingers around Georgina's miniature as some of her ire returned.

"Lady Gordon." His voice was cultured and smooth, but as bland as the rest of him. "I am Edward de Lacey. You wished to see me about James Wittiers?"

She put the miniature into her reticule. "Yes, I do," she replied. "I am not certain if you are aware of it, sir, but you have done me a grave disservice."

A slightly raised brow was his only reaction. "I fail to see how that can be possible, madam. We have never met, to my recollection."

"This morning I was in the offices of Mr. Wittiers. It took me weeks to secure an appointment with him; he is very much in demand, you see." He looked unimpressed, and unmoved. Even a little bored, to her eyes. Francesca's poise slipped, and she plunged along with her grievance. "He agreed to take my case. We discussed it at some length, and at the end he agreed to handle the matter for me. He excused himself for a moment, and never returned. His clerk came in shortly after to tell me that Mr. Wittiers had been called away on an urgent matter and wouldn't be able to assist me after all. He recommended I seek other counsel."

"It sounds to me as though your complaint lies with Mr. Wittiers," said the infuriating man in that cool tone.

"He left in response to your summons!" She could hear her voice rising and fought to control it. "Before your note arrived, with its noble crest, he was willing to help me. And then suddenly he was gone, leaping to do your bidding and leaving my case without so much as a word!"

"Again," he said, "your displeasure should be directed at Wittiers, if he has treated you so abominably."

"No," she retorted, flinging out one hand. "That won't do any good. I know his services are well and truly lost to me now—lured away by your title and your money. But I want you to know that you have cost, not me, but an innocent little girl her best hope of happiness."

"Madam—" he began, but Francesca had lost all hold on her temper.

"You disclaim all responsibility," she charged, jabbing a finger at him, "but through your interference with *my* solicitor, a child, my niece, has been wrongly kept from me and now spirited away, to God knows where, in the custody of a cold and possibly cruel woman, and I shall be forced to waste precious days and weeks searching for another solicitor and an investigator to find her!"

"I sent a note to Wittiers asking him to call upon me when he found it convenient," said Edward de Lacey, as calmly as before. How that calm infuriated her. "How he arranged his schedule to find a convenient time, I do not know. Why he turned you away, I do not know. I was by no means ready to engage him blindly, and thought it entirely possible that he might not suit my purposes."

She narrowed her eyes. "And did he?" she asked softly.

He looked back at her with implacable eyes. "That is not your concern."

She caught her breath. Slowly she crossed the room until she was just a few feet in front of him. "How dare you," she whispered. "I—I should insist that *you* help me now."

The man had the nerve to smile. It was a flat, dry smile, with only a spark of amusement in his eyes to indicate it wasn't forced. "Should you?"

"It would be only fair," she said wrathfully. "Since you have snatched away my solicitor."

"He wasn't really 'your' solicitor, though, was he?"

"He agreed to take my case!"

"Apparently he changed his mind."

"Through your interference!"

"Oh?" He rocked back on his heels, then abruptly leaned toward her. She refused to give ground, but had to look up to meet his eyes. They gleamed like polished silver, as if he enjoyed this, and she caught a whiff of his soap. He smelled very masculine and very rich, with nothing of hard work about him. "Then win him back," the coldhearted devil replied. "Steal him away from me, Lady Gordon."

"But no." She raised her eyebrows at him. How she hated that tone of voice, partly mocking, partly daring, and underpinned with amusement because he knew she would fail even if she tried to do as he suggested. "I am sure your case is much more important than an innocent little girl whisked away from her only living relation by a greedy stepmother. The more I think about it, it is much more appropriate that I seek aid from someone who has only to snap his fingers to bring people running to his bidding. And since you will have Wittiers to do that bidding, you should be able to spare a few hours of your time to attend to my trifling little need."

He stared at her in silence for a moment. That was all the time it took for her to realize what she had just said, and how incredibly stupid she must seem to this man. But it was too late to retreat now, so she kept her chin up.

Then he smiled again. In spite of herself, Francesca couldn't help noticing he looked much more attractive when he smiled like this. "You," he said, "are quite a woman."

"It's the Italian side of me," she replied, as if he had just paid her a great compliment.

"Indeed. I have rarely—" He paused with a sharp glance at her. "—*never* seen such blatantly managing behavior."

Francesca tipped up her chin, smiling warmly at him. She knew the fight was lost but didn't want to leave with her tail between her legs. "Then shall I see you tomorrow, to begin our search?"

"I think not." Still smiling, he bowed his head. "Good day, Lady Gordon."

"I shall never forgive you for such heartless refusal," she called after his departing back.

He glanced at her. "Nor should you," he said gently. "Good-bye, madam." He opened the door and walked out, leaving it open.

"Good riddance, you mean," she said on a sigh. She pressed her fingers to her forehead as a servant appeared in the doorway.

"May I see you out, my lady?" he inquired, polite but firm.

Francesca held her head high. "Thank you." She followed him with regal hauteur through the silent, elegant house until he swept open the imposing front door for her. She marched down the steps, climbed into her carriage, and told Mr. Hotchkiss to take her home.

Then she let her head fall back with a crack against the carriage seat. What a spectacular, and complete, disaster.

Chapter 5

The Earl of Halston, Louisa's father, had taken a comfortable home near Belgrave Square for the Season. The butler showed Edward into the house, and then came back to tell him Lady Louisa was in the garden, and would he care to join her there? Of course he would. He stepped out into the enclosed garden and called her name.

"Edward!" Louisa came down the path, her eyes shining and her cheeks pink. "What a surprise!"

"A pleasant one, I hope." He raised her hand to his lips and inhaled deeply. Louisa smelled so delicately feminine, of lilacs and spring and tea, just like a woman should smell. As always, he was very pleased with his choice of wife.

His fiancée laughed. "Of course! I hope you will stay to dinner as well; Mama will be devastated if you do not."

He shook his head. "Tonight I cannot; perhaps another evening." He tucked her hand around his arm, and she fell in step beside him. "My father died last week."

She bowed her head. "Papa saw the notice in the paper. I am so sorry, Edward."

Edward nodded. "Thank you. We had anticipated it

for some time, of course, because of his failing health, but still . . ." An unexpected sting of loss made him pause to regain his composure. "My brother and I have come to town to settle some affairs of his." There was an understatement.

"Of course," she murmured. "It was good of you to come see me at all, when you must have so much to do."

He smiled wryly. "On the contrary, it was the only thing I wished to do. The rest is far from pleasant, and only the sight of you brings me any peace."

She smiled at him. They were so well-matched, he thought; she understood that he needed calm and peace more than anything right now. Unbidden, the thought of Lady Gordon popped into his mind, all flashing eyes and exuberant gestures. That woman was the very last thing he needed, even aside from her outrageous demand that he drop everything and leap to her assistance. He hoped she had hired a new solicitor already, just so she wouldn't be back to plague him again with her passionate entreaties and alluring voice, to say nothing of that gleaming hair and magnificent bosom— He stopped his thoughts with a slight shake of his head. He was mad to find anything about that woman alluring, particularly when he had a woman like Louisa at his side.

"You know I am always here when you wish to see me," Louisa told him now. "As any good wife ought to be." Then a shadow fell over her face. "We must put off the wedding again, mustn't we?"

Edward sighed. On his honor, he had to do just that— not only to observe some mourning for his father, but to clear away this messy problem before it could become a real scandal. "We must, unfortunately."

Louisa's expression fell, but then she rallied a smile for him, although less brightly than before. "I understand. Next fall will be a fine time to marry. Mama will have no more concerns about my trousseau not being ready in time."

"I knew you would understand." Edward laid his hand over hers. Their engagement had lasted over a year already, and never once had she pressed him on the matter. A model of peace and tranquility, his Louisa.

They walked along the path in companionable silence. "Do you have a great deal to do?" she asked. "His Grace was always so thorough in his planning."

"Indeed. I suppose most of it is rather routine." Edward paused, debating. He hardly wanted his father's shameful secret to become common knowledge, and it made him angry all over again to speak of it at all. But Louisa was his fiancée, his future wife and mother of his future children. If he couldn't confide in her, in whom could he confide? He brushed aside the echo of Gerard's warning. Her brother had never warmed to Louisa, although he readily conceded all her advantages. He thought her too meek and mild; Gerard admired a woman with high spirits and a ready wit, and had no appreciation for Louisa's quiet dignity. Fortunately, she was marrying him, not his brother, and she suited him perfectly. They were two of a kind, he and Louisa.

And in all fairness, he owed her the truth. On the slim chance he and his brothers were unable to tidy away his father's mess, it was only fair that Louisa know his new circumstances.

"There is only one issue that concerns me," he said,

making up his mind. Louisa would stand by him, at least until he discovered the truth. "It seems my father kept one rather large secret from us all, and it will cause us some trouble to sort out."

"Oh dear." Her face filled with concern. "How dreadful."

It certainly was. "I cannot believe Durham could do such a thing," he said, suddenly finding he wanted to tell her. She would understand, as Gerard and Charlie couldn't possibly understand, how it felt to be kept in the dark. "Not the act itself, perhaps, but that he could keep it secret for so long—from *me*. I never failed to do my duty as his son, and then to learn—"

Louisa stopped walking and took his hand in hers as Edward closed his mouth, aware that his voice was rising in temper. "What is it?" she asked. "Surely it cannot be so bad that you and His Grace cannot work it out." She smiled at him. "I have tremendous confidence in you, Edward."

He stared at her hands, so small and soft on his clenched fist. "It is disgraceful," he said in a low tone. "My father was married before my mother—decades ago, to a woman whom no one has seen in almost sixty years. But they were never divorced, and Durham didn't know what happened to her when they parted. He assumed she was dead when he married again, but he was never certain—or never had solid proof. He may have been certain in his own mind; he never spoke a word about this to me or to either of my brothers, and yet now we must find this woman and learn if her marriage to him might invalidate Durham's marriage to my mother."

Saying the words caused the familiar surge of fury, and he paused to brutally press it away. Being angry wasn't going to help anything. "I've already engaged a solicitor to examine the legalities. After so many years, it's unlikely she is still alive, or would come forward to press a claim now, but it is something we must prepare for. If a single stone is left unturned . . ." He sighed. " . . . it would be a disaster."

She didn't say anything. Edward looked closely at her; she had gone alabaster pale and hardly seemed to breathe, her gaze glassy and fixed on his face.

"Good God," he exclaimed, catching her in his arms. "Are you about to faint?"

"No," she said, her voice a thin gasp. "I—I don't think so. Oh, Edward, that cannot be true!"

"No matter how hard I wished and prayed, it has not evaporated like a bad dream," he replied. "I hated to burden you, but it was only fair to tell you. But you must promise me to keep it in confidence. It will be unpleasant enough to wade through my father's distant past without gossip spreading like a plague through the town."

Again she didn't reply. Louisa turned out of his arm and stumbled away to a bench, fanning one hand in front of her face. Edward felt suddenly awful for telling her; he could see how hard it hit her. He sat beside her on the bench and waited for her to recover.

"And—And you are certain nothing will come of it?" she asked at last, her chest still heaving as if she'd run a mile.

"Absolutely," he answered immediately. "The solicitor agrees."

Louisa dipped her head in a shallow nod. "That is good," she murmured. "Oh, Edward—how terrible for you if it did not!"

He sighed. "Terrible indeed. The title was never to be mine, but the rest . . . My brothers and I wouldn't be destitute, as Durham left us modestly provided for, but losing Durham would be a mighty blow." And they would still be bastards. Edward knew it wasn't nearly enough recompense.

"That—That was very thoughtful of him . . ."

"Yes." There was nothing else to say about it. It was only a small amount. Much of Durham's income was tied to the estates that produced it, and most of them were entailed. They couldn't be left to anyone but the next duke, and if that person should wind up being someone other than Charlie . . . he and Gerard would lose their share of the income as well. And worst of all, the entail on some of the properties ended with Charlie—or whomever assumed the dukedom next— and it had been their father's explicit wish that Charlie give each of his brothers an estate of his own: the Sussex property to Edward, and a similar one in Cornwall to Gerard. His expectations had been very grand indeed, until a few days ago.

After a few moments Edward stirred. He still had things to do, and couldn't linger in the garden with Louisa. His terrible news had thrown a pall over their time together in any case. "I must go, Louisa. I'm sorry to have brought such unhappy news, but I couldn't keep it from you."

"No," she said thinly. "No. I—I am glad you told me. What a dreadful secret to keep!"

He glanced at her sideways, unsure if she meant it would be dreadful to keep it a secret herself, or that his father had been dreadful to keep it from him. "But you will keep it in close confidence?"

"Oh!" She looked up at him with wide blue eyes. "Of course I will—not a breath of it shall pass my lips."

Edward smiled at her. "Thank you." He pressed a kiss to her knuckles.

"But Edward," she said anxiously, "how much longer must we put off the wedding, do you think?"

He turned her hand over, tracing one fingertip gently over the delicate veins in her wrist. "A few months, at least—six, perhaps, for proper mourning."

"Oh." She sighed. "I see." She got to her feet, tugging her hand free of his grasp. "I had better go in," she said, glancing over her shoulder toward the house. "Mama will be getting curious, and I will have to tell her . . . about the postponement, that is . . ."

"Of course." He rose and reached for her. Normally Louisa accepted his kiss with a blush and a smile, but this time she lifted her face with an almost tragic expression. He brushed his lips against hers, dismayed to feel them tremble. "I'll speak to your father to explain about the postponement," he told her. "You don't have to say a word if you don't wish to."

"If you like," she whispered, looking at him with glistening eyes. "He isn't home at present. Oh—Oh, Edward!" She shivered and took a step forward into his arms.

"There, now," he said, holding her lightly and patting her on the back. "I'll call on him tomorrow. It will come out all right."

She stood rather stiff and still in his loose embrace, then stepped back. "I hope so. I—" She bit her lip. Her face was still very pale. "Good day, Edward."

"Good day, dearest."

She closed her eyes at the last word, but then rallied a smile for him. Edward bowed and left, appreciating all over again that he had chosen the ideal bride. Her father, Earl Halston, would understand he must observe some mourning for his father, but they could still be married by Christmas. As for the rest . . . he devoutly hoped no one need ever hear about that.

Francesca woke with a mood as gloomy as the day. After returning home yesterday she'd reviewed her lists of solicitors again, and remembered what each man had said to her. Alconbury had come by and tried to persuade her to come to the theater with him that night, saying she was in dreadful need of raising her spirits, but she couldn't bear even that. She'd sent him on his way, and consoled herself with a few glasses of wine. It had struck her very hard that Ellen had taken Georgina, even harder than the loss of Wittiers. At least before, she'd known where Georgina was, even if she hadn't been allowed to see her. Now she didn't even have the hope of seeing her. What if Ellen had run off to America? Or to the Continent? It would take forever to track her down, particularly if old Mr. Kendall remained blithely indifferent to her concerns about Georgina's care.

Her housekeeper brought the morning post and newspapers with her breakfast. Francesca sat at the table and flipped through them, barely looking at each one. She didn't feel like accepting invitations now, and she couldn't bear to answer her aunt's letter. Aunt Evelyn had been more mother to her than her real mother, raising her from the time she was five. She put Evelyn's letter aside with a twinge of guilt and drank her tea. Her head hurt. She hadn't slept very well, and no doubt there were dark circles under her eyes from it. She thought about going back to bed, just for a little while.

"Lord Alconbury's sent a posy of violets," said Mrs. Hotchkiss, setting the flowers in the center of the table. "Quite pretty, I think."

Francesca sighed. "Very pretty. And so thoughtful of him."

"Such a gentleman," murmured Mrs. Hotchkiss as she bustled out of the room with the empty teapot.

Francesca smiled wryly. Her housekeeper thought she should marry again, and had decided Alconbury was the right man. He was certainly pleasant enough: handsome, charming, and intelligent. She simply couldn't imagine going to bed with him, though, and right now thoughts of men and marriage were the farthest thing from her mind. Everything except Georgina was far from her mind, it seemed. She turned over the newspapers, barely seeing the page. Unless Ellen had published her new location in the papers, there wasn't much that could catch her interest . . .

Except for what was printed.

Francesca read the opening lines in shock, then snatched it up for a closer examination. It was Gregory Sloan's gossip sheet, which was so often wrong it was only suitable for kindling. He paid outrageous money for the most salacious rumors, and then rushed them into print, often without any effort to substantiate them. She wasn't even sure why she subscribed to it. But there, in bold black print, was the heartless and aristocratic Edward de Lacey's name.

THE DURHAM DILEMMA, it read across the top of the page. "Rumors are swirling about town that the late Duke of Durham may have left his sons an unexpected, and much unwanted, inheritance," the story began.

The duke, who died only a week ago, contracted a secret marriage several decades ago. One can only wonder why it was kept so secret until now, when the dukedom and all its wealth are poised in the balance. Perhaps because that marriage was still lawfully binding when the duke married his duchess? Perhaps because all three Durham sons would be totally disinherited if it were discovered? But it seems the Durham sons are not unaware of this dark secret. Lord Gresham, the eldest—and perhaps future duke—has taken to his bed and not been seen in over a week. Lord Edward de Lacey is suddenly and unexpectedly in town, consulting solicitors. Surely the appearance of Augustus de Lacey, the cousin who would be heir presumptive, cannot be far off. And one can only wonder what society will make of this dreadful dilemma . . .

The piece went on, wandering into ever more incendiary suppositions, but Francesca's mouth had fallen open by the third sentence. Her mind whirled. Well, that certainly explained why Lord Edward summoned Wittiers. She had expected it was some ordinary matter of money or property. This was far more serious, involving not only money and property but his standing in society and the life he had been born to expect, to say nothing of his very name. Of course, she was doubtful even James Wittiers could argue a dukedom from someone else's grasp if there were evidence it rightfully belonged to that person, but in Lord Edward's place, she would have used every leverage at her disposal to secure Wittiers's services, too.

And perhaps . . . She eyed the size of the letters screaming across the front page. She thought of Sloan, tall, big, loud, and hawk-eyed. If this edition sold well, he'd print more about this Durham dilemma tomorrow, and the day after. If Lord Edward had ever looked crossly at his scullery maid, Sloan would probably have her sad story in his paper by the end of the week.

Perhaps that handed her a bit of leverage as well.

She jumped up from the table and gave a hard pull on the bell rope. "Mrs. Hotchkiss, I must go out," she said when the housekeeper hurried in. "Immediately."

"I'll send Mr. Hotchkiss for the horses at once," replied the woman, startled. "Will you be changing?"

Francesca looked down at her comfortable morning dress. "Oh, goodness, yes. I want to look breathtaking. I've just gotten a second chance with Edward de Lacey!"

It was barely an hour later that her carriage turned once more into Berkeley Square. The facade of the Durham residence looked even more imposing under the roiling black clouds above, but today she walked sedately up the steps and rapped the knocker, firmly but not nearly as hard as her heart was pounding behind her ribs.

This time she told the butler it was imperative that she speak to Lord Edward on a matter related to their conversation the previous day. She held her breath, hoping that Lord Edward hadn't told his servants not to admit her again, and when they did so, she switched to hoping he would agree to see her. By the time she was shown into the same blue room to wait, her stays felt way too tight and she had to clasp her hands together to keep from wringing them.

Today she only waited a few minutes before he strode through the door, as severe as she remembered. She noticed the black band around his sleeve. Perhaps mourning accounted for his dark, plain clothing. His expression was as imperturbable as it had been yesterday, but she smiled as he closed the door behind him.

"Lady Gordon." He bowed, his gray eyes steady on her.

"My lord." She curtsied. "I have come to apologize."

"Indeed." His gaze flickered over her. Francesca knew she looked her best today, in a rich green walking dress with golden ribbons. There was no overt admiration in his gaze, only examination, but it made her feel more confident all the same to know there was no fault with her appearance. "I assure you, that is not necessary."

"But it is," she said with feeling. He meant that she needn't have come again; she meant that she had made a mistake in approaching him so intemperately to begin with. There very much was a need for her to apologize.

"I was very out of temper yesterday, and spoke imprudently and impolitely."

"Not at all," he replied, proving himself a better liar than she had anticipated. "I am delighted you have found other aid. Now—"

"No," she said gently. "I still have need of your aid—but now, I believe, you may be in need of mine as well." She drew out the page of newsprint from her reticule. "Perhaps you have not seen."

For a moment he just looked at her with those cool gray eyes, measuring her. Francesca waited patiently, holding out the paper. She knew his type, this straight and proper gentleman. He'd see his name in the newspaper, and the shocking rumors attached to it, and be furious. Men dueled over such things. Lord Edward would rage about a bit, and when he calmed down she would make her offer. Unless he was a very great fool, he would see the sense of it at once. And then she would have the chance she so desperately needed.

He took the newspaper, smoothing the curled edges and pulling it flat. His eyes never left her, as if he waited for some flicker of temper as an excuse to dismiss her again. Today, though, she was on her very best behavior. Yesterday she had been half mad with frustration and outrage and even fear, but today she was given a reprieve, and she meant to make the very most of it. Today, nothing he said or did would make her lose her temper, even if she had to bite off her own tongue to keep silent. Francesca met his gaze evenly, keeping her face arranged in a modest, serene expression, and waited.

Finally he looked at the newspaper, his gaze dipping

away from hers. His eyelashes looked absurdly long from this angle, she thought in surprise, thick and dark against his cheeks. Her Aunt Evelyn used to say every woman had some feature to be proud of, be it a lovely neck or good skin or fine eyes; she wondered if Lord Edward de Lacey was proud of his long, beautiful eyelashes, and had to press her lips together to avoid smiling at the thought.

He didn't look up for some time, more than enough to have read the offending piece several times over. She had unconsciously tensed in anticipation of an outburst, but his face didn't change, and he didn't move. He could have been carved of marble for all the reaction and emotion he showed, even though the paper had all but called him and his brothers bastards and imposters. She was just beginning to wonder if she had grossly misunderstood things when he spoke.

"Very well, Lady Gordon," he said without looking up. "You have piqued my interest. What bargain have you come to offer?"

"I am acquainted with Mr. Sloan, who publishes this newspaper. He has come to my musicales on a few occasions." He had propositioned her as well. She said a sincere prayer of thanks that she had declined him gently and not laughed in his face. One never knew when a shred of goodwill might be needed. "I can arrange a meeting to persuade him to print a retraction."

Lord Edward was silent for a long moment. "I could sue him for defamation."

"He would never print a retraction then," she said. "He is . . . somewhat stubborn when confronted." Sloan was an ambitious man who'd worked his way up from nothing to a position of some power. Of course, he'd done it by printing the most scandalous gossip and salacious stories in his gossip sheets, which were consequently in hot demand. If Lord Edward filed a suit, Sloan would react like a caged bear and print everything he could find about the de Laceys, even if he libeled himself right into debtor's prison. That, Francesca was certain, would help no one, least of all her. "But I believe, because of our acquaintance, he would listen to me."

"And you could persuade him to retract this?" He slanted her a dry look. "No doubt he will be reluctant to withdraw such a shocking story."

"I can persuade him," she said, ignoring any whisper of doubt in her mind. If she couldn't persuade Sloan, she would have nothing to entice Lord Edward into helping her.

He turned and walked away, his footsteps echoing in the bare, beautiful room. At the window he stopped, feet braced apart and hands clasped behind his back, the newspaper still between his fingers. Only when he took a deep breath and rolled his shoulders back did Francesca see any sign of tension in him. She had to admire that, given what Sloan had printed in his gossip sheet. She never found it easy to keep such tight rein on her thoughts and feelings; in Lord Edward's place, she would have broken something by now, most likely.

"And what service would you ask of me, in thanks for this favor?" he asked after a few minutes, turning his head slightly to ask over his shoulder.

Francesca took some eager steps forward before catching herself. "I require help with a legal matter.

My niece, Georgina, has been living with her step-mother since her father's death. My sister, her mother, died two years ago. Her father had promised to name me in his will but he did not; there is no legal guardian living. I am godmother to Georgina, and I would like to raise her now that both her parents are gone, but her stepmother refuses to allow me even to see the child, and has moved house without telling anyone where they went. I want to find my niece and have her given into my care."

"I am not certain I see how I could help you at all."

She sidled a few more steps toward him, but moderately this time. "James Wittiers was the only solicitor who didn't shake his head in regret or patronize me for being a hysterical female. If you merely help me find another reputable solicitor who will take my case seriously, I would consider it very fair repayment."

He half turned, not quite facing her, and cocked his head. "You wish me to interview solicitors for you?"

"No," she said, her voice trembling ever so slightly as hope dug its shiny talons into her heart. "I wish you to help me interview solicitors. They have all dismissed a woman alone, of no great standing and no great fortune. I have funds to pay," she rushed to assure him. "I am not asking for charity. I merely need . . . consequence."

He inhaled deeply, still staring fixedly across the room, not toward her. Francesca studied his profile, hardly daring to breathe. He had a firm jaw, which was now tensed tight, and a slight crook to his nose that wasn't apparent from straight on. Somehow the thought of him fighting and having his nose broken at some point in life made him seem more approachable, more like her and less the exalted son of a duke. He also has a nice mouth, a small part of her noticed. She remembered the way he had smiled at her yesterday, at the end, and thought to herself that he would be a very dangerous man if ever roused to passion. And for some reason she found the image very attractive.

She stopped her wayward thoughts with a guilty flinch. She wanted his help in her quest to find Georgina. She had no business wondering what it would be like to see him in a passion, or what it would take to arouse him so. She must have become lonelier than she'd thought since Cecil died. If she wanted a man, Lord Alconbury could be hers in a matter of hours, and he was amusing, charming, and attracted to her. And obviously, since she didn't want Alconbury enough to take what he had frequently hinted she could, she didn't want a man at all. Especially not this dark, somber man who needed to smile more.

"I presume you have a list," he said at last. "Of solicitors."

"I— Yes." She gathered her wandering wits. "Four or five names."

He nodded slowly, his head sinking lower until he had an almost brooding air. "Bring Sloan," he said, very quietly. "As soon as you can."

"Of course," she said, even as her heart skipped a beat. "I will send word the moment I hear from him."

Finally he turned to her. "Thank you, Lady Gordon." He put out his hand. "I believe we have an agreement."

She put her hand in his. "I'm sorry it began under these circumstances," she said honestly, with a flicker of her eyes toward the newspaper he still held.

Without looking at it, he folded the paper in half and put it behind his back. "Indeed," was all he said.

Francesca was impressed. The man must have ice in his blood, or perhaps in his belly; his hand was certainly warm enough, wrapped around hers. She could feel the warmth and strength of his grip even through her gloves. His fingers pressed hers for a moment, and then he released her.

"Good day, sir," she said, her voice gone oddly breathless.

He studied her. His eyes weren't cold, flat gray at all; there were shards of blue in them, like glimpses of clear sky between clearing clouds. "Until later," he replied.

Chapter 6

E dward stood at the window for a long time. His caller appeared on the steps below. Even on this dark and cloudy day her hair shone like a new penny. He hadn't noticed that gleam when she was in this room, just a few feet away from him. Next time, he'd have to look more closely at her hair and not be so distracted by the rest of her.

And there was plenty to distract him. On the street below, she spoke to her coachman, one gloved hand gesturing eloquently as the man nodded. She was pleased; every line of her figure radiated it. If he could see her face, no doubt her eyes would be glowing and that lovely flush of color would have risen as before, when he told her to bring Sloan. It put him in mind of fresh peaches or newly bloomed roses, soft and pink and begging to be touched. His eyes tracked the curve of her cheek, visible beneath her bonnet, but it was too far to see if his mental image was correct. Her shawl had slipped down one shoulder, exposing the skin of her bosom, as pale as fresh cream next to the dark green of her dress. At least his memory of her bosom had proved highly accurate. The fashionable gown she'd worn this morning

had shown off those assets even better than the severe
dark dress yesterday. Lord Gordon, whoever he was or
had been, was a fortunate fellow.

She finished speaking to her coachman and stepped
into the carriage with a brief flash of trim white ankle.
The driver closed the door behind her and climbed up
on his box. The horses started off, and Lady Gordon
was gone—for now.

He supposed he ought not to think of her at all, especially not with this fascinated awareness, but thinking
of her was preferable to thinking of anything else—
particularly his fiancée, Louisa, who had told someone
his secret after vowing not to. His first incredulous
thought, on reading the newspaper Lady Gordon had
brought, was that someone spied on him, or that Wittiers had been indiscreet, or that one of his brothers let
something slip after too much wine. But buried in the
dregs of the story was mention of his engagement—or
rather, his recently broken engagement. Since even he
hadn't known it was broken, the source could only be,
somehow, Louisa. He'd been on the verge of calling
on her father this morning when Lady Gordon arrived.
Thank heaven she had, since it saved him from making
a damned fool of himself for presuming he could trust
his own bloody fiancée.

The cheap gossip sheet crumpled in his fist, and he
forced himself to smooth it out and read it once more.
Edward seethed at the thought of having to beg the man
who printed it for a retraction, even though he knew it
was his best hope of salvaging matters. A quick retraction would allow him to deny the horrible truths printed
in front of him, or at least turn a repressive eye on any

gossipers. If Lady Gordon could effect one, he would indeed be in her debt, although some damage had already been done.

Slowly, deliberately, he ripped the paper into shreds. The ink left smudges on his fingers, as if the malice on the page were seeping into him like some poison. He crossed the room to the fireplace and tossed the pieces into the grate, then rang the bell. "Lay a fire," he instructed the footman who came. "At once." He wanted a bonfire, to obliterate that rag from his home.

The servant bowed and hurried off. Edward scowled at his stained hands, and went upstairs to wash. Fervently he wished he were still in Sussex. There he could have gone for weeks without needing to see anyone or face any whispers. In London he doubted he could go anywhere now without encountering someone who had heard the rumors; rumor, his father used to say, was the only thing that spread faster than contagion.

The truth of that was borne out within a few minutes, when Gerard returned. Edward heard his brother's voice, and then his footsteps in the hall, as he was scrubbing the last trace of ink from his hands. With barely a knock on the door, Gerard barged in. "What the bloody hell is this?"

Edward glanced at the familiar page of newsprint in his brother's upraised fist. "A piece of rubbish. I'm surprised you read such things, Gerard."

His brother flushed. "I don't—except when my own name is in them and people hail me from passing carriages to ask if I'm about to flee the country with the Durham silver plate."

He sighed and reached for a towel. "I'm sorry for

that. It was as rude a shock to me as it was to you."

Gerard narrowed his eyes. Edward said nothing; he wouldn't have to. Gerard was more perceptive than people gave him credit for. His brother bent his head and read the newspaper as though searching for something, then winced. Edward knew what part he had read, or finally grasped. "Damn. I'm sorry, Edward," he said quietly. Nothing more. Charlie would have made some mention of being right about Louisa, or at least kept speaking about the matter when he wanted to say nothing at all about it. Gerard knew when to keep his mouth closed. Edward had never appreciated that about his younger brother more than he did now.

"No apology is necessary," he replied evenly. Pity was useless.

Gerard cleared his throat and folded the newspaper. "How should we respond?"

"I've already had a suggestion. It may be possible to persuade the printer to issue a retraction."

"That will cost a pretty penny."

Edward thought of Lady Gordon's gleaming hair and luscious bosom. If this Sloan fellow were half as fascinated by her as he was . . . "Perhaps not. It may only cost me a personal favor."

Now his brother was intrigued. "To whom? Not that I feel inclined to offer this gossipmonger anything, mind you."

He smiled thinly. "Nor I. No, the favor would be for an intermediary who wishes something else from me."

"What?"

He hesitated. For some reason, he didn't want to tell Gerard about Lady Gordon. She was exactly the sort of woman his brother liked; if nothing else, Gerard would applaud her boldness in offering her bargain, although Edward imagined he would admire many other things about her as well. "Nothing very exciting," he said vaguely. "A legal problem."

That squelched his brother's interest. "Ah. Then you don't plan to visit the printer?"

"Stay out of this, Gerard," Edward warned, seeing his brother flex his hands. Gerard's temper was a little too hot for this situation. From what Lady Gordon had said, Sloan required delicate manipulation. Even if she had merely told him that to gain his assistance, he was fairly certain it wasn't wise to beat a man with a printing press.

"What? I only want to help."

That was probably true, but they would almost certainly disagree on the method of help. He just gave Gerard a speaking look. Beating up the printer wouldn't help their cause at all. "In that case, I've got the papers you want downstairs," he said, changing the subject to one they both approved. "Father's reports as well as the blackmail letters themselves. I hope you see something in them that Pierce missed."

They went downstairs to their father's study, which still smelled faintly of his tobacco. Edward couldn't help feeling as if some part of his father's spirit lingered there as they looked through the four brief letters to Durham, threatening the exposure of his long-ago marriage to Dorothy Cope unless the sum of five thousand pounds, all in gold coin, was left near a certain gravestone in the churchyard of St. Martin's in London. They reread all the reports from Durham's investigators as well, which

Edward privately thought very thorough. He didn't see much for Gerard to exploit.

"This isn't much to go on," Gerard finally said, echoing his thoughts.

Edward shrugged. "You don't have to go after the blackmailer."

His brother's expression hardened. "Oh, I'm going after him. This bloody thief has already caused us a lot of trouble and now started a scandal. He'll regret sending these." He sat back and stared thoughtfully into space. "I wonder if someone was sent to watch the churchyard other than on the dates specified in the letters."

"Father made no mention of it." Edward glanced through the long, detailed letter from his father to be sure. Durham had written out a summary of his actions as best he could recall them, and made no mention of watching the graveyard. Edward still wished he had known at the time, instead of later, but he could read between the lines of his father's shaky, scratchy scrawl. Durham had died with a terrible weight on his heart. "If he did, nothing must have come of it."

"I could try leaving a package at the gravestone and see what happens," Gerard murmured. "Or chat up the rector and see who's been lingering about the church lately . . ."

"I leave you to it, then." Edward rose. "I've got a few things to attend to." Sending a note to Earl Halston, principally, to verify that his betrothal was indeed over.

"No doubt." Gerard got up to leave, folding the letters and reports carefully. "Edward . . ." His head bent over his task, he didn't look up as he spoke. "I have no proof, but Halston is reputedly in a very tight spot. A fellow was telling me last night at White's that Halston hoped to have his daughter wed before the end of summer. The promise of your marriage to Louisa has been keeping his creditors at bay, but . . ." He cleared his throat, fiddling with the papers before shoving them into his pocket. "That is to say, ending it might not have been Louisa's desire."

But she hadn't brought herself to confide in him about it either way, as he confided in her. And she had explicitly promised to keep his confidence. Edward felt that betrayal more sharply than any mercenary behavior on Louisa's part. He could have understood and perhaps even accepted a severe financial crisis, if she had just told him. He could have understood if her family recoiled from the scandal. But a broken promise was something else. "Thank you, Gerard," he said quietly.

His brother coughed, then murmured a farewell and left, his face set in that determined expression that made Edward wonder if perhaps Gerard might succeed where Durham had failed. It didn't change what he meant to have Wittiers do, but it would be rather gratifying to see the instigator of this disaster punished in some way.

The reply to his note to Halston was swift in coming. The earl was polite, but said that given the unexpected upheaval in Edward's life, it was only natural that he must withdraw his consent to the marriage, as a concerned father. Edward wondered if his concern or Louisa's had been the prevailing factor, and how exactly a gossip sheet had gotten wind of the break before he himself was told. He had promised Louisa he would call on her father at the earliest convenience; would it have been too much to expect to be told to his face, and not made to look like a jilted idiot in front of all London? Apparently so.

He was still brooding over it when the butler brought another note. This one was in a round, vibrant hand that conveyed energy. Without even breaking the seal, Edward knew it was from Lady Gordon.

> *Dear sir,*
>
> *I have prevailed upon Mr. S to call on me this evening before dinner. I believe it will put him more at ease to call at my home instead of yours. It would be best if you arrived earlier, so that we may discuss our circumstances. If you could join me at six o'clock, I would be much obliged.*
>
> *Humbly yours,*
> *F. Gordon*

He wondered how she had persuaded Sloan to come. He wondered what circumstances they would have to discuss. And most of all, he wondered what the F stood for.

He arrived promptly at six that evening. Her home was a quaint little town house not far from Russell Square, nothing to the quiet elegance of Berkeley Square but appealing nonetheless. The footman ran up the stairs ahead of him to rap the knocker, and the door was almost instantly opened by a neat, middle-aged housekeeper.

"Come in, my lord," she said, holding the door as Edward walked in. "Lady Gordon is expecting you." And indeed, the lady herself appeared as he was shedding his coat and hat.

"Good evening, sir." She dipped a curtsey. "Thank you for coming."

He barely heard what she said. Her hair, shining as brightly as before, was arranged in loose, seductive waves that looked as though a man had been running his hands through it, and she had just caught it up in a few combs. Tendrils curled around her temples and at the nape of her neck, teasing that fine, fair skin he had remarked earlier. Her gown looked ordinary until she moved, when it swirled and caught on the curves of her hip and waist. He had thought it was some dark silk, but realized instead it was thin black net draped over a gown the color of flame that shimmered with her every movement. The image of a living flame, smoldering beneath a respectable facade, caught his imagination and fixed him in place. What else about her burned?

She cocked her head to one side as he stood staring at her. "I hope my note wasn't abrupt," she said. "You said you wished to see him as soon as possible—"

"Yes!" Edward gave himself a mental shake and bowed. "Good evening, Lady Gordon. Your note was perfectly timed, and I have no complaint."

Her expression eased into a smile. There was something about the way her chin dipped and the way her eyes sparkled that made it look rather coy and seductive. Or perhaps that was his imagination, which seemed to have sprouted wings and soared out of its normal range tonight. She held out one hand toward a pair of doors standing open. "Won't you come in? We have some matters to settle first."

Edward followed her into the room, trying to ignore the swish of her skirt as she walked before him. It was just a business arrangement between them, he reminded himself. The way she moved—and smiled—was a distraction he would have to ignore. The housekeeper who had admitted him closed the doors of the room, and they were alone.

"May I offer you a drink?" she asked as they sat down, she on a small settee and he on a facing chair. A tray filled with a number of crystal decanters was on the table beside her. Lady Gordon entertained gentlemen often, from the looks of things.

Normally Edward only drank after supper, but tonight he took one more look at those loose curls trailing over her shoulders and said, "Please."

"Perhaps I should tell you about Mr. Sloan first." She poured a glass of brandy and held it out to him.

Edward took a sip and nodded. "By all means, if you think it necessary."

"His father was a stevedore," she began. "He wanted more out of life, so he cast about for something profitable. Publishing the scandalous secrets of people above him—and to his mind, that includes nearly everyone—not only made him money, but brought him some status as well. He is fiercely proud of his achievement; he is rich, as he wanted to be, and he has made his money off the troubles of aristocrats and other proud people, the sort who have always looked down on him." She hesitated a moment, rolling her lower lip between her teeth. "If you brought a suit against him, he would react very badly, even if it meant his own ruin."

Edward inclined his head. "I grasp your meaning."

A sigh of relief slipped through her lips, and she smiled. "Fortunately, I have an acquaintance with him. Not a close one, really, but cordial enough that I believe our association will sway his inclination. However, to make the most of our chance, it would be best if Mr. Sloan believes you to be a close friend of mine."

"Ah." *How close?* whispered some devil in his mind, the devil that was still preoccupied with the lines of her collarbone. Her incendiary gown didn't cover them at all. "How do you suggest I proceed?" he asked to drown out the insidious little voice.

A bit of that flush he had admired earlier rose in her cheeks again, although her expression remained the same. "You might call me Francesca, instead of Lady Gordon. Permit me to call you Edward a time or two. Allow me to insinuate we have known each other for some time, and have a special affection for each other. I promise not to go so far that he will begin to print rumors of our attachment," she rushed to add, watching him closely. "Just enough that he will view it as a favor for me as well."

Her name was Francesca. How unusual—but then, she had mentioned something about being Italian, even though she looked and sounded every inch an English-woman. "I have no objection," he said. He probably should have one, especially since he quite liked the sound of his name in her husky voice. A business arrangement, he thought again; business only. *Francesca.*

"Very well." She wet her lips. "I should probably beg your pardon now for anything I might say. I have a lamentable tendency to get carried away in the heat of the moment, and say more than I intended. I've been thinking all day how to persuade Mr. Sloan to issue a retraction, but it will have to be decided by how he reacts."

"If you can persuade him to retract, publicly and prominently, you may say almost anything you like," Edward said dryly. "I shan't be offended by what is, for all purposes, a performance."

Her eyebrows went up slightly in surprise. "Quite right!" A pleased smile spread over her face. "How fortunate we see it the same way."

He smiled faintly. "If we did not, I wouldn't here, would I?"

Her lips twitched but she didn't look away. "I really am very sorry for haranguing you yesterday."

"There is no need for regret." He paused, then decided there was no reason to stop himself. They were on a more intimate footing tonight already. "I gathered you were under some strong emotional influence."

Her lips parted, and she took a deep breath before answering. "Yes. But I ought not to have succumbed to it."

Edward dismissed it with a wave of one hand. "No, no. When one's family is endangered, there is no stricture that cannot be broken. In your place I would have done the same."

"I very much doubt it," she exclaimed, and then looked as though she wanted to snatch the words back.

He cleared his throat. "Yes, well. Perhaps not *exactly* the same . . ."

She gave him a look, her eyebrows raised and her lips slowly curling. It was an intimate smile, one lovers might share over a private joke. Edward resisted the urge to shift in his chair, and instead took another sip of his brandy.

"All right, I might have done something utterly different," he conceded. "But only in deed, not in spirit." He paused, watching her expressive face glow with subtle amusement. "I truly am very sorry for your difficulties over your niece. I hope the girl is not in any danger."

She blinked several times, very quickly, then straightened her shoulders. "Thank you," she said. "I hope not, too."

Now that he was staring at her, he seemed unable to stop. His eyes roamed over her face, beautifully flushed, and her gleaming hair, so glorious against her skin. The other day, when she railed at him for stealing her solicitor, she'd been magnificent, in the manner of an avenging Fury. Francesca Gordon in a passion was quite a sight. The little devil that had invaded his mind tonight couldn't stop comparing her to Louisa, who went pale and silent in emotional upset. Francesca—he really mustn't become accustomed to thinking of her as such—reacted with anger and action. She stormed his house, the home of a total stranger, and upbraided him for inadvertently ruining her hopes. She said she would never forgive him, and smiled wickedly when he called her a managing female. By God, one could have a rousing good row with a woman like this, and then . . .

Edward closed his eyes and inhaled to quell the images springing to his mind in vivid, sinful detail of how they could get over an argument. He didn't want to have an argument with any woman, no matter how sweet the reconciliation. He admired women like Louisa, who knew when to hold her tongue and be tactful and agreeable. It kept life orderly and predictable.

Unfortunately, tonight would likely be none of those things. And Louisa, who was so perfectly suited to him and claimed to love him, had broken their engagement in the most public, humiliating way possible.

He looked at his hostess. She was a handsome woman, with spirit and courage. If she could achieve what she promised tonight, he would be happy to line up every last solicitor in London for her inspection. Then he would bid her farewell, and that would be the end of their association.

Francesca . . .

With one twist of his wrist he drained the last of his brandy.

"May I pour you some more?" she asked. Flame silk flickered at him as she leaned toward the tray with the decanter. The firelight shone on her hair as if it were a mirror. Edward felt as dry as tinder.

"Absolutely."

Chapter 7

Francesca was quickly discovering that she wasn't quite as prepared for this evening as she had thought.

She wasn't worried about Sloan. He had replied to her note with a great deal of warmth and alacrity. He might not be anticipating the same evening she was, but he would be here, and she refused to consider the chance that she might fail to persuade him. If nothing else, Sloan appreciated the value of having people in his debt, and this would put her—and Lord Edward—very much in his debt.

But inviting Lord Edward to her house, and seeing him there, was more jarring than expected. From the moment he first stepped into the house, darkly somber in his evening clothes, he seemed to take in everything in a glance before fastening his attention on her, and now he sat and watched her over his brandy glass with those inscrutable gray eyes. Francesca felt on edge. He looked taller here in her bright, cozy parlor than in the chilly blue salon in Berkeley Square, where the high ceiling dwarfed them both. She had dressed very carefully for tonight, in one of her favorite gowns that made her feel strong and beautiful. Female beauty was a form of power, and tonight she needed every advantage she could find. It was meant much more to beguile Gregory Sloan than Edward de Lacey, but the longer she sat under Lord Edward's regard, the more aware she felt of every whisper of the silk against her body. She could almost tell when he was looking at her; her skin seemed to tingle. There was nothing offensive or importunate in his gaze. He just watched her with a directness she wasn't used to, as if she were of immense interest to him. Not even Alconbury fixed his attention on her so completely.

And strangely, she didn't find it bothersome, just unsettling. As if someone who should have taken no notice of her had suddenly become deeply interested. She didn't know how to respond to his interest. Of course, he was interested in what she could do for him, and perhaps in what he would be required to do for her. She was a little surprised when he asked about Georgina, but she could hear the sincerity in his voice when he spoke of family. Of course, his family had been threatened as well, so perhaps he understood, in a way, how she felt and why she acted as she had.

She was glad when he accepted more brandy. It gave her something to do, and at the same time another excuse to look at him. Even as he was, at ease with a brandy in hand, he looked controlled and reserved. She hoped he would remain so, at least as long as it took her to convince Gregory Sloan to print a retraction. If he were to lash out at Gregory and begin an argument, her whole plan could end in disaster.

Fortunately, the guest of honor arrived then, a go(

quarter hour before she had specified. Francesca rose to her feet at the sound of the door knocker, smoothing her hands over her skirt and composing herself for the following performance, as Lord Edward had called it. He rose as well. Without a word he moved to the fireplace and leaned one elbow against the mantel, as if he were a welcome and frequent guest in her home. She gave him a nod of approval, then turned as Mrs. Hotchkiss opened the door for Sloan.

He strode in with a look of victory about him, but stopped abruptly as he saw Lord Edward. Francesca went toward him, hands outstretched. "Mr. Sloan," she said warmly, "how lovely of you to come by."

He raised her hand to his lips. "As if I would refuse any invitation from you."

She laughed lightly, ignoring his implied meaning. "A lady must never presume these things. But here— there is someone I particularly wish you to meet. May I introduce you to my friend?" At his curt nod, she turned to the other man. "Edward, this is Mr. Gregory Sloan. Gregory, may I present Lord Edward de Lacey?"

His expression stiffened at the name, but Sloan bowed every bit as politely as Lord Edward did.

"May I pour you a drink?" Francesca asked her new guest.

Sloan said nothing for a moment, his eyes on Lord Edward. "My dear Francesca—" he began softly.

"Oh, yes, you know I had an ulterior motive in inviting you tonight." She poured a generous brandy and pressed the glass into his hand before seating herself.

"But really, Gregory, how could you print such things and not expect to stir up a tempest?"

His eyes darkened, just a little, but Francesca saw it. A mask slid over his features, almost as an actor slipping into a part. Sloan lifted one shoulder as he took the chair opposite her, where Lord Edward had been sitting a few moments ago. "It was business, my dear. Nothing but business."

"As if that excuses everything," she murmured.

"In my world it does," he replied, and took a large swallow of his drink.

"Would you print such things about me?" she asked in reproach. He just looked at her. "Because it was every bit as distressing to me as it was to Edward."

"I told you not to pay it any mind, my dear," said Lord Edward, to her surprise. He left his post by the fireplace and came to sit beside her on the settee. It wasn't a large piece of furniture, and he made no effort to keep his distance. Francesca's pulse jumped as their shoulders bumped, and she had to stop herself from inching away.

Sloan looked between the two of them. "I'd no idea you were even acquainted with his lordship," he said stiffly. "Even so, I cannot withhold every bit of news just because it affects you or any other friend of mine. I'd have nothing to print."

Francesca felt the tension spring up in Lord Edward's arm, so close to hers. "I do understand, Gregory," she said quickly. "You know I read your naughty paper every day—such a bad influence you are." She pursed her lips in a teasing imitation of a grimace, and Sloan smiled a little. "But in this case I had to speak to you. You must admit it was rather shocking and exceptional, what you wrote, and bound to cause quite an uproar. And Edward and I have known each other for some time," she added. She tilted back her head to flash a brilliant smile of warning at the man in question. "He's simply not in town much."

Lord Edward smiled back at her. "To my regret. The moment I saw your face yesterday, I couldn't remember why I stayed away so long." To Francesca's shock, he was looking at her as if they were much more than friends, with that dangerously attractive smile she had noted before—and warned herself to be wary of. Flustered, she yanked her attention back to Sloan, who was watching with a mixture of skepticism and interest.

"I won't deny your scandal sheets are very amusing," she said to Sloan, "but this time you've gone too far. Where on earth did you hear such lies?" She wagged a finger at him in mild admonition. "Someone will bring a suit against you one of these days."

His eyes turned on Lord Edward, amused and a little mocking. He leaned back in his chair, almost gloating. "Not this time they won't. My source was sound."

Francesca burst out laughing. "Oh, don't be silly! Of course Edward wouldn't dream of doing such a thing— my friendship runs both ways, you know, Gregory darling." She gave him a meaningful smile. "But one day you'll cross a hothead who won't have my good counsel to restrain his foolish impulses."

A dull flush rose in his cheeks. "Then I don't know what you wanted to discuss."

She had thought about this, and realized she would

have to toss Sloan some sop. If she tried to get him to retract every word, he'd dig in his heels like a mule. She knew she should have broached this earlier with Lord Edward, but it was too late now and she would have to take a chance. "Well, of course, I'm sure your source had his sources," she began, choosing each word with deliberate care. "Not everything was a *complete* fabrication, you understand—but on the key point, your source has sadly misled you. I think you should retract the parts that could come back to haunt you. After all, people buy your papers because they believe them to be true. If it should appear that you print anything, even that which is demonstrably false . . ." She made a helpless gesture with one hand, letting her words trail away.

"Oh?" Sloan sat forward, expression sharpening. It made him look a bit like a rat, sharp-nosed with quivering cheeks. Francesca didn't even want to think what he would have looked like had she accepted his proposition, but she had a bad feeling it would have been very much like this. "Which parts are false?"

"I understand your position, sir," said Edward unexpectedly. Francesca glanced at him from the corner of her eye without altering her expression, even as her mind raced. Oh dear, what was he about to say? He had agreed she would handle this . . . But Lord Edward moved to the edge of the settee and set his empty glass down on the tray. "Your source is obviously a member of the Halston household." Sloan sat back warily and jerked his head in a single nod. Lord Edward sighed. "I had hoped to keep it out of the papers," he said to Francesca with some regret. "I only spoke to her yesterday."

"Of course," she said, playing along, trying to think what the Halstons had to do with this.

Sloan stared at him, stone-faced. "Then you're not engaged to Lady Louisa Halston."

"Not any longer."

"She broke it off?"

Lord Edward flicked one hand. "A gentleman cannot possibly answer that question."

"Oh, Gregory, must you dig for more information?" cried Francesca. "I won't have my drawing room made into a gossip mill for your paper." Good Lord—she had hardly paid attention to the bit about a broken engagement, but she now had a terrible suspicion Lord Edward had discovered it was over when she showed him the gossip sheet. She couldn't tell a thing from his expression, but surely no man would appreciate being jilted, let alone in the gossip papers. She remembered how he had stood so stiff and still at the window that morning, his shoulders tensed up, and her heart softened a little. What a dreadful way to learn such a thing.

"I'm not digging, Francesca dear," said Sloan, still watching the other man with a calculating expression. "Just verifying what I was told by someone who assured me it was sound and true in every way."

"I've no wish to call anyone a liar publicly. Lady Louisa was very upset yesterday," said Lord Edward in his cool, crisp voice. "I am sure some strong emotions sprang out of our conversation, and that is perfectly understandable. But I really cannot allow this . . . slur on my family to stand unchallenged. My brother has taken to his bed because of a broken leg. I hired a solicitor to see to some of my late father's rather complicated and extensive affairs. There is nothing exceptional about either event, and to knit these matters into a full-flown scandal is really beyond the pale."

Sloan's eyes narrowed. "What do you suggest?"

"Nothing," replied Lord Edward, "except that the story you were told may have been amplified to increase its value."

"Hmph." Sloan shot a dark glance at Francesca, as if blaming her for the undermining of a scandal that might have provided a legion of profitable stories. She returned his look with one of sympathetic disappointment, as if he only had himself to blame. Which he did, mostly, although apparently with some help from a vindictive woman. Why had Lady Louisa Halston jilted Lord Edward? Or had he dropped her?

Lord Edward leaned back, looking at ease. "I presume Lord Halston was compensated for his story. He's been in financial difficulties for some time, and no doubt this additional distress overset his mind. But in essence, he sold you a bill of goods." He paused. "If I were to make good your loss . . ."

Sloan was silent for a moment, calculation visible in his eyes. "Two hundred pounds," he said at last. Francesca gasped, and he cut a harsh scowl at her. "I suppose it's right fair of you to make compensation, as you say, for any loss I may have suffered."

Edward raised one eyebrow. "And for my loss?"

"I'll print a nice retraction on the front page tomorrow morning, of all those rumors about your father's secret marriage." Sloan's eyes glittered. His accent had degraded rapidly, and now he sounded almost like the dockworker he had once been. "Will it please you, Franny m'dear?"

Mouth still open from the whopping sum Sloan had demanded for his retraction, Francesca scrambled for a reply. Lord Edward said nothing, so she stammered, "Y-Yes, I— That sounds eminently fair to me. See, Edward," she added, recovering to turn to her other guest. "Didn't I say Gregory was a reasonable man?"

"And very right you were, my dear," he replied with a smile. He laid one hand on hers and pressed lightly. Francesca wasn't sure if it was in thanks or in warning, but she felt it to the tips of her toes. "I would be lost without you."

Sloan's mouth turned down at the corners. He lurched to his feet. "When will I have the money?"

Lord Edward didn't move from his seat. "Shall we say, first thing tomorrow morning?"

"Aye, after you get your morning papers." Sloan snorted. "Understood."

Francesca jumped up. "Oh, there," she said with a smile. "A pleasing resolution! I knew we could find one. Thank you so much for coming, Gregory; it was such a pleasure to see you again."

He gave her a look. "I'll just bet it was," he said under his breath. "Perhaps our next visit will be less about business."

She gave a low laugh. "Of course! You can't imagine I enjoy talking about business." She walked him into the hall and bade him farewell, smiling brightly until Mrs. Hotchkiss had shown him out and closed the door. Then she placed one hand against the wall for a moment as her knees went weak. She could hardly believe that had worked, even if not the way she'd anticipated. Two hundred pounds! Edward hadn't batted an eye at the figure, but it was a large amount of money. She hoped he wasn't put out by that bit of extortion. Had Gregory really paid so much? Francesca considered the magnitude of the scandal suggested, and thought he might well have paid close to that amount. If true, and if the news could be doled out one drop at a time, enlarged upon and embroidered from time to time, he could publish it every day for months.

But now that danger was averted—from Gregory Sloan's newspaper, at any rate. She had made no promises regarding any other gossip rags, and Edward hadn't mentioned them, either. And as soon as Gregory Sloan printed his retraction, Edward would help her find a fierce and able solicitor so she could rescue Georgina.

Francesca took a deep, fortifying breath, trying to forget how he sat so close to her and looked at her so familiarly. Out of the blue she wondered if he had taken it very much to heart that his fiancée had thrown him over. The girl must be soft in the head. Edward de Lacey was shockingly attractive when he smiled, as rich as the very devil, and she was sure she'd never met a more proper gentleman . . . Not that it was any of her business why his fiancée had sold gossip about his family to a scandal sheet—even for two hundred pounds—or why the girl had cried off at all, let alone without having the courtesy to tell him in person. Francesca told herself it would be only decent to allow him to nurse his heartbreak in quiet dignity.

Then she almost laughed at herself, spinning a sad

story out of nothing. For all she knew, it had been an arranged marriage without a speck of affection, and he was only angry that it had gotten in the papers. His personal affairs and motives weren't her concern, and it was mildly embarrassing that she had to keep reminding herself of that. And they still had business together, this time hers. She turned and went back into the parlor.

Chapter 8

Edward poured himself another glass of brandy the instant the door closed behind Sloan and Francesca, then swallowed half of it in one gulp. For two hundred pounds, Lord Halston, who would have been his father-in-law, had sold his private embarrassment to the meanest gossip rag in London. Thank God Gerard had told him about the earl's difficulties this morning, or else he never would have believed the man could have done such a thing. Of course he had known Halston wasn't nearly as wealthy as Durham; nobody was. Of course Louisa's marriage into the Durham family would have bolstered her family's fortunes a great deal; that was no secret, either. He knew all that, and yet still, like a damned fool, had given Louisa his heart, his respect, and his confidence, thinking he had hers as well.

In return she told her father what she had promised to keep secret, and one of them decided it wasn't even worth waiting to see if this potential scandal led to ruin or just a large legal bill for Edward. He had thought her so much better than that. He had thought she genuinely cared for him. He tossed back the rest of his brandy and eyed the decanter, itching for another drink even though he could feel the heat of the liquor in his blood already. Perhaps they ought to put Charlie in charge after all, for it seemed he wasn't half as perceptive as everyone— including himself—thought.

His hostess came back into the room, almost radiant in triumph. "That went rather well, I think," she said, going to the table and pouring herself a small glass of sherry. "We shall see in the morning, of course, but I trust everything was to your satisfaction?"

"Yes." He forced himself to shake off his simmering anger at Halston and focus on Francesca Gordon. It was less difficult than it should have been. As much as Edward tried to deny it, she was fascinating, both in appearance and manner. She was nothing like Louisa, who had been his idealized model of womanhood for years now, and yet there was something about her that pulled at him. Perhaps it was the fact that she offered to help ameliorate his scandal, where Louisa had helped cause it. Or perhaps it was something else. He didn't want to think about it too much.

She smiled and raised her glass in salute to him. "To a successful partnership, my lord." The loose cluster of curls at her crown trembled as she tipped back her head to drink. The skin at her neck was smooth, and looked as velvety soft as a fresh peach. Garnet earrings winked at her ears. And when she smiled at him again, her upper lip glistened with wine. He could almost taste it on his tongue . . . and he couldn't help thinking that he was no longer an engaged man.

When she looked at him inquiringly, he held out his glass without hesitation. Somehow prudence and moderation seemed vastly overrated and unrewarding tonight. He watched the light play over her face as she poured more brandy into his glass. No, "handsome" wasn't quite the right word for her. Neither was "beautiful," really, but she certainly wasn't plain. Her nose was a little too prominent. Her mouth was wide and full. Her eyes, when she glanced up at him, were the color of good brandy and bright with delight. And her hair, in the candlelight, was most definitely some shade of light coppery brown that appeared to have a glow all its own.

"Yes," he said, forcing his thoughts back into safer paths. "Very successful, indeed. Sloan was as susceptible to your persuasion as you promised, and I am in your debt. Tell me how you wish to proceed in finding a solicitor, and I shall make the arrangements at once. I don't allow my debts to languish." The sooner he satisfied his obligation to her, the sooner he would be free of the need to see her, which would in turn dissipate the urge to touch her.

She crossed the room to the fireplace and took a paper out of a carved box on the mantel, then came to sit beside him. He had unconsciously chosen the settee again, and when she sat with a swirl of silk, her skirts billowed over his feet. He could feel the sweep of the flame-colored flounce brushing his ankle.

"I have made a list," she was saying. "I inquired with most of these gentlemen already, but made little headway. It is my hope that one of them will reconsider."

Edward tried to ignore that little rustle of silk against his ankle. He could feel it even through the fabric of his trousers. He could smell her perfume as well, some fresh, rich scent that made him think of dark gardens in the moonlight. The brandy seemed to have heightened his awareness of every sensation, unfortunately.

He swallowed the last of his drink, and reluctantly put the empty glass on the table. He needed to marshal his thoughts into order and stop thinking about the texture of her skin and the taste of her lips, neither of which he would ever have cause to learn in truth. He took the list of names and studied it. A couple of the same solicitors had been suggested to him as well, although none with as high a recommendation as Wittiers. "Very well. I'll arrange it."

She blinked. "What? You—You'll just arrange it, like that?"

"I'll send a note to these two"—he indicated the names he recognized—"and have them call. They were also recommended to me, so I presume they are sufficiently qualified."

"Oh," she said in a surprised tone. "I presumed as much . . ."

"Never presume competence." He folded the list. "May I keep this?"

"Of course."

He made the mistake of looking at her. Perched on the edge of the settee, hands clasped on her knee and lips parted, she was staring at him as if he were both alarming and wonderful, as if she might throw her arms about him in gratitude. Edward cleared his throat. "Have you any objection?"

"No," she murmured. "None at all." Her expression didn't change.

He found himself unable to turn away from her when she looked at him like this. "Any suggestion to add?"

"No, not yet." She seemed about to say more, then stopped herself.

He leaned forward. "Oh? You look . . . puzzled."

She wet her lips. "I'm very sorry," she said in a hushed, rapid voice. "About your fiancée. I didn't realize . . . when I first read the piece . . . I didn't attach as much significance to that as I did to the rest."

Her face was so expressive. He could see no shade of calculation in her clear gaze, no artful manipulation. She looked genuinely sympathetic, her eyes soft and sorry. There was something very appealing about her frankness. It formed a seductive, and dangerous, combination with her other attractions. It was bad enough that he should be fascinated by her hair and her bosom and the way her skirts brushed so intimately against his leg; to find her even more attractive would be madness. "Neither did I," he said at last, when he could speak with his normal detachment. "And you really must stop apologizing, particularly for things you bear no responsibility for."

"Not personally responsible, no," she agreed. "But I wouldn't want you to think I rushed to confront you with that evidence; my attention was wholly caught by the other charges . . ."

"The 'Durham Dilemma,' as Sloan put it?" Edward sighed. He knew that damned phrase would be on everyone's lips whether Sloan printed his retraction or not. "I would rather that phrase sink into oblivion. A broken betrothal is a minor furor compared to the thrill of a potential scandal like that."

"Yes," she murmured, "but it can still wound."

It had. Not that he would allow himself to give in to

the sting of it. He said nothing, as his thoughts weren't very suitable for a lady's ears.

Of course, Lady Gordon was like no other lady he had ever met. And that was also not worthy of comment, Edward told himself.

She cleared her throat at his prolonged silence. "You will notify me when the solicitors respond? I really am anxious to begin. Heaven only knows where Ellen's taken Georgina by now."

Edward jerked out of his thoughts. He had business with her, he reminded himself yet again. He was a bloody fool to sit here brooding on Louisa's betrayal and his hostess's charms when he owed Francesca Gordon a great deal, and had no business with her except finding a suitable attorney. "Of course. I shall send to them tomorrow, and notify you."

She walked him to the door and bade him good-night. The evening seemed colder once he left the house, and Edward buttoned his coat as he walked down the steps to his carriage. He caught one last glimpse of her, still standing in the bright rectangle of her doorway, her hand lifted in farewell as his driver started the horses. He raised his own hand before realizing what he did, and then spent the entire ride home trying not to think that it would only be a few hours before he saw Lady Gordon again.

Chapter 9

The first thing Francesca did when she woke was rush downstairs to read Gregory Sloan's paper. To her relief, he had kept his word and printed a retraction. It was quite a humble one for Sloan, and she hoped Lord Edward was satisfied. He had appeared to be, last evening. He'd thanked her and been far more gracious than she had expected from their first meeting. In fact, he'd been a great deal warmer, even when Mr. Sloan had gone and it was just the two of them on her settee.

She was still at the breakfast table when the knocker sounded. For an instant a wild thought flashed through her mind that it would be Lord Edward, and she leaped to her feet in alarm at being still in her morning gown with her hair loose. She should have told Mrs. Hotchkiss to delay, so she could run upstairs and dress more appropriately, or at least put up her hair. But a moment later Henry Alconbury came through the door, beaming brightly. Her shoulders relaxed in relief and she smiled back at him.

"Good morning," he said, coming to give her a kiss on the cheek. "I see you're rising early now."

She laughed and resumed her seat. "Were you trying

to catch me unprepared? I retired early last night, if you must know."

He stepped back and inspected her face. "This is at least two nights in a row you've kept early hours. It's quite unlike you, my dear. I hope you're not making yourself unwell." He had come by the other night when she was sunk in despair over losing both Georgina and James Wittiers's services, and he had worried over her then, too.

"No," she assured him. "After last night, I am much better." She reached for the teapot. "Would you like some tea?"

He made a face but nodded. Mrs. Hotchkiss had followed him silently into the room, and rushed to set out another cup and saucer, and Francesca poured him a cup. "One of these days I shall corrupt you into drinking coffee," he said, dumping sugar into his tea.

"Never," she scoffed. "Coffee is a vile drink."

Alconbury rolled his eyes. "Mrs. Hotchkiss, you must conspire with me," he said to the housekeeper, who was still straightening dishes in the sideboard. "I shall not be satisfied until I am served coffee in this house."

Mrs. Hotchkiss shook her finger at him. Francesca knew Mrs. Hotchkiss thought Alconbury could do no wrong, so she ignored it. "Now, sir, you'll not be costing me my position. Lady Gordon wants only tea, and tea I shall serve."

"Traitor," he said mildly. "I shall bribe you later."

Mrs. Hotchkiss sniffed. "There's only one way you'll be telling me what to serve in this house, my lord, and that's not it." Alconbury gave her a beatific smile. Mrs.

Hotchkiss put up her chin and marched to the door, where she turned around and sent Francesca a meaningful look over his head. She might as well have cried out, *Marry him, madam!* Francesca said nothing and waved one hand in dismissal.

"What has improved your situation?" Alconbury asked as the door closed behind the housekeeper. He sipped his tea with an air of long-suffering. "Has Ellen written and agreed to let you see Georgina again?"

Francesca sighed. "No. But I have great hopes of securing a solicitor very soon, and then I intend to hire the best investigator in London to find them."

"Oh?" Surprise lit Alconbury's face. "That's quite a turnabout. Not two days ago you were sunk in gloom over solicitors, and now you've got one?"

She hesitated. "Not quite. But I expect to, in a day or so."

"How did you manage that?" He reached for the sugar, despite her severe look, and added more to his tea.

"I found a gentleman in need of my assistance, and offered to help him if he would help me in turn. We struck a bargain."

For a moment Alconbury's face froze. His startled blue gaze flew to meet hers. Francesca just raised her eyebrows; he was not her husband or her father, to criticize her actions—and she had done nothing shocking or improper anyway. Not that she was about to confess to him, at any rate. Alconbury picked up his teacup and took a long drink. "Who would that be, my dear?" he asked, his voice carefully light. "I thought I was your gentleman in need."

She laughed. "Yes, ever in need of something! It was

just a trifle, but it put him in my debt, which shall suit me very well indeed." Of course she had maneuvered to create that debt, but that was beside the point. Another thing she didn't feel moved to reveal.

"Indeed," he said. His jovial manner had dimmed noticeably. "Who is it?"

"Lord Edward de Lacey." She poured herself more tea, more for the occupation than because she wanted more to drink. Alconbury, for all his good looks and general charm, had become a bit too proprietary toward her of late. It would do him good to realize she was still her own person, and capable of solving her own problems.

Alconbury's forehead creased as he tried to place the name. "De Lacey?" he murmured, then repeated it incredulously as comprehension dawned in his eyes. "Edward de Lacey? Of the Durham de Laceys? Of the Durham Dilemma?"

"*Tsk*, Alconbury. You know better than to believe Gregory Sloan's rubbish."

"I don't care if it's rubbish, you should be careful about getting tangled up with that sort!"

"Why?" she asked just as sharply. "What sort do you mean—wealthy, aristocratic, and with such consequence everyone rushes to do his bidding at once? Because that sort of help appeals to me very much right now." He scowled. She relented, a little. "Then what do you know about him, not his family? For it's only Lord Edward I've dealt with, and he's been utterly unremarkable—very civil and completely proper."

Alconbury was not persuaded. "I don't know much—yet—but to be in the gossip papers—"

"As if one can control that!" she exclaimed. "I'd have no friends and no amusement if I shunned everyone in the gossip papers, and that includes you, my dear sir."

He waved one hand. "That's different."

"Yes, I daresay it is," she agreed wryly. "You land in the gossip papers because of your outrageous behavior, while people like Lord Edward arrive there due to the actions of others."

"That's not what I meant." He sighed. "What I should have said was, men of that sort are accustomed to getting what they want, no matter whom they harm in the process. They would think nothing of taking your assistance and then never finding a convenient time to render you theirs."

Francesca pursed her lips. It hadn't occurred to her that Lord Edward might break his word—not that she would allow him to do so. She had faced him down once before, and wouldn't hesitate to do it again if necessary. "I shall keep your warning in mind."

Alconbury closed his eyes for a moment. "Very well. I see your mind is made up, and that I cannot change it. Dare I ask what you did to obligate him to you?"

She smiled and held out Sloan's scandal sheet. "The 'Durham Dilemma' was sadly exaggerated, it appears."

He read the paper. "You—*you* persuaded Sloan to print this?" he asked in astonishment. "Francesca, what did you have to promise *Sloan*?"

"Nothing," she replied. "I asked him very sweetly, and he indulged me."

Alconbury looked as if she'd clubbed him in the head. "Gregory Sloan doesn't do favors without getting something in return. You know that."

"And yet I promised him nothing." She paused, shooting him a look of mild warning. "Lord Edward struck that bargain, and it was solely between the two of them."

He passed his hand over his face. "So now Sloan will be keeping his eyes on you, and you'll be hounding de Lacey to fulfill his promise to you. How did you manage all this in the space of a day?"

"You make it sound so nefarious."

"Don't you see that it could be?" He jumped to his feet instead of laughing. "I don't know much about Edward de Lacey, but his brother is the Earl of Gresham—or now Duke of Durham, I suppose—and he's a regular hell-raiser. A rake of the highest order, a daredevil, a spendthrift who's done his best to run through the Durham fortune . . . They're not a good family to tangle with."

"I shall be fine," she said firmly, trying to curb her growing impatience. Alconbury had been so sympathetic all the previous times she'd confided in him about her troubles; what had gotten into him today? "Lord Edward promised to help me secure a solicitor. I asked nothing more, and he certainly offered nothing more. Once he does so, I expect we'll never have cause to see or speak to each other again."

He paced to the window and stood in silence for a moment, staring out at her garden with his hands clasped behind him. "Don't you think," he said quietly, "that perhaps your quest to raise Georgina is becoming impractical?"

Francesca felt as if she turned to stone for a passing second. "What do you mean by that?"

"I mean . . ." He made a frustrated gesture with both hands. "John Haywood didn't name you as her custodian. You've had trouble finding a solicitor willing to plead your cause. Now Ellen's taken the child, and you might spend a fortune on investigators before finding her, without any assurance you would be able to take her in even when you do. Isn't it time to consider leaving this search to Mr. Kendall?"

"John didn't name Ellen as custodian, either." She had to say the words very precisely to avoid losing her temper entirely. As it was, her fingers clenched into a fist around the butter knife, and her chest hurt from the sharp, angry beating of her heart. "I found one solicitor who believed my case had merit, and I shall find another soon, one who will take the case and win it. Georgina is my sister's child, left without a father or mother, and I will not abandon her because of the expense, certainly not to the derelict oversight of Mr. Kendall!"

He must have heard the rage in her voice, for in a moment he was beside her on his knee, covering her fist with his own hand. "I never meant you should abandon her. I know how you care for her. But Francesca . . ." His fingers stroked along the taut lines of hers. "Georgina needn't be your only family. You deserve to have your own children—and a husband—to love."

She supposed, dimly, that could be construed as a marriage proposal. Unfortunately, she was still shaking with fury over his suggestion that she give up on something, *someone*, so dear to her. Alconbury had plenty of family—his mother, three sisters and a younger brother, a growing pack of nieces and nephews. She could laugh at his bemoaning their demands and the headaches they caused him because she knew he loved them all, to some degree. But it meant he couldn't know what it was like to lose everyone; her father died when she was a child, and her mother left her behind for Italy. Her husband died after only a few years of marriage. She had loved her sister Giuliana even if they only became well acquainted later in life, but Georgina absorbed all the love she would have given her own children, if she'd had any. And the thought of quitting her search now, when she didn't even know if Georgina was well or where she was, was harsher than a slap in the face. Alconbury didn't understand her at all if he thought she would do that for him, even if she had been madly in love with him. Which she most assuredly was not.

At her silence, he squeezed her hand. "You know I adore you. I don't want to see you hurt, or worn down by a long legal battle that may well be impossible to win. You'll drive yourself mad over this."

Losing Georgina would carve away part of her heart and soul. It was impossible to think of quitting the fight. She slid her hand out from under his. "Then I shall have to win quickly."

His shoulders fell. Alconbury looked at her gravely. "And I suppose this de Lacey fellow is part of your plan to do that."

As if on cue, someone rapped the knocker on the front door. Again, irrationally, Francesca's heart shot into her throat at the thought that it might be Lord Edward, appearing as if summoned by Alconbury's talk of him. She heard Mrs. Hotchkiss answer the door, then a murmur of voices before the door closed. She realized she was gripping the edge of the table, and got to her feet just as her housekeeper opened the door.

She was alone, with a letter in her hand. "A message for you, my lady."

Francesca recognized the crest on the seal as she took it from Mrs. Hotchkiss and tore it open. Her eyes flew over the brief message, and she exhaled in relief. "Yes, Lord Edward is part of my plan," she said in belated answer to Alconbury's skeptical question. "And he appears to be working out splendidly."

Chapter 10

Edward expected it to take a couple of days to find a solicitor for Lady Gordon, which meant there was no time to be lost. He sent notes to two of the names on her list he recognized the next morning right after breakfast, requesting their presence in Berkeley Square. Both replied with alacrity that they would wait upon him in the afternoon, and Edward dashed off another note to Lady Gordon. With any luck, either of these solicitors would agree to take the case, and the fascinating, alluring, unpredictable Francesca Gordon would be out of his life before he slipped and did something stupid.

He had to send a footman out specifically to hunt down a copy of Sloan's gossip rag. Edward hated funding anything of that sort, but he had to know if Sloan had kept his word and printed the retraction. And yes, there it was. On the bottom of the page, naturally, rather than blazoned across the top as it had been yesterday, but at least it wasn't small type that no one would ever read. "It has come to the Editor's attention that the Durham Dilemma might be quite easily solved," Sloan had written. "We have learned that the broken engage-

ment, of some several month's standing, between Lady
Louisa Halston and Lord Edward de Lacey may have
helped ignite the rumor of that gentleman's imminent
fall from Good Society . . ."

It was hardly the groveling confession of error
Edward privately wanted, but it would have to do. He
gritted his teeth and wrote the bank draft to Sloan, then
touched the corner of the scandal sheet to the candle
flame and flung it in the grate, watching until the paper
curled in on itself and blackened to a pile of cinders.
If only the words could be so easily burned from the
consciousness of everyone in London.

His brother was quick to remind him they couldn't
be. Gerard arrived home from his morning ride in a
towering bad temper, not mollified by the retraction in
the least. Unlike Edward, he'd gone out the night before
and gotten an earful of the gossip, which was, predict-
ably, centered on their troubles.

"The Durham Dilemma!" Gerard scowled. "That's
what they're calling it; it's not just some smoky business from Durham's youth, it's a scandal of national
concern!"

"Not really," Edward replied. "It merely has all the
elements of a novel—clandestine marriage, a long-lost
wife, a deathbed confession after decades of secrecy, the
ruination of us three . . . It would be nearly irresistible
to most people, I daresay, if it were a melodrama on the
stage, let alone real. Fortunately, it has been retracted."

His brother grunted. "What did that cost you?"

"Two hundred pounds."

"Yesterday you said it would cost you a favor, not two
hundred pounds. Were you able to pay it off instead?"

"What does it matter to you?" Edward asked, a little sharply. "I said I would tend to it, and I did." He resisted the urge to look at the clock. He'd told Lady Gordon to arrive only half an hour from now, and already his nerves were drawing up in anticipation. He'd find her a solicitor today if he had to drag Pierce to London and put him on the case. It was wrong—unnatural, even—to look forward to seeing a woman so much.

Gerard raised his head at Edward's tone. "What does it matter to me?" he repeated. "It's my name being dragged through the mud as well! I'd like to know what you had to promise in exchange for this pathetic, half-hearted retraction—which, by the by, is hardly kind to you, as it implies you abandoned poor Louisa." He waved one hand at the gossip sheet he'd brought home with him. Edward wished he would stop bringing additional copies into the house.

"I've promised to help secure a solicitor's services," he said tersely, ignoring Gerard's last shot. "On a completely unrelated matter. Two of them are supposed to call in less than an hour, so you'd best be off."

"At least tell me who our mysterious accomplice is." Gerard stayed in his chair and looked stubborn. "I'm rather grateful to the fellow, even if his help cost two hundred quid as well as this favor."

"Actually, it was a woman," said Edward as levelly as he could. "And we should be quite grateful to her." It was time to change the subject. "I don't suppose you learned anything at the churchyard."

His brother flipped one hand. "Of course not. Unless it's the rector blackmailing Father, there's been no one unusual at the church these six months, and the grave

in question is ancient and overgrown. No one's left anything or asked for anything left there. Tell me about this
woman."

"She's calling today to meet with the solicitors—"

"She's coming here?" Gerard's interest was well and
truly roused now, and thoroughly diverted from the
blackmailer and his letters. "Soon?"

Edward stretched his fingers to keep from curling
them into a fist. He had no reason to be proprietary
about Lady Gordon. "Yes."

"Splendid!" Gerard lounged in his chair with an
expression of pleased speculation. "I should thank her
myself."

"I thought you were setting off for Somerset at any
moment in pursuit of that blackmailer."

"I have a few things to tidy up in London first. Writ-
ing to my commanding officer, of course, to get permis-
sion for a longer leave. Had to get my horse reshod. I
might need a new pair of boots as well, now that I'm
in town . . ."

Edward raised his eyebrows. "Excellent. I'd no idea
you were staying in town for so long. Perhaps you'll be
good enough to query these solicitors for me, so I can
attend to other things." Just because he was in London
with a cloud hanging over the Durham estates didn't
mean there was no work to be done. It had simply followed him from Sussex, and was stacked on his father's
wide mahogany desk right now awaiting attention. The
fact that he hadn't been able to attend to it because he
was awaiting Lady Gordon's arrival only made the work
seem more pressing.

"We all know you'll do it much better than I could."

Gerard gave him a wicked look. "But I should *so* like to meet our benefactress."

"Hmm." Edward shook his head. "Dodging the dull part, as ever."

"I've spent the last day chatting with a rector and skulking about a graveyard," his brother replied. "I think I've earned a look at this woman you obviously want to keep hidden away for yourself."

Edward inhaled, but caught himself in time. Snapping back at Gerard that he was not trying to keep her hidden would only make it appear that he cared whether Gerard met her. Which was certainly not his concern. Much. "Very well. She'll be here soon."

Lady Gordon arrived a short while later. Edward got a strange feeling as he introduced his brother to her. She wore some dress of blue that seemed to float around her like a cloud. Her hair had been tamed into a modest knot, although a few wisps still teased her neck. She looked utterly respectable, but Edward could tell from Gerard's face that he wasn't nearly as impressed by her matronly propriety as he was by her siren's voice and her lush mouth and her direct manner. He watched his brother's expression change from curious to surprised to enthralled in a matter of seconds, and almost expected Gerard to offer to interview the solicitors after all. But when Blackbridge came to announce Mr. Fowler, Gerard merely bowed and excused himself, sparing only a darkly amused glance at Edward on his way out.

For a moment he and Lady Gordon were alone. It was both a blessing and a curse, he thought, as she turned on the sofa to face him and a stray beam of weak sunlight caught her glorious hair again. Even primly pinned down as it was, it still glowed like something Titian would have painted.

"Thank you for acting so promptly, Lord Edward," she said. "I had to wait four days to see Mr. Fowler the first time."

"I wouldn't have dreamed of delay." What would her hair look like down? He pictured a waterfall of coppery waves spilling over her bare shoulders, down her bare back . . . God Almighty, he had to stop doing this.

She smiled rather wryly. "Of course," she murmured. "I'm sure not."

Edward supposed there was more than one way to interpret that, but he hoped she had chosen an innocuous reason rather than the truth: that he was looking forward to the end of their association because he was far too attracted to her for his own good. He was disgusted with himself for being so intrigued by her, and he was horrified at the flicker of possessiveness that burned his chest when Gerard bowed over her hand, holding onto it for a moment too long. Theirs was a temporary acquaintance, born of unfortunate circumstances and desperation on both sides. In a matter of days—even hours—it would be over, and she would never walk through his door again. And he would never admit to thinking about her again. Ever.

Fortunately the butler showed in Mr. Fowler then, and Edward turned his attention to the solicitor. He intended to sit back and let Lady Gordon present her case, look appropriately approving of her hopes, and then shake Mr. Fowler's hand after he agreed to represent her. After a few introductory words, he did just that, explaining that it was Lady Gordon's case they had summoned him about. This was reasonable, he told himself. She knew the particulars, and he did not. She would be employing the man, and he would not. But after a while it became clear that Mr. Fowler's interest had been caught by the prospect of working for him, and not for her.

He watched, narrow-eyed, as the solicitor gently but inexorably beat down Lady Gordon's every point. The man was good at making an argument; he was just choosing the wrong side to argue, for Edward's purposes. When at last Lady Gordon nodded and said she understood if Mr. Fowler was still unable to take her case, Edward had enough. He got to his feet when the solicitor did so.

"May I have a word, sir?" The attorney nodded. "You must excuse me a moment, my dear," he said to Lady Gordon, and led the solicitor from the room.

In the corridor he closed the drawing room door. "What is the fatal flaw in her case?" he asked without preamble.

"Ah, well, there is no single fatal flaw, my lord," replied the man carefully. Fowler was a tall, broad-shouldered man with bushy black hair and sharp, shifty eyes like a weasel's. "But the will is not in her favor, she has never lived with the child—"

"The guardian named in the will is dead, and the trustee of the child's funds seems rather derelict in his duty. What argument would there be against bestowing custody of the girl on her aunt?"

Fowler scratched his chin. "The girl has been living with a mother."

"Stepmother."

The attorney shrugged off the distinction. "Unless there is hard evidence the stepmother has been abusing the girl, the court will likely not be moved to alter that arrangement. Lady Gordon, my lord, does not present a maternal appearance."

Edward raised an eyebrow. "She is a respectable lady with her own income and home. She is the girl's family by blood."

"She is a widow," said the solicitor. "She hosts parties with foreign guests. And . . ." He wiggled his eyebrows suggestively.

"Yes?" he prompted when the lawyer said no more.

Fowler cleared his throat and lowered his voice. "My lord, you must understand my position—may I speak bluntly?" Edward gave one short nod. "This is an argument between women. I've never been partial to female clients; invariably they require too much delicacy and consideration. The law is not for the female sex, sir. It is too harsh and critical for a woman's moods."

Edward turned toward the room they had just left, where Lady Gordon waited. Of course Fowler hadn't seen her as he had, but he had never thought women were the weak, overwrought creatures other men sometimes did. "I saw no sign of hysteria or undue delicacy of mind. I thought she had a good grasp of the law and had considered very carefully how her case might succeed."

"But would she be the same when she suffers defeats and reverses? I am not equipped to deal with weeping women, sir." Edward tightened his jaw, wondering what it would take to make Francesca Gordon dissolve into tears. He had a feeling she'd shoot a solicitor before she sobbed on his shoulder. Fowler must have taken it as understanding, though, for he leaned slightly forward. "She appears to be a woman of strong emotions, sir—a rather tempestuous temperament, if you will, and I have no stomach for it."

"I see," said Edward coldly. "Yet if *I* wished to hire you to find this child . . ."

The man hesitated, but Edward had seen the spark of speculation in his eyes. Fowler didn't want to deal with a woman, but he'd be happy enough to take Edward's money. "Thank you, Mr. Fowler," he said before the solicitor could reply. "Good day."

Francesca Gordon was on her feet when he went back into the drawing room. "What is wrong?" she asked. "What did you say to him?"

"Nothing." Edward closed the door behind him. "He isn't suitable after all. Mr. Hubbertsey will be here shortly."

She was quiet for a moment. "I didn't like him much anyway," she said at last.

"Nor I," said Edward under his breath. "Perhaps I should speak to Mr. Hubbertsey first. I think I've got the details in hand by now."

Lady Gordon gave him a narrow look. "Why?"

"You wished to borrow some consequence, did you not?" Unconsciously he straightened his shoulders and flexed his hands as he returned to his seat.

She frowned. "Yes . . ."

"Then let us ladle it on," he replied. "As a trial."

She still looked dubious, but nodded. When Mr. Hubbertsey was shown in, Edward explained the case. By now he had heard it enough times he was beginning to have a vague interest in the girl at the center of it. He couldn't help but pity a child who lost her parents so young. He remembered too well the grim atmosphere that pervaded the house when his mother died, just before he turned eight. Gerard, only five—as old as Lady Gordon's niece when her mother died—had refused to believe the duchess was dead, and so Durham had taken all three sons into the room to see her. Edward hadn't wanted to; like Gerard, he wanted his mother to wake up and be herself again. The sight of her so still and gray had been the biggest shock of his life, but at least his father was there, patting him on the shoulder as he tried unsuccessfully not to cry. And this little girl had lost both parents in short order and was now divided from her only living relative. It was quite right that he provide what assistance he could, Edward told himself. His father would have expected no less of him.

Unfortunately, Mr. Hubbertsey soon proved as unsatisfactory as Mr. Fowler. He barely looked at Lady Gordon when he first came in, but as Edward described the case, the man's eyes slid her way. On guard after Fowler's dismissive attitude, he saw weary annoyance flash across the solicitor's face. Edward was not a man to waste time on anyone who would refuse him in the end, the moment Mr. Hubbertsey's demeanor shifted to one of subtle regret, Edward thanked him and dismissed him. Blackbridge, following instructions to wait close at hand, showed the man out almost before the solicitor realized what was happening.

Lady Gordon stared fixedly across the room, hands knotted in her lap. "Was he also unsuitable?"

"Yes."

"How?"

"He wasn't going to take the case."

She unfolded her hands and smoothed her palms over her skirt. She inhaled a long, controlled breath. He could feel her emotions like another presence in the room, pulsing bright with anger and frustration. Lady Gordon was trying not to lose her temper again. Perversely, Edward wished she might fail, which surely only proved how vital it was that he conclude this business as quickly as possible. "How do you know?"

"I could tell."

"How?"

"By the way he looked at you," he retorted. "Neither he nor Fowler wishes to deal with a woman."

A series of expressions flashed across her face in short order—humiliation, fury, despair—leaving her flushed that intoxicating shade of pink. "I see," she said tightly.

He simply couldn't imagine being in her position, rejected not for any weakness of her case or inability to pay, but just because of general traits attributed to her sex. As galling as it must have been to be refused at all, it seemed a hundred times worse, in his eyes, that she had been refused on specious grounds. He almost wished Fowler would come back for a moment, to see how little hysteria there was in Francesca Gordon. From what she'd said, she must have endured similar scenes several times over before today, perhaps even worse. For the first time, Edward appreciated why she accosted him over Wittiers and then contrived to secure his help. In her position he would have done—in fact, had done—just the same when it was his family in question.

"Who were the other solicitors recommended to you?" he asked.

She pulled another copy of her list from her reticule and handed it to him, then surged to her feet and paced across the room. Edward read the list again with new skepticism. It was composed of respectable, experienced solicitors, the sort he would hire. He had accepted it blindly before, thinking only to find the first man who would take her case. But that sort of help would be hollow; she wanted to win her case, not merely have it heard. She cared very deeply about the child at the center of the matter, and he reluctantly acknowledged he would feel rather callous if he didn't make a real effort to help her, particularly after she fulfilled her part of the bargain so promptly and efficiently.

Unfortunately, that would take more time than expected, not to mention throw him into her company a great deal. It sounded very simple when she first presented it—he had found a solicitor within two days of arriving in London, after all—but now it was clear he would have to devote more thought and energy to her. To *helping* her, he reminded himself at once. The less attention he devoted to her eyes and her voice and the way she moved, the better.

He got up and crossed the room. She turned at his approach, her eyes glittering like polished amber. Just like the other night, she put him in mind of a fire, banked by propriety but still smoldering with energy and feeling and . . . passion. "I fear none of these men will prove satisfactory."

Her eyebrows arched slightly as she glanced at the

list in his hand, held out for her to take. "You know that by reading their names?"

"If Fowler and Hubbertsey were the two most likely candidates, I see no point in wasting time with the others."

A deeper color bloomed in her cheeks. Her eyes remained fixed on the list although she didn't reach for it. "I see."

She thought he was rejecting her as well, as the solicitors had. Edward hoped she never knew how unlikely that was. "Perhaps we should consider other . . . possibilities."

She looked at him, and her lips parted. For a moment the only other possibilities that ricocheted through his mind had nothing to do with solicitors. She took a step closer. "What other possibilities?"

He took her hand in his and closed her fingers around the discarded list. "Possibilities that do not involve anyone on this list."

Her head tilted suspiciously. "But I was told I needed a solicitor."

Edward gave her a slight smile. "Whoever advised that did not, perhaps, fully comprehend your circumstances." Her hand still rested in his. For some reason, she didn't pull away, and he didn't release her. He wasn't even sure he could release her, not while she was looking at him like this.

"Very well," she murmured after a moment. "What do you think I need, then?"

If he had been a less sensible man, Edward might have lost the thread of the conversation right there. Instead he found himself playing along, taking shameless advantage of the chance to linger close enough to see every little flicker of her eyelashes, every rapid beat of the pulse at the base of her throat. "I know what you want," he replied. "But you must decide what you are willing to do to get your niece back."

The intrigued light in her eyes cooled to determination. Her hand curled into a fist in his, crumpling her list. "Whatever it takes."

His feelings exactly—whatever it took to satisfy his obligation to her and thus relieve the insidious temptation of her company. This time he made himself let go of her hand. "Excellent. I'll send word."

"I shall be anxiously awaiting it." She looked at him again with new interest, even warmth. "Thank you for everything, Lord Edward."

When she had gone, Edward went into his father's study. He took his seat behind the desk, mindful of all the work waiting for him in neat stacks on the wide mahogany surface, but instead of taking it up he found himself staring out the window as rain began to spatter the glass. It was the honorable thing to do, he told himself; Francesca Gordon had helped him, and now he was obliged to repay the favor. If only he could keep his thoughts on that honorable thing, and away from the almost irresistible urge to touch her, he would be fine.

Blackbridge came to announce Wittiers. Edward nodded and pushed aside his wayward thoughts. There was another reason he should finish soon with Lady Gordon; he needed to concentrate on securing his inheritance. Even this morning, when he talked about the blackmail letters with Gerard, he had been distracted from that one all-encompassing goal by Francesca's imminent arrival. *Lady Gordon*, he reminded himself.

Wittiers came in and got straight to business. He had begun preparing the petition Charlie would need to present to make his claim to the dukedom of Durham. The main problem, of course, lay in documenting the pedigree that would establish Charlie as the sole and un-disputed heir. As Wittiers explained, the petition must be accurate and truthful in every way they knew. The evidence of a prior marriage in Durham's own hand was very much a problem, especially as word of it had gotten out in the gossip papers and everyone would be looking to see how Charlie's petition explained it away.

"Surely rumor can't stand as evidence," Edward said sharply.

"Of course not, my lord," Wittiers replied. "In our favor, there appears to be no record of the marriage in any family Bible, let alone an official register, and your late father states they did not live as man and wife; indeed, he says that it was a secret marriage, performed just before such ceremonies were outlawed some sixty years ago. That will suggest it was not entirely legal to begin with, and that your father suspected as much. Additionally, any witnesses who might have known them then are unlikely to be found after so many years, which will forestall any allegation that they were known to be married. And of course there is no shred of evidence that she ever approached him again, seeking support or recognition, despite a powerful motive to do so once he assumed his title."

"But my father did acknowledge the marriage. In his eyes it was a legal union."

"Yes," Wittiers conceded. "It would be best if we could verify the date of death of the lady in question."

Edward closed his eyes for a moment. "My brother has undertaken to discover more about her. My father didn't leave us much information."

"No, he did not," murmured the solicitor. Edward had given him copies of Durham's letters. "That is both good and bad. But I have persevered in the face of such challenges before, my lord."

Edward nodded. That was why he had wanted Wittiers, after all. Challenges seemed to inspire him, and his reputation as a solicitor was founded on winning them. "Do you recall a woman by the name of Francesca Gordon?" he asked abruptly.

Wittiers's eyes narrowed, then he nodded once. "I believe so."

Edward realized he was drumming his fingers on the arm of his chair, and flattened his palm against the leather. "I have met Lady Gordon and heard about her case. She approached you about it at one time."

Nothing marred Wittiers's smooth expression to indicate he was surprised at this turn of conversation. "Indeed she did, sir."

"What did you think of the merits of her case?" When Wittiers hesitated, Edward added, "I understand you came close to accepting it."

"I do recall that case." Wittiers seemed to sit straighter and his expression grew more focused. "I did consider accepting it, as a challenge. Custody of a child, I believe? It would have been a difficult argument to make, and the chances of success were uncertain, but I believed I could win it." He smiled, a rather wolfish look. "I don't take on cases I don't believe I can win."

"Of course." Edward studied him. "And what did you think her chances were?"

"One in five," the man answered promptly. "The will was not in her favor, the child's guardian was not testifying on her behalf, and the child was not known to be in any danger."

"Ah." So low—and this was Wittiers's assessment, who had almost taken the case. The others must have given her no chance at all. How unsurprising she'd had difficulties. "I wonder what you think the chances of my case are."

"Much better, my lord—three in four, at least. Rumor, and a letter from a man of advanced age on his deathbed, are all that suggest any fault in your brother's pedigree. And if no one else files a credible claim, it is all but assured. Half the titles in England might be contested, if these are judged valid reasons to withhold one. There will be a strong prejudice in Lord Gresham's favor."

Just as there was a strong prejudice against Lady Gordon, it seemed. Again Edward felt the faint scrape of injustice. One chance in five was far from impossible. Wittiers couldn't be the only solicitor in London with a certain arrogance regarding his own abilities to win difficult cases. "I am relieved to hear it," he said. "Keep me informed of your progress."

Wittiers was on his feet and bowing. "Of course, my lord."

When the door closed behind him, Edward's eyes fell again on the stacks of correspondence and bills waiting on the desk. His business agent would arrive at any moment to begin working through them. Just because the Durham estate was in danger of being disputed was no excuse to neglect it. Wittiers was quite sure they would prevail, and Edward knew he would only create more work for himself in the future if he shirked his duty now. Besides, he had too much care and pride in the family estates, and in his own contributions to them, to simply turn his back on them now. When Mr. White, the Durham business agent, tapped at the door, Edward called him in at once and began arranging the most pressing items in front of him.

But as the man sat down, Edward paused again. "Mr. White."

"Yes, my lord?" The agent was a model of competence, hardworking and honest. His pen was already poised to note whatever Edward said.

"Find a reputable man who investigates private matters. He must operate with great discretion and the utmost reserve; I don't wish anything I am about to ask to become public knowledge."

"Of course not, sir," White murmured. "I understand you completely."

Edward hesitated again, rubbing one finger along his upper lip. He probably ought not to do this . . . But perhaps nothing would come of it. "He is to locate a woman named Mrs. Ellen Haywood, widow of one John Haywood. Her brother may be living with her as well; his name is Percival Watts, and he is, I believe, an artist—a painter. They recently resided in Cheapside but have disappeared. If they are in London, I want to know where, and if they are not, I want to know where they've gone. I'm particularly interested in the whereabouts of a girl living with them, a child of about seven years named Georgina. He should do nothing other than report to me what he finds, and under no circumstances can he alert anyone to his, or my, interest."

White's pen scratched for a moment, and then he looked up. "Will that be all?"

"No," said Edward, even though he knew without a doubt he shouldn't be doing this. "I also want to know everything he can learn about Lady Francesca Gordon."

Chapter 11

Francesca left Berkeley Square torn between humiliation and hope. The interview with Mr. Fowler was bad enough, but when Lord Edward abruptly sent off Mr. Hubbertsey, too, she wanted to throw something, or crawl under the sofa. Somehow it was much worse to be rejected in front of Lord Edward, for all that he sat there with his gray eyes as cold as a winter's sky and called both attorneys unsuitable. When he returned her list and declared them *all* unsuitable, Alconbury's warning about being brushed aside had echoed in her ears. And wouldn't Lord Edward have ample reason to turn her away? He might well think her delusional and tiresome, unable to convince a single attorney in London to take her case.

But he didn't send her off with empty regrets and murmured hints that she look elsewhere for assistance. He offered to think of other possibilities, ones that wouldn't involve humbling herself to beg solicitors to reconsider her case. Francesca was wild to know what he meant by other possibilities, even as she tried to keep her surging hope at bay. Alconbury, who was no naive innocent, had assured her she needed an attorney to

handle the matter. Alconbury had suggested most of
the men on her list, the ones Lord Edward dismissed
as unworthy of his time. Of course, Alconbury never
interviewed anyone with her, as Lord Edward had done,
or assured her he knew what she wanted. Lord Edward
didn't shake his head and sigh when she declared she
would do anything to get Georgina back; he smiled,
the vaguely predatory smile of someone who was accustomed to getting what he wanted. Her opinion of him
was a great deal warmer for that.

All the way home she wracked her brains for other
options. Giving up, as Alconbury had suggested, was
unthinkable. She could try again to bring Mr. Kendall to
see the justice of her goal, and secure his help; perhaps
he would be moved by Ellen's recent disappearance. Of
course, he had shown little to no interest in Georgina so
far, despite her strongly worded pleas, and as he would
be abroad for the next several months, he could hardly
get the results she wanted in the near future. She supposed she might hunt Ellen down and kidnap her niece,
but that would unleash a whole new set of troubles. So
what other choices would Lord Edward propose?

Not for the first time, she had some very unkind
thoughts about John Haywood. He had been a charming fellow, handsome and easygoing and always ready
to laugh, but at heart he'd been a weak man, easily
led by others. Giuliana's more forceful, practical personality had complemented his in every way, and her
fortune certainly made their life easier. But once her
sister died, Francesca had almost seen the backbone
melt out of John. He forgot to pay bills for months,
then lavished money all about in a way that would have

put the Prince Regent to shame. Money ran through his fingers like water. She thought his servants must have begun stealing from him, he spent so heedlessly and with nothing to show for it. He spoiled Georgina outrageously—even Francesca, who adored the tiny girl, knew he went too far in indulging her, but her diplomatic suggestions were all brushed aside. John's marriage to Ellen brought some order back into the household, but not enough. Ellen had the restraint and moderation John lacked, but not the strength of character to impose it on her husband. John never found time to change his will, not even after he promised Francesca that she would have the raising of his daughter in the event of his death, nor even after he'd married again and his wife was expecting a child. John hadn't had much to leave, it was true, but to have been so careless of his duty to his new wife and to his children, both Georgina and his future offspring, was almost unforgivable, in Francesca's opinion.

And now he was dead, and Ellen was hiding his daughter away. In her softer moments Francesca felt some pity for Ellen, who had been left a widow with two infant sons and very little money—again thanks to John and his inability to economize even the slightest bit—but that sympathy never lasted long once she thought of Ellen's actions since. Ellen had been in the room when John promised Francesca that she should have the care of Georgina; Ellen had known his wishes and then deliberately obstructed them. For that alone she could never forgive her.

Mrs. Hotchkiss divined from one look at Francesca's face that the interviews had not gone well. "I took the liberty of preparing tea, madam," the housekeeper said as she took Francesca's hat and pelisse. "I'll bring it right up."

Francesca nodded. "Thank you, Mrs. Hotchkiss." She went into the drawing room and sank onto the sofa. When the housekeeper brought in a tray a few moments later, she mustered a smile. "You always know just what I need."

"Not that you always take my advice," the woman murmured with a pleased smile as she fussed over the tray. The Hotchisses were worth every farthing of their salaries, Francesca thought gratefully.

"And that is what I admire about you, Mrs. Hotchkiss. You offer your good advice so freely, and then bring me tea and sympathy when I choose my own doomed path anyway."

"Never doomed," said the housekeeper loyally. "I'd never say such a thing, madam." She handed Francesca a cup of tea, perfectly prepared.

Francesca swirled the spoon in the tea and watched the steam curl and billow around it. "It certainly seems like it today," she said with a sigh.

"Things will look vastly improved tomorrow, I'm sure. But until then . . ." Mrs. Hotchkiss tilted her head at the brandy decanter. "Maybe just a drop, in your tea?"

Francesca shook her head. "No, not today. I think a clear head will serve me better. It appears all my well-laid plans may come to naught."

"Well, I'm sure you'll come up with a new plan, madam. And Mr. Hotchkiss and I will do everything we can to help. It would be so lovely to have a child around the house, to say nothing of two or three."

She narrowed her eyes at the housekeeper, whose face was blandly innocent. "I have only one child in mind at the moment, not two or three. Let us not get ahead of ourselves."

"Of course not! I was thinking of Miss Georgina. She might be lonely without other children around; that was my only fear."

"Hmm." Francesca sipped her tea. "I could get her a puppy. Or a parrot."

"A parrot!" Mrs. Hotchkiss swelled with indignation. "No, Lady Gordon, I beg you. Nasty, smelly birds, parrots. And they bite! Not at all suitable for children, I should think. Lady Cartwright, my former mistress, had a parrot. It was terribly noisy, madam, squawking at all hours like it was being tortured to death—which some people might have considered doing, mind you. You'll reconsider once the young lady is here, mark my words." She nodded her head for emphasis, then bustled from the room, muttering, "A parrot, indeed!" under her breath.

Francesca's smile over the housekeeper's tirade against parrots faded quickly. Teasing Mrs. Hotchkiss about the animals she might buy to amuse Georgina was completely pointless if she couldn't even visit her niece. And without a solicitor, knowing where Georgina was would only be small comfort, because Ellen could run away to parts unknown again and she would be powerless to protest.

She would have to wait and see what Lord Edward proposed. He had looked so confident when he put her list back in her hand . . .

That night she tried to keep her mind off Georgina.

Perhaps Alconbury was right; she was in danger of driving herself mad over attorneys and wills and other things far beyond her control. That would certainly not help her cause. So she joined some friends at the theater, laughing and talking and losing herself in the farce onstage. Alconbury came by between acts, bringing glasses of champagne and a beaming smile.

"What a relief it is to see you enjoy yourself again!" He brought her hand to his lips. "I was afraid I overstepped myself the other day and spoiled our friendship."

She laughed, and took a sip of champagne. "You did overstep yourself, but fortunately for you, I am a forgiving sort of woman." Of course, it was much easier to forgive him when Lord Edward supplied all the affirmation and sense of purpose Alconbury lacked. She was mildly startled to realize how inconsequential Alconbury's disapproval felt compared to Lord Edward's support.

"It is just one of many things I adore about you." He grinned. "In fact, there are so many, I feel positively weak at the knees . . ." He started to sink down, as if falling to his knees. His expression was smiling, but his eyes were serious—and determined.

Francesca gasped, then made herself laugh again. "You were quite put out with me the other day, and well did I know it. A true gentleman would say nothing more of the matter, and merely be pleased to see me taking your advice to go out at nights."

"Well, I've always been a true gentleman, haven't I?" He leaned closer. "Even when I didn't want to be."

She met his eyes. "Don't be ridiculous," she said,

smiling, but more in warning than humor. "You're a thoroughgoing scoundrel."

"No." He held up one hand. "I won't be. Not while you are caught up in finding Georgina and winning custody of her. Just know that . . . know that I respect your desire to do this, and I'm always ready to lend my support, in any—and every—way you need." She stared at him in surprise. He had listened to her troubles and given his advice when asked, but never offered to take up the fight with her. He smiled, and ducked his head to kiss her cheek. "Remember that, Francesca. You don't need to turn to people like de Lacey."

So that was it. Oddly, she felt more relief than dismay that his motives sprang out of jealousy and not from any newfound conviction she was right about Ellen and Georgina. It meant nothing had really changed between them. "Good night," she said lightly. "I appreciate your offer of support very much; you may be sure I shan't forget. It was so kind of you to come see me, but I don't want to keep you from the play." Thankfully, the drama was beginning, and there was no excuse for Alconbury to linger. He pressed her hand once more and left to return to his own box, and Francesca turned her eyes to the stage, even though it was harder to concentrate on the performance now.

A week ago she would have been overjoyed to hear Alconbury pledge his support and assistance. She knew he thought her battle would be long and difficult, although he had never suggested surrendering altogether until the other day. But now that he was offering all she wanted, for whatever reason, she didn't feel like taking it. He was ridiculous to be jealous of Lord Edward, who had never done anything more forward than take her hand and hold it. Perhaps a few moments longer than necessary, although it hadn't been unpleasant at all. Quite the contrary, as he had strong, lovely hands, and a light touch. Francesca realized she was rubbing one thumb along the back of her other hand, imagining his fingers cupped around hers again, and reached for her fan.

Sally Ludlow, her hostess and friend, changed seats to sit beside her. "He's besotted," she teased. Francesca started, still thinking of Edward de Lacey. "Poor Alconbury," Sally added.

"Infatuation," Francesca whispered with a dismissive flick of her fan.

Sally glanced at her shrewdly, and raised her own fan to cover her words. "Nonsense," she said as the crowd roared with laughter at the actors onstage. "He's in love, and you know it as well as I do."

"You're wrong," Francesca returned quietly. "He's very fond of me, I grant you, and I of him—but we're not that suited to each other. Ours is a light, frivolous affection that would never survive the hardships of marriage."

They applauded as the lead actress swept onstage. She had carried the play thus far, and the audience quieted in anticipation. "He's hinting that he wants to marry you," Sally murmured. Francesca didn't reply. "I take it you plan to refuse . . . ?" she added, a lilt of surprise making it half a question, half a statement.

"He hasn't asked me." Francesca kept her eyes on the stage. "There has been nothing to refuse."

"Indeed." Sally was watching her in the dark theater. "You had better prepare yourself, for he intends to."

Francesca smiled as if it were no matter one way or the other. "Thank you for the advice."

But she knew Sally was right. Sooner or later she would have to confront Alconbury's unspoken proposal, particularly if he were telling other people it would become a formal one soon. He'd been patient and light-hearted about it so far, but obviously something about her association with Lord Edward piqued him. Francesca knew she was being a coward, but she dreaded telling Alconbury no, once and for all. He was a very dear friend. He was amusing and clever, an excellent dancer and a good listener. He always had a kind word and a handkerchief ready when she was in low spirits. She wasn't sure she could have done without him these last two years, since her husband died.

For a moment Francesca felt the echo of Cecil's loss. Cecil, she was sure, would have been very much in favor of bringing Georgina into their home, since they had no children of their own. He always agreed with what she wanted. Several years older than she, he'd said he waited a long time to find a woman like her, and it was a pleasure to indulge his young wife. The six years of their marriage had indeed been indulgent, as Cecil introduced her to the world of politics, the arts, and a social whirl quite different from her quiet upbringing. Francesca had said at times that Cecil was training her to be the wife he wanted, but he corrected her; he was showing her how to be the woman she should be. Francesca supposed she had never lacked a strong will, but Cecil showed her how to channel it appropriately.

Alconbury once joked that Cecil would rue the day he gave Francesca her head, for he'd never get the bit between her teeth again. She had exclaimed in indignation, but Cecil just laughed.

What would Cecil think of her now? Would he approve of her method of getting help, or would he be appalled that she'd invaded Lord Edward's home and rung a peal over him for perfectly defensible actions? Would he agree with Alconbury that she should consider quitting the search for Georgina, or would he applaud her vow to let nothing stand in her way? Would he want her to encourage Alconbury?

Alconbury was irrevocably entwined with Cecil in her mind. They had been two of a kind: genial, witty men who made her laugh and who weathered her tempers with good humor. He'd been so often at their home, Cecil declared he was more family than friend. When Cecil had gone out that last terrible morning, never to return, it had been Alconbury he took with him, and Alconbury who brought the devastating news of Cecil's death home to her.

No one had been a stronger, steadier presence in her life than Alconbury since then. But she knew his feelings had taken a turn somewhere along the line—or perhaps had always tended in this direction—and hers had not. Selfishly, she wished they hadn't. She wanted things to go on as they had been, even though she knew that was wistful thinking on her part, as well as unfair to Alconbury.

The crowd around her erupted in applause, and Francesca forced her mind back to it, clapping dutifully as the actors made their bows. Sally had warned her Alconbury would make his intentions clear soon, but the man himself had promised not to press the matter while she was caught up in her search. Until then, Francesca decided, she would cast her lot with Lord Edward. She knew what sort of help she could expect from Alconbury. With Lord Edward . . . anything was possible.

Chapter 12

When the knocker sounded early in the morning two days later, Francesca was sure it was Alconbury, come to demonstrate his helpfulness. He had a habit of calling on her early, even without any extra motivation. She hadn't been able to get away from the question of his intentions at the theater; after he left her, two other acquaintances, people who didn't know each other, had asked if he'd finally proposed. She had smiled and brushed it aside, but knew she would have to face it eventually. Sooner or later he would broach the subject, and she felt awful for wishing it would be later—or never.

Since she was in the hall, having just come downstairs, she went to answer the door herself. With such a small staff, it would be ludicrous to wait for Mrs. Hotchkiss, who was laying out breakfast, to come do it for her. She braced herself for whatever Alconbury would say today, and opened the door.

Much to her surprise, it was Lord Edward de Lacey standing on her front step instead of Henry Alconbury. "Lady Gordon," he said with a small bow. "Might I have a few moments of your day?"

"Of—Of course," she stammered. Good heavens; what could he want? It was unspeakably early for a call.

He stepped past her into the narrow hall. Mrs. Hotchkiss had come hurrying behind her, and now jumped to take Lord Edward's hat. Francesca caught sight of herself in the mirror opposite the drawing room. Dear Lord, she looked like she had just rolled out of bed—which was very nearly true—with her hair almost tumbling down her back, wearing a soft and comfortable morning dress that was at least two years old, and without a spot of powder on her face. She frantically tried to smooth her hair into a neater knot, since there was nothing that could be helped about her dress or face. As she twisted a loose tendril around one finger and tucked it behind her ear, Lord Edward doffed his hat and turned to hand it to Mrs. Hotchkiss, facing the mirror. His gaze met hers in the glass, and Francesca froze. For a moment they seemed connected by that shared glance, hers wide and flustered, his thoughtful and intense.

As usual, she had no idea what he was thinking. But as his gaze seemed to trace every blushing inch of her face in the mirror, she no longer thought his eyes were cold. In fact, for a moment she thought they were exactly the opposite.

"Won't you come in?" she said, abandoning her hair. Without waiting for a reply she turned and went into the drawing room—anything to escape that piercing gray gaze. "Please sit down."

"Thank you." He sat on the settee when she took the chair directly opposite it. "I apologize for not sending a note first. I happened to be nearby and acted on impulse, mindful of your desire for haste."

"Think nothing of it, sir." She gave him a warm smile, feeling more in control of herself. Or at least her outward demeanor; her heart, unfortunately, still thumped like a carnival drum inside her chest. When he crossed one leg over the other, his knee was very close to her own. She really ought to rearrange the furniture in here, to provide her guests more space. "I'm very much in your debt after the other day, and don't require such formality as a note."

"No," he said, studying her. How did he do that, she wondered; how did he keep his face so inscrutable? She kept her own pleasant smile pasted to her lips even though it was harder than ever to maintain a facade of serenity under his regard at this close distance. He rested one hand on his knee, and the remembered sensation of his fingers around hers flashed across her mind. She had barely remarked it at the time, but now she seemed unable to forget it.

Unfortunately, while she was concentrating on her own poise, he had still been speaking. " . . . Very much the opposite, I believe. I am still in your debt, having failed to locate a suitable solicitor, as promised."

Francesca blinked a few times. Her brain felt slow today, as if she'd not fully woken yet. He was still in her debt? She must have missed something he said at the beginning. "Ah . . ."

He raised an eyebrow. "That is what you wished, is it not?"

"Y-Yes," she said, thinking madly, "but—"

"You rendered me a service, and so far I have not been able to do the same for you. Personally, I found the solicitors we spoke to the other day . . ." He paused, his mouth tightening. " . . . disappointing."

She flushed. "Yes—"

"I have been considering your object, and, if I may, should like to make a recommendation or two." He paused again, searching her face. "You may reject anything I say, naturally."

She was anxious to know what he would say, but something about his demeanor put her guard up. Was he about to suggest, like Alconbury had, that she give it up? That she should believe what the solicitors were trying to tell her about her difficulties, and accept that she couldn't win? Francesca sat up straighter, bracing herself. "Of course, sir," she said, her voice cool even to her own ears. "I would be glad to listen to your advice."

A faint smile touched his lips, as if he heard her unspoken addition that listening didn't mean agreeing, but he didn't say anything about it. "I've come to believe securing a solicitor first may be too tedious and slow a process. Given that your niece has disappeared and her stepmother may be contemplating removing her from London, even from England, locating her is more important than hiring a lawyer, who will only file a petition. Without the child herself, even a successful petition is useless to you."

She narrowed her eyes. If the court approved her petition, surely they would force Ellen to produce Georgina. "Go on."

"Once you locate her, you are in a far superior position. I believe you said the stepmother has no legal claim to the child, either? And she is aware you are planning to contest her care?" Francesca nodded at his arched brow. "Then she will know it looks bad that she's taken the child and left you no word. If we can locate them, she may be willing to listen to reason, and negotiate a solution to everyone's problems."

Francesca digested this in silence for a moment. One thing she had to concede: he wasn't at all suggesting she give up. But what he *was* saying . . . "I'm afraid Ellen hasn't shown much interest in negotiating with me."

"And yet you can be so persuasive," he murmured.

She didn't let her expression change even though she could feel the warmth blooming in her cheeks again. She would never live down her first impulsive visit to him, apparently. "I have *tried* to speak reasonably with her. I don't always lose my temper and corner people in their homes, you know." He seemed to find that amusing, from the way his eyes lit and his mouth crooked just a bit. She had to bite back a smile in return, relieved that he was amused. "I first offered to take Georgina just before the twins were born. I thought Ellen would be relieved at having one less child to care for. Instead she grew very upset and said she couldn't think about it then. I said nothing and let it go. The next time I visited, I found Ellen in tears, with laundry hung all about the house, the two babies wailing in concert, and Georgina hiding under the stairs with her fingers in her ears." She paused, wondering what Georgina was enduring now. "I may have been a bit more insistent that time in my offer, but Ellen simply refused to listen, and asked me to leave. We've barely exchanged a civil word since, and the last several times I called she wouldn't even let me see Georgina."

He tilted his head back and looked at her for a moment. "But what did you offer her?"

Francesca's mouth firmed. "Nothing! She knew Georgina's father wanted me to raise her, but she refused to let me take her."

"Then why has she refused to give up the girl? She has contravened her late husband's express wishes, at no small burden to herself. Why?"

She saw what he was getting at. "I believe she is dependent on the annual maintenance for Georgina's care, to run the household. It isn't a large sum, but her husband was almost destitute at his death, and left her nothing in the way of a widow's portion. Her useless brother Percival refuses to take employment because he is an 'artist,' even though he lives with them and might be expected to help support the household. I do know they left their last lodgings after falling behind on the rent."

Lord Edward's smile was vaguely victorious, but not unkind. "Then you know what could persuade Mrs. Haywood."

Francesca closed her eyes for a second against her instinctive urge to refuse. "Are you suggesting," she said with forced calm, "that I *buy* my niece from her?"

His chin dipped and his eyes grew a little cooler. "Rather blunt language, but in a way, yes. I am."

Her first instinct was to laugh; he must be joking. Her second instinct was more profane, and would have branded her no lady if she said it out loud. Buy Georgina? Reward Ellen for stealing her niece by giving her money? She'd rather stack the banknotes in the fireplace and burn them one by one. "I'm not sure I can agree to that," she said in a frigid voice. It was the politest response she could make.

"I understand it might look like appeasement," he said. "Or certainly not the appropriate consequence for her actions. But I assure you, a legal battle will cost you a great deal of money. Would you rather give the money to a solicitor, who may not win your case in the end and whose tactics may forever embitter this stepmother against you, or give it to the stepmother, in exchange for her promise—legally binding, of course—to relinquish all claim to the girl?"

It sounded so reasonable when he put it that way, which Francesca found wildly annoying. She didn't want to be reasoned into bribing Ellen. She wanted Ellen punished, or at least judged by a court to be in the wrong. Her hands balled into fists in her lap. "I would have to think about it," she said. For a very, very long time.

"Of course." He was unperturbed by her distinct lack of enthusiasm. "In the meantime, since I have failed to locate a suitable solicitor, may I see to hiring an investigator? The child must be located before anything else can be accomplished."

That also sounded reasonable, and fortunately was more in accord with her feelings. Thank God he had given her some sort of acceptable suggestion. "Thank you, yes. You must be sure to send me the bill, though."

He smiled. "Naturally, Lady Gordon. I have not forgotten you don't want charity."

She looked down at her hands, still clenched together, and took a deep breath, then let it out slowly. She must be more appreciative; he had done more than she asked him to do, and was offering further assistance. Just because she didn't like his advice didn't mean it had no value, and certainly she should be appropriately grateful it was offered at all. "I will consider your other suggestion as well. I am very grateful for your thought on the matter."

"I realize it must go against your every inclination," he said. "I'm aware that you've been quite . . . dismayed by Mrs. Haywood's actions. But the only thing that matters is the result. You're willing to spend the money already; why not try a more direct path to your goal? And once you have the girl and the stepmother has waived all claim, your case will be far, far more likely to succeed in court. It would be a simple matter for any solicitor to file a petition for you then."

She rolled her lower lip between her teeth. "It certainly couldn't make it harder," she muttered.

"It was a difficult undertaking from the beginning," he agreed. "Wittiers acknowledged he would have considered it a challenge to win."

"I know," she said on a sigh, then frowned in bemusement. "You spoke to James Wittiers about me?"

Lord Edward's face changed, as if he regretted telling her that. He sat back in his chair, looking stiff and aloof again. She hadn't even realized he'd leaned toward her as they spoke. "I hoped to discover what merit he had seen that other solicitors had not. I asked his professional opinion of your case—"

Francesca smiled ruefully. "I'm sure I don't want to know what he said."

He paused for a moment, giving her a sharp, uncertain look, then cleared his throat. "Not much. He thought it would be difficult, but not impossible, to win in court. That led me to consider how you might get what you want without going to court at all. Whether you succeed in court, or simply remove any obstacle to your desire, the result is the same."

Francesca was struck speechless. She'd thought she had to follow the rules to get what she wanted. Alconbury had assured her it was a job for a solicitor, and she believed a court appointment as Georgina's custodian was the surest, best way to protect her niece. It never occurred to her to scheme and manipulate events to get Georgina. It never would have occurred to her that Lord Edward, cool and proper aristocrat, would suggest she do so.

Although that's exactly what she had done to get Lord Edward's help. No wonder he was amused at her resistance now. It was pure stubbornness on her part, she knew. She didn't want Ellen to profit in any way from her treachery, let alone profit directly from her own purse. But if she looked at it coldly, and a bit more calmly, she realized Lord Edward was right. Having Georgina back would far outweigh the grudge she bore Ellen Haywood, eventually. Money was behind Ellen's actions, and money, in large enough quantity, would pry Georgina out of her clutches. And it would certainly be faster than waiting for the courts to take up any petition.

She looked at Lord Edward with new awareness. Perhaps she'd been luckier than she knew when he whisked Wittiers away from her. Her reckless gamble in confronting him had certainly borne far more fruit than she had expected. His proposal wasn't at all what she had planned to do or asked of him, but instinctively she felt it was a better plan. She had tried to go about it so properly, when perhaps what she needed was a bit of ruthless manipulation.

On impulse she reached out and clasped his hand. "Thank you, sir. Your visit today has been a revelation."

His fingers tightened in her grasp. "How so?"

Francesca laughed, a little embarrassed. "You've shown me the error of my ways. I was so furious at Ellen, I lost sight of my real object. Of course you're right; it would be far more efficient—and effective— to give the money to Ellen in exchange for custody of Georgina, no matter how noxious it will be to do it."

"I hope the joy of your niece's company would wash away the distaste."

Slowly she nodded, thinking of Georgina's infectious giggles, her bright eyes, her sweet nature. "Yes," she said softly. "It would. I said I would do anything to keep her safe, and I don't intend to retreat from that now."

He looked at her with something like approval in his eyes. "Very good. I'm glad to hear it."

She smiled at him, and after a moment he smiled back. His eyes really were more blue than gray, she thought. His mouth was also quite appealing, now that she looked closer at it. His whole face changed when he smiled like this, as if they were equals, even intimate friends.

Abruptly she grew very conscious of his hand in hers. His fingers had closed around hers in a sure, firm grip, as if he liked holding her hand. It felt absolutely lovely, and very . . . right. Her mouth grew dry as her mind fastened on the feel of his skin against hers and the way his eyes, bluer and warmer than ever, seemed to peer straight to the bottom of her soul, where—much to her shock and dismay—a small but potent flame of attraction burned brighter by the moment.

With a start, she released his hand and got to her feet. She must remember herself. A moment of physical awareness meant nothing, not even when coupled with the new understanding and cordiality between them. Lord Edward rose as well, his expression as composed as ever. She took a deep breath; she was such a fool, first browbeating and extorting the man into helping her, and now letting herself find him attractive. It was nigh impossible that he would feel the same about her. He was the son of a duke, while she was a widow of no great fortune or rank. "Thank you for offering to find an investigator," she said, to refocus her thoughts. "I trust it will be easier than hiring a suitable solicitor?"

A hint of that dangerous smile still softened his mouth. "I don't expect any trouble."

Francesca believed it. Most likely he never did. That must be the secret to his controlled manner; if one knew things would come out as desired in the end, there was no reason to lose one's temper. It must be nice to have such assurance. She just lifted her hands and sighed as she walked with him back into the hall. "I've been through quite enough trouble already. I devoutly hope there's no more to be had, and all will be smooth from here on out."

Lord Edward took his hat and cane from Mrs. Hotchkiss. "I don't doubt there will be difficulties, Lady Gordon," he said. "We simply won't be daunted by them."

Francesca's heart leaped. This was what she needed, someone who believed she would win in the end. Of course, he meant more that *he* would triumph, and since he was now on her side, that also meant she would triumph, but she didn't care. Let him take all the credit; let him direct the whole damned search if he pleased, she thought as she bade him farewell and he went down her steps, moving with his usual unhurried grace. When she had Georgina safely in her care, by hook or by crook, by court declaration or by bribe, she would turn to Lord Edward, whatever he had said or done to her in the meantime, and have two words only for him:

Thank you.

Chapter 13

Edward wasn't quite sure what prompted him to call on Francesca Gordon this morning. In retrospect, he ought not to have done it. She had opened the door herself, looking unlaced and a bit rumpled, her shining hair barely caught up off her neck, and he almost forgot what brought him to her door. There had even been a moment, when their eyes met in the mirror as she was fingering a stray coppery lock, when he was in serious danger of casting all common sense aside and threading his hands into her sunrise-bright hair and kissing her, just to see if she could possibly taste as good as she looked.

Fortunately the moment had been only that—a moment—and then she looked away. It was a good reminder, actually; she wanted him to help her, not kiss her. Edward was taken aback by how persistent that urge was. It was one thing to see a beautiful woman and feel a spark of attraction, and quite another to be so strongly drawn to a woman who was neither beautiful nor demure, who flashed her temper at him with regularity, and who wasn't above manipulating him to her will. That last point alone made her utterly unsuitable as a lover, he told himself . . . and then had to shake his head, several minutes later, to dislodge the erotic images his mind conjured up at the thought of Francesca Gordon as his lover.

The carriage drew to a halt in front of Charlie's house, the Portland stone facade brilliant in the sunlight. It was far grander than Francesca Gordon's modest brick home in Bloomsbury, but he felt much less anticipation as he walked up the front steps of this house. No doubt Charlie would give up the place and move into Berkeley Square as soon as Wittiers completed his task, if not sooner. Edward rather hoped it would be later. He wasn't sure he and Charlie would rub on together very well beneath the same roof.

The footman had run up to knock, so the butler was already opening the door when Edward reached it. He could never picture his brother opening the door himself, let alone looking so informal as Francesca had, soft and rumpled and relaxed. He wondered if she routinely opened her door that way in the mornings. Perhaps he should call on her again, unexpectedly and early, to see . . .

No. He most certainly would not. He hadn't even needed to do it this morning. It was just one of those strange impulses that wouldn't fade, like an itch that only grew more agonizing until it was scratched. But now he had done it, and reasonably, the urge should go away. Hopefully soon.

The butler showed him into the breakfast room, where Charlie was still at the table. "Ah, good morning," he hailed Edward in a cheerful tone. "Have a bite?"

"Thank you, no. I've already eaten." He took a seat at Charlie's wave.

"Just coffee," Charlie told the footman standing at attention by the sideboard. "Then you may go."

When the footman had set his coffee in front of him and bowed out of the room, Edward turned to his brother. "How is your leg?"

Charlie shrugged as he sliced off a bite of kidney. "Still attached."

"Much improved, then," Edward replied, making Charlie cough as he chewed. "I'm glad to hear it."

Charlie took a long sip of coffee and eyed him. "Why are you here?"

"To inquire after your health, of course." Edward raised his cup, and Charlie snorted. "And to let you know how the solicitor is getting on."

"Ah," said Charlie. "I thought you'd come to tell me about Lady Gordon."

It was Edward's turn to almost choke. He put his cup down hard, with a sharp clink of china on china, and coffee splashed into the saucer. He glared at his brother as Charlie grinned wickedly back. "Gerard has been here."

"Indeed he has, and he was a font of information. She's quite fetching, I hear, although Gerard wasn't very clear about how she related to our pressing issue." For a moment Charlie gave him a hawklike stare worthy of their father. "Not that I begrudge you the pleasures of her company, of course."

"It's a simple business arrangement, nothing more." Edward kept his voice cool and even, refusing to let any hint of his less-than-businesslike thoughts about Francesca Gordon color his tone.

Charlie leaned back in his chair and nodded with false solemnity, his eyes glittering with amusement, as if he saw right through that.

"She did me—or rather, *us*—a great service, and in return I am helping her with some small matter of hers." Edward shrugged with what he hoped would pass for indifference. "There's nothing more in it." *Yet*. He took another sip of coffee to hide his unease over that last, unconscious, word his mind had added.

"She did 'us' a great service." Charlie looked positively fiendish with glee. "Edward, you exceed even your own high standards, coaxing attractive widows into *our* service. You've surely done quite enough already to defend the family name, certainly more than I've done. I've been very remiss, haven't I? Let me help. Send her to me, and I shall be glad to repay any service she's done 'us.' Gerard tells me she has the most glorious figure—"

"Charlie," Edward barked in spite of himself.

His brother burst out laughing. "Good Lord, Ned, if you could see your face! Of course I won't steal your redheaded widow. I daresay she's a great deal more lively than Louisa Halston—I always did say that girl was cold, you know I did—and if anyone deserves a bit of fun, it's you. You're well rid of the Halstons, and ought to revel in your escape by embracing the wilder pleasures of life for a change." Still grinning, he picked up his fork again and turned back to his breakfast.

Edward had known Charlie wouldn't let Louisa's de-

fection pass without comment. Unlike Gerard, Charlie
delighted in causing trouble and making people squirm.
Unlike Gerard, Edward refused to take the bait and have
an argument. He concentrated on his breathing until
the urge to say something scathing in reply passed.
"If I didn't expect you to put yourself out over losing
Durham, rest assured I won't expect you to do anything
on Lady Gordon's behalf. Gerard made the same offer,
and then nearly ran from the room when he heard what
she wanted of me."

"Why, what does she want?"

"An introduction to an attorney," said Edward in a
repressive voice. "Speaking of the same, I came to tell
you how Wittiers progresses, should you care."

"Of course I care," said Charlie. But his brother
seemed to have lost interest for the most part. His eyes
wandered to the newspaper spread open beside his plate,
which he must have been reading before Edward's arrival. He turned a page and scowled at something
printed there. "Damned decent of you to keep me informed. How is he proceeding?"

Dutifully, Edward recited what he had discussed with
the solicitor, but he doubted his brother listened to half
of it. Charlie glanced at him and nodded from time to
time, but otherwise busied himself with his breakfast
and the newspaper—which, Edward couldn't help noticing, was one of those appalling scandal sheets like
Sloan printed. For some reason, that rubbed him raw.
He had no objection to managing the legal fight to claim
and keep Durham, nor to running the several estates
that produced his and his brothers' wealth, nor even to
doing it all alone. But it galled him that Charlie couldn't

even pay proper attention to him because he was so interested in the sort of rubbish that would ruin them all. Finally, Edward pushed back from the table and stood up. "I won't keep you from the latest *on dits*," he said in a cutting tone. "If you want to know more about Wittiers's progress, by all means call in Berkeley Square whenever you like."

"I heard every word you said," Charlie replied without glancing up. "Don't kick up at me, I'm a wounded man."

"Yes, I remember, three great brutes who shoved you down a staircase," said Edward dryly. "Over a woman."

"And left me an invalid for weeks, casting me upon the scant sympathy of my relations." Finally his brother leaned back in his chair and looked at him. "Gerard is off to the wilds of Somerset. He came to say good-bye."

"He told me this morning." Their brother was still determined to find the blackmailer. Edward wished him much luck.

"Perhaps he shall solve the entire problem with a well-placed pistol shot."

Edward pinched the bridge of his nose for a moment. "Yes, everything will be so much better when Gerard is in the dock for murder." He let his hand fall and shook his head. "And even if he did kill the blackmailer, it wouldn't solve our problem. I expect Cousin Augustus to knock on the door at any moment, sniffing around for some grounds to file a petition of his own for the title. Wittiers is turning London upside down looking for any record of Father's clandestine marriage so he can know how to counter it, but having no luck at all. Thanks to rags like that one"—he poked one finger at

Charlie's paper in contempt—"everyone is murmuring about the shocking secret, and it wouldn't take much to fan those murmurs into a blazing scandal that could stain our names forever, no matter which way things go. Anything we do or say outside the strictest bounds of propriety would merely heap fuel on the embers."

Charlie's face had lost its mask of lazy boredom. His eyes were almost compassionate as he said, "I never imagined Louisa would do such a thing, Edward."

The name spit him like an arrow through the heart. He took a deep breath against the surge of bitter fury. "I was mistaken to tell her. You and Gerard were right, and I was wrong." He didn't say that often. Another deep breath. "And I don't want to talk about it."

Charlie nodded, and for once let it go. Edward said good-bye to his brother then and left. He had so far managed not to think about Louisa's actions constantly. It hurt too much to think of the woman he had loved, honorably and faithfully, betraying his confidence and jilting him without a qualm. He wanted to know why. He wanted to demand she explain herself, even though he had no desire to repair the breach now. He wanted to know how he could have been so deceived in her character; he had thought her loving and loyal, trust-worthy enough to hear his darkest secret and keep it so. Perhaps Gerard was right, and her father had forced her to do it because of money. Of course, a little voice in his head whispered that Halston couldn't have known unless Louisa told him in the first place. Whatever led to the cancelled engagement could never have happened until she told her father.

He tried to shake off his brooding thoughts when

he reached home. Blackbridge took his hat with reserved dignity, quite unlike the cheerful housekeeper in Bloomsbury. Now that Gerard was gone, the house was as silent as a tomb, and somehow felt as cold and as dark as one, too, after the bright, warm rooms Lady Gordon kept. Edward strode into the study, still in a foul mood over Charlie scraping open the wound that was Louisa, and vastly annoyed at his inability to stop thinking of everything connected to Francesca Gordon. He had his own worries and duties and responsibilities, and he would not allow Louisa or Francesca or anyone else to interfere with them.

Mr. White came from the small adjoining office when Edward rapped at the door. "Have you got the plans for the new wing at Furnlow?" he asked abruptly, sending the estate agent scrambling for the architect's letters and drawings. Furnlow was the estate in Cornwall promised to Gerard. A year ago, perhaps sensing his time was growing short, Durham had declared it too small and damp, and engaged an architect to renovate the old manor house and build a new modern wing. Gerard was in Spain then, fighting Bonaparte, and Durham grew frail in a shockingly short time, so it fell to Edward to supervise most of the planning. To abandon it now would seem an admission of defeat. With ruthless intensity he went over every line of the drawings, sending several changes and recommendations back to the architect. Then he turned to the other estate business, dealing with queries from his bankers, the butler in Sussex, the estate manager in Lincolnshire, and a host of smaller concerns. By the time he reached the end of it, evening had fallen, the bright sunlight outside the windows slanting and then fading to deep purple shadows.

Edward rolled his shoulders, stiff after leaning over the desk for so long. "That will be all, Mr. White."

"Yes, my lord." The agent was gathering up his notes when there was a tap at the door. White went to answer it.

"My lord, there is a man to see you: a Mr. Jackson," announced the butler.

Edward glanced at White. "The man you instructed me to hire, sir," Mr. White said. "I told him to report as soon as he discovered anything."

"Show him in," Edward told Blackbridge.

A few minutes later a short, slim fellow—looking more lad than man—slipped into the room. He had a round face and innocent blue eyes, and for a moment Edward wondered what the bloody hell White had been thinking to hire this boy as an investigator. Of course, appearances could be deceiving. "Yes?"

Mr. Jackson bowed politely, his eyes fixed on Edward. "I've come to make my first report, as you wished, sir," he said. He had the face of a boy, but the voice of a man. "I've written it up as well." He held out a sealed packet of papers, which Mr. White took and laid on Edward's desk.

"You work quickly," Edward remarked.

Jackson smiled, an expression that sharpened his features into something cunning and dangerous. "I aim to please."

"Is this regarding the child or the woman?" Edward nodded at the packet in front of him.

"Mostly the woman. I've got my ear out about the

others, though. I should know more in a few days."

"Ah." Edward's eyes strayed to the packet again. "Is there anything you have to report not included in here?"

"No, sir. I can report any way you like, as often as you'd like."

"Excellent," Edward said. "Time is of the essence, especially regarding the child, so report as often as you have something. You may leave it with White if I am not in."

"As you like, sir." Mr. Jackson bowed, and slid silently from the room.

"Expeditious," Edward said.

White nodded. "He came very highly recommended, my lord, for his quickness and his discretion."

"Indeed." He stared at the packet for a few more minutes before rousing himself. "You may go, White."

Alone at last, Edward got up and walked to the window. For some reason, he was unaccountably loath to read Jackson's report even as his fingers itched to tear it open. He supposed a better man would do nothing, and simply keep the sealed report for future reference. Of course, he reflected, a better man wouldn't have asked for it in the first place. Now that he had it, it seemed pointless not to read it. He retrieved the report from his desk and opened it, leaning against the window frame and holding the page up to the dying light.

Francesca Gordon was the daughter of an Englishman and an Italian opera singer, a soprano of some modest fame. Her father had been a country gentleman who made a small fortune when coal was discovered on his property in Cornwall, and who died in an accident at his mines when his daughter was a young child. After his death, the singer went back to touring the Continent, and Francesca was raised by her father's sister in Cornwall. At the age of approximately twenty-two, she married a baronet, Sir Cecil Gordon. Sir Cecil was fifteen years older than she, but it appeared to be a happy marriage. They lived a modest but comfortable life in London, moving in a wide circle of acquaintances and holding frequent salons. Sir Cecil died just two years ago in rather murky circumstances, but Lady Gordon was still known for her entertainments, although on a smaller scale. She kept a house in Bloomsbury with a married couple called Hotchkiss for staff, plus a woman who came in to cook and a charwoman. For the last several months Lady Gordon had often been seen in the company of Lord Henry Alconbury, a well-to-do baron who was widely expected to marry her before the end of the year.

Edward's brows descended as he read that last part, and he flipped the page impatiently. There was more about Lord Alconbury, which he skipped, and a few remarks about her salon. She didn't keep the most elegant company, but there were evenings of literature, poetry, and music. She was not overtly scandalous, but neither was she a model of propriety. She had Whig leanings and Catholic sympathies, probably because her mother had been Catholic. She attended the theater and the Ascot races. She lived within her means.

He tossed the report back on his desk. Jackson was worth every penny of his fee for finding out so much so quickly. Edward turned the various pieces over in his mind even though he had no idea what he would do with his new knowledge. There was nothing to alter his opinion of her, really, although that bit about Lord Alconbury interested him more than it should have. Perhaps it would help cure his unreasonable interest in her if he thought of her as an engaged woman . . . or perhaps not. Surely Jackson would have mentioned it if they were firmly betrothed, which meant she was still unattached. Still, it was something to keep in mind, should his control begin to falter as it had today.

No, by far his best course of action would be to press Jackson to find the child, and avoid all unnecessary contact with her until then. Once Francesca Gordon had her niece, he would never have to see her again. Distance would cure his fascination, even if nothing else seemed able to.

Chapter 14

~~~∽∞∾~~~

E dward's discipline held firm. He sent only a short note to Lady Gordon informing her that he had hired an investigator and would notify her as soon as there was any news. She replied in a similarly brief note, which he read several times before tucking it away in his desk, even though there was no reason to keep it. Then he carried on with the demands of the estate, feeling rather reassured of his own restraint. He *was* able to control his interest in her. Perhaps it was only natural he should have found her so intriguing, given how they had encountered each other. But that's all it was, a passing intrigue, and he was above such things. Aside from a few surreptitious rereadings of her note, and a jolting moment when he thought he saw her on Bond Street through his carriage window, he successfully shut Francesca Gordon out of his mind.

For four days, anyway.

He was on his way out, striding toward the hall with gloves in hand, when the butler caught up to him. "There is someone to see you, my lord," said Blackbridge breathlessly. "Mr. Jackson."

Edward stopped in his tracks. Had the investigator

brought more news about Lady Gordon? Or was it about the little girl? "Yes," he said, tamping down the surge of interest in the first question. "Show him to the study. I'll see him at once."

By the time he reached the study, Thomas Jackson was already waiting. He stood by the window, cap in hand, looking like a chimney sweep today. Edward closed the door behind him. "You have something?"

"I do." Jackson dug a packet of paper out of his pocket. "You asked me to report as soon as I learned anything."

Edward took the papers without looking at them. "Have you located the child?"

"No, but I've had some success on her uncle."

"Ah." Edward regarded him a moment. Locating the uncle—Percival Watts—was nearly as good as locating the girl herself. Perhaps his association with Francesca Gordon was about to end, sparing him any further contact with the lady. He had hired Jackson because of his reputation for quick, reliable, and discreet work, but now he found himself wishing the man had been lazier, or at least less efficient.

Beneath his shaggy black hair, Jackson's blue eyes were piercing and intelligent, waiting. "Won't you sit down?" Edward waved one hand at the sofa. "Perhaps you should tell me yourself." Then he would have the opportunity to question the man at once, if there were any discrepancies or oversights in the report.

Jackson sat on the edge of the small sofa. Edward dropped the report on his desk and faced his investigator, bracing himself for the inevitable. "Mr. Watts is a painter," said Jackson. "He aspires to be a good one, and has taken studies at the Royal Academy. He's put forward a number of paintings for exhibit, but remains a probationer."

"Meaning?"

"He's been up for membership and wasn't elected. It seems his paintings don't suit the public taste, nor the Academy's. The man I spoke to said he'd heard Watts had taken up portraiture for an income, but also that Watts was rather dismal at it, and hadn't been very successful."

"So he can be located through the Academy?" Edward frowned. "Someone must know where he lives, then."

"None I could find," Jackson replied. "He stopped attending sessions at the Academy last year, and none of his mates have seen him since."

"What about this man who told you about the portraiture? He must know someone who's seen Watts."

"It was several months ago, in the winter, that the man heard Watts was painting portraits. He knew the story because one patron complained about his finished portrait and refused to pay." Jackson shrugged. "This fellow had heard it was a decent portrait and the same faults would be found in the sitter's mirror, but the damage was done to Watts's reputation. He hasn't been to his regular haunts in some time, and no one seems to know where he's gone."

"I see," Edward murmured. "Is he likely to have left London? Does he have family in the country to whom he might return?" If Watts and his sister had a place to go stay with relatives, it was quite likely they would have done it, since it appeared they were extremely low on funds.

"All anyone knows is that he was living with his widowed sister in London. My source believed Watts was reared in the city, but that might not be reliable. If he's got family elsewhere, no one's the wiser."

Edward nodded thoughtfully. "So he's got no obvious place to go, no ready income, and is likely with his sister still. It stands to reason he would have to sell his art—and quite likely wants to do so. Commissions? Private exhibitions? Arrangements with discreet art dealers?"

"I'm looking for them all," Jackson said. "Commissions are hardest to discover, being between the two parties. I'll put the word out to the art dealers I know—"

"No," Edward said, holding up one hand. "I'll do it." He suspected any art dealer who knew where Watts was might also have been persuaded to keep the information to himself, especially should anyone like Jackson come sniffing around for him. If Watts and his sister were hiding from Francesca, they would be on guard against someone asking questions about their whereabouts. A wealthy lord looking to purchase paintings, on the other hand, would be hard for a penniless artist to refuse, no matter his wariness.

Jackson must have followed the logic. "Aye, that might be more effective," he agreed. "As you like, m'lord."

"Keep looking for Mrs. Haywood; it's possible she and Watts have gone separate ways and she's taken the child with her. I care nothing for finding Percival Watts if the girl isn't with him."

Jackson nodded. "And the other woman? Shall I still keep an ear out for Lady Gordon?"

The sound of her name caught him unawares, like

a sharp jab to the stomach. He clamped his lips together to hide any unwitting reaction to it. "No, I have quite enough information about her." Anything else he wanted to know, he would have to learn himself. Or rather, he would have to restrict his untoward interest in her, and not allow himself to dig further, no matter how insatiable his curiosity felt. He was already perplexed and displeased with himself for having set Jackson on it in the first place, and was not going to add to his sins in that way.

Jackson gave him a long look, but only said once more, "As you like."

Edward nodded and dismissed him, but then he remained in the study. If he were brutally honest with himself, it was possible he had been able to keep from thinking about Francesca Gordon only because he knew Jackson would return sooner or later, when he would have both reason and need to think of her again. It was the only way to explain why he hadn't told the man to go see Lady Gordon herself with news of Mr. Watts, Mrs. Haywood, or Georgina, but to return to him. Of course he didn't want Jackson to let slip that he had wanted to know about her as well, but Edward acknowledged, reluctantly, that his motives were even murkier than that. Now he would have to call on her and tell her this news, including the part where he volunteered to contact art sellers himself in hopes of drawing out Percival Watts. And if he knew the woman at all, she was quite likely to want to accompany him. Edward found himself wondering how many dozens of art sellers there might be in London, and knew he was in trouble.

With a sigh, he pushed himself away from the desk.

At least he was able to admit his failings. Perhaps the awareness of them would help him keep his head when he came face-to-face with his own personal Circe.

It was an endless week for Francesca. At first she anxiously awaited word from Lord Edward, but after a message that he had hired an investigator, there was nothing. No note indicating progress, no note indicating failure.

It was difficult to adjust to waiting after she had spent so many weeks actively hunting for a solicitor and then engineering Lord Edward's assistance. Every morning she woke thinking of ways she might locate Georgina, and how much she might have to pay Ellen to relinquish the girl, only to remember that she must have patience. She must wait until the investigator had done his job. The more she pursued Ellen, the farther Ellen might flee. The best move was to lie in wait, then spring in and catch her and Percival unawares. She had to remind herself of this every day, though, because every day that passed with no word seemed longer than the one before.

But . . . Oh, if only Lord Edward would call on her. Surely he could spare an hour to come by and reassure her that all was proceeding well. She had taken his advice—against her own inclination—and then he had gone off and left her to sit and wait. Did he not realize she couldn't carry off his cool, calm restraint on her own? What seemed so logical when he was explaining it came to appear more and more intolerable when he was absent, with no word. She began to spend as much time thinking about him as she did about Georgina. She even caught herself looking for Lord Edward's face on the street, listening for the jangle of his harness at her door, and considered inventing an excuse to call on him just so he would have to tell her *something*.

Making it even more trying, Gregory Sloan called upon her, his ruddy face sharp with determination. Francesca gave a mental groan at his appearance, but this was hardly unexpected. She rallied a bright smile and welcomed him into her drawing room. It wasn't long before he got to the point.

"I know you put one over on me," he said with a significant glance. "About the Durham affair."

"I don't know what you mean." She sipped her tea, secretly relieved he wasn't the dissembling type; she'd rather get it over with.

Sloan snorted with amusement. "You don't know! My dear Francesca, you're far cleverer than that. You knew all along Edward de Lacey wanted that rumor extinguished not because it was false, but because it was true."

"I'm sure I have no idea if it's true or not," she said blithely. "He assured me it was false, and I took his word as a gentleman and a friend."

"A friend," he repeated with a piercing look. "How dear a friend?"

She just lowered her eyes and smiled demurely. Sometimes it was best to say nothing.

"Right," grumbled Sloan. "I hope your friend told you all about his engagement."

"The one that no longer exists?" She waved one hand. "Yes, I knew of it."

Gregory Sloan leaned toward her, and something like compassion softened his face. "Did he tell you he was in love with her? It was arranged by her family because the Halstons are in financial trouble; the earl's concealed it for years, but now he stands on the brink of ruin. He told his daughter to do everything in her power to entice de Lacey, and that's what's held his creditors at bay these last two years. But Lord Edward was in love with her, and won't get over her soon."

Francesca made a face. "Who told you that—Lord Halston himself?"

Sloan grinned. "Not quite—a footman in the house, who's owed six months' wages. He had it from the butler, who's also owed wages but hasn't decided whether he wants to publish his story or not yet."

"A servant who's owed wages: the most objective, reliable source of all."

"If I trotted every Halston servant through your drawing room and they all told the same story, you still wouldn't believe it," he said in amusement. "Nor, I think, do you really care what the truth is."

"About the Halston finances?" She gave a little shrug. "I confess I do not."

"No, about de Lacey's engagement to Louisa Halston."

This was becoming tiring. "Perhaps I find it charming he was in love with his fiancée—and if so, the more fool she was, for discarding him. There aren't enough marriages of love. I think it's very romantic."

"Hmph. Even the fact that she must not have loved him as well as he loved her?"

"Oh, what difference does it make?" she cried impatiently. "It's broken off now, and I suspect irrevocably."

He narrowed his eyes on her. "That sounds deter-

mined of you. Tell the truth: are you setting out lures
for him yourself?"

Francesca's mouth fell open. "Of all the— Mr. Sloan,
I'm appalled you would say such a thing. Of course not."

"You were quite anxious to put down that rumor
about him—except of course the part about the broken
engagement."

She set down her teacup and regarded Sloan with
reproach. "As I recall, Edward himself told you the engagement was broken. I certainly wasn't aware of it until
you printed it in your paper, and it wouldn't have made
a shred of difference to me whether it was broken or
not when I asked you to reconsider. I can't believe you
would accuse me of such a thing."

"Hmm." He had a quizzical expression. "Of course,
once he was free of this young lady, using your influence with me would be one way to secure his gratitude
and regard."

Of course it was; that was why she had acted as she
had. It hadn't been for the reason Sloan thought—the
very thought of it, setting out to seduce Edward de
Lacey! He was undeniably handsome, and would certainly turn many women's heads, even without a title
and fortune. He was intelligent and practical, which
couldn't be said of every man. Francesca had no patience for useless people, and Edward de Lacey was far
from an incompetent wastrel. He had a ruthless streak
as well, although she had to admire that, since he had
deigned to use it on her behalf. And when he held her
hand in his, she seemed to feel it with every nerve in
her body.

But he was too restrained for her: too cold and far

too superior socially, at least for the moment. She might have wondered what it would take to arouse him to a passion, or what it might be like to kiss him—he did have a lovely mouth—and she might have even succumbed, once or twice, to wild curiosity about why his fiancée jilted him so rudely, but that didn't mean anything. That was just her energetic imagination, galloping away from her at times, not an actual plan to seduce.

And no one could be allowed to think so. The last thing she needed was Sloan poking around in her affairs, stirring up rumors about her intentions toward Lord Edward. She leaned forward in her seat and crooked her finger. Sloan lurched toward her, his eyes lighting up in incipient triumph. "You're right," she whispered. "It suits me much better that he's not engaged to Louisa Halston." Francesca knew a fiancée might have objected to her presence, and thus scuttled her hope of Lord Edward's aid. "I don't know why or how it happened, but I had nothing to do with it. And as for 'setting out lures' for him . . ." She shrugged. "I never really thought of it, even though I shall always think fondly of him." If Edward de Lacey found Georgina for her, she would bless his name every day for the rest of her life. "But really—you think I arranged for him to speak to you solely to win his regard?" She pursed her lips and tried to look hurt. "That doesn't speak very highly of me, or my personal charms, does it? As if a man wouldn't spare a second look at me unless I extorted it from him!"

Sloan's face eased as he grinned in repentance. "Ah, Franny, you know I didn't mean it that way! I just can't resist this little puzzle; some stuffy, top-lofty aristocrat, who doesn't spend much time in London at all, sees his life fall apart, and in the blink of an eye you're his dearest friend, ready to do battle to protect his reputation. Caring for the wounded—or in this case, the penniless disinherited? Seizing your chance to gain a new husband, taking your chance he'd still be a titled wealthy one? Or something else?"

"Something else," she said gently. "And that's all I intend to tell you, after you all but said I must be blackmailing him into visiting me."

"Well." Sloan's eyes dipped briefly to her bosom. "I don't miss what's in it for him, to call on you. I wonder what's in it for you to receive him. The man's about to lose everything, my dear."

She laughed lightly. "And wonder you shall, impertinent man." She rose and put out her hand. "It was a pleasure to see you again, Gregory," she added in pointed dismissal.

He looked disappointed. "Very well." He bowed over her hand. "I hope to repeat the pleasure soon."

Not very soon, she thought. "Good day," she said aloud, walking him to the door and smiling until the door closed at his heels. Then she rolled her eyes and let out an exasperated oath. First Alconbury, now Sloan. "Heaven spare me suspicious men!"

"There's nothing that scoundrel can do to you," sniffed Mrs. Hotchkiss. "More tea, madam?"

"Yes, please." Francesca went back into the drawing room and collapsed on the sofa, draping one arm over her eyes. "It's enough to make one become a hermit."

Her housekeeper just chuckled and went out to get a

fresh tea tray. When she came back a short time later, Francesca reluctantly sat up. "Thank you, Mrs. Hotchkiss. I would be driven to drink if not for your tea."

"Shall I bar the door, then?" the housekeeper asked with a sympathetic expression. "For I do believe we're to have another caller soon."

She groaned. "Lord Alconbury?"

Mrs. Hotchkiss cocked her head. "No, I don't believe so. It was a carriage I heard, not Lord Alconbury's horse . . ."

Francesca paused, wary but filled with hope. "Who, then?"

The knocker sounded. Mrs. Hotchkiss raised her eyebrows in question, and Francesca nodded quickly. Perhaps, just perhaps, it would be a message from Lord Edward. She heard the door open, and then—her heart jumped into her throat—it was his own voice in her hall. She rushed to the doorway, a wide, expectant smile on her face.

"Lady Gordon." He handed his hat to Mrs. Hotchkiss and bowed. "I hope I've not called at a bad time."

"Not at all, sir," she said with fervor. "You are always most welcome!"

His head went up a bit, and a flicker of surprise brightened his eyes. Francesca flushed, belatedly realizing how enthusiastic she sounded, but she just smiled and held out her hand, welcoming him into her drawing room. He walked past her, very tall and smelling of some subtle, rich cologne in his superbly cut coat, and she hurried to perch on the edge of her chair.

"I've spoken to the investigator," he said at once. "He's discovered—"

"Georgina?" she said, clasping her hands tightly together as if in prayer.

His expression became a shade graver. "Unfortunately no, not yet. But he has located traces of Percival Watts, the girl's uncle."

"He's no relation to her at all," said Francesca over the anxious thumping of her heart. "But go on."

Lord Edward's mouth quirked. "Of course. I misspoke. But you told me Mr. Watts was an artist, and my investigator traced him to the Royal Academy, where he submitted some paintings."

"He's a member?" Francesca was astonished. She had only ever heard Percival was a struggling artist, not elected to the Royal Academy.

"No, but he was acquainted with people there. He studied there. By the accounts of those who know him, he's still trying to work as an artist, but having a difficult time of it." He paused. "The investigator believes he may be trying to sell his paintings through art sellers in London or private exhibitions. However, an investigator poking about, asking questions, may cause the man alarm. The last thing we wish to do is provoke him into deeper hiding. I suggest it would be better if I made discreet inquiries with the art sellers, intimating I might like to purchase one of Mr. Watts's paintings. The prospect of a patron may entice him out of hiding."

"Oh, yes," Francesca breathed in excitement. "That may well!" Then she colored. "But of course you didn't bargain for such involvement! I'm very grateful for your assistance, but surely I can make those inquiries myself—"

He raised an eyebrow. "And what will Mr. Watts

think when he hears a copper-haired lady is looking for him?"

Francesca stopped, deflated. "Of course. He would suspect it was I."

"There's no link, however, between our names," Lord Edward went on more kindly. "And, at the risk of sounding quite pompous and important, my name is the sort any artist would be glad to attract. That is why you pursued me, is it not? My . . . consequence?"

She straightened self-consciously in her seat. "Yes, among other things. But I don't wish to impose *overmuch* . . ."

Now he was definitely amused. "No, of course not. But I make the offer freely. You may decline, of course."

She rubbed one thumb over the other, watching him watch her. Curse Gregory Sloan; now all she could think about was what it would be like if she did decide to seduce Edward de Lacey, and what heartbreak he might be suffering over his lost fiancée. Part of her was trying to forget every last word of that conversation. The other part of her was distracted by the way Edward's gray eyes seemed almost luminous today as he studied her. He was much more handsome than she'd first thought, Francesca realized. As if it weren't enough for him to be a duke's son and immensely wealthy. Why *had* Lady Louisa broken off with him? Had it only been the fear he would lose his fortune? Silly girl; there were so many other ways a man could be attractive . . . and desirable . . .

She took a deep breath and forced her mind away from the suddenly impure direction her thoughts had wandered. The last thing she should do was allow herself even to think about seducing Edward de Lacey. She needed his help too badly to ruin things by affronting him. From now on she would behave with perfect poise and restraint, and remember that it was only a business arrangement between them, no matter how conscious she might feel of him as a man.

"Thank you," she said. "That's very generous of you. I am more grateful than you can know."

His smile was brief. "Not at all. It is what we agreed."

It was far more than that, and for the first time she wondered why he was offering. "Yes, but I did not ask this. And you must really send the investigator to me. I intend to pay his bill, and there's no reason for him to trouble you about this search anymore."

Lord Edward tilted his head back almost warily, as if he were considering what to say next. "It's no trouble," he said after a moment. "I feel some sympathy for the little girl."

"That's very good of you, sir," she replied, "but I must insist."

"He is . . ." He paused. " . . . a rather rough character. I'm not sure it would be safe for him to visit a lady."

"Surely he can send written reports instead. I shall have Mr. Hotchkiss in the house any time he's expected."

"I'm not certain he can write notes and reports." Lord Edward cleared his throat. "Really, it's no trouble."

She gave an awkward laugh. "I see. I begin to feel like such a pest to you! I never meant to exact *this* much effort . . ."

"I do not take my debts lightly, Lady Gordon," he said firmly. "And I have already assured you I don't feel aggrieved."

If she kept arguing, it would be rude. She made herself smile and unconsciously settled her shoulders in a more relaxed posture. "Then I have no choice but to continue expressing my gratitude, do I?"

He inclined his head. "That is also unnecessary," he said, but she could see he wasn't as adamant about this as about sending the investigator to her. Good heavens, what sort of man had he hired? A rough, illiterate, dangerous man who couldn't be trusted in her house? Well, as long as he ran Ellen and Percival to ground, she supposed it didn't matter who the fellow was.

"At least allow me to come along and help as I may with querying art sellers," she said. "I simply cannot sit and wait another week or two with no word, while you do all the work." He just looked at her, his gray eyes unreadable. "I must insist," she said firmly. "She's my niece, and as grateful as I am for all your assistance, this is my cause."

"Of course," he said as if he had expected this all along. "I wouldn't dream of refusing you."

Chapter 15

Francesca thought of herself as someone who appreciated art, at least as well as the average person. When Cecil was still alive, they attended art exhibitions and amassed a modest collection of paintings and drawings. But she also admitted that had been mostly Cecil's doing. Her true love was music, and in any event she'd never had large sums of money to spend on paintings.

Edward de Lacey, however, walked into an art gallery as if he expected to buy every canvas in the place. The proprietors seemed to recognize on sight he was a man to be waited on, and would all but rush across the room to welcome him.

At first she merely watched in amusement, and then it grew tedious. No one wanted Lord Edward to walk out of his shop without making some purchase, and they would send their assistants scurrying to bring out ever more items that might please him. But once Lord Edward said he was looking for paintings in a style similar to what he had seen in the works of Percival Watts, by Mr. Watts himself if at all possible, Francesca was ready to leave. For the first time she saw an advantage to being inconsequential. At least then one could conduct business quickly and be out the door, without the need to pretend appreciation of yet another portrayal of the Sabine women.

Edward seemed to realize this as they left one establishment. "Shall I drive you home?" he asked, his gray eyes studying her closely.

"Of course not." She opened her parasol and tried to look fresh and optimistic. "There are plenty of places left to visit."

"Ah," he murmured. "I feared you were becoming bored."

Beyond reason. She pinned a determined look on her face. "Never."

"Then you're the only one," he said, to her surprise. "I thought that last fellow would never stop talking."

She tried to swallow the smile, but it escaped anyway, along with a bit of laughter. Lord Edward's eyes gleamed at her as he extended his hand to help her back into his curricle. "None of them are reticent. I know that's a good thing for our purposes, but it does become tiring."

He handed a coin to the boy holding the reins and swung into the seat beside her. It was an elegant carriage, smart and expensive, but not the outrageous vehicle some gentlemen drove. "I think we shall have time to visit only one or two more today. I hope that is acceptable."

Even in her impatience to make progress, she'd had enough for one day. She exhaled a sigh of relief. "Of course."

He just smiled and set the horses in motion. As they drove, Francesca watched his hands on the reins. She had always liked men's hands, whether they were the elegant hands of a gentleman or the strong hands of a working man. Lord Edward's hands, in his pale leather driving gloves, were both elegant and strong, steady and sure as he guided the pair of horses through the busy streets. She remembered how his fingers had felt the other day, when she impulsively grabbed his hand and he folded his fingers around hers. A wicked part of her brain, the part infected with improper thoughts about him, wondered what those large, strong hands would feel like on her. How he would hold her, if he ever kissed her. She told herself it was wrong to think such things, but the thoughts had plagued her for days now. And when she wasn't careful, she found herself very agreeably lost in contemplation of them.

She caught herself doing it now, and jerked her eyes away from his hands. This was dangerous. She could strangle Gregory Sloan for planting such ideas in her head. Of course, she had noticed the man was attractive before Sloan's comments. She had spent an unpardonable amount of time wondering about the state of his heart after being jilted by Louisa Halston. And there had been that moment, in her house just a few days ago, when she almost thought he might be just as aware of her. But for Sloan to suggest she was angling for him herself . . . well, that was just ridiculous. Even if his fingers did flex and straighten almost sensually as the reins slid between them, and her stomach felt tied in knots by the sight.

"How long do you expect it will take to discover something?" she asked, to distract herself from his hands.

"If anyone knows how to contact Mr. Watts, I doubt

they'll waste much time," he replied. "The prospect of a generous commission should be strong motivation."

"Then we may have word of him in a few days, which should lead us to Georgina," she said, thinking out loud. "And then I shan't trouble you anymore." She glanced at him at the same moment he looked at her. "I cannot say how much your help means to me," she added in a rush. "It's far more than I ever expected."

His gaze shifted to the front again. "You have told me so. There is no need for continued gratitude, Lady Gordon."

She was quiet for a moment. "I'm not accustomed to relying on others to help me. I don't like feeling helpless."

The corner of his mouth curled. "I would never have thought you so. But I comprehend your meaning." He paused. "I dislike unfairness. Your case was rejected by Fowler and Hubbertsey not because of the case itself, but because they didn't wish to work for a female. They were quick to judge you a hysterical woman, despite any evidence to the contrary."

"You're too kind," she said with a rueful smile. "I have hardly shown you my retiring and demure side."

"Do you have one?" He pulled up the horses and turned to look at her with interest. A market had taken over the next street, and they would have to walk.

"Of course," she said serenely. "All women do."

He jumped down and tied the horses, then offered her his hand. His fingers closed securely around hers as she stepped down from the carriage. She could feel the warmth of his flesh through his glove and hers. He retained her hand in his even after her feet were both on the ground. She tipped up her head to see him regarding her with that probing gaze that made her want to squirm. "How . . . intriguing."

"Mine may be somewhat smaller than most," she added in a confessional way.

He was watching her as they began making their way through the market. "Perhaps you will show me someday."

She arched her brow at him. Part of her realized that this felt like flirting, which was the last thing she would have expected from Edward de Lacey. She also realized she liked it, despite all her vows that it was to be purely business between them. He was hardly the stiff, cold fish she'd first assumed. He had such a lovely mouth. What would it be like to kiss him? she wondered. It would be a terrible shame if he couldn't kiss well.

She was being wicked, thinking such things. Nevertheless, she allowed a wicked little smile to play across her lips. A *little* flirting was harmless. "Are you certain you wish to see it? Often men say they prefer it, but find it . . . disappointing."

"I never said I would prefer it," he replied. "Merely that I would like to see it before trusting in its existence."

"How unkind you are, implying I haven't been ladylike."

"Never. Perhaps . . . perhaps I prefer you this way," he said, giving her a speculative look.

Francesca laughed to cover her jolt of surprise, and the even more startling thrill that raced through her. He was definitely flirting back. It was completely unexpected, and she wasn't quite certain she was wise to indulge in it, but . . . there was that thrill. And the persistent thoughts about kissing him. "Perhaps?"

Slowly he smiled, with a definite hint of promise. "Perhaps . . ."

What he would have said next, she never heard. They had been walking rather aimlessly and desultorily toward an art gallery open to the public. The market was busy, and their progress slow. But in the midst of the crowd, when she wasn't even watching for it, Francesca caught a sudden glimpse of a little girl with long dark curls and a thin, mischievous face with familiar dark eyes. "Georgina," she said in shock. Before the thought had even fully formed in her mind, she plunged instinctively off the pavement after the girl. "Georgina!"

She barely heard Edward's startled exclamation behind her. She pushed past a flower seller and shouldered her way through the bustling market. The dark-haired girl had vanished, and she paused to scan the street anxiously. "Georgina!" she screamed.

From the left came something that sounded like "Franny." Georgina had always called her Aunt Franny, her young tongue tripping over the full name. Francesca wheeled in that direction and started forward again, finally catching a glimpse of a tall thin man with untidy blond hair. He carried a large portfolio under one arm and was all but running away from the place where she stood. Francesca's mouth compressed; it certainly looked like Percival Watts, although she couldn't see if he had a child with him. She grabbed up her skirt and rushed after him, heedless of everything but finding the girl who had caught her attention.

The street twisted and turned, then ran down a hill

rather sharply, leaving the market. Francesca nearly slipped on the cobbles as she hurried down the narrow lane. She ran through two more streets and then burst into the main road and jerked to a stop, searching again. Where, where, *where* . . . ? Her eyes snagged on a flash of blond. There, on the other side of the street, the fair-haired man was still hurrying away, and—her heart seized—he held the hand of a young girl, a girl with long dark hair.

Oh, dear God—she was so close. Francesca bolted after the pair, right across the busy road. A horse reared as she flew in front of it, and the rider shouted at her. She threw up one hand in apology and ran on, darting past a cart and around a carriage. A flashy phaeton almost ran her over, and she had to scramble backward out of the way of its glossy wheels, losing precious seconds as the driver fought to keep his high-strung horses under control. She finally reached the opposite side of the road and paused again, her heart slamming into her ribs from her frantic race. She pressed one hand to her breast and turned in a complete circle, scanning the streets for the blond man or the dark-haired girl. Around her bustled a sea of people, but not those two particular people. She hurried down the street in one direction, then spun and ran in the other, looking down every side street, to no avail. They were nowhere to be seen.

A trickle of sweat ran down her neck, into the valley between her breasts. She was perspiring like a laborer, had just made a complete fool of herself running through the streets, and had nothing to show for it. Anguish squeezed at her already tight chest until she thought she would faint of it. She pressed her hands against her sides and tried to catch her breath. What if that had been her niece, and she'd scared Percival into running off with her again? What if they left London? What if she had just squandered her best chance to see Georgina again?

A familiar carriage pulled up beside her. Edward de Lacey jumped down, his face like stone. She could read the fury in his eyes and turned her head away, not ready to face his censure when her own disappointment was already making her sick to her stomach. She didn't protest when he took her by the arm and led her to the carriage. Without a word he almost shoved her up into his curricle, then climbed up beside her. With a snap of the reins they jerked forward, and she had to grab the edge of the seat to avoid lurching into him. Her gaze roved the streets as he drove, desperately searching for another glimpse of that small pale face in the crowd, until finally she had to close her eyes in despair.

She blinked when the carriage stopped. He'd brought her home without speaking a word on the way, but she had a feeling he was about to deliver a blistering reprimand. She didn't want to hear it. She was a grown woman, and ought to be allowed to contemplate her reckless stupidity without being scolded like a child. At this second, when her disappointment was so raw it hurt to breathe, she just wanted to be alone for five minutes so she wouldn't fall apart in front of him. She gathered her skirt in one hand and jumped down from the carriage, running up the steps and through the door Mrs. Hotchkiss held open for her, right into the safety of her drawing room.

That wasn't the end of it, of course. He followed her.

She heard the rumble of his voice as he spoke to Mrs. Hotchkiss, and she heard him close the drawing room door. She braced her shaking hands on the back of the sofa and focused on her knuckles. Another minute, maybe two, to compose herself . . . Dear God, had it been Georgina? Had she jumped too quickly to that conclusion because she so desperately wanted it to be true, or had she come within a few arms' lengths of recovering her beloved niece? The doubt, the worry, the fear all fed on each other, devouring her from the inside until she thought it would drive her mad. She said a silent prayer that she wouldn't burst into tears or start throwing things while Edward was here. Just this once, she wished he would be angry enough with her to just leave.

But of course he was not.

"What the bloody hell were you thinking?" he demanded, sounding more coldly furious than she'd ever heard him sound before. "You could have been killed! What sort of fool are you, running through a busy street like that?" Francesca dug her fingers into the sofa until her knuckles whitened, trying to hide her silent acknowledgment that he was right. She hadn't thought at all—that glimpse of a girl who could have been Georgina had wiped caution and sense from her mind and left only frantic determination in its place. Now she realized the folly of her actions, even through the writhing mess of disappointment and dismay inside her. She had been foolish, yes, and rash.

But she had never shied away from the consequences of her actions. She sucked in deep, miserable breaths until her pulse slowed to a normal, heartbroken, rate. He could have just let her run off into the crowd. Instead he followed, probably saw her dangerous dash across the busy road, and then scooped her up and brought her home. She owed him more than this. Slowly she pried her fingers out of her sofa cushion and stole a look over her shoulder at him.

Edward was still scolding her, his handsome face dark with passion. Francesca tried to stamp out that last thought, but it had already taken root and sprouted a dangerous weed in her heart. She had finally roused him to a passion, right at the moment she was at her weakest, when she would have given anything for a diversion from her increasingly desperate, and hopeless, search. And now his words were like spikes driven into her conscience: she had been foolish, and rash, and perhaps cost herself a chance to find her niece. She had endangered herself and him both, because of an impulse. He had helped her when he was under no obligation to do so, and today she had only shown him how foolish that was.

"Have you lost your mind, madam?" He stalked up to her when she said nothing. "You can't just—"

Francesca whirled around and kissed him. Up on her toes, one hand braced on his shoulder, her mouth to his. She felt his jerk of surprise, felt him start to pull back, and she put her hand on his jaw to hold him, very lightly, in place. His lips were firm and warm against hers. For a moment it was like kissing a statue, and she felt the first scratch of humiliation that she had kissed a man who didn't want her, but then he made a harsh noise of surrender, a split second before his arms swept around her and *he* was kissing *her*. His fingers bit into her flesh as he fitted her body against his. His mouth slanted and opened over hers, demanding and longing at once. It was the kiss of a man who had denied himself for too long, and it was all she could do to hold on, shocked that it felt so utterly right.

His arms tightened and he lifted her, swinging her around until her back was against the wall. His hands, free from having to hold her to him, slid over her body as if he owned every inch and wanted to leave no doubt in her mind of that fact. Francesca shuddered as his fingers curved around her breast, the edge of his thumbnail scraping over her nipple. She arched her back, pressing her hips into his as she gripped the lapels of his jacket for balance. His weight pressed into her, pinning her to the wall and making her vividly aware of the magnificent erection growing harder by the second against her belly.

Oh God. He wanted her. It might only be desire born of anger and the moment, but it stripped away the last of Francesca's rickety sense of decorum and restraint. She kissed him to stop the flow of his words; she knew she'd been a fool. But she also kissed him to quiet the urge to discover what his lips would feel like against hers. It was a mad, lunatic urge, one she didn't understand and had tried to banish, and she'd been fairly certain—hopeful, even—that he would recoil in alarm and slay that terrible urge once and for all. Instead . . . oh, heavens . . . Instead he kissed her back as she had never been kissed in her life, and now she feared the urge would never die.

His hand left her breast and slid down the slope of her ribs. She could feel the heat of his touch even through her stays and dress, and then his long fingers splayed over the small of her back, right at her waist, and pressed her to him. She had the sense of being drawn into him, as if their bodies would meld into one if only all these wretched clothes were out of the way. And it felt so right, so necessary, she couldn't even think why it would be wrong at all if that happened. She pressed into him, kissing him back with all the bold recklessness she had tried to contain for too long.

With a sudden grunt he tore his mouth from hers and twisted out of her arms. Francesca sagged against the wall, barely held up by her shaking legs. She kept her eyes steadfastly closed and managed to turn away from him. Reality flooded back over her in a cold wave. Out of the blue she remembered that he had been engaged to another woman just a few days ago, a woman he allegedly loved very much, and she had a terrible feeling she knew what made him push away from her. It was her own fault—she never should have flirted with him and allowed herself to have such dangerous thoughts about him. She was a Jezebel to have kissed him so boldly in the first place. She told herself she deserved any set-down he gave her, and that she had only herself to blame if he never spoke to her again. But she also wished with every fiber of her being that he wouldn't say Louisa Halston's name, not now. Let him regret the kiss for any other reason, but not that one.

"I apologize," he said in a low, savage voice very unlike his usual refined tones.

"There is no need," she whispered.

"It won't happen again."

Mutely she shook her head. It was too much to hope something that glorious would happen to her again.

There was a long silence. "It absolutely *cannot* happen again," he said, as if his previous statement hadn't been strong enough.

She wet her lips. They felt full and sensitive. She could still feel his mouth against them. "Are you persuading me, or yourself?"

For a long moment there was silence. She still hadn't opened her eyes, unable to face him. And then, quiet but unmistakable, came the sound of the door opening, and closing.

It released the spell that seemed to have frozen her in place. Her knees unlocked and she managed to walk unsteadily to the sofa before collapsing onto it. She covered her face with both hands. What had she done? He might never want to see her again. And she felt a terrible sense of loss that had nothing to do with the help she originally wanted from him.

Edward drove as if the hounds of hell were chasing him away from Francesca Gordon's house. He gave his grays their heads and even flicked the whip to push them, and took the road out of London. He needed out of the city, away from her, out of range of the urge to turn around and go back for another kiss. A sane man would have kept right on driving, straight back to Sussex, where his normal, orderly life could proceed without any interference from copper-haired temptresses who twisted him in knots even when he told himself he was on guard against it. Today she'd sent him veering from heart-stopping fear when she plunged into a road teeming with traffic, to fury that she acted so thoughtlessly and dangerously, to shock and then raging desire as she kissed him, first softly and then as deeply and hungrily as he kissed her. God, how she kissed him. His hands shook as he loosened the reins and the wind threatened to take off his hat as the curricle sped along.

Why had she done it? Surely she knew better than to toy with a man like that. Had she only kissed him to distract him from upbraiding her? His jaw tightened as he thought about it. He hoped that wasn't it. Perhaps, in retrospect, he shouldn't have scolded her so harshly. The woman he knew would not appreciate it . . . but that woman also wouldn't have hesitated to tear into him in kind. The Fury who invaded his house to lecture him about stealing her lawyer would have lashed back at him today, and probably tossed him out of her house at the end. That woman he was prepared for, and able to resist—at least, he'd been able to so far, just barely.

But this woman . . . Edward felt a flicker of alarm as he recalled, in lush, exquisite detail, how she fit so perfectly into his arms. How her lips parted under his, hot and wet. How her breast filled his hand. How she clung to him, and pressed against him, and made those tiny sighs of desire and encouragement, urging him on until he could have lost his mind and carried her upstairs to strip her naked and—

The horses had slowed to a stop, their sides heaving with exertion. The curricle was sitting in the middle of the road while he sat lost in thought about the erotic, passionate interlude he had so narrowly avoided. Or lost. It was unnerving that he couldn't decide if he had avoided something terrible or lost something wonderful. Even more unsettling, he didn't know how he'd react if presented with the same chance again. It was best, of course, if such a situation never happened again, because then he might . . . might . . .

Might what? He felt a sheen of perspiration on his forehead. What might he do if Francesca ever kissed him again? He would most likely kiss her back—obviously he didn't have the strength of character not to. She was impulsive and outspoken and daring, all things he didn't admire in a woman . . . and yet he was both charmed and fascinated by her, even knowing he shouldn't be. Every man must have a weakness, he supposed, and for some reason she was his.

No, if she kissed him again, he would step back and tell her it was improper. Nothing could happen between them. It was certainly something she shouldn't do again. It was very wrong of her to kiss him, with that single touch of her fingertips on his jaw to stop his instinctive retreat. Yes, if not for that touch he would have stepped back at once and then . . . Edward shuddered. He would have seized her again for a truer, deeper kiss, just as he had done in reality. Just as he still wanted to do now. Just as he had been thinking about doing almost since the moment he saw her.

He couldn't blame Francesca. His desire for her was a bonfire, piled high and waiting for just a spark to ignite it. It was hard to blame her for the blaze when all she had done was strike the spark.

The reins slid through his fingers as the horses began stretching their necks. Edward fought to reassert his reason, and make some sense out of the day. Francesca wasn't a foolish woman. She was a bit impulsive, but not reckless. She must have seen something to make her go tearing through the crowd and fling herself into the

Strand. She had screamed "Georgina"; could she possibly have seen her niece in that throng? Could Percival Watts have been at the gallery, and they missed him by minutes? Edward wanted to find the man, but not accost him in the middle of the street where he would likely be on guard, particularly if he had the little girl with him, particularly if Francesca did anything to set him off—like chase him through the streets screaming the child's name. He hoped it hadn't been Percival Watts she'd seen, just because it would make things more difficult if the fellow took fright and went deeper into hiding as a result of her pursuit.

Of course, the longer it took them to find the girl, the longer he would be thrown together with Francesca.

He tightened up the reins and turned the horses to go back to town, this time at a more rational pace. He wasn't going back to Francesca's, not now, not when he couldn't promise himself he would act with honor and restraint. The image of her leaning against the wall, her bright hair disheveled, her bosom heaving, her mouth soft and pink from his kiss . . . He cursed under his breath that he couldn't even control his own thoughts. He would call on her tomorrow, or the next day, or sometime next week, however long it took for the taste of her mouth to fade. By then he would have marshaled his thoughts into proper order again and regained his dignity and sense of honor.

It would be much easier to do that, of course, if he could stop wondering how far she would have let things go if he hadn't walked away.

Chapter 16

❦

After four drafts Francesca managed to compose a note the next morning to Lord Edward, apologizing for her actions. She didn't specify which actions, so when his reply came, she had to take a deep breath before opening it. But he said nothing of kisses or offense; he accepted her apology and tendered one of his own for scolding her so harshly. Then he asked if she would like to attend another gallery the next day.

Francesca let out her breath in relief. Thank heavens. She honestly hadn't known what to expect. He had flirted with her, very mildly, and most definitely kissed her back, but that didn't mean anything. Her heart leaping, she replied in the affirmative. It was a great consolation that he was still willing to help her. She had learned her lesson and wouldn't do anything inappropriate again.

That week she saw him every day. He took her to galleries open to the public, and private collections whose owners only admitted friends and acquaintances. They visited art dealers and the Royal Academy. She learned more about the art world than she had ever cared to know, but none of it was directly helpful. No one could—or would—tell them where Percival Watts was, or where he was likely to be found. The few people who knew anything of him professed that he had drifted out of his usual haunts over the last few months, and then disappeared entirely a few weeks ago. Coupled with the investigator's lack of progress tracing Ellen Haywood and Georgina herself, it was very lowering for Francesca's spirits.

But Edward was undaunted. He seemed far too calm to her increasingly frustrated eyes, but soon she grew to depend on that. Because of his unshakable confidence, she was able to keep herself in check. He was certain this would yield results, and she had promised to trust him. His assurance soothed her impatience, as much as it could be soothed.

"I can't stand this," she said as they left a gallery in Pall Mall. "I don't think we'll ever find him this way."

He helped her up into his curricle. "Perhaps not." He retained hold of her hand until she looked at him. "Would you prefer to sit quietly at home and wait for Jackson?"

She pulled her hand free. "No, but what do you mean, it may not?"

"It may not. Jackson may be the one to find her. I notify him of every trace we uncover of Mr. Watts, and it may be one of those scraps of information—seemingly useless and outdated when we learn it—that eventually leads us to your niece." He took the reins and jumped up beside her.

"Perhaps," she grumbled. "I do wish it wouldn't take so bloody long, though!"

He just smiled, and curled his fingers around her

hand, resting on her lap, as he set the horses in motion. Francesca felt the tips of his fingers brush her thigh, and then the weight and size of his hand resting on her leg. Before she could stop it, a vivid memory of that kiss flashed through her mind, followed by more. She bit her lip hard, but the images only grew more erotic, of his hands on her, of his lips on hers, of even more wicked things.

Oh dear. She had tried so hard to forget about that kiss. All week she had behaved with perfect propriety, not making one flirtatious comment. Neither had he, which was, she told herself, confirmation that it had been a momentary lapse on his part. If only she could convince her body that it was never to be repeated. As his hand stayed on hers, and the carriage jostled over the cobbles, she could feel every touch as if her dress and petticoats weren't even there. And it unleashed a growing hunger for more inside her.

After a few moments he seemed to sense something. He glanced at her. Francesca kept her eyes fixed ahead, but she could feel the blush on her face. A moment later he released her hand, but his fingers stroked over hers in a lingering way that only sent more heat spilling through her. She sucked in a deep breath and forced a bright smile to her lips, determined to pretend it had never happened.

Edward looked at her for a long moment. She braced herself for a reminder that nothing could happen between them. His gaze flickered to her mouth. "Would you . . ."

She had to swallow and wet her dry lips. "Yes?"

"Would you like to attend the gallery at Cleveland House this evening?"

It never occurred to her to refuse. She wanted to see him too much. "Of course."

She dressed carefully in a dark red gown that evening. She told herself there was nothing wrong with wanting to look her best, but as she came down her stairs to meet him, her pulse jumped anyway. He looked up and saw her. Heat flashed in his eyes for a moment before he masked it, but she saw it, and something inside her ignited in reply.

Cleveland House held the late Duke of Bridgewater's collection of art. Francesca had never seen it, even though the gallery admitted guests, and some of the works were quite renowned, but tonight she found herself unable to appreciate it. She was too aware of the man beside her. He had flirted with her; he had kissed her; he obviously didn't mind seeing her and touching her. Perhaps she should just seduce him and be done with it. The temptation became like a fever in her brain.

"Do you not care for painting?" Edward asked as they strolled through the rooms.

"I confess I don't have a true eye for it." She paused to examine one artist's signature, which included a looping W. Watteau, not Watts.

"What is a true eye for art?" He led her on to the next painting, a large canvas portraying the goddess Diana interrupted in her bath by Actaeon. "Do you like this painting?"

"Yes," she said. "I like the light and shadows."

"But?" he prompted.

Francesca hesitated. "I should not admit to anything else."

"Indeed. What else?" He stopped walking and turned toward her, looking down at her with interest.

She smiled to hide the sudden leap in her pulse. "You will think me hopelessly uncivilized, so I won't tell you."

"Now I must know." His attention was fixed on her completely now, his posture inclined toward her, his eyes intent on her face. Once, she would have found it unnerving, wondering if he was trying to intimidate her. Now she found it secretly exhilarating. She recalled the feel of his skin under her fingers, the solid strength of his body against her, the taste of his mouth, and a little smile crossed her lips.

"Must you? On what grounds, sir?"

"On the grounds . . ." He paused to study her. "On the grounds that your expression is too intriguing. It is . . . mysterious. I shall be tormented by wondering what it might mean."

"Tormented?" She raised her eyebrows in delight.

"Mercilessly," he murmured, not looking at all upset by the prospect.

Even though she had told herself not to think of it, her imagination refused to heed her reason. What would it be like to kiss him again? Would he stand by his declaration that it must never happen? Or would he give in to the attraction that almost shimmered in the air between them? She had gone from not liking him at all to being keenly attuned to his every subtle change of expression, and the way his mouth moved when he spoke to her. She could sense when his mood changed, and she was entranced by this slightly roguish, naughty side of him tonight.

"Well." She glanced around and lowered her voice. He leaned nearer, until his cheek was very near her own and she could smell his shaving soap. Just being near him made her feel reckless and wicked, and she wanted to tempt him to feel the same. "I have the most impertinent thoughts at times. I find myself thinking of new titles for pieces which would surely appall those with a natural love of art, to say nothing of the artists."

"New titles?" he repeated.

"Yes." She faced the painting in front of them again, one of the celebrated Titians. "I look at this and think, 'The Perils of Bathing Outdoors.' Diana will turn the intruder into a stag, but really, she should have built a bathing house if she didn't want to be spied upon. Don't you think a goddess could have at least borrowed some screens?"

He looked nonplussed. He turned to inspect the painting again, then back to her. "You," he said, "are shocking."

She waved one hand in modest acknowledgment. "Tell me the thought never occurred to you."

"No," he said slowly. "It never did, although I could not tell you why. I certainly shall think of that every time I recall this painting."

Francesca made a penitent face. "I apologize for ruining your enjoyment of it."

"On the contrary, you have significantly embellished it." He tucked her hand closer around his arm and began walking again. "What would you call this one?"

She contemplated it for a moment. " 'Fair Warning.' "

His eyebrows shot up. "The lady is fascinated by the man in his prime," she explained, "without realizing he wants a wife to care for his children and parents there in the background."

He cocked his head. "I don't think that's what the artist intended you to see."

"Of course not," she agreed. "But it's what I see when—"

"When you are feeling mischievous," he finished when she stopped. "Mocking the finest art ever created."

"Don't be ridiculous, Edward," she said, laughing. "I am not mocking it." He glanced at her curiously, intently. It took a moment for Francesca to realize what she'd said. A blush warmed her face. She cleared her throat. "Forgive me. I did not mean—"

"No," he said quietly, still watching her in that probing way he had. "By all means, call me by name, Francesca."

He said it as if he were whispering it over her skin. Her body reacted on instinct, although she was somewhat embarrassed to admit she had already been primed for this. She was attracted to him, more and more every time she saw him, and she hadn't been able to stop thinking about that kiss, that wicked, wonderful kiss. In her stronger moments, she told herself kissing him had been an unmitigated disaster, because now she not only thought about kissing him, she thought about seducing him. Or being seduced by him. She didn't have time for an affair right now, certainly not with a man of his station who would . . . who would . . . Oh, Lord, it would be easier to remember the arguments against it if he would stop looking at her like this. She made herself smile, trying to hide the potent attraction heating her blood. "As you like, Edward."

They walked on. Francesca struggled to keep her mind on what they had come to do, but it was clear to her they wouldn't find any connection to Percival Watts here. It was a magnificent collection—in spite of her lighthearted comments, she recognized that—but contained nothing like the rough, hazy landscapes she remembered seeing in Percival's painting studio. Still, she found herself reluctant to go. Far from appearing appalled by her impudent names for the paintings, Edward was intrigued. His hand fell on hers more than once to keep her by his side. He prodded her, and she grew more daring. She named one somber portrait "The Tobacco Hunter," opining that the fellow looked desperate for a smoke on his pipe. She pronounced a man in one painting an obvious rogue, only to have Edward point out that she was slandering David, God's chosen king. It took her breath away, to share a guilty but unapologetic grin with him, as if she were slowly pulling him out of his proper deportment with her own less-than-proper behavior.

It gave her a hint of a wicked side to Edward de Lacey, and that only attracted her more.

They wandered through the rooms, some badly lit and others so filled with paintings it was hard to take them in. The conversation flowed easily now. She had never seen Edward smile so much, and it was making her dizzy. All her protests to Alconbury and Sloan that it was just business began to seem as thin and frail as old lace. She wanted to see him smile—at her. She craved that heady thrill when he laughed at something she'd said. And most dangerously of all, beating beneath her skin like an echo of her pulse, was the desire to see him in the deepest throes of passion.

She had almost forgotten why they were here when Edward stopped abruptly. She had no choice but to stop as well, since her arm was still wound around his, even closer than when they had arrived. She glanced up at him in surprise, and her throat clogged up at his expression as he stared at a woman across the room. Instinctively she just knew who was ahead of them.

Lady Louisa Halston was every bit as beautiful as the gossip sheets said. Slender and delicate, her hair was the color of fresh butter, and spilled from her crown in perfect ringlets. Her gown was up to the minute in fashion, and flattered her coloring and her figure. Francesca could only see her profile from where they stood, but it was very nearly perfect. Her nose was not too large, her chin not too pointed. She stood with her head tilted slightly to one side, studying the painting in front of her with a thoughtful air as her companion spoke and gestured to it.

"Oh, dear," Francesca said in a too-quick voice, casting about for any reason to leave. "These are all portraits. I don't think Percival had much of a hand for portraits . . ." She trailed off as Edward's arm tensed.

"Nonsense," he said in a smooth, cold tone, all trace of levity and irreverence gone. "Don't be so hasty." He turned away and led her to a portrait near the window, of a lady in green.

Dutifully, Francesca examined it. "Lovely."

"Is that all you have to say?"

She glanced sideways at his grim face. "Yes," she said. "I don't feel like mocking her."

He didn't comment on her choice of words, just walked on. She wondered if he wanted to see his former fiancée. He certainly wasn't taking action to avoid her, as he marched them along the room. Then she wondered if perhaps she shouldn't take it out of his hands and feign a sudden headache. He would have to take her home if she swooned to the floor in pretend illness.

But then it was too late. They turned toward the next room, and came face-to-face with Lady Louisa and her companion. By now a number of other people in the room had noticed, and Francesca dimly heard the buzz of whispers that quieted down. She took a deep breath, not knowing what to expect.

Edward felt Francesca's tension, but was helpless to reassure her. It was all he could do to keep his emotions battened down after catching sight of Louisa on the opposite side of the gallery. She was still as beautiful as ever, still the same sweet image of ladylike perfection. Suddenly he regretted not going to see her after the end of their engagement, just so he wouldn't have been caught so unprepared this evening, when he had readily allowed himself to be drawn in by Francesca's outgoing charm and slightly risqué sense of humor. He forgot all about looking for connections to Percival Watts as they grew more and more at ease. When she slipped and called him Edward again, he felt something like elation humming through him. He would definitely kiss her again, tonight. And this time he wouldn't force himself to walk away. Whatever happened after that would be . . . inevitable.

That was when he caught sight of Louisa. Like a bucket of cold water thrown in his face, he suddenly felt again all the anger and shock at her betrayal. He steeled himself to it, but still felt it burning at the edges of his mind as Louisa and her companion finally met them.

"Good evening," Edward said. He bowed his head. "Lady Louisa."

"Good evening, de Lacey." The Marquis of Calverton's eyes gleamed. He was two decades older than Edward, a few inches shorter but a fit, physical man. Durham once bought several brood mares from Calverton's stud farm, and the marquis had driven a hard, ruthless bargain. Edward respected him for that, but he also never forgot his father cursing Calverton's name after some especially sharp haggling over one mare. "And good evening to you, Lady Gordon," Calverton added, to Edward's surprise. He glanced at her to see a gracious smile on her face as she dipped a curtsey.

"How good of you to remember, my lord."

He regarded her with entirely too much interest for Edward's liking. "You are hard to forget, my dear."

She laughed. "You flatter me."

"May I present my betrothed, Lady Louisa Halston." Calverton shot a keen glance at Edward at the word "betrothed," but he'd been prepared for that; indeed it seemed the only reason Louisa would be out with him. After all, Calverton had a large fortune, and it was indisputably his. "Louisa, this is Lady Gordon," the marquis added. "She used to have some of the finest singers in London at her salons."

Louisa hadn't looked away from Edward since he said her name. Finally she shifted her gaze, to greet Francesca with reserve and propriety. Edward noticed how fragile she seemed next to Francesca. Louisa was slim and pale, holding herself regally still. Francesca seemed to shine with hidden heat, from her glowing hair to her vivid red gown to the warmth of her smile. Francesca was warmth and energy, where Louisa was quiet and peace. Seeing them both at once, he didn't know what to think. Instinctively he still felt the comfort of Louisa's serenity, but now he had discovered he craved—much more than he would have ever guessed—Francesca's vivacity.

"What do you think of the pictures, Lady Gordon?" Calverton asked.

"Quite impressive," she replied. "How do you find them, Lady Louisa?"

Louisa raised her eyes to Edward's. "Magnificent," she said quietly.

He had once imagined that soft blue gaze meeting his every morning and night. If not for a blackmailer, he would still be betrothed to her; it would be her hand on his arm this evening instead of Francesca's. He and Louisa would have walked through the gallery in polite, dignified appreciation, and not once thought of a cheeky new title for any piece. He would have thought it a lovely evening . . . but it wouldn't have made him feel the way he did with Francesca, as though he'd ingested a bit of liquid lightning.

Francesca was still chatting easily with Calverton. Louisa was silent, smiling politely, her wary eyes flicking back to Edward from time to time. By God, he had loved this woman, and she was engaged to another man within days of jilting him. Perhaps it should have made him feel better, this proof that Gerard had been right about her and her family, but it didn't ease the cruel shock of seeing how very deceived he had been in her.

"It was a pleasure to make your acquaintance, Lady Louisa." Francesca's voice broke into his thoughts as she discreetly pinched the inside of his arm, where her hand still curled familiarly. "And to see you again, my lord."

He snapped his eyes away from Louisa. "Good evening, Calverton. Lady Louisa."

Calverton put his hand possessively at Louisa's back and smiled. "And to you, de Lacey. Lady Gordon." With a polite half bow, he led Louisa away. Edward didn't watch her go, but he caught a breath of her scent, lilacs, and closed his eyes against the memory. He liked lilacs.

Francesca cleared her throat. "I do believe we've seen most of the paintings here. I didn't see anything that might be Percival's work."

Right. Percival Watts. Edward forced his mind to the reason they were here tonight. He had brought her thinking it would help in her search, not end with him facing his faithless fiancée. It wasn't Francesca's fault at all, but the evening felt ruined, and he took the escape she offered. "Are you ready to go?"

She glanced at him, her eyes dark. She made no attempt to revive the lighthearted fun they had shared earlier. "Yes."

He headed for the door, Francesca walking beside him without another word.

Chapter 17

❧⟶ ∽∾ ⟵

The ride home was almost silent. Francesca didn't know what Edward was thinking, but she could guess. The few glances she stole at his profile told her all she needed to know. Something inside her almost wept at how remote he looked, and she had to bite her lip to keep quiet. By now she knew Edward wasn't the sort to get angry and swear or punch someone. Instead he became cold and silent, as if retreating inside some internal fortress no one could breach.

In this case, she could almost understand that. She would never forget the expression that flashed ever so briefly across his face when he saw his former fiancée. Lady Louisa Halston was beautiful, true, but more importantly—and more cruelly—Edward had truly cared for her. The pain in his face was too deep, too personal, to spring from anything else. He must have trusted her. And in return, when he most needed her confidence and support, Lady Louisa broke off their engagement and sold his private scandal to Gregory Sloan. Everything must have been for money. Francesca knew the man Lady Louisa had been with. The Marquis of Calverton was in his early fifties, a proud, rather haughty man with an immense fortune and an illustrious title. He had already buried two wives and needed another, since he only had three daughters. He'd visited her salon a few evenings when she had an old friend of her mother's in to sing. She hadn't disliked him, but neither had she liked him. He was too calculating for her taste, too aware of his position and everyone else's. He was nothing like Edward, not by half. If Lady Louisa cared for anything other than money and position, she was likely to regret her new choice of husband.

Not that it was her concern whom Lady Louisa married. She didn't care a bit . . . except for the small voice inside her heart that practically sang with triumph that Lady Louisa *had* seen fit to jilt Edward. Her loss would be someone else's gain . . . perhaps even Francesca's. At least for a little while.

They had reached her home. The horses stopped; the carriage dipped as the footman jumped down from the back. Edward stepped down when the servant opened the carriage door, holding out his hand to help her alight, a gentleman to the end. She took her time gathering her skirts to climb down. Her personal desires had been doing hard battle with her common sense and cold practicality, but now there was no contest. She would be a liar to say she hadn't been waiting for this chance for a while now, and she didn't even pretend she had the discipline to keep herself from seizing it.

"Would you like to come in for a drink?" She glanced up at him. In the lamplight his expression was set and composed, his eyes shadowed by the brim of his hat, and she had no idea what he would reply.

"Perhaps not tonight," he said.

Francesca stepped closer and laid her hand on his arm. "Perhaps tonight is the perfect time," she said quietly. He looked down at her, the light catching his gray eyes and turning them to silver. Something flickered there as he caught her meaning. She met his gaze for a moment longer, just to leave no doubt, then turned and walked unhurriedly up her steps.

The Hotchkisses had already gone to bed, since she told them not to wait up for her. They had a small apartment behind the kitchen, close to the mews. She let herself in with her latchkey, leaving the door open behind her. If he didn't follow in a minute or so, she would close it and pretend nothing had happened. It hadn't, really, and if nothing continued to happen, she could carry on as before.

She was pulling off her gloves when the door closed. Her heart skipped a beat as he stepped up very close behind her and fingered her shawl. His gloved fingers brushed her bare shoulders, and she shivered as he lifted the silk shawl away and cool air rippled over her skin. A moment later she heard the unmistakable swish of fabric as he shed his coat and hung it up, and that unleashed a different sort of shiver. He was staying.

Trying to ignore the sizzle of anticipation in her veins, she went into the dark drawing room and poured two glasses of wine. Her hands were unnaturally steady, for all that she had just invited a man into her home to seduce him. Francesca considered herself a modern, independent woman, but she'd never done anything like this. Cecil had been dead for two long years. She hadn't been with a man since. And now she found herself almost melting from the hot burn of desire inside her—for Edward de Lacey of all people, whom she'd accosted like a shrew and who had probably viewed her as a mild annoyance, if not worse. For the man she had thought made of marble, with ice water running in his veins. That didn't mean she hadn't been attracted to him, of course, just that she ought to have been able to ignore it. And she had . . . mostly . . . until now.

She turned. He stood in the doorway, arms folded across his chest, watching her with an intensity that made her heart jump. If she had ever doubted he felt the same pull toward her that she felt toward him, now she knew. She held up one of the glasses of wine. "Sherry?" she asked, her voice huskier than usual.

Slowly, he crossed the room and took the glass from her hand. His gaze never left hers as he set it down on the table beside her. She had to tip back her head to meet those eyes, now as turbulent as a stormy sky. His gaze seemed to be asking something, seeking some answer without asking a question. Francesca was pretty certain her thoughts and feelings were written on her face, and after a minute the probing nature of his stare changed to one of purpose. He stripped off his gloves, one at a time, and dropped them to the floor. She dimly heard them hit the carpet as he raised one hand and fingered a loose lock of hair at her temple.

She could feel the heat of his skin, so close to her cheek, and unconsciously she turned her head, leaning into his touch. Edward made a soft, guttural noise in the back of his throat as she rubbed her cheek into his palm. With quick, efficient movements he pulled the combs from her hair until the whole mass tumbled down around her shoulders. Then he dug his fingers into her hair and curled them around the nape of her neck, holding her in place as he pressed his cheek to hers.

It seemed she had waited an eternity for this. She splayed her hands open against his chest and inched closer to him, pressing into the warmth and strength of his body. He said something inaudible, the barest rumble in his chest, and she let her head fall back even more into his cradling hands. Since the day she'd kissed him, she had wanted to feel this again, his arms around her and his heart pounding hard at her touch. Something inside her wanted to purr and stretch like a cat and rub against him.

His thumbs stroked over her cheekbones, moving over her flesh as delicately as the brush of a butterfly's wing. The pads of his fingertips pressed on the back of her skull, tipping her face up. Francesca closed her eyes, and her chest grew tight as she waited for his lips to touch hers again. *Kiss me*, she pleaded silently. She didn't know how she could stand to wait another minute for it, even as his hands skimmed over her skin, his fingers sure and deliberate. He traced her temples, smoothed along her eyebrows, and drew his fingertips down her jaw, exploring each arch of bone and dip of flesh with the barest of touches. She could feel his breath on her cheek, close enough to warm her skin but still too far away. It was exquisite and unbearable all at once.

And then, finally, his lips brushed the corner of hers. Francesca inhaled sharply, hardly realizing she'd been holding her breath, and sensation rushed in with her breath. He kissed her gently, almost tentatively, at first, his lips barely touching hers. She swayed toward him, trying to lean into the kiss and deepen it, only to be held in place by his hands, still twisted in her hair. Without a thought, she surrendered to his control. She had wanted him so badly, knowing it was wrong and unseemly to do so, that now she was almost afraid to move and break the spell. Even as his lips settled on hers a sliver of worry poked at her mind, that he would pull away and turn from her and declare once again that nothing could ever happen between them.

Of course, he'd said that almost a week ago. And she had seen the memory of that kiss smoldering in his eyes more than once since then. Clearly he had failed to persuade himself any more than he had persuaded her.

With unhurried care his mouth pulled at hers, exploring, shaping, and then finally opening to taste hers. She moaned at the first stroke of his tongue against her own. He tasted like wine, the rich warm flavor of port still clinging to him. That must be why she felt tipsy and off-balance, she thought, as if the room had begun tilting from side to side like a ship at sea. She could grow drunk on kisses like this.

He looked at her, his eyebrows raised. Francesca gazed boldly back, and ran the tip of her tongue along her upper lip. Edward inhaled a harsh breath, and then he was kissing her again. There was less control in this kiss. His hands flexed around her neck, and he ran his palms down to cup her shoulders and slide along them, then down her spine. He spread his hands wide over the small of her back, pulling her hips into his. Her back arched as he bore her backward until her shoulders pressed against the wall. She could feel the damask wall covering against her bare skin. The thought flitted away as his hands kept sliding, down to grip the curves of her bottom, to lift her to her toes and drag her even tighter against him. The length and breadth of his erection seemed branded on the skin of her belly, right through her clothes and his. The steady hum of desire inside her grew louder and more strident until it seemed to drown out her heartbeat, shutting out all thought and doubt. Not that she had much of either left; he wouldn't be here if he didn't want her, and she'd had plenty of time to think about how much she wanted him. She let go of his shoulders so she could wrap her arms around his neck, trying to hold him to her in this breathless little cocoon of desire. Her left foot lifted of its own volition to rub lightly along the outside of his calf.

His breath caught and he laughed quietly. He released her bottom and hiked up handfuls of her skirt. The fabric of her petticoats spilled over her thigh as he reached down and grasped her knee, lifting it almost to his waist. Francesca shuddered as cool air hit her bare leg in intimate places. Her blood was already running hot and fast just from the thought of him touching her there.

The heel of her shoe knocked against the narrow table beside them. He inhaled roughly and raised her knee farther, until he propped her foot on the table. She melted against the wall and clutched at him for balance as he stroked the flat of his palm leisurely down her calf, then circled around to slide up her shin. In the still darkness of the room, the soft shush of his bare hand over the silk of her stocking seemed to reverberate in her bones. He dipped his head, his lips whispering over her temple. His fingers paused. She shivered as he pressed, lightly, on the inside of her knee, opening her until he could move that last little step forward and ease his hips into the embrace of her legs.

Francesca gulped as his body moved against hers. He flexed his spine, rocking his hips into hers, and she spasmed in painful pleasure as the length of his cock rubbed against her most feminine spot. God, he was going to kill her if he kept moving at this languorous pace. It must have been an hour since she walked through her door, and so far he had barely kissed her, yet she felt ready to burst into flame at any moment.

She pushed her hands down his collarbones, forcing the elegant evening jacket back. He gave a low growl, but shrugged out of the coat without a word. She yanked and ripped at the buttons of his waistcoat as he kissed a scorching path along her temple and his fingers continued to play up and down the side of her leg. Her hands were shaking by the time she got the last button undone and tugged the waistcoat off. Edward cooperated enough to pull one arm free and then the other, but otherwise his attention seemed locked on touching every last inch of her skin, from the top of her head to the arch of her foot, after he slipped her high-heeled slipper off and tossed it aside.

But at least she could touch him now. With a few pulls, the front of his shirt came free of his trousers. Now it was his turn to tilt back his head and exhale as she slid her hands up the warm, firm planes of his chest. He let her explore for a moment, and then shifted his weight forward without warning. She was pinned between the wall and Edward, her hands trapped under his shirt, balanced on one increasingly shaky leg. She squirmed a moment before realizing she was stuck, fol-

lowed closely by the admission that she liked it very
much and that it was, in fact, exactly what she had been
hoping to achieve. This was what she'd wanted to rouse
from Edward: passion, dark and thrilling and purposeful. She just hadn't expected to be so excited by it—
his touch seemed to send sparks radiating across her
skin, through her flesh and into her bones. It wasn't the
wild ecstasy of pent-up need that she felt, but the controlled, relentless exploration of a man who would not
be rushed. She hated his restraint even as it was twisting
her into excited knots from the anticipation.

Edward held her there, cupping her jaw with one
hand to hold her face up for his kiss, his other hand
gliding over her leg, slowly working its way across her
thigh. His hips still rocked against hers with a gentle
but persistent pressure. He kissed her deeply, his tongue
possessing her mouth as thoroughly as he was about to
possess her body. Francesca moved against him, her
breath rasping in her throat as she tried without success
to impart some of her own frantic need to him.

His fingers slid up over her knee, pausing to finger the
ribbon of her garter. A moment later the ribbon eased
and slipped away, and he was sliding her stocking over
her knee. Her muscles jumped and relaxed as he stroked
down her thigh, over her hip, and finally, blessedly, between her legs. She let out her breath in what was nearly
a cry of relief and pleasure. Oh God—after waiting so
long for him to touch her, she thought she might shatter
at the next stroke of his wicked, talented fingers. He
knew how to touch her, and where, and how firmly . . .
how could he make her come undone so easily? After
wanting him so desperately, she was about to climax

within seconds after he touched her. She didn't want that. She wanted him to feel the same pleasure, the same madness, the same abandon she felt.

With Herculean effort she twisted in his grip. "Stop," she gasped. "I can't take it—make love to me, *now*, damn it . . ." She dug her fingernails into his flesh and raked downward, recklessly glad when he muttered a curse and recoiled. She took advantage of his momentary distraction and whipped her hands out from under his shirt. "You can't play with me all night like that." She curled her fingers into the fall of his trousers and felt for the buttons. "I'll go mad . . ."

His smile was hard and slow, his eyes glittering as if he'd intended to drive her mad all along. He said nothing as she unbuttoned the trousers, and merely arched his neck and groaned as she finally wrapped her fingers around his erection. Francesca's heart was leaping; she felt dizzy. This was her darkest fantasy come true: Edward standing half undressed and disheveled, his arms braced beside her shoulders, his head thrown back in ecstasy, his hips rocking back and forth to slide his length between her hands.

And it wasn't enough. She reached up with one hand and pulled his head down, sealing her lips to his. There was no pretense of delicacy this time. His mouth opened against hers and she tasted him again, more intoxicating than before. She could easily find herself addicted to the feel of this man's mouth on hers. His member was hot and thick in her grasp, still thrusting against her palm, and she wrapped her fingers more snugly about him, running her thumb over the blunt head and down the velvety smooth shaft.

Edward growled deep in his throat. He pulled on her knee, hooking it over his hip. The heavy crimson silk of her skirt rustled as he dragged her up, off her feet, still pinned against the wall, until she kicked her other leg free of the petticoats and curled it around his waist. She had to release him for a moment to shove the bulk of her gown aside, and he took advantage. He shifted his grip, holding her up easily, and then she felt him step forward, angle her hips toward him, and push deep inside her.

For a moment she felt light-headed, and had to grab his shoulders to steady herself. Her body was ready for him, but she still felt stretched and invaded and utterly conquered. He adjusted his hold on her, then started moving. Her body seized every time he drove into her until she was shaking and almost sobbing. His breathing had grown harsh as well, and when she brushed her hands over his face, his skin was damp. He shifted again, anchoring her knee at his waist and tipping up her chin, still thrusting into her hard enough to shake the watercolor hanging on the wall nearby. At the first touch of his lips on hers, Francesca felt the floor drop out from under her as a hot, heady climax roared along her veins. Her back arched and her head fell back as it pulsed through her. Edward rested his forehead on the exposed line of her neck, and a few moments later she felt his breath against her throat hitch and pause as he stiffened in the throes of his own release.

She managed to drape her trembling arms over his shoulders to keep from falling. It took real effort to turn her head to the side and press her lips to his cheek. His chest was heaving as hard as hers, but he was still holding her up. She had finally succeeded in making him lose his control, it seemed. If only it hadn't cost her every last pretense of disinterest.

Francesca laid her temple against his. Her fingers combed through his short dark hair, ruffling it as she had longed to do from the start. "I don't want tonight to end," she confessed in a whisper. There was no point in trying to hide it now.

He raised his head and looked down at her. His eyes were mirrors for the silvery light that came through the window. For the first time since walking through her door, he spoke. "This is only the beginning," he said, and kissed her again.

Chapter 18

The clock chimed two before Edward felt even partially restored to his usual state of mind.

He hadn't intended to make love to Francesca up against the wall of her drawing room. Well, maybe he had; it certainly crossed his mind while he stood beside his carriage after she invited him in with desire burning in her eyes. In that minute of deliberation and hesitation, he imagined making love to her on the floor, on the sofa, on a table, on a bed, and even against a wall. It successfully drove away all thoughts of Louisa, and by the time he dismissed his driver and followed Francesca into her house, he'd already been hard. He *had* intended to make love to her. The wall was simply available when she kissed him with all the heat of a torch put to kindling.

In the hours since, he'd made love to her twice more, although they made it upstairs after that first time. If he had expected their coupling to be tamer the second time, he'd been wrong. Francesca undressed him with a thousand sensual touches that twisted him into knots of desire so tight, he actually threw up the skirts of her gown and had her again, bent over a chaise longue. By the time he got her naked, he had recovered enough to let her control things, but he was going to have to buy her a new gown. The red one was absolutely ruined. Patience, it turned out, was highly overrated at times.

And now he lay with her in bed, her back to his chest, his body relaxed and sated as his mind began to emerge from the fog of lust and urgency that had enveloped him. He would have been pleased not to have rational thought return; then he could have spent the night as he was, stretched out next to the most fascinating, irresistible woman he had ever met, idly running his hands over her bare body. But somehow, reason crept back in, pricking him hard. After behaving like a wild animal for the last few hours, he supposed he owed her . . . something. An explanation, or a declaration. It was obvious that he wanted her, and equally obvious that she wanted him. One night, though, was not enough. Already he was thinking how they would go on. But he hadn't planned anything about this relationship. If he wanted it to continue, it was only fair that he be honest with her now.

"That was my fiancée," he said, choosing the most obvious starting point. "At Cleveland House, with the Marquis of Calverton."

She twisted her neck and gave him a faint, dreamy smile. Her copper hair spilled across the white sheets and her pale shoulders, silky soft against his arm. "I know."

Yes, she would. "Ah, of course. Sloan's paper."

"That, and gossip, and innuendo, and the expectant silence that filled the room when you and she met." She rolled her eyes. "Nothing is secret in London."

"No," he murmured, pressing a kiss on her shoulder.

"I suppose not." How long until *this* was public knowledge? Charlie would never let him hear the end of it. Oddly, he didn't care.

She turned away. "I thought you handled the encounter very well. The lady will have no reason for embarrassment or reproach."

He barely caught back a snort. "I am sure that will please her."

She was quiet for a moment. "Was this the first you saw of her since : . . ?"

"Yes." He trailed the backs of his knuckles over the full curve of her hip. Her figure was ripe and lush and utterly perfect, in his view, quite unlike the slim, willowy Louisa. Not that he had ever held Louisa naked in bed, nor even—come to think of it—been driven half mad with thinking about it.

There was another long silence. "Did you love her?" she whispered.

Edward paused. "Yes," he admitted. "I did." He thought he had, anyway. The feeling was distant and dim, barely remembered and hardly significant. Love was hardly necessary in the sort of marriage he had expected with Louisa, but he had refused to marry a woman he wasn't fond of. Perhaps that was all it had been, and he'd mistaken it for love.

Francesca rolled over to face him. "Do you still?"

He stared at her face. It seemed an odd time to ask that question, as they lay naked together, twined in the sheets of her bed after several hours of scorching lovemaking. But then, perhaps it wasn't. Perhaps it was the best time. He ran his fingers down the slope of her arm again to thread his fingers through hers. "No." He raised her hand to brush his lips across her knuckles. "Do you love Baron Alconbury?"

She gave a gasp of laughter—surprised, he thought, but not uneasy. "Alconbury! Where did you hear about him?"

"Rumor," he murmured. "Whispers. According to gossip, he wants to marry you."

She lifted one shoulder, but her smile faded. "Perhaps he does. That doesn't mean I want to marry him."

"But a man doesn't let it be known he wishes to marry a woman without some indication she would accept him. We aren't such foolhardly fellows as that." He continued kissing her hand, spreading her fingers against his own. She had beautiful hands, graceful and strong. Her fingers were almost as long as his.

"Is that how it was when you proposed to Lady Louisa?" Her siren's voice had grown husky again as she watched him caress her hand.

"Yes." He pressed his lips to her wrist, feeling the soft, strong beat of her pulse. "My family has known hers for years. Her father gave my father to understand that she was very fond of me and that he would look favorably on our union. My father suggested I see if she suited me."

"And then you fell in love with her?"

"It was a good match." He shrugged. "I called upon her a few times, and discovered we got on rather well. Our temperaments agreed. I came to care for her. By the time I proposed to her, it was a foregone conclusion; she knew I would ask, and I knew she would say yes." He placed her hand flat against his chest, holding it to his skin with his own hand for a moment. He stroked her arm to her shoulder, then down the bare curve of her side. "So why would Alconbury think you might accept his offer of marriage?"

She said nothing for a long moment. Edward waited, content to keep running his hands over her soft skin. He thought he could easily spend a year exploring just the dip of her waist below her rib cage. "My husband died only a month after my sister," she said softly. He listened in silence; he already knew a few bare facts, but not how she saw them. "I wasn't prepared for both. Giuliana had a difficult confinement, and the doctor warned her . . . Well, it was heartbreaking, but not a complete surprise when she died laboring to birth her child. But Cecil—my husband—Cecil agreed to act as a second in a duel, and somehow he ended up getting shot. He hadn't said a word to me about any of it, and the friend who inveigled him to do it fled to the Continent before I could question him—or shoot him myself. It was a cruel shock. One day he was here, hearty and sound, and the next . . ." Her eyes were shadowed and sad.

Edward's fingers slowed to a stop and his jaw hardened. How could a man leave his wife so? And dueling, of all the damned foolish things to do. He wondered why Jackson hadn't unearthed this rather lurid detail.

She took a deep breath. "Alconbury brought me the news. He tried to stop that idiotic duel, and held Cecil's hand to the last. I would have been lost without him these last two years. He's been a good friend to me."

"I am glad he was." Edward brushed a loose lock of hair back over her shoulder, his fingers lingering in the silky copper strands. "But you don't love him." He returned to the main point, the one that concerned him the most.

She looked at him with a clear, open gaze. "If I did," she whispered, "I would not be here with you."

"No?" He raised one eyebrow. The attraction between them was incendiary—strong enough to overcome his honorable intentions. He'd wanted her before he knew she was a widow, before he'd been charmed by her, before he'd even liked her. If Louisa hadn't jilted him, he never would have been here with Francesca, either—but he would have thought about it.

"Of course not. I had to work quite hard to lure you here," she replied with a short laugh. "Why would I have wasted all that effort if I'd wanted Alconbury instead?"

"You lured me here," he repeated, beginning to smile. How had he never guessed how seductive it could be to know a woman wanted him enough to lure him? His fingertips glided down her shoulder. "I didn't realize I was being pursued and manipulated . . ."

"You were taking too long to seduce me," she said, unrepentant. She shifted her weight, stretching languidly beneath his touch. "I grew impatient."

"My dear Lady Gordon, I had no idea you wanted me from the moment we met." He pressed closer to her, turning her onto her back. "You might have mentioned it earlier . . ." He stroked down the center of her chest, and pressed his lips to her collarbone.

"Oh, not from the moment we met! I thought you were too dull initially." She arched her neck and sighed as he kissed his way toward her throat. "Too restrained . . . too colorless . . . too quiet . . ."

He laughed softly. His fingers skimmed the plane of

her belly, teasing her navel and tracing her ribs. "And now?"

"Hmm." She tilted her head to the side and studied him with a playful expression. "A little less restrained than I thought."

"Yes, you've been a thoroughly corrupting influence." He cupped the swell of her breast. "I feel utterly . . . debauched."

"Is that a complaint?" Her smile was pure, knowing, sin.

Edward rolled on top of her, bracing himself on his elbows. "Did it sound like one?" He kissed her.

"You should take it as a taunt." She wound her arms around his neck and one leg around his waist as he settled his hips between her thighs. God almighty, he wanted her again, just as badly as he had downstairs. Then, he had put off any thought of consequences and repercussions. Now, he could see only that they were both free to want each other as desperately as they did. How fortunate that was . . .

"Which part?" He slid his palm down her belly to touch her. She sucked in a sharp breath, but her hips rose against his, and when he pushed his finger inside her, she was wet.

"To be . . . less quiet," she gasped. Her body began to undulate beneath him. Edward slid another finger inside her, still stroking the spot that made her tremble and gasp.

"You want me to scream?" he whispered against her mouth. "As I intend to make you scream?"

"Yes," she moaned. She clasped his backside in both hands and squeezed. He resisted her urging. He wanted to make her scream, to see her come apart in his hands. She didn't know it, but he had already come apart in hers. He just wasn't the sort to shout about it. He also wasn't the sort to want to make a woman scream, even in the grip of passion, but somehow he wanted to see Francesca so enraptured she screamed out her pleasure to the heavens.

"Then scream for me." He devoured her face and throat with open-mouthed kisses, drunk with the taste of her. He pushed his fingers in and out of the slick tight channel of her body. His thumb circled and pressed the sensitive nub hidden in her wet nether curls until she was shaking.

"Oh God, wait," she begged, twisting her head away. She clutched at his shoulders. "That's too . . . Stop— *stop* . . ."

"Stop?" Edward took his hand away. Her eyes flew open, dilated with passion and shock, and he thrust deep and hard inside her. She writhed under him, her hips meeting his on each pounding stroke, until he felt her body begin to clamp around his. His ballocks drew up with impending climax, so deliciously tight it hurt. He clenched his teeth, wanting to drive her over the edge before giving in to his own release, but she was already there. She tossed her head from side to side and scored his chest with her fingernails. He felt the ripples of her orgasm pulling his out of him as she gave a high, keening cry. He plunged deep inside her one last time, and seized her in his arms as his release broke and rushed through him like a blazing inferno.

"You cried out," she said weakly as he rolled to one

side, taking her with him, their bodies still intimately connected.

"Did I?" It was a struggle to form the words. Edward felt a satisfaction like he had never felt before, soft and heavy and peaceful. It was more than just the lovemaking, although that was certainly part of the reason he felt so blissful. Francesca was right about him—he *was* too dull and colorless and quiet and restrained. Until she came along, he had never realized how much so, and he certainly never felt any urge to change. But with her, he felt like a different man, an unsettling and oddly liberating feeling. All he really knew was that he had never in all his life felt so happy that he could have shouted it to the sky.

"You did," she murmured, curling against him. "It was glorious to hear." Her gleaming hair, now wildly disheveled, tickled his chest as she tucked her head under his chin. His entire body felt exposed and sensitive, as if he'd shed a tough outer skin. Perhaps it was the rigid restraint he had cultivated his entire life, the shield he'd worn against the slings and arrows of life. Perhaps it was his good judgment deserting him for good. Whatever it was, he felt damned good without it.

His lips curved into a grin as he pressed one last kiss on her forehead. "Sleep," he whispered. "You can wring another cry from me tomorrow."

Her shoulders shook gently with laughter, and then she was quiet. Edward gathered her close, settling them both more comfortably before falling with her into Morpheus's embrace.

Chapter 19

Francesca woke slowly, drifting out of the deepest sleep she could recall in months. Without opening her eyes she stretched and rolled over. She felt comfortably easy in body, clear and refreshed in mind. A night of making love could do that to a woman.

She smiled as remembered sensation flooded through her. Edward was still here, she knew, sensing his presence even before she saw him. "Good morning," she mumbled.

"The finest morning of my life," he said, sounding as relaxed as she felt. She pried open her eyes and gazed up at him. He was sitting in a chair pulled up beside her bed, his elbows propped on his knees. He wore no cravat and his jacket was unbuttoned, but otherwise he was fully dressed. "You're beautiful in your sleep," he added with a faint smile.

Francesca blinked in surprise. "How long have you been watching me sleep?"

"Since the sun came up."

It was barely light in the room now. She gave a hesitant laugh. "You're an early riser."

"Yes," he acknowledged. In the soft dawn light his eyes were dark smoky gray. "Always have been."

"Hmm." She stretched again, and tried to smother a yawn. "I much prefer to lie abed in the mornings."

"Indeed." His gaze drifted down the length of her body as she arched her back. The covers had slid to her waist, and Francesca made no effort to pull them up. She liked the way her skin tingled under his scrutiny, and rather boldly hoped it might lead to a more physical study. Edward made love with a focused thoroughness that made up in intensity whatever it might lack in spontaneity—and she was happy to spark any spontaneity needed. "I was somewhat tempted to do the same myself, this morning," he said softly.

She gave him her most seductive smile, in spite of her sinking heart. "Then why are you already dressed?" She knew the answer, of course; he was ready to leave, not wanting anyone to see him emerging from her house in the first hours of the new day. It was a time-honored thing for a man to slip out the door like a thief in the night. She was probably fortunate he had stayed until morning.

He met her eyes. "In case you wished me to leave."

She never wanted him to leave. Francesca's mouth went dry as that thought flashed through her mind. "Why would I wish that?" She made herself laugh, making light of the moment. "I hardly thought my actions were unwelcoming thus far."

He didn't smile. "Because you are a widow. Because you might wish to avoid any unpleasantness from your neighbors and from the gossips. Because you might want time to yourself, to think about . . ." He paused.

" . . . how things should proceed . . ." He cleared his throat. " . . . between us."

Her lips parted in amazement. The unflappable Edward de Lacey was at a loss, picking over his words. And those words implied he wasn't ready to leave of his own wish, but out of respect for hers. She pushed herself up against the pillows and tucked the covers under her arms. "That is very considerate."

"If I go now, through the kitchen, no one but the coal man would see me." He fixed a steady look on her. "I will not be affronted if you ask me to go."

"To sneak out, you mean." Francesca twisted a fold of the sheet around her finger. She wished he wouldn't be so gentlemanly, even as her heart fluttered at his deference and solicitude for her wishes. She hadn't prepared herself for this when she invited him in last night, but she realized that had been her mistake. She knew who Edward was and how his mind worked. He was hardly the sort of man to flaunt their affair, especially not after being subjected to vicious gossip himself.

But she still felt there was room between flaunting and hiding, and that was the path she meant to take. "I won't ask you to leave—unless you wish to keep it secret," she added quickly. "I suppose you did not intend for this to happen last night, and if you prefer that no one know—"

"Francesca," he interrupted her, "I have nothing to hide. I'm not sorry for one moment of last night— except, perhaps, that it was over in far too few hours."

Her lips curved in irrepressible happiness. "Neither am I." She leaned toward him without conscious thought. Edward closed the gap and took her face in his hands to kiss her, deeply and sweetly. Joy blossomed inside her, just to be with him and see this new side of him.

"But I don't want to subject you to any unpleasantness," he said, still running his fingers through her bedraggled hair. "If you would like to make our association known to your acquaintances, before it becomes generally recognized . . ."

He wanted to know if she wished to tell Alconbury first. Like a lightning bolt, Francesca realized it. After the way Lady Louisa had treated him, he didn't want Alconbury, her good friend and rumored suitor, to suffer the same rude shock, nor her to be called callous or capricious. Her heart gave a little throb at his thoughtfulness, even for a man he might have viewed as a rival. "I'll tell Alconbury today," she whispered. "I never led him to believe he and I would ever be lovers or more, but he deserves to know about . . . this . . . from me."

"He does." Edward smiled wryly. "Do be gentle, when you break his heart."

She laughed, although a part of her felt a rush of sadness. This would change her relationship with Alconbury. He had been so good to her, so good *for* her. She couldn't imagine life without him dropping by for breakfast, escorting her to the theater, listening to all her woes and offering his shoulder when she needed one, making her laugh at the littlest thing. But she sensed he wouldn't do any of that once he knew Edward was in her bed at nights. She treasured Alconbury's friendship, and she recoiled from the thought of causing him pain.

"Then I take it there's no need for me to slink through the kitchen now?" He had wound her hair around his fingers and was pulling her inexorably toward him.

"No, although if you want to go, I could not stop you." She traced his lips with one finger. "I still can't decide why you got dressed."

Edward laughed quietly as he moved from his chair to the bed. "That can be soon remedied. Or . . ." He stripped away the duvet and swept her naked body with an openly admiring, lustful gaze. "Perhaps not. We managed quite well enough with clothing last night."

"And without," she reminded him.

He clasped her hands in his and straightened his arms, stretching her out flat on the bed as he loomed over her. "Variety, my dear," he whispered as he lowered his head to her breast. "And patience."

Francesca quivered as his tongue flicked over her nipple. Heat rushed through her even as her skin puckered into gooseflesh. He alternately licked and blew light puffs of air across her nipples, first one then the other, until she was twisting in his grip and begging him to go on. "More," she gasped. Her breasts ached from his teasing.

"Like fresh raspberries," he muttered. "Plump and pink and ripe." He took one nipple between his teeth and bit down lightly. Francesca gave a strangled little scream, and then moaned as he finally sucked it into his mouth.

Edward lifted his head after a few minutes and smiled darkly at her. "You like that."

"Yes," she choked. "Oh, yes. More, *please . . .*"

"More?" He dipped his head to the other breast. "God, you're sweet . . ."

She whimpered and nodded, even though her whole body had convulsed as he suckled again with long, steady pulls and quick little nips of his teeth. She couldn't escape; he held her in place for his torment, even though escape was the last thing on her mind. She arched her back, pressing up into his hot, sinful mouth as he tasted her. When her breasts were aching with sensation, he began working his way down, kissing the ridges of her ribs and licking the underside of her breasts, his breath hot against her skin. Slowly his fingers untangled from hers until his palms slid down the length of her arms and she was free . . . to plunge her fingers through his hair as he kissed lower and lower down her abdomen.

Then he kissed the inside of her thigh and rose from the bed. "Stay there," he commanded. Francesca raised her head and frowned, then blushed as she watched him walk across the room to the washbasin and wet the towel. Blessed saints. She hadn't washed last night. She remembered him cuddling her against his chest, his arms around her, and then the next thing she knew it was morning. What a way to start their first day as lovers . . .

Edward peeled off his jacket and dropped it on top of her discarded red gown, still lying across the chaise. "Someday I'll have you in the large copper bathtub at Lastings. It's nearly large enough to swim in."

"What is Lastings?"

He crawled back across the bed to her. "My family's estate in Sussex. It should be mine someday." He held the towel over her belly and squeezed. Water dribbled onto her skin, and Francesca sucked in her breath.

"That's cold," she gasped.

"Is it?" Lazily, he trailed the wet towel over her skin.

She squirmed at first as the cold drops ran down her hips and between her legs, until Edward dipped his head and began kissing again, his mouth a heated contrast to the water. By the time he swirled the towel down over the curls between her thighs, she was shaking with renewed lust, incoherently urging him on. He looked up long enough to flash her a smile that promised unspeakable things before he sealed his mouth over that delicate nub that radiated pleasure through her whole body.

She might have screamed. She might also have fainted; it was hard to tell. The blood pounded so hard in her ears, she couldn't hear anything else. He was—*Oh, Mother of God*—and his tongue—now his fingers—

He drew the climax from her as if he had all the time in the world. Francesca fleetingly wondered how she had been so wrong about him; he was no more a restrained and dull gentleman than she was a nun. He was driving her wild, and he was still fully dressed. The inequity of it surfaced in her mind and ballooned to paramount importance. She had started this affair, and she would not relinquish . . . Good Lord, how did he know to do *that*? Her body drew up tighter, ready to burst into flames, and she gulped in a deep breath to stave it off. She was going to retain some element of control . . . even if it killed her . . .

With enormous effort she dug her elbows into the mattress and wriggled away from his beautifully wicked tongue. "Take off your clothes," she demanded in a ragged tone.

"No." He cupped one hand under her knee and tugged. "I want to taste you."

"I want to taste *you*," she threw back at him. Edward

paused, his eyes flying to hers. She scooted farther back, sitting up as she did. "Let me show you."

Unresisting, he let her pull him to his knees. Francesca unbuttoned the fall of his trousers and took him in her hands. She circled her fingers around his cock and slid up and down the length. She looked up to see him looking down at her, raw hunger burning in his face. "Close your eyes," she whispered. He swallowed hard, but obeyed.

Francesca whisked the discarded towel around his erection, paying him back for the cold water. Edward cursed and lurched backward, but froze as she tossed the wet towel aside and replaced it with her mouth, taking him right into the back of her throat on one stroke. His hands fisted in her hair as she drew back, then plunged forward again.

He stopped her after a few minutes. "I always knew your mouth was made for sin," he said, breathing heavily. "But I want to feel you . . ." He pushed her onto her back, and fitted himself against her opening. "Come for me, darling," he said, thrusting hard inside her. "Now."

She melted. The cloth of his trousers rasped against her bare legs as his weight bore down on her. She gripped his waistcoat in both hands as the buttons scraped across her skin, her belly, her breasts. Their bodies moved together, against each other, inside each other. And when she came, a rich sweet rapture, he was the one who shouted.

He washed her again, later, when the sun had come up and the room was bright with morning. Francesca was used to dressing herself in the morning, but found it was a different experience with a man in the room. Cecil had been an early riser as well but was usually already gone riding in the morning by the time she awoke. He certainly never sat and watched her choose her dress, or helped her into it. And ever since, she had been alone in the mornings.

"It ties on the side," she tried to explain. Edward was examining her simple morning dress and undergarments with his usual intense interest, which was making it difficult to get the dress on. "This piece just wraps around and ties there."

"Really," he murmured. His hand was under the dress as if examining the construction but in reality exploring the way her body felt in clothing. His fingertips ran along the narrow band of lace edging the top of her stays, right along the swells of her breasts. "So simple. So tempting."

"Surely you've taken off a woman's dress before." She laughed, even though she didn't want to think of him undressing Lady Louisa or any other woman.

"Not as many as you might think. My brother Charlie was the one who could get under a girl's skirts before Gerard and I even knew what a petticoat was." He spoke absently, his attention still absorbed in her undergarments. He circled behind her, still stroking his hands over the lines of her stays, her half-fastened dress hanging loosely from her shoulders. It threatened to slide off altogether as he ran his palms up her belly to cup her breasts, his thumbs rasping over the sensitive flesh exposed just above the garment. Francesca's breath hitched in her chest as she watched his every action in the mirror before her. He glanced up, and she just caught the edge of his wicked smile as he lowered his mouth to her neck.

"Your brother sounds like a terrible scoundrel," she said breathlessly. "Is he?"

"Yes." He pulled her backward, into him, until her bottom was against his hips. For a man who had made love to her five times in the last twelve hours, he seemed remarkably vigorous.

"Are you close with your brothers?" She wavered on her feet. It would be so easy to lean against him, give one little shrug of her shoulders and let the dress fall . . . He was playing havoc with her intention to keep her wits about her. She wanted to know more about him, but . . . oh dear . . . his fingers were *so* talented . . .

He paused. "Yes," he said in a cooler voice.

Francesca sensed she was trespassing, but she wanted to know. Edward had heard all about her family, from Giuliana's tangled life to Cecil's shocking death. "Does that mean not really?"

"No." His hands had stilled now. "We are close . . . comparatively speaking."

"Compared to what?" she persisted. "I never knew my sister until she was grown, so I don't know how it usually is with siblings."

His hands fell away from her breasts and he stepped away. "Neither do I." She heard a flicker of grimness in his tone, but she couldn't see his face in the mirror anymore.

She cleared her throat. "I'm sure it's vastly different, from family to family."

Edward folded his arms and looked at the floor. "We are not close in the manner that I have observed between sisters. Or in the way that people of a different class might be, with no duty and obligation dividing them. We have a common heritage and responsibility to it, and I think we each, in our own ways, try to uphold it."

She turned to face him. "Duty and obligation weigh you down a great deal."

He met her gaze. "Yes."

She felt the gulf between them then, and turned away, pulling her dress into place and fastening it with nearly steady fingers before going to her dressing table to finish her toilette. She wished she hadn't asked about his brother at all, even as she wished he would reveal this one thing about himself. Perhaps it was an omen for their new relationship. Perhaps he was happy enough to share her bed and indulge the desire that had been smoldering between them for days, but wanted her kept far away from anything to do with his family—which was, she acknowledged, far superior to her own in station. Was she to be his lover who could know him as he really was, and hear his hopes and worries and frustrations as well as his pleasures and amusements? Or the mistress who would get to see him only when he found it convenient, and then just for a few hours of physical pleasure? She didn't want to be merely a mistress; it implied dependence, and a restricted role. She was an independent woman with means of her own. She hadn't invited Edward into her house because she wanted his money or protection. She just wanted *him* . . . but not on any terms.

As she twisted up her hair, she could see Edward in the mirror. His expression had settled into the reserved, cool cast she remembered from their first meetings—

when she thought he needed to smile. She poked some pins into her hair and fiddled with the brush for a moment. Perhaps she was being too hard on him. She was rushing to conclusions about his feelings for her based on one action, when he might have a very good reason for growing quiet and grim. He hadn't seemed like this a few hours ago, when they were relaxed and easy in bed together. Perhaps he cared deeply for his brothers, and they didn't return the affection, or caused him a great deal of trouble, or any number of other things. Perhaps— Oh dear, she was truly an idiot for not thinking of this earlier—she had reminded him about the potential problem with his inheritance. That would certainly cause her to become grim and quiet, if she were in his place. Yes, she told herself firmly, she was being a fool, and was likely at fault to begin with. She took a calming breath and forced herself to let go of any hasty resentments. There was no reason to fly into a fit and ruin their relationship before it had a chance to begin.

"You'll stay for breakfast, won't you?" She got up and went to the wardrobe to get a light shawl. It was too warm for a fire, but still cool upstairs.

Edward looked at her as if she had startled him out of his thoughts, and for a moment said nothing. Francesca just waited, eyebrows arched hopefully. "If you wish," he said.

"I do." She smiled, partly in relief. "Very much so."

It felt so natural to walk down the stairs with him. He held the door for her, and then pulled out her chair. Mrs. Hotchkiss had laid out some dishes, rather more than usual. Francesca suspected her housekeeper already knew she had a guest. When the woman bustled in a moment later with a fresh pot of tea, her suspicion was both confirmed and denied. Mrs. Hotchkiss wore her usual beaming smile, but it vanished the moment her eyes landed on Edward. She recovered at once and set the teapot down in front of Francesca as usual, but gave her a questioning look when she had gone around behind Edward, where he couldn't see. Francesca just shook her head a tiny bit. If Mrs. Hotchkiss had expected Alconbury, then she hadn't been paying very much attention.

"Tea?" she asked Edward. He had taken the seat at her left, pushing the chair to the side so he was facing her more directly.

"Thank you, yes."

"Or perhaps coffee?" she asked on impulse, and recognized the spark of craving in his eyes. "Mrs. Hotchkiss, could you please bring some coffee?" She knew Mr. Hotchkiss liked coffee in the mornings, so there was bound to be some in the house.

Her housekeeper's brow wrinkled in surprise. "Yes, madam."

"It's not necessary," Edward said smoothly. "Tea is lovely."

"No trouble at all, sir," said Mrs. Hotchkiss, setting down the toast and hurrying from the room. "I'll have it ready in no time."

"You must tell me where you purchase your coffee," Francesca said to him as the door swung shut. "I understand there is a great variation."

Edward smiled. "You don't have to buy coffee just for me. I'm quite content with tea."

"Perhaps I want you to be more than content," she said as she prepared herself a cup of tea. "So you'll be tempted to breakfast with me again."

"I most certainly shall," he replied. "But it won't be because of the coffee." She glanced at him, sitting so comfortably at her table, watching her with heat in his gaze, and felt her heart give a hard thump. She could become accustomed to this all too easily.

Mrs. Hotchkiss came back after they had filled their plates, a steaming cup in her hands. "I just brewed it, sir," she said, setting it in front of Edward.

He leaned forward and inhaled deeply, a blissful expression on his face. "Thank you. A fresh cup of coffee is good for the soul."

"And the head, says my husband." The housekeeper nodded emphatically. "Good, strong coffee." She gave Francesca a mildly surprised but approving look as she bustled back out the door.

Edward poured cream into his cup. "Her husband, I presume, is also part of the household?"

"My coachman." She smiled ruefully. "A very small staff of two."

"Why would you need more?" He sipped the coffee. "Particularly not when one can make coffee so well. Great God. Mind you don't invite my brother for breakfast. Charlie is fiendishly particular about his coffee and would steal her from you in a heartbeat."

There it was, another mention of his brother, but this time Francesca resisted temptation. "Heresy, sir," she said lightly. "Mrs. Hotchkiss is invaluable to me. I would fight desperately to keep her."

He drank more coffee, then set the cup down. "I was

unfortunately abrupt upstairs. You must have formed an idea that I don't care for my brothers."

She felt his gaze on her, and concentrated on her toast. "It's not my place to say anything about it."

"Your place," he repeated. "No, perhaps not. It is my place to tell you—you've certainly been forthcoming about your family. I am . . ." He paused. "I am not in the habit of talking about mine. I suppose because many people know of us—sometimes too much, to some unfortunate effect—and also because I've spent most of my life in the country, where one is generally afforded more privacy. There aren't so many people I feel compelled to share my private thoughts and feelings with." He paused again. "It does not come easily to me."

"I understand," she said. "You don't have to—"

"No!" He shook his head ruefully. "See, I've done it again. It's too easy for me to act coldly and quash any overtures." He drank more coffee. "I do care very much for my brothers. In consequence, they vex me greatly, and no doubt I repay them the favor in full. My father raised us to compete with each other, but also to develop our own strengths. Our mother died when we were all young, and my father . . . He was a rather forceful personage, to put it mildly, and he refused to raise weak, insipid sons. Gerard, whom you've met, bought a commission in the army and has been killing Frenchmen ever since. I gravitated toward the books, the accounts, the running of my father's properties, where I might wage my battles with bankers and solicitors."

"And Charles?" she asked when he stopped.

Edward sighed. "Charlie pursues pleasure. He's very

good at it, from what I hear, perhaps because he devotes his every waking moment to it."

"And that's why you had to hire Wittiers," she said slowly. "Because your brother was too . . . ?"

"Drunk? Occupied chasing women? Unconcerned that we might all lose everything? Yes."

"Surely not," she exclaimed. "He is the eldest!"

"The heir," agreed Edward. "The one who has most to lose if this blasted mess can't be untangled to the House of Lords' satisfaction. Gerard has his captaincy, at least, and I suppose I could scrape along, but Charlie . . ." He shook his head and finished his coffee. "Wittiers has been solely my undertaking. Gerard has his own ideas about how to solve the problem—he's much too impatient to let a lawyer handle it—and Charlie won't do anything at all, so it fell to me." A faint frown crossed his face. "I didn't mean to steal Wittiers from you."

Francesca bit her lip. "Well, you were quite right to point out that he chose to cast me aside in favor of your case. My complaint did lie with him; you merely happened to take the brunt of my anger."

Edward raised his eyes to meet hers. "You can't know how exhilarating I found it."

She laughed as she sliced the top off her egg. "You called me managing."

He leaned forward. "You called me heartless."

"You didn't give me what I wanted."

His gaze heated. "I have endeavored to improve."

Mrs. Hotchkiss came back into the room then, so Francesca settled for sharing a small, wicked smile with him. There were no words to express how much he had improved in her opinion since that first day, anyway. She wasn't quite sure how he had done it. Her opinion of him had been so low, so venomous, she couldn't even notice how attractive he was. Or how charming. Or how wicked, beneath his reserved, proper exterior. Or how capable and thoughtful and tender. In short, how utterly right for her he was . . .

She stopped that thought before it could take hold. It was too soon even to wonder what the future might hold for them. They both had greater purposes to pursue— he, his inheritance, and she, Georgina—and neither was willing to set them aside. Francesca wasn't a timid woman, but she recognized that there were many obstacles to a life with Edward. He was the son of a duke, for one thing, accustomed to the wealth and dignity of the nobility, while she was the daughter of a slightly scandalous opera singer and a country squire. She was determined to find her niece and raise Georgina as her own, while he was responsible for the Durham estates, which she sensed were enormous and enormously demanding. As much as her heart tripped over itself when he smiled at her, or touched her hand, or said her name, a small, cold voice inside her whispered that all affairs began this way. Their passion might be a nine-days' wonder, a flame that flared brilliantly for a short time then burnt out, leaving them both a little charred.

But a short time later when Edward said he must leave, and Francesca walked him to the door, that voice went quiet. She held his coat, allowing herself one last stroke of her hands down his shoulders and arms as he pulled it on. He turned to face her, still shrugging the fine wool coat into place. He looked almost ready to go out for the evening again, aside from his cravat folded into his pocket; almost as if the previous night hadn't happened. She summoned a smile, telling herself not to be so maudlin. "Good-bye."

Edward's eyes met hers. He walked toward her, closer and closer, until she took an involuntary step backward into the wall. He cupped his hands around her jaw, one thumb brushing her cheek. "Good-bye," he repeated. "For now." He kissed her, his tongue sweeping into her mouth so sensually she quivered, and echoes of his love-making rippled across her skin. "What are your plans this evening?" he asked, dropping light kisses over her mouth between words.

"What?" She pressed into him, her arms around him beneath the layers of jacket and coat. "Tonight?"

"Yes, tonight. I want to see you again."

"Oh, yes," she sighed, and then bit her lip. "Oh, no, actually. I promised to attend the theater with the Ludlows."

"Covent Garden?"

"Yes . . ." It was hard to think, let alone speak, as Edward continued kissing her so lightly, so teasingly.

"Then I suppose I must let you go. For now." His mouth descended on hers again.

She clung to him. "I'll send a note to Mrs. Ludlow with my regrets."

He laughed quietly. "No, my dear, you should go. I'll find a way to see you."

She looked up at him, half drunk with desire, and reason trickled back in. She was acting like a girl in the grip of her first calf love. She took a deep breath, a little surprised at herself for losing her composure so quickly again, and smiled. She released him, smoothing his lapels back into place where she had crumpled them. "I should like that very much," she said as calmly as possible.

A trace of amusement still on his face, Edward gave her a scorching look, as if he knew very well that he was leaving her tense and longing for more. "Until then, my dear."

She closed the door behind him and slumped against it, her fingertips brushing down her throat, following the trail his lips had so recently traced. Perhaps she should have had more affairs, just so she would be practiced in how to act. Already she was in danger of throwing off all reserve and aplomb and letting herself fall madly, dangerously, passionately in love with Edward de Lacey. That, she reminded herself, would never do, but somehow it felt like a distant and trivial thing to worry about when she was so happy.

She went back to her breakfast, mildly surprised to see she had eaten anything at all. Edward's coffee cup still sat on the table, and a rather silly smile curled her lips as she regarded it. She must tell Mrs. Hotchkiss to seek out the best coffee in London this very day.

Francesca was still at the table when the knocker sounded at the door. She caught her breath, but it was not Edward's voice in the hall. Alconbury, most likely, from the way he was laughing with Mrs. Hotchkiss. Oh dear, so soon . . . But it was best to get it done with. She owed him the courtesy of learning it from her, before she and Edward were seen in public together and everyone guessed they were lovers just from the blissful look on her face. When he came into the room a moment later, she got to her feet and smiled at him. "Good morning, Alconbury."

"A very good morning to you, Francesca dear." He stopped suddenly and sniffed, and a delighted grin split his face. "God bless my soul—do I smell coffee? Have you finally come to your senses and taken it up?"

"Er . . . not really." She took her seat and rang the bell. "But I shall have Mrs. Hotchkiss fetch you some at once."

He laughed. "That's better than nothing, I suppose! I've longed for this day for months, you know, to be served coffee at your table . . ." His voice ran out. Francesca glanced at him from under her eyelashes and saw that he was staring at Edward's coffee cup. The smile had left his face. Oh, dear.

"You must tell me where to buy the best coffee berries," she said. "Do sit down."

A muscle twitched in his jaw. He circled the table, deliberately taking the seat opposite the one Edward had occupied. "I see I'm not the first to have morning coffee with you."

"You must take it as a compliment, an overdue acknowledgment I ought to have served it sooner."

"But not to me," he said quietly. Francesca closed her mouth and devoted herself to crumbling the remains of her toast. Oh, *dear*.

"Henry," she said at the same moment he asked, "Dare I inquire who won you over?"

She blushed, and his shoulders fell. "Ah," he said. That was all.

She pushed back her plate and turned to face him.

"Henry, you must know it was never meant to be, between us."

"No," he said in a queer tone. "I don't suppose I did know."

She reached for his hand, but he folded his arms in clear rejection. She clenched her fingers, then tapped them on the table. "I haven't encouraged your affections that way," she tried again. "Your friendship has meant the world to me—I never would have survived the last two years without you."

"Hmph." He arched one eyebrow skeptically.

"I know you may not approve of my actions," she forged onward, "but I hope you can respect my decisions. I hate it when we disagree, and I never wanted to hurt you." He just looked at her, his eyes shadowed with anger and hurt. She sighed. "Truly I didn't. This wasn't something I planned—"

Alconbury sat forward, his face taut with urgency. "Then listen to me—I hesitated to confront you with this earlier, because you swore it was just business between the two of you. I had a hard time believing it but I trusted you to guard yourself. Now I see—the bloody bounder no doubt planned all along to help you only to get into your bed!" She started to protest, but he put up one hand to quiet her. "Edward de Lacey is the very model of a cold, uncaring aristocrat. I've asked around, you see. His father, the Duke of Durham, was well-known as a hard-driving, domineering man who wielded his considerable power to his advantage, ruthlessly at times. His duchess died some twenty years ago or more, and it's no secret he raised his sons in his own image, with no moderating maternal influence. Edward is the son most like him, according to all accounts, and I've seen nothing to alter that image."

"Alconbury," she said firmly, "you're condemning a man based on gossip. You would know better if you met him."

"I don't want to meet him," Alconbury snapped. "This man is too far above you, Francesca! He won't think anything of discarding you for a more eligible woman of his own class—like Louisa Halston. That was a marriage based on money and power and rank, not any finer emotion such as you might think you feel. At best you'll only ever be an amusement to him, enjoyed and quickly cast aside. He'll never marry you, no matter what he says now."

"He hasn't asked me to marry him," she said without thinking.

Frantic hope sprang into Alconbury's eyes. "But I will." He was off his chair, down on one knee, reaching for her hand. "Francesca, darling, you know I adore you. I have for years. Marry me."

Her chest felt squeezed in a vise. "Stop," she said, her voice low and rough. "Please don't . . ."

"I'll do whatever it takes to find Georgina," he promised. "We'll raise her as our own child, and, God willing, several more. We can be happy together; we already are! I can give you the life you deserve, and should have had all along."

"No," she whispered. The word scraped harshly against her throat. Everything he said was like a thorn pricking deep into her flesh. "I'm sorry, Henry . . ."

"All right," he said a little desperately. "I can accept that for now. At least tell me you aren't in love with him. At least assure me you've kept your head."

She opened her mouth, but found she didn't know the answer. Did she love Edward? It was surely too soon . . . but she was in real danger of it. The man Alconbury described was nothing like the man she knew, the man who had made such sweet love to her last night, the man who made her heart thump and her stomach leap with just one of his rare smiles, the man who could reason her out of her stubborn moods and absorb her temper with calm patience. Would he stay with her as long as she wanted him, maybe even marry her? She didn't know. But was she willing to chance the terrible fate Alconbury warned her of, just for the joy of Edward's company, however transient it might be?

She didn't know.

Her silence went on too long. Alconbury let her hand slip out of his. He sat back on his heels, looking drained. "Francesca," he said in despair. "I can't bear to watch you do this to yourself."

"How can *you* do this to me?" she cried, clapping one hand to her chest. "I would never upbraid you so for your interest in any woman, yet you give me all the credit of a simpleton and scold me like a father would his daughter. Do you think me blind? A fool? Utterly incapable of determining my own life? Don't treat me like a child, Alconbury. I can make my own decisions, for good or for ill—just as you can. I only ask you to be my friend!"

He put his hands over his face for a moment. "Very well," he said at last. "Very well. You decide your course. But as your . . . *friend*, I can't help but look after you. If—when—he throws you over, I'll still be here, still your friend. Remember that."

She felt like crying. It would never be the same between them, no matter what, but it was too painful to say. "Thank you," she whispered. He nodded. Heavily he got to his feet and was gone, with barely a mutter of farewell. The door closed and she was left alone with the ache of his disappointment, and the terrible unanswered question about Edward, filling her mind.

Chapter 20

Edward walked home from Francesca's house. He waited for the contentment humming through his body to fade and die out, but it didn't. Perhaps it was the natural rejuvenation after making love so thoroughly and so many times. It might have been due to the anticipation of seeing Francesca again that evening and repeating the exercise. But somehow he couldn't shake the idea that he'd lost some outer shell, that Francesca had stripped him in more ways than one. The morning breeze felt fresh against his face. Instead of striding briskly along, mentally tallying the work that must be done today, he studied the people he passed. London held an extraordinary variety, from the black-faced chimney boys scurrying along with their long brushes to the apple-cheeked vendor selling pies from a cart, his hoarse voice ringing out over the rumble of carts and wagons: "Fresh pies! Hot meat pies, ninepence!" He had never seen this part of town without a pane of glass separating him from them. How novel it was, like a brave new world opened before his eyes.

He smiled at himself for that image. It was a brave

new world, fresh and exciting and almost gilded with gold. All due to Francesca.

Blackbridge must have been watching for him, because the butler swept open the door as he reached the top step. "Welcome home, my lord," he intoned, taking Edward's hat and coat. "Mr. Wittiers has called, and awaits you in the blue salon."

Edward inhaled deeply. Yes, he must get back to work and shoulder his duty again, but somehow it felt easier after the bliss of last night. "Excellent. I'll see him shortly. Has White arrived yet?"

Blackbridge followed him up the stairs. "Yes, my lord. He is in his office working."

"Very good." At the top of the stairs Edward paused and swung around, seeing the house with new eyes. It felt so formal and cold after Francesca's cozy little home. He wasn't about to paint everything bright yellow, and obviously he couldn't replace Blackbridge with Mrs. Hotchkiss, but he could make some small change, surely. "Why are there no flowers in the house?" he asked abruptly.

Blackbridge had stopped short on the stairs. He blinked at Edward's query. "None were ordered, sir."

"Every morning, a fresh bouquet here, and there, of whatever is in bloom," Edward directed him, pointing. "Something bright, Blackbridge."

"Yes, my lord." Blackbridge bowed, but not before Edward caught the flicker of surprise on his face.

He hid his amusement and went into his rooms, where his valet had already laid out a fresh set of clothing, as if Edward came home every morning still wearing his evening clothes of the night before. Not that his servants would ever say a word about it, but a whisper must have gone around the house when the coach returned last night, leaving him at Lady Gordon's home.

"Will you bathe, my lord?" Mills asked.

Edward shrugged off his jacket and handed Mills the crumpled cravat from his pocket. "No, not this morning. Just a shave—but quickly."

Half an hour later he walked into the blue salon, freshly washed, shaved, and attired. "Mr. Whittiers," he said as the solicitor leaped to his feet. "You have been waiting. My apologies."

"It is nothing, my lord." Wittiers bowed. "I have news."

"Indeed." Edward waved one hand at the chairs before the fire, seating himself across from the solicitor. "Good news or bad?"

Mr. Whittiers's mouth pursed. "Complicating—not unexpected, but unwelcome just the same. I have heard your distant cousin Augustus de Lacey plans to petition the Crown claiming his right to the dukedom of Durham within the next fortnight."

"Ah." Decidedly unwelcome news. "I presume you have prepared for this—as it is, in your own words, not unexpected?"

"Of course. I proceeded as if it would happen and took the liberty of making a few inquiries into your cousin's situation. He will have some trouble proving his pedigree; there is at least one birth of questionable legitimacy in his lineage, and he does not have the luxury of descending directly from a recent holder of the title, but must reach back at least three generations. Additionally, he will have to present evidence that disputes Lord

Gresham's claim, and I have found that exceptionally difficult to come by. Our petition is nearly ready. I want but another few days to satisfy myself on a few points and refine the language." Edward said nothing when the lawyer paused. "I stand by my earlier predictions regarding the case, my lord," Wittiers added. "It means the matter will not be decided quickly, however."

Edward nodded. "Very good, then. Do what must be done."

"Can you provide an insight into any weakness of his claim?" Wittiers moved to the edge of his seat. "Any suggestion where we might look for fault?"

Edward was having the hardest time keeping his concentration fixed on this topic. He certainly should— Augustus was a rogue, an infamous reprobate who would desolate Durham if he ever got his spendthrift fingers on it. The mere thought of that man reaping— and wasting—the fruits of his labors should have sent him into an icy, resolute fury. Perhaps it did accomplish that, but the fury was muted, lessened somehow. He no longer had the pervading sense that everything he was and everything he wanted was bound up in Durham. He was still firmly determined to hold onto his inheritance by every means at his disposal, but perhaps . . . just perhaps . . . if the unthinkable happened and Augustus prevailed, or the estate was cast into abeyance, it wouldn't mean the bleak existence he had imagined. Thirty thousand pounds had been left to him outright; it was nothing to the enormous wealth of Durham, and it didn't include Lastings, the estate his father had intended for him, but it could be enough for a quiet life, particularly if he shared it with a woman already in possession of her own home and modest income . . .

"Augustus doesn't really want the title," Edward said, mentally closing off that line of thought. "He wants the money. His own fortune varies widely, from what I hear, ranging from barely solvent to deeply indebted. I imagine his solicitor wouldn't be anxious to wage a long and difficult suit, knowing he'll never be paid if Augustus is unsuccessful. And—to be blunt—he may not be paid to his satisfaction even if Augustus triumphs. My cousin is far better known for his willingness to evade debts than for his rectitude in paying them." He glanced at Wittiers. "I assume you are acquainted with the solicitor he has engaged."

"Indeed, sir, I am." Wittiers smiled his cold, cunning smile again. "We are colleagues, rather adversarial ones, but professional men nonetheless. There aren't terribly many solicitors in London who are suited to argue before the Committee for Privileges in the House of Lords."

"No." Edward closed his eyes for a moment. He must focus his mind on this, and stop thinking how appealing it was to consider a life with Francesca. He had known the woman less than a month. They had been lovers less than a day. He was planning too far, assuming too much. He was actually weighing his entire life and heritage against the bone-deep pleasure he found in her arms.

"Then I leave it in your hands," he told Wittiers. "Between professional colleagues, of course. Submit my brother's petition as soon as practicable. Perhaps the Crown will indicate preference, and that will deter Augustus from proceeding. But regardless, we don't intend to retreat, whether Augustus contests our petition or not."

"Of course not, my lord."

"I want this in motion within the week, to give no hint of doubt or hesitancy. I still believe we hold every advantage, and mean to press them all. If Augustus is intimidated, so much the better, but there's no need to do so overtly."

"Yes, my lord." Wittiers looked delighted with this aggressive instruction.

Edward nodded, rising to go. "Good. I expect to hear from you in a few days."

He went to the study, sobered by the conversation. This could grow into a war. He was still confident Charlie's claim was stronger than anything Augustus could present, but that didn't mean the decision would go to them. There was a long and delicate path they must take through the process, and now that there was an opposing case, anyone in the House of Lords could cause trouble. Edward thought he personally had no real enemies, nor did Gerard, but Charlie was a different story: an aggrieved husband, a thwarted rival, anyone Charlie had bested or slighted . . . They couldn't award the dukedom to Augustus just to spite Charlie, but if there was any doubt under the law, members of the Committee for Privileges could be influenced in their recommendations. At worst, they could deem Augustus's claim solid and superior and recommend he receive the title, but they could also forward a recommendation that neither Charlie nor Augustus had a claim beyond reproach. Durham could be left unsettled, tied up in legal snarls that might last a century. That, Edward realized, would be just as awful as losing it outright. And despite his growing feeling that he could possibly survive without Durham and be happy in Francesca's world, he didn't intend to lose his birthright without a fight. If Augustus provoked a battle royale, he would meet his cousin on the field.

After such a late start, he drove himself hard all day. He went over every report on his desk with Mr. White and kept his secretary busy as well. The footmen came in to light the lamps before they were done, and Edward leaned back from the desk with no small amount of satisfaction. There was something very fulfilling about accomplishing so much in short order. He wondered if Charlie would ever want to take the reins of Durham from him, and then shook his head at the fancy. That was unlikely, and Edward was both sorry and glad. Part of him thought his brother should have to work, somehow, for the luxury of his legacy, to live up to his responsibilities and duties as well as enjoy its benefits. But part of him was also well-pleased with his own role in the family. He liked running the estates. He liked the order of it, the exactitude and discipline it required of him. It had brought him his father's respect, his brothers' gratitude, and his own satisfaction as the estates thrived and prospered under his hand. It was the perfect situation for them all. He was the middle son, the spare; in another age he would have been given to the Church as a boy. In another family he would have been relegated to kicking up his heels with no responsibility except to wait, ready to take the heir's place if necessary. None of that would have suited him at all. Without the running of Durham, he would be as useless as . . . well, as useless as Charlie.

On that happy thought, he closed the last ledger. "That will be all, Mr. White. And you, Mr. Deane," he added to his secretary.

White bowed as he collected his papers. "Yes, my lord. Good evening."

"Thank you." Edward rubbed his hands along the arms of his chair, thinking of his plans for the night. He had worked hard all day because he intended to leave everything concerning Durham behind until tomorrow morning at the earliest. Discipline deserved a reward. "A very good evening to you, too."

It didn't take much effort to locate Francesca. She had mentioned the Ludlows and Covent Garden, and the theater manager was all too pleased to tell Edward which box the Ludlows had seats in. He was also pleased to sell Edward the rest of the tickets for that box; it wasn't a new play, and only half the seats were sold. Edward would have preferred to have her all to himself, but it was better than nothing.

He arrived halfway through the first act. The grand entrance hall was nearly empty, and only a few late arrivals lingered in the saloon upstairs. Edward climbed the stairs to the second tier and walked around until he reached the Ludlow party's box. Silently he turned the knob and slipped inside.

He paused a moment to allow his eyes to adjust but saw her at once. She sat in the second row of seats, beside another couple. Her gown was dark and bared her shoulders. A silver pendant gleamed in the candlelight, drawing his eye down the smooth skin of her throat to the swells of her bosom. He inhaled a quiet, unsteady breath and caught the faint scent of her perfume. Just a few hours apart, and it still took him by surprise how much he wanted her.

He took the seat next to her, glad it was unoccupied. She cast a very slight glance at him, then another, longer and shocked, as she gasped. "Good evening, my dear," he breathed, catching up her hand and bringing it to his lips. Over her knuckles, he watched her face change from startled to self-conscious, and then almost immediately ease as her lips curved in delight. He raised one eyebrow. "Am I welcome?"

She flipped open her fan and swished it energetically in front of her face. "Most certainly," she said behind the fan. "Merely unexpected."

The lady in front of them turned around, the feathers in her headdress bobbing indignantly. "Shh!"

Edward gave Francesca a private little smile, and she returned it with glowing eyes. It was pleasure enough to sit by her, for now. He turned his face to the stage, conscious of every breath she took and every rustle of her skirt when she shifted her body. She was glad to see him. A little part of him had wondered if, just perhaps, he shouldn't declare his interest in her so publicly, so soon. But as soon as she smiled at him in that intimate way she had, as if they alone shared some delightful secret, that lone point of pause vanished. He leaned back in his chair and allowed his thoughts the luxury of wandering.

Francesca was exquisitely conscious of him beside her. She had barely heard him come in, but now Edward seemed to fill the box, and surround her with the warmth of his body and the faint scent of his soap. On the other side of her, Sally Ludlow nudged her elbow three times, obviously seething with curiosity, but Francesca ignored her. It was all she could do to keep her eyes fixed blindly on the stage. He'd said he would find a way to see her, so she had hoped . . . But her expectations had been limited to hoping he would come to her again tonight. A bottle of the best brandy sat in her drawing room, and the finest coffee in London waited in the kitchen. She'd even given Mrs. Hotchkiss explicit instructions to ask him to wait if he should arrive while she was still out, and plotted how she could plead a headache if Sally and Mr. Ludlow wished to stay out late.

But now he was here beside her, in a very public setting, giving no indication he was taking pains to conceal their affair. Her thoughts ran in circles: Why? Did he not care for public opinion, and did what he wanted to do? That didn't fit with the man she knew. Did he want people to know, for some reason? That idea made her heart flutter wildly, despite what Alconbury would say. Or . . . and this last was almost so unspeakable, she hardly dared allow herself to think it . . . did he want to be discreet and private about their affair, but simply couldn't keep away? The thought that he might have spent the day thinking about her, thinking about when he would see her again, wishing away the hours until he could—in short, if he had spent the day as she had—was almost enough to crack open the Pandora's box inside her heart where she had stowed Alconbury's despairing question: Was she falling for Edward de Lacey?

She still had no answers and didn't want to think about it yet. For whatever reason, Edward was here with her now, and she was determined to enjoy it without wasting the night wondering why. The next time Sally nudged her, she just turned to her friend with a confident smile and a speaking look. Sally's eyebrows drew together in faint worry, and she glanced at Edward again before giving Francesca a slow nod of acknowledgment.

At the intermission she made the introductions. Edward greeted the Ludlows with his normal reserved but excellent manners. Sally and her husband didn't seem to know what to make of him, and conversation was strained and fitful. Mr. Ludlow was a laconic man at the best of times, but Sally wasn't at all the quiet or shy type. Yet even she seemed somewhat cowed by Edward, though he did nothing Francesca could see to intimidate. When the other people in the box got up to take a turn in the saloon or fetch some refreshments, she saw Sally poke her husband in the side before getting up to join the others. Francesca bit the inside of her lip as they left. As much as she craved being alone with Edward, it gave her a bit of pause to see her friends practically flee his presence.

If Edward remarked anything, though, he didn't show it. "I surprised you this evening."

"Yes." There was no point in denying the obvious. "But happily," she added, unable to keep a small smile from her face. And it was true. Whatever his reason for coming here tonight, she was wildly glad to see him— more so than she had expected to be, and far more so than she wished to admit just yet. There was plenty of time to contemplate the dangers of her actions. There was plenty of time to resurrect her defenses. Tonight still sparkled with the first thrill of fascination and discovery, too glorious and breathtaking to resist.

Edward's expression grew more intense as she admitted she was pleased to see him. He shifted in his chair, turning to face her and leaning toward her as he laid his arm across the back of her chair. "I'm quite relieved to hear it." His fingers brushed her bare shoulder. "I worried you would find it . . . unseemly."

She had to laugh quietly at that. "You find things unseemly far sooner than I do, sir."

His eyebrow went up. "Do I?"

"Yes."

"Hmm." His fingers were tracing a delicately sensual circuit on her skin. Francesca's mind leaped ahead to when he would be able to do that all over her body, not just the top of her shoulder, and a hot rush of longing went through her. "And yet," he went on thoughtfully, as if touching her had no impact on him at all, "you're back to calling me 'sir.'"

She met his gaze evenly, even though her nipples had puckered into hard buds and she longed to arch her spine and beg his wicked, wonderful fingers to wander all over her back. "What should I call you, my lord?"

His posture tilted toward her again. She could see the striations of blue in his eyes, even in the dim theater light. "What do you want to call me, Francesca?" he asked softly. "I give you leave to do as you desire . . ." His fingertips swirled over the nape of her neck. "With my name."

Darling. Lover. Mine. The words clogged in her throat, and she had to resort to a brilliant smile to cover the pause while she scrambled for a neutral answer. "'Edward' should do."

He smiled slowly, as if he had seen her hesitation and suspected what caused it. "That will be a good start."

The door of the box opened, and Francesca wrenched her eyes away from Edward's. She was a fine one, wondering madly what it meant that he joined her so conspicuously tonight, then allowing herself to be seduced by nothing but the touch of his fingertips on her shoulder. She glanced over her shoulder, expecting to see Sally and Mr. Ludlow returned to take their seats, wondering if she should feel glad they had saved her from herself or annoyed that they had interrupted.

It was Alconbury. He carried a glass of champagne in each hand and wore a look of determination. The cloistered feel of the box vanished as she was abruptly reminded that what had seemed a deeply intimate moment in fact happened in broad view of a theater full of people. The vast majority most likely hadn't even noticed what occurred in Box 26, second row, but someone would have. Someone had. And now he was here, looking girded for battle.

Edward withdrew his arm from the back of her chair and his hand from her neck before he rose. Alconbury saw it, though, and his eyes were grim even as he gave her a wide smile. "Good evening, Francesca dear. So sorry to be late joining you tonight." He stepped forward and handed her one of the glasses, leaning down to press a light kiss on her cheek.

For the brief moment that her face was blocked from Edward's sight, Francesca scowled at Alconbury. "Stop," she hissed.

He just tipped his glass to his lips and swallowed

half his champagne before turning to Edward. "How do you do, sir? Henry Alconbury, at your service." He gave a brief bow.

"Lord Edward, may I present my friend, Baron Alconbury," Francesca interjected, laying a slight edge on the word "friend" as she got to her feet. Lord, what to do? Edward's face was inscrutable; he could be amused, vexed, or anything in between. Alconbury had been drinking, she could tell, which meant he would be overly exuberant and liable to say anything. She set down the glass he had handed her, annoyed enough not to drink it. "Alconbury, may I introduce to you Lord Edward de Lacey."

"A pleasure, sir." Edward bowed just as briefly as Alconbury had.

"Ah, the infamous de Laceys." Alconbury grinned. He took another generous gulp of his wine. "I saw your brother Gresham lose two hundred guineas at White's last month. Bought a round for everyone in the place afterward. Capital fellow."

"Yes," said Edward with no apparent trace of concern. "That would be like Gresham."

Francesca took a deep breath. "Are you enjoying the performance, Alconbury? I thought you declared you would never see this play again."

"My mother wished to see it." He gave a shrug and a guileless, self-deprecating smile that would have melted most female hearts. "You know I try to make my mother happy. Family is so important. However . . ." He lowered his voice and looked at her warmly. "I must confess the sight of you has been the only thing preventing me from running screaming from the theater. If I must suffer Hamlet's madness yet again, at least I have had the pleasure of seeing you as well."

She laughed in spite of herself. He was pouring it on rather thickly. "I'm not certain I appreciate the comparison. But it was so kind of you to visit me for a moment." The door opened, and other occupants of the box returned, settling into their seats in the front row. "Perhaps it will improve on you this time," she added, silently urging Alconbury to go.

He made an exaggerated face of disdain. "I doubt it, unless poor Yorick's ghost would come back to slay the rest of the cast."

"Likely not," she said, and Alconbury laughed.

"Then I suppose I must resign myself, although you have extinguished my last hope for entertainment tonight." He took her hand and raised it to his lips. "Until tomorrow?" he asked, a fond smile on his lips.

"I think not," she replied, tugging at her hand. "I daresay you will have a wretched headache tomorrow."

"I'll come to you for a cure." He refused to let go of her.

"Good night, Alconbury," she said firmly. Francesca gave one last pull, and he released her hand, but she had tugged too hard; her elbow flew back and she heard a clink. "Oh, dear," she said on a sigh. "I believe that was the wine." She picked up her skirt and brushed at the spilled champagne.

"Oh, let me . . ." Alconbury scrambled after the wineglass.

"I'll fetch some more," Edward said. "Pardon me, Lady Gordon. Alconbury." And he was gone, slipping out the door before she could say she didn't want any more wine.

But it was a moment she could use. "You must stop this," she said as Alconbury used his handkerchief to dab the spilled champagne from her skirt hem. "Henry!" she snapped when he wouldn't look at her. "Please!"

He stood much too close to her. "Francesca, I don't think you realize what you're doing," he said with none of his earlier joviality. "Wait—you'll see how much public censure this exposes you to by tomorrow."

Her mouth compressed. Perhaps he was right. Perhaps she would find herself in too deep and regret ignoring his advice. But right now all she could think of was how much she disliked being maneuvered and condescended to, and how infuriating it was that he wouldn't listen to her. "Good night, Alconbury."

A shadow crossed his face. "I don't want this to divide us," he pleaded, very quietly. "But . . . You don't want my advice. I can see that. Somehow I shall try to keep it to myself."

"Thank you," she said through stiff lips.

His face fell. He nodded. "I'll see you tomorrow. Good night, Francesca."

She swallowed. "No. Not tomorrow." Not only did she need some space from Alconbury's increasingly smothering attentions, there was a chance—she hoped a good one—that Edward would still be at her house in the morning. But either way, she didn't want to see Alconbury.

For a long moment he just stared at her with a bit of wounded surprise, as if trying to read her thoughts. Francesca raised her chin and met his gaze straight on.

She didn't have to explain herself. Let him make of it what he would. "Very well," he said at last. "Another time, then." She nodded once, and he left.

She stood looking down at her damp skirt and sighed. The door opened again a few moments later and Sally edged inside, her eyes darting around. When she saw the men were gone, she hurried to Francesca's side. "Are you well?" she demanded. "I saw Alconbury leave, looking as if he'd been beaten. And where is . . . ?"

"Lord Edward went to fetch wine. And no one beat Alconbury but himself." She dropped back into her chair.

Sally rushed to resume her own seat. "Francesca, what's going on? I thought you were nearly engaged to Alconbury—"

"I was not," she said sharply. "Just because he let people assume—"

"You're right." Sally squeezed her hand. "I assumed. But you said Lord Edward was merely helping you find Georgina; what is he doing here tonight?"

Francesca took a deep breath but couldn't stop the flutter of joy the thought caused. "I don't know, Sally. But I do know . . . I am very happy he is."

Chapter 21

E dward strolled toward the saloon, intending to
allow Francesca plenty of time to speak to Baron
Alconbury. It was clear to see Alconbury was half mad
in love with her, and growing frustrated by her lack
of reciprocal feeling. Edward couldn't quite admire the
man for invading her theater box and making a show of
his affection, but he had a fair amount of sympathy for
someone who was discovering his love was doomed to
end badly. He suspected Alconbury had just begun to
grasp that fact, and wasn't taking it in stride. That was
understandable.

If Alconbury didn't accept it soon, however, he would
make him. Even Edward's patience was not endless.

The crowd began to thin as people filtered back into
the galleries and boxes for the rest of the performance.
He so rarely came to town, let alone to the theater, that
it took Edward several minutes to realize what was happening. A pair of women, some years older than he, put
their heads together and nearly turned their backs to
him. He overheard a rush of whispers, and then they
both peeped over their shoulders with sharp eyes as
he passed. A couple strolling along stopped short and

became very interested in a painting on the wall when he walked by them. A woman averted her eyes when he looked her way.

Only when he saw a man he knew quite well, and nodded politely, did it become clear that he was being snubbed. The man, Lord Danvers, didn't look away from him, but his face flushed and his answering nod was barely noticeable. Edward's eyes narrowed but he didn't pause. It was unavoidable that some gossip would accrue to his name, retraction or not. He hadn't heard any of it yet, but that was most likely because he hadn't gone out in society out of respect for his father's death.

He took another turn of the room, on watch for it now, and saw subtle signs everywhere as people moved past him returning to their seats. And most of these patrons weren't even of his class, which he knew would be even colder to someone about to lose his elevated status. This was why he didn't like London. He wondered what Charlie had seen and heard of the gossip, and for once envied his older brother the ability to laugh off everything. Forgetting all about the wine he had ostensibly come to get, Edward turned on his heel and walked back toward the box. At least Francesca seemed indifferent to the scandal.

"Edward."

He paused, not certain if he had heard his name or not. The corridor was almost empty now, and he could hear the applause beginning for the opening of the next play.

"Edward!" whispered the voice again, and this time he placed it.

Louisa Halston was standing in one of the curtained

alcoves off the corridor. Her face was pinched up pleadingly as she stared at him. When he faced her, she made a small beckoning motion with one hand. He didn't move. What could she want now?

"Please, Edward," she said, her voice breaking on his name. "I just—I just want a moment, to explain . . ."

Slowly he crossed the corridor. She stepped back into her hiding place, making space for him. He leaned one shoulder against the corner, blocking her from view without stepping into the alcove himself. "Good evening, Lady Louisa."

She flinched. Her soft blue eyes were red at the edges, and her skin looked almost transparent. She was still beautiful, but now she looked like she was made of glass, about to shatter. "What must you think of me?" she said quietly. "I'm so very sorry, Edward."

A gentleman would have made it easier for her; a better man would have acknowledged, at least to himself, that he was glad she had jilted him. But enough residual hurt remained that Edward asked levelly, "Sorry for what?"

Louisa swallowed. "For—For what happened between us."

He tried to remind himself she was only twenty-one years old, and had nothing like Francesca's bold spirit. "Why did you tell your father?"

"I had no choice," she said in a quavering voice. "He asked me what you had come about that day—I had to tell him the wedding was postponed, and then he questioned me about it for almost an hour until I broke down and told him what you said. I didn't know he would act as he did, but . . . but I did suspect he would want to call off our engagement. You must know—you must understand . . . We are in dire straits, about to lose everything!"

Edward took a deep breath. The Halstons didn't live as though they were on the brink of ruin. The colder, ruthless part of him thought the earl might have taken steps to economize before finding himself in dire straits. "Then why did you give me your word?"

"I wanted to," she cried. "I wanted you to trust me, and I wanted to be worthy of that trust. When I gave my word, I did mean to keep it. Please believe I did. But you of all people must know that family comes before any promises to others!"

Edward remembered his brothers telling him not to confide in Louisa. He had rejected their arguments because he cared for her enough to expose his family's ugly secret, to inoculate her against it. And yet . . . he had acted out of a sense of obligation, really. He had trusted her, yes, but he told her because he thought it would be unfair to keep it from her. He hadn't rushed to tell her because he needed her comfort or wanted her advice. It had been his duty as a fiancé, and so he'd done it, just as he would have fulfilled any other duty to her when she was his wife.

Duty and obligation. He had been taught to revere both and never would have considered flouting either. How very odd that a terrible family scandal and losing his future wife would have shown him how confining duty and obligation could be, and how free one could feel without them.

"Why did you wish to marry me, Louisa?" he asked softly. "Was it just the money, to save your family?"

Her lips parted in dismay. "No! Of course not! I cared very much for you, Edward. We're so alike, you and I, both so dutiful and sensible. We always got on so well together, with no discord or even disagreement between us. I always imagined us leading quiet, peaceful lives together. And it was easy to think so, since it was such an ideal match in every other way as well. Our families agreed."

Perhaps she *was* just like him. Those were exactly the reasons he had chosen her, after all. She had come to care for him because everything indicated she should, much the same way he had cared for her. And those were all the reasons why he would never have really loved her.

It was a revelation. He had cared for her, he truly had, but it couldn't have been love. He felt betrayed when Louisa broke his confidence, rudely shocked at the form of his dismissal, and furious over the gossip it stirred up. But for the loss of Louisa herself, he felt nothing of heartbreak or anguish. He was like Romeo, despairing of fair Rosalind's affections only until he saw Juliet and discovered what he really wanted.

"I do understand," he told her. He took her hand and raised it to his lips for a light kiss. "I wish you every happiness, Louisa."

Her eyes filled with tears. "Oh, Edward," she whispered. "I do feel we would have been so *happy* together, if only . . ."

A thin smile crossed his face. He was quite sure it would have been a shadow of real happiness, even if neither of them ever realized it. Louisa had unintentionally done him a great favor by stripping that away from him before he discovered how shallow "contentment" could feel. "Do you? Perhaps. But we're both sensible, as you say. We must each find our happiness elsewhere now."

She nodded, despite a rather tragic expression. Edward felt a flash of pity for her, knowing she wasn't nearly as able to pursue her own happiness as he was. He was free to return to Francesca, while Louisa's father would undoubtedly marry her to Calverton or some other peer wealthy enough to save the Halstons from destitution. There was nothing he could do about it, though. Louisa was the only one who could, and she had most likely chosen her course already. Duty and obligation. He pressed her hand once more. "Good-bye, my dear."

"Good-bye," she whispered. "Thank you for understanding."

Edward bowed his head, and then she was gone, slipping past him to hurry back to her family. He watched her vanish around the corner, and silently wished her true happiness, perhaps as much as he himself was in the process of discovering. He turned back toward Box 26, and his heart sped up in anticipation.

Edward was gone so long Francesca began to wonder. Perhaps Alconbury's visit had put him off somehow. Perhaps he had encountered someone in the saloon outside who made him reconsider his public appearance at her side. She knew she should be discreet and patient, but she couldn't bear it. She sat through the first two scenes of *Hamlet* without hearing a word of them, and was just about to cast all dignity and restraint out the window and go see what had happened when the door at the back of the box opened. He slipped into the chair beside her, and she expelled a long, silent breath of relief.

They sat in silence until the end of the act. As the audience applauded he leaned toward her. "Francesca." His whisper was little more than a breath across her cheek. "I want you."

Her heart jumped. She turned her head, keeping her eyes on the stage. "Now?" she murmured through her smile.

"Yes."

Oh my. Her heart thudded so hard against her ribs, she could hardly breathe. "Here?" The people in front of her shifted, and she prayed they wouldn't turn around and notice her, flushed and trembling with a desire that had roared to life inside her at his words.

She felt Edward's amusement. "Come with me." He put out his hand, and she barely remembered to grab her shawl as she placed her fingers in his and let him lead her from the box. As he opened the door she glanced back and gave Sally a helpless little smile. Her wide-eyed friend just shook her head in farewell.

He didn't say anything as they walked through the theater corridors, deserted and quiet now that the play was in progress. In the entrance hall downstairs Edward sent a page running for his carriage. He was still holding her hand, and Francesca felt very conscious of it, even though there was only theater staff around to see.

"Will your friends miss you?" he asked suddenly.

"Ah—no, no, not terribly." She hadn't been thinking of the Ludlows at all.

Edward glanced at her. "Will they disapprove of our leaving together?"

She blinked in surprise. "I don't think it's their place to disapprove, but no, I don't think they shall."

"They wouldn't think you should have chosen Lord Alconbury?"

Francesca felt her cheeks flush. "Perhaps. But that was never going to happen."

"Really," he murmured with another keen glance. The page reappeared, waving to indicate the carriage was waiting. Edward led her outside and handed her into the vehicle. When he closed the door behind him, cutting off all outside light and noise, Francesca felt enclosed in some private world with him.

"Would you never have reconsidered Alconbury's suit?" Edward took her hand and began peeling off her glove.

"I—well, no, I don't believe so . . ." She inhaled sharply as he kissed the inside of her bare wrist, sucking lightly at the tender skin. "Why?"

"He seems a very eligible suitor. You already like him very much, and it's clear to see he would fall on his knee at a moment's notice, if you encouraged him."

"Oh, yes, he's very eligible." She watched, transfixed, as his dark head bent over her hand. Her eyes drifted closed as his wicked lips moved with light torment over her skin, higher and higher up her arm. His fingertips drew delicate patterns in the wake of his mouth until her whole arm felt shivery and crackling with sensation.

"Then wouldn't it make sense to encourage him?"

"Stop talking of sense," she whispered.

He laughed quietly. "You must acknowledge the effort it's costing me. When you're near, my darling, all my sense goes missing and I can't think of anything but this . . ." His lips touched hers. "And this . . ." He kissed her again, sliding his hands into her hair. "And the things I long to do with you."

"Let's talk of that instead." She tried to pull him back to her, but Edward laughed again and ducked his head to her neck, nipping gently at the sensitive skin beneath her ear until she was writhing with desire.

"I have just recently realized the distinction," he breathed against her ear, "between *want* and *need*. I always knew what I wanted, but until you, I never knew what I needed."

"And that is?" Dimly she felt the carriage slow to a stop.

Edward's slow smile caught the light as the door opened. "You. In every wicked way I can have you."

"Then you'd better come inside," she whispered, touching his cheek. "It will take a while."

He dismissed his coachman. Francesca's blood surged through her veins as they went inside her house, where she sent Mrs. Hotchkiss off as quickly as Edward had sent off his carriage. In a more rational state of mind she might wonder what he'd been thinking to bring up Alconbury, but instead all she could think of was his last statement, ripe with the promise of sensual pleasures. What did he have in mind? She felt like a girl again, desperately curious about the mysterious, wicked, wonderful things this man could do with a woman. Good heavens, if she'd guessed that stiff and proper Edward de Lacey had such dark depths to him, she would have seduced him at once, that first night he came to her house to see Sloan.

He followed her upstairs as if it were completely

normal. Strangely, it felt normal, as though he belonged in her house, in her bedroom. Even when he closed the door behind him, there was no awkward awareness.

She went to her dressing table and sat down to remove her jewelry. In the mirror, she watched Edward take off his coat and waistcoat, and unwind his cravat, his eyes fixed on her. He came up behind her and put his hands over hers as she reached for the clasp of her necklace.

"Let me." He unhooked the necklace and let it fall into her lap. With the same lack of urgency he pulled the pins from her hair until it fell loose around her shoulders. He caught the length in one hand and twisted it all to one side, so he could press his lips to the nape of her neck, sending goose bumps racing down her arms. Francesca swayed in her seat and gripped the edge of the dressing table. She couldn't have moved for anything, as his mouth whispered over the slope of her shoulders, nipping at her earlobe, lingering at the side of her neck. And she could watch every action in the mirror, which seemed to double the effect of everything he did.

"Stand up," he whispered. His silver eyes gleamed at her in the mirror. He slid one hand, palm down, over her shoulder and down the bare skin of her bosom until he could flick undone one small button at the side of her breast that held her dress closed. She gazed at him defiantly, then leaned back.

His head bowed as he studied the expanse of skin above her bodice. He flicked another button loose, then curved both his hands over her breasts. She inhaled sharply and pressed against him; she could feel his erection surge against her shoulder blades. His hands flattened on her breasts and he rocked his hips against her back. "You do nothing for my gentlemanly instincts," he said, his voice grown rough.

"I don't care for them at the moment." She arched an eyebrow at him in the mirror. "They proceed too slowly."

"Good," he growled. In a few seconds he had undone the rest of her gown and peeled it down her arms. Francesca pushed herself to her feet, expecting to step away from the dressing table, but Edward stopped her. He kicked the chair from between them and stepped up close behind her, pinning her to the table. He let her shove the gown down over her hips, but by the time it hit the floor he was already winding his fist in the hem of her shift, twisting it around his hand until he had pulled the whole thing to her waist. He anchored her to him with that hand, his arm solid muscle around her waist, and slid his free hand down her belly.

"Too slowly, you say?" He laughed softly as she opened her mouth, then only moaned as his fingers slipped between her thighs. "I shall have to try harder to please you, I see . . ."

Francesca couldn't speak. She couldn't look away from the mirror, where his every action was reflected back to her. The lamplight gleamed on the gold ring he wore as his long, strong fingers stroked the soft curls between her legs, then probed deeper to touch her so delicately, so perfectly, she quivered like a plucked violin string. But he knew her body better than that; he gentled his touch. He petted her until she melted. He played with her until she was panting, pushing her hips into each stroke. He curved one finger high up inside her until she almost screamed. He moved against her, grinding his erection between the curves of her bottom, and she writhed in his grip, casting her arms backward around his neck as she felt herself nearing the brink.

"Feel what you do to me," he whispered, pressing against her so she could feel every rock-hard inch of him. "You drive me mad, Francesca . . ."

She gave him a reckless smile, even though she was all but draped over his chest, held up only by his arm around her and the tips of her toes as she arched into him again. "I don't believe it . . . You're still clothed . . ."

His answering grin was savage. He yanked his hand out of the folds of her shift, letting her back down onto her feet. He pulled open the collar of his shirt and then tugged the whole shirt over his head. She stared breathlessly at his reflection as he reached for the fastenings of his trousers. "Put your hands on the table," he rasped. She leaned over and spread her feet, and then he rubbed the blunt head of his cock against her before sliding deep inside.

She shuddered and almost climaxed right then. Edward scooped one arm around her chest, his hand cupping her breast. His other hand went back to her sex, his fingers opening her to his merciless pleasuring as he began thrusting hard into her from behind. "Open your eyes," he commanded. "I want you to see what we are together . . ."

Francesca pried open her eyes and tried to focus on the image in her mirror. She looked wanton and voluptuous, fully exposed by the man who surrounded her inside and out. Her hair swung loosely around her in time with his pounding possession, and she braced her fists on the dressing table to drive herself backward, hard, faster, deeper into his strokes. She could see his fingers moving between her legs, drawing those internal threads of rapture tighter by the second until she thought she would break from the tension. She watched his hand fondle and grip her breast even as the sensations arrowed straight to her belly. And over her shoulder, his face, now dark and taut, his eyes glowing like moonlight as he took her right over the edge of sanity into oblivion.

Edward felt her climax, and bared his teeth in raw male triumph as her head fell back and Francesca let out a long, thin cry of release. He pushed deep and held himself there, relishing every contraction of her body around his. But he couldn't take it for long; watching her expression in the throes of ecstasy sheared away the last bit of control he had. He shifted his grip to her hips and rode her hard until his own climax engulfed him, drowning any other thought.

For a long moment there was only the sound of her soft, half-gasping little breaths, and the thud of his heart, loud in his ears. He had never felt this . . . this liberation, this unfettered contentment. Not with another woman, not after a hard day of accomplishment, not after a brilliant business maneuver, not even after beating his brothers at anything. His body was wrung out with physical satisfaction, his mind felt fogged and sluggish, but his heart . . .

"If this be madness," came Francesca's weak voice from behind the shining veil of her hair, "lead me to Bedlam."

"Perhaps tomorrow. I don't think I can make it further than the bed." He took another deep breath as she laughed, and the vibrations rippled through her body into his. "I could stay here forever," he added, almost to himself, as he brushed aside her hair to nuzzle the back of her neck.

She raised her head and gave him a sultry look. "Forever! How many wicked plans do you have?"

"You have no idea," he murmured, easing away from her. He reached around and began untying her stays.

"Perhaps I have wicked thoughts of my own as well."

"I willingly submit myself to them all." He stripped off the stays and then her shift, leaving her in just her stockings. "Tell me about these ideas. How wicked are *you*, my dear?"

She laughed again. "Until tonight, I would have said more wicked than you! But now . . ." She began leading him toward her bed. "I shall never look at that dressing table in quite the same innocent way."

"Nor me?" Suddenly serious, Edward caught her face in his hands. "You said you would never reconsider Alconbury's suit; you say he is only a dear friend to you. What am I?"

The answer shone in her expressive eyes before she glanced away with a blush and an awkward laugh. She cared for him, beyond their intense physical attraction, beyond the cooperation they had begun to find Georgina. Any latent fear that she might have been using him, for any reason, was laid to rest. She started to stammer an answer but Edward stopped her. He knew what he needed to know.

For the better part of a fortnight he took Francesca every place he thought might amuse her. She protested at first, but he persuaded her she needed to do something besides hunt for Georgina. They went to the theater, the opera, and Pidcock's Menagerie. They visited the Tower, to see the king's jewels and arms, and the British Museum to see the antiquities. Every day Edward fell more and more under her spell. He still got reports from Jackson on the search for Georgina; he still oversaw Durham business with Mr. White and directed Wittiers on the petition to claim the dukedom for Charlie; but never far from his mind was the next time he would see Francesca. The more he was in her company, the more he wanted of it.

One night it came to him that this was what happiness was. Lying in her bed with her in his arm, sated and content, he embraced the feeling that had been steadily growing stronger and stronger. He had never been shy about pursuing what he wanted, once he determined it was worth pursuing. He pulled Francesca snugly into both arms and kissed her shoulder.

"Come away with me," he whispered. "Tomorrow, just for the day. Let me take you to Greenwich, or Richmond, anywhere out of London. I want to get away from the city."

"Greenwich!" she exclaimed, twisting to look at him in surprise. "That is, *yes*, of course, anywhere . . . But what—"

He kissed her until she melted in his arms again. "Will you?" He smiled as she stared up at him somewhat dreamily and nodded. "Good."

"What is in Greenwich?" she asked playfully as his kisses wandered down her jaw and neck. "What are you plotting now, Edward?"

"Something wicked," he murmured as he bent his head to her breast, settling his weight atop her until their bodies fit together as perfectly as they always did. "But . . . something wonderful."

He was plotting how he would keep her with him. Forever.

Chapter 22

The next morning Edward left early. Barely awake, Francesca mumbled a protest when he rose with the sun and dressed, but he merely whispered that he had plans to make before whisking her away for the day. Then he kissed her, and she almost succeeded in enticing him back into bed, but he merely laughed under his breath and promised to let her have her way later.

But when the door closed softly behind him, she found herself unable to go back to sleep, even though she knew her face would show the signs of another sleepless night of sin. She was hopelessly in over her head. Alconbury had warned her that Edward wouldn't marry her or even stay attached to her for long. At the time she had brushed it aside, because she didn't need Alconbury's advice and because she didn't want to think about the end of her affair with Edward when it was just beginning. But it had been several days, and Edward was at her side more than not. Everyone had remarked it. And now the thought refused to be swept away, although she still didn't have an answer to Alconbury's other question, about what she truly felt for Edward.

When he showed up in the theater box unexpectedly,

she had been taken off guard by how happy it made her. When he squired her about town as if he had no interest in being anywhere else, it only made her want more. Even with Alconbury's warning lingering in her ears, she was still helpless against the lure of Edward's company. No doubt she would have invited him into her bed even if he'd told her outright that he only intended a brief affair.

The trouble was . . . she didn't think he intended that. The trouble was, he'd asked her to go away with him. He questioned her about her feelings for Alconbury, as if to make certain she wasn't in love with another man. He gave every impression of courting her even though they were already lovers. The trouble was, she'd gone and lost her heart to him, stunningly swiftly but no less completely, and she wanted him to tell her at Greenwich that he had done the same for her. And if he didn't . . .

With a scowl, Francesca threw back her covers and got out of bed. She really was her own worst enemy at times. Here she found herself in love with a handsome, wonderful man who was obviously deeply attracted to her, who never patronized her or belittled her in any way, who was able to overlook her more outrageous actions, and all she could think about was what awful thing he might be about to tell her. She opened her wardrobe doors and rummaged through her clothing. Today she was going to take things as they came, and not set herself up for any disappointment. If Edward only told her he cared for her, well, that was still good news. If he told her he wanted to keep making love to her, that was also good news. She reminded herself that Edward was not like her; he was methodical and rational and not likely to lose his head over a woman in a matter of weeks, no matter how combustible they were together in bed. She remembered his description of how he became engaged to Louisa Halston, a process that had taken months or even years.

"He called me managing," she told her reflection in the mirror as she held up a green dress in front of herself for inspection. "That is not a compliment." Even though it sounded like one when he reminded her of it in her breakfast room the other day.

"But then he said he wanted to see me again," she went on, casting aside the green dress and reaching for the russet and cream one. "And then he did so, very publicly." Which was not a declaration, but many people would think it one.

"If he doesn't wish to see me anymore . . ." She stared at her own face in the mirror and had no words for the stark expression she found there. "There is no reason he must continue," she whispered.

Good heavens, what did Edward mean by this outing to Greenwich?

She finally chose her sapphire blue riding habit, in case he meant for them to ride, and went downstairs. Mrs. Hotchkiss met her at the bottom of the stairs and held out a note.

"This is just come for you, madam. May I say you look very well this morning?"

Francesca smiled at her housekeeper. In spite of her furious wonderings, she did feel very well, with hope and nervous anticipation fluttering inside her chest. "Thank you. I'll be going out today."

"Shall I have Mr. Hotchkiss bring the carriage?"

"No, that won't be necessary. I shall be going with Lord Edward." The older woman nodded without blinking an eye and bustled out to bring breakfast.

Francesca opened the note at the table. Sally Ludlow wrote that she hadn't seen or heard from Alconbury since the scene in the theater a few nights before and she was worried. She asked, tactfully, if Francesca had any idea what might have happened. Her postscript belied any true concern, though, as it begged her to be kind to Alconbury when next she saw him, and remember that he really did love her.

She sighed. Everyone was so quick to assure her one man was in love with her, just as they assured her the other man was not and never could be. How much easier things would be if her feelings had fixed on the man who loved her. Or rather, if the man her feelings had fixed on was the man who most assuredly loved her.

Alconbury, she knew, would be fine. The day after Edward had joined her in the Ludlows' theater box, Alconbury sent her a lovely little posy of daisies. *Apologies for last night—wishing you every happiness,* the card read, signed only with his swooping initial. She hadn't seen him since. Whether that was because she had been so often with Edward, or because Alconbury was avoiding her, she couldn't say.

She quietly folded Sally's note. She was fortunate to have such friends. She hadn't seen the Ludlows, either, since that night at the theater; they moved in different circles than Edward. Since he had begun squiring her around, she hadn't seen any of her usual companions, in fact. She hated to think that she must give up her friends to be with him, or that she must keep the two separate. It was another obstacle she didn't feel like facing, not yet.

She expected Edward might need a while to make his preparation, so it was a happy surprise when she heard the jangle of harness and the creak of a coach outside just an hour after she finished breakfast. She flew up the stairs to retrieve her hat and was just starting back down when the knocker sounded, a hard, rapid pounding. Mrs. Hotchkiss, already on her way to the door, hurried forward to answer it.

"Where is Lady Gordon?" Edward surged through the doorway and almost grabbed Mrs. Hotchkiss. "I must speak to her at once!"

"I'm here," she said, startled. "What is it?"

He looked up at her, his face breaking into a fierce smile. "Jackson has found Georgina."

Francesca's knees gave out at the unexpected response. Georgina . . . She had been so caught up in thoughts about her own situation, she hadn't even thought of her niece today. The guilt hit her at the same moment relief did. She collapsed with a thump on the stairs, still clutching her hat. "Where?" she whispered. "Where is she?"

He strode past Mrs. Hotchkiss and took the stairs two at a time until he reached her. "Bethnal Green."

All the way on the other side of London, but still close enough. She nodded, unable to speak. Thank the blessed Lord Ellen hadn't taken Georgina far away; that had been her deepest fear, and now that it was put to rest, she said a swift prayer of thanks. She would have her niece back in a matter of hours.

Edward cupped her cheek in his hand. "You look about to faint—Mrs. Hotchkiss, bring some sherry."

"No." She wrapped her trembling fingers around his wrist. "I'm fine. I'm going this instant to fetch her."

"Of course. My carriage is outside." He helped her up, and they went down the stairs.

"Have you really found her?" asked Mrs. Hotchkiss anxiously as Francesca tied on her bonnet. Francesca nodded, too overcome to speak. The housekeeper exclaimed in delight, and shooed her out the door when Edward opened it. "Godspeed," she cried. "Bring back the young miss as soon as you're able! And sir, oh, God bless you, my lord!"

She felt overcome as they hurried into the carriage and Edward told his driver where to go. "I cannot wait to see her again," she said softly when he was beside her and they were on their way. "She's the sweetest child, Edward. I've missed her so desperately."

"I know." He pulled her into the circle of his arm. "Does she look like you?"

"No, she's the image of her mother. Giuliana took after our mother, while I inherited my father's coloring. Georgina has dark hair and fair skin like Giuliana did." She smiled. "Even when Georgina was an infant, my sister despaired that she'd gotten our mother's nose as well. I could see no sign of it, but she grows so quickly. I wonder how much she will have changed since last I saw her?"

"You'll soon find out," he said, squeezing her shoulder.

"I know. I can hardly believe it . . ." Her voice failed her as she thought of how she had almost despaired of ever seeing this day. And without Edward, she might still be waging her quixotic battle to secure a solicitor.

"And it is all thanks to you," she went on as tears sprang into her eyes. They were tears of elation, but Edward pressed a handkerchief into her hand. "I cannot thank you enough, Edward, for all you've done— for helping me, and comforting me, and your sage counsel—"

"My part was a small one," he said. "It was your determination that mattered."

"Indeed." She laughed weakly and wiped the tears away. "My determination won nothing until it got the better of me and I invaded your house to rail at you about Wittiers."

"You are too harsh on yourself."

"I was frantic with worry. Ellen had just vanished, and I had no idea—the neighbor told me Georgina looked thin." She turned to him in alarm. "Did the investigator say how she looked? Is she well? Is she hurt? If Ellen's mistreated her, I swear I'll call the constables on her!"

"He said she looked well," said Edward in a soothing voice. "There's no cause to worry about that yet."

"I don't think I can offer her money if she's been beastly to Georgina," Francesca went on. "Even unintentionally. Why, it's surely abuse to keep a child in squalor when she has relations who would gladly care for her!"

"Jackson said nothing of squalor. Don't leap to conclusions."

"I am not leaping to conclusions," she exclaimed. "I'm trying to prepare myself for what we might find."

Edward shook his head. "But are you prepared for what you must do?"

"Of course! We talked several times about it—I even agreed to bribe Ellen to return her to me."

He gave her a look of admonition. "That may not be the most tactful way to put it."

Francesca flipped one hand impatiently. "Of course I wouldn't call it such to her face."

"Then what will you say?" He put up one hand as she scowled and opened her mouth to respond. "Remember that if you offend her, she may refuse just to spite you, even if the arrangement you offer is entirely in her favor."

Yes, that seemed very possible. Francesca closed her eyes for a moment and struggled to control her feverish impatience. "Very well. What should I do?"

"Stop assuming the worst." She pressed her lips together. Edward held up one hand, his expression set and determined. "Also, most importantly, you must not act as if you want this more than anything."

She cringed. "Impossible."

"No," he said firmly. "You're perfectly capable. When you brought Sloan's paper to my home and offered to procure a retraction, you managed to be cold and practical."

She glared at him. "I was not! My palms were damp and I was biting my tongue the entire time."

"But . . . ?"

"But I knew you wouldn't help me if I lost my temper again," she admitted through her teeth.

"Not true," he said, to her surprise. "I wanted that retraction very badly. Never underestimate your opponent's desires. But you offered a fair bargain, one I had no choice but to consider, and then you let me realize that. For all I knew, you might have had a list of other men you planned to approach with the same request, and if I'd said no, you would have walked away."

She frowned. "But that won't work with Ellen. She has the one thing I want—Georgina—and she knows it. If she refuses, I can hardly approach someone else with the same offer."

"Very true, but you must approach her as if you *want* to strike this bargain with her. Your other course of action is to go to the court, which would be very expensive for both of you. Each of you stands a roughly equal chance of losing, which would mean bearing the expense as well as losing the child and her income. Tell her you want to avoid that, to benefit you and her alike. Show some compassion, even if you must feign every ounce of it, for her circumstances."

"I have tried to, really I have—and I *do* feel some sympathy for her. But you didn't see Georgina as I last did, teary-eyed and unhappy, begging me to take her home with me. You didn't hear Percival shouting that he would call the watch on me if I didn't get out at once. You didn't hear Ellen declare that she would never give up Georgina—" She stopped, breathing hard.

"Have you any idea how I longed to plant my fist in Gregory Sloan's face?" he asked, a hard twist to his mouth. "Or barring that, to sue him into penury? And you asked me to sit calmly by and listen to you *charm* him."

She inhaled deeply, seeing his meaning. "A performance."

"Precisely. Nothing more, nothing less." He took her hand in his and held it as they left the heart of London, as the busy streets and tall buildings gave way to narrower roads and scattered houses. Bethnal Green was a quieter town, hardly a town at all to Francesca's eyes. It seemed an eternity, but finally the carriage stopped before a small cottage, set back from the road in a large garden. The whole coach swayed as the footmen jumped down, and Francesca straightened her spine, mentally preparing her script.

Edward glanced at her as his servant opened the door. "Are you ready?"

"One thing," she said. "Will you keep Percival out of the way, if he's there? I believe he encourages the worst in Ellen's behavior toward me, and I confess I despise him as much as he does me."

"Of course."

She grasped his hand as joy and nerves made her heart thud. He helped her down, and together they went through the gate into the garden. Belatedly, Francesca realized there were more footmen than usual in the Durham livery; two had jumped down from the back of the carriage and another had climbed down from the box. The driver had tied his reins and was watching everything with unusual alertness, and she just caught the gleam of a pistol barrel on the seat beside him. She glanced up at Edward, whose face had settled into austere, almost autocratic lines, the hauteur of a man who would not, *could* not be denied. It was like advancing on the enemy with a small army at her back.

There was no way Ellen could thwart her now.

A small black dog came running to meet them and ran circles around them, yipping loudly. Before they reached the front door a woman opened it.

In the split second before recognition dawned on her face, Ellen Haywood appeared almost friendly. She looked rather well, to Francesca's mild surprise, no longer thin and worn but with some color in her face and her blond hair neatly coiffed. But the minute she met Francesca's eyes, that color faded from her face and she moved to slam the door.

"Mrs. Haywood." Edward had gotten his hand on the door before she could close it, and now pressed it inexorably open. "A moment of your time, please."

"How do you do, Ellen?" asked Francesca. Now that she was face-to-face with her nemesis, her nerves vanished, fading into icy calm. This was the moment she had been waiting for, and with Edward—and his tall, muscular footmen—close at hand, she felt rather invincible. "May I introduce my friend? Lord Edward de Lacey, this is Mrs. Ellen Haywood." Dismay filled Ellen's face as Edward bowed his head. "May we come in?"

Ellen stared at her, panic in her eyes. "How did you find me?"

Francesca lifted her eyebrows. "Were you hiding?"

The other woman's blush was confession enough. Edward had kept her from closing the door, and now she reluctantly stepped back. "Come in, then," she said bitterly. "I suppose I have no choice."

No one replied to that. Francesca caught the subtle signal Edward made to his servants, who silently slipped off through the garden. One remained by the door. Ellen noticed them as well, from the way her eyes darted from the footmen to Francesca and Edward. Visibly tense, she gestured toward the parlor, a neat but somewhat shabby room.

"Why are you here?" Ellen blurted out as soon as Francesca seated herself.

"I would like to see my niece," Francesca replied tranquilly. "Is that too much to ask?"

Her calm demeanor seemed to unnerve Ellen even more. Her wide eyes flew to the door and back, as if she expected someone else at any moment. Francesca prayed it was Georgina, and only kept her seat with great effort.

"Georgie's not here," Ellen finally said. "She's out."

"I will wait." Francesca drew off her gloves and settled in her seat more comfortably. "In fact, I'm glad she's not here. I wished to discuss something with you privately."

Ellen's face burned. Her skin was already somewhat browned, as if she spent her days outdoors. "No."

Francesca paused. "No?"

"No, you won't take her." Ellen raised her chin, her eyes flashing despite the rapid rise and fall of her chest.

For a moment Francesca regarded her. Ellen was clearly braced for another screaming row, not for her to be calm and reasonable. Francesca knew she had only herself to blame, for losing her temper before, but now she had the benefit of hindsight and resolve, to say nothing of Edward's practical advice. "How difficult this year must have been for you," she said sympathetically. "How are your sons?"

Confusion flashed across the other woman's expression. "Very well."

Francesca nodded. She could almost feel Edward's approval, bolstering her restraint, encouraging her onward. "They must be quite a pair now, if they have John's looks and temper."

"They do," said Ellen slowly. "Both are the image of their father." Maternal pride was showing through her suspicion.

She smiled a little. "Then they're fortunate boys. John was always one of the most amiable men I knew. And they must have grown so much! They were just creeping around the floor when last I saw them."

Ellen fidgeted with the edge of her apron. Her wary eyes darted to Edward again. "They're walking now."

"Children grow so quickly," Francesca said. "I was amazed by how rapidly Georgina changed from week to week, even as an infant." She paused as a real swell of emotion constricted her throat. "No doubt I shall hardly recognize her now."

The color fled from Ellen's face. "You won't take her," she said again, her voice rising. "I won't allow it! How can you even ask such a thing?"

Francesca's fingers were numb from clenching so hard as she clung to her calm with every bit of strength she possessed. "It was her father's wish that I raise her, in the event of his death," she reminded Ellen. "My sister would want her only child to grow up with family. I have loved Georgina since the day she was born as if she were my own daughter, the child I was never blessed with in my own marriage."

"I don't care," said Ellen, her voice shaking. "I'm sorry you never had a child, but you can't take mine."

"She's not your child, though, is she?" said Francesca before she could stop herself. Edward, who had been silent so far, stirred beside her. She bit her tongue and forced her temper aside as she gentled her tone again. "But you have two sons, young boys who need you very much. Someday you'll want to send them to school, or to learn a trade. I want to help you provide for them."

"No, you don't," Ellen cried. "You just want to take Georgie!"

"I do want to take her, to raise her as her father, your husband, wanted her to be raised. My first thought was to hire a solicitor, to petition the court on my behalf." Ellen looked horror-struck. "I believe I would prevail," Francesca went on, evenly but firmly. "I'm well able to take care of a child. Her mother was my sister, and her father agreed I should take her, as Georgina's nearest blood relation and godmother. And I love her every bit as deeply as a mother could. But solicitors don't work for free, and such a course would be hard on your family as well as on me. It occurred to me there might be a more beneficial way to solve our differences."

Ellen shook her head. Tears winked in her eyes.

"I was prepared to spend a great deal of money on a solicitor and court costs. But that would only benefit the solicitor. A widowed mother with two infant sons would have a far greater need for the money," Francesca said softly. "I know Georgina's inheritance provides an annual maintenance for her care, which you would lose if she left your household. I understand your position, truly. And I'm proposing we both benefit: I will raise Georgina, and in return I will give you the two thousand pounds I would have spent filing petitions in the Court of Orphans."

She had considered the amount carefully. Georgina's

allowance was one hundred pounds per annum, which meant one thousand pounds over the next decade she might be expected to live with Ellen. Francesca didn't think it would be persuasive enough to offer merely to replace that amount; there was no clear benefit to Ellen in that. But Ellen had two young sons. The income from two thousand pounds, invested wisely, would replace that hundred pounds a year indefinitely and still leave the principal intact for schooling or an inheritance for the boys. It was a great deal of money, enough that Francesca knew she would feel the pinch of losing it, and she was all but holding her breath as she waited for Ellen's response.

The woman was clearly torn. She bit her lip until it turned white, and twice dashed tears from her cheek. Just as she opened her mouth to speak, there was a commotion outside. The little dog was barking again, and Francesca heard voices—including Georgina's high, young voice. She was on her feet in an instant, turning toward the door.

"Percy!" screamed Ellen. "Percy, no! Take the children and go!"

Edward was already out the door. More voices, male this time, sounded in the corridor over the barking, and then Francesca heard what she had dreamed of every night. "Aunt Franny?" cried Georgina. "She's here?"

"Yes, dearest," she called, as evenly as she could manage. There was a patter of footsteps, and finally Georgina herself appeared in the doorway, taller and thinner than before, but clean and healthy-looking, her face bright with delight.

"Aunt Franny!" She rushed across the room and

threw her arms around Francesca, who held her close, too overwhelmed to speak. Her heart seemed about to burst, and her eyes were wet. At *last* . . .

"I missed you so," Georgina said, looking up at her with shining dark eyes. "Why didn't you come see me before?"

Behind them, Ellen began sobbing. Francesca tried not to listen, because then she would think about the lies Ellen must have told Georgina to explain why she hadn't come to visit in so long, and she didn't think she could maintain any semblance of poise if she allowed that. "I missed you very much, too," she told her niece. "I wish I had been able to visit sooner."

Georgina hesitated, then gave a very philosophical nod. "I understand. Mama told me adults have great responsibility and cannot spend as much time as they'd like visiting."

Francesca drew in a deep breath to stave off the fury at Georgina's calling Ellen "Mama." Or at Ellen telling Georgina that she was too busy to visit, when it was Ellen's own actions that had prevented her from coming. "I'm never too occupied to see you," she said instead. "And my heavens, how you've grown! You look more and more like your mother."

Georgina smiled widely. "Do I? I remember Papa saying she was very beautiful."

"She was, darling," Francesca replied softly. "Just like you."

"Ellen." Percival stood in the doorway, looking defeated. He shot a black look at Francesca before turning back to his sister. "Ellen, come here a moment."

She seemed afraid to leave the room. Her eyes darted

from Francesca and Georgina back to her brother. "Now, Percy?" she whimpered.

He nodded. "Yes, now. You have to let Georgie talk to . . ." He paused, his face puckering up as if tasting something bitter. "Let Georgie talk to her aunt."

Georgina sensed the tension. "Why?" she asked in alarm. "Why should I talk to Aunt Franny, Uncle Percy?" When Percival said nothing, she looked to Ellen. "Why, Mama?"

Ellen Haywood put her hands behind her back. "There's no reason you shouldn't, Georgie," she said, her voice cracking. "Since you haven't seen her in a while."

But Georgina was worried now. "Aunt Franny?" she appealed. "Can Mama stay?"

"No, no," Ellen said at once. "I'll just . . . I'll just be outside with Billy and Jack." She hurried across the room, and Percival put his arm around her as she slipped through the door. Francesca just saw Ellen cover her face with both hands before Edward stepped forward to reach for the door. He paused long enough to give her a long look, his expression somber and serious. The door closed with a click, and they were alone.

"What is wrong, Aunt Franny?" Georgina's thin face was lined with fear. "Why did everyone leave?"

"So we can have a bit of a visit. No one's left, dearest, they're just outside the door." Still holding the girl's hand, Francesca led her over to the sofa. "I didn't mean to stay away so long," she began. She didn't want to upset Georgina even more, but she couldn't bear to let her niece think she'd abandoned her. "I wanted to visit very much. But when you all left Cheapside, I didn't know where you'd gone."

Georgina's eyes got wide. "Oh, that was frightening," she confessed in a tiny voice. "Uncle Percy said we had to leave very quickly and we must be very quiet, too. Jack cried because we forgot his favorite blanket."

"Mrs. Jennings told me."

"Hmph," said Georgina, looking shockingly like Giuliana when peeved, two thin lines dividing her eyebrows and her eyes flashing fire. "*She* was glad to see us go. She was rude to Mama and she always complained I swept dirt onto her steps when I never did."

"I didn't like her, either," Francesca said in a confidential whisper, which made Georgina smile cautiously. "But I was so sad to hear you'd gone, and not even told where. I missed you, and have been trying to find you. I came as soon as I knew where you were."

"I'm so glad you did!" Her sunny smile disappeared quickly, though. "But are you going to argue with Mama again? I don't like that."

"No." Francesca steadied her voice. It was killing her to hear another woman called "Mama" by her niece. "I've come to bring you home with me."

She had expected Georgina to be surprised, even nervous about leaving. She had prepared herself for childish worries or fear. It had been a while since Georgina had seen her, and longer still since she had been to her home. Of course it would seem frightening to a child. She was not prepared for Georgina to frown in bemusement and ask, "Why?"

"Well, darling, your parents wanted me to. Before your mama died, she and I used to talk about you—she loved you so very much. She wanted to take you to Italy, where she grew up, and to see the great opera houses of

Europe, where your grandmama used to sing. When she died, it nearly broke my heart, but I remembered all she wanted for you, and knew she would want me to take you all those places, since she never could. And your papa agreed; he always said I should take you when you were a little older. He used to say he could tell you were an Italian at heart, even when you were a very small girl." Georgina's small, shy smile encouraged her. "Do you remember my house? And Mrs. Hotchkiss, who used to make Savoy biscuits for you? We've prepared a room for you of your very own, right upstairs from my own. Mrs. Hotchkiss is horribly afraid I'll buy you a parrot, but otherwise she cannot wait to see you again."

"A parrot?" Georgina wrinkled her nose. "Parrots are loud."

Francesca laughed. "So said Mrs. Hotchkiss!" She tilted her head to better see her niece's face. "We shall have a capital time together, even without a parrot."

"Oh, but . . ." Georgina frowned again. " I don't want to leave Mama and my brothers."

"But darling, she isn't truly your mama," said Francesca gently.

Georgina's mouth puckered. "I don't want to go, Aunt Franny."

"You'll be so much happier," Francesca went on quickly, thrown off stride by this unexpected refusal. "You won't have to sweep the steps or work in the garden. You'll have nice dresses, and music and drawing lessons, and whatever else you wish to learn. We'll learn Italian together, for when we go to Italy."

"No," said her niece, mutiny in her eyes.

"Now, Georgina." Francesca decided to be firm.

"The last time I saw you, you begged me to take you home with me."

"I did not!" the girl declared, seeming genuinely shocked by the idea. "I don't want to leave Mama and Billy and Jack!"

"Your father wanted me to raise you, dear. You must accept his decision." Francesca hadn't expected this to be so difficult. Georgina wasn't responding to her very reasonable and enticing plans as she should, but then, she was a child, and had been somewhat willful her whole life. Perhaps it had been a mistake to ask her opinion at all. It really wasn't up to her where she lived. "I've already spoken to Mrs. Haywood about this. She knows your papa wanted you to come with me."

Georgina's face grew red. She jumped to her feet. "You did not!" she cried. "Mama would never say I should go with you! She loves me!"

"Of course she does. So do I." Francesca's temper was stirring in reply, no matter how hard she tried not to let it. "Be reasonable, Georgina."

"If you loved me you would let me stay!"

The floor seemed to list beneath her feet. "You shall still see everyone here," she said, trying to calm the girl. "Not every day, but we'll visit."

Tears gathered in Georgina's eyes—of fury, not grief. "Mama won't let you take me away. She needs me. You only want me to come with you because you can't have any children of your own; Uncle Percy said so!"

Francesca gasped as the cruel words hit her. "That is *not* true," she snapped. Curse Percival Watts and his spiteful tongue. This would be going much better if Percival hadn't poisoned Georgina against her. She made a great effort to moderate her fury and return to the initial joy of their reunion. "Georgina—why must we argue? I thought you would be pleased. We used to get on so well!"

Anger still darkened Georgina's face, but her chin trembled. "You didn't want to take me away then."

"I did, darling," she said, only to wish the words unsaid as real fear blanched Georgina's face.

"No," shrilled her niece. "No! Mama!" She turned and bolted for the door.

"Georgina, please," Francesca cried, but it was too late. Georgina flung open the door and threw herself into the waiting arms of Ellen Haywood.

Chapter 23

❦

Edward watched Percival Watts huddle over his weeping sister. The deep sobs wracking Ellen Haywood's shoulders weren't quite what he would have expected of someone merely losing an income. Not for the first time, he wondered what Francesca would do if her plans went awry. Unless he was very much mistaken, Mrs. Haywood was deeply attached to the little girl—perhaps as much as Francesca was.

He had begun to suspect it when he cornered Percival Watts in the back of the hall with the children. Watts had obviously just come from the market, with a large basket filled with packages on one arm and a towheaded toddler in the other. Another little boy, a replica of the first, had been holding hands with a slim, dark-haired girl Edward guessed, rightly, to be Georgina. The children all looked well, and had been chattering gaily until Mrs. Haywood's scream. Watts had already turned to flee when Edward caught him. The man glanced through the open door, saw the footman run up, and slumped in concession. Edward explained things swiftly and firmly, and Watts just nodded, looking sullen and resentful. By the time he sent the little boys into another room and went to the parlor door, Georgina had already run in to Francesca, and Edward could hear the happy sounds of reunion.

But then Mrs. Haywood came out. Edward saw her face crumble with grief, and his small suspicion burgeoned into a great apprehension. He tried to give Francesca a glance of warning, but she was glowing with happiness and triumph, holding Georgina's hand. He closed the door and tried to stifle that feeling of impending disaster.

"I suppose you've come to help her steal Georgie away." Percival Watts suddenly turned on him with a venomous look.

"Sh-She offered m-me two th-thousand pounds, Percy," sobbed his sister. Her face was blotchy and red.

Watts snorted. "Oh, brilliant. She wants to *buy* a child?"

"She wishes to make things fair," said Edward.

"Fair? How is it fair that she should sweep in like some lady of the manor and throw her money to us poor, ordinary folk, and we should be grateful for her condescension?"

Edward arched one brow. "How fair is it to keep a child from her only family, in defiance of her father's wishes?"

"We're Georgie's family," Watts shot back. "Who the hell are you, anyway?"

"Edward de Lacey, at your service." Edward fixed his coolest stare on the man.

"Percy." Mrs. Haywood's sobs had subsided. "Stop. Percy . . . she means to take Georgie, and I don't know how we can stop her. She said she would go to court if I didn't accept her offer. What should we do?"

Watts glared at Edward. "We can't afford to fight her there," he muttered.

His sister clutched at his sleeve. "Perhaps if I talk to her . . . apologize . . . perhaps she'll relent . . ."

He scowled. "She's too selfish for that."

"I see why it was impossible for you and Lady Gordon to deal cordially," said Edward dryly. "Misperceptions abound."

"You didn't see the way she behaved," snarled Watts.

"Your actions have not commended you, either."

"Then what do you suggest, sir?" Mrs. Haywood swiped the corner of her apron across her eyes.

"He'll take her side," muttered Watts.

"Hush, Percy," she snapped at him. "I'll take help from any quarter, if it will help me keep Georgie."

Edward studied her a moment. Grief had settled on her face, but there was still hope in her eyes. "She loves Georgina," he said gently. "Very much. Whatever else has passed between you and her, she wants only her niece's happiness."

Mrs. Haywood's chin quivered, but she nodded.

"If you want the same—whatever is best for Georgina—you might acknowledge that to her. Then you'll have the same goal in mind, and needn't work at cross purposes any longer."

Mrs. Haywood's eyes closed and she swayed on her feet. Her brother muttered something as he reached for her, but Edward didn't hear what. His ear had caught the sound of raised voices from the parlor. Watts's head came up as he, too, heard it. He shook his sister, whose eyes grew large as she listened. In the sudden quiet of the hall, Georgina's high voice was audible, though indistinct, through the parlor door. She sounded agitated, even angry. Edward thought he heard the name Percy, and then the lower murmur of Francesca's voice.

"They're arguing," whispered Mrs. Haywood unnecessarily.

"No!" rang Georgina's voice, followed by rapid footsteps. "No! Mama!"

Ellen Haywood was on her knees, arms open, by the time Georgina burst through the door. She hugged the girl to her, tears leaking down her cheeks again, as Francesca appeared in the doorway, her face ashen. Edward's heart fell.

"Mama, I don't want to leave you!" sobbed Georgina into Ellen's shoulder. "Don't make me go!"

Mrs. Haywood rocked her back and forth, crooning softly. "You don't have to go with her, Georgie," said Watts, glaring smugly at Francesca.

Edward didn't wait for her response. He seized Mr. Watts by the arm and bundled him back down the hall. "Let me go!" demanded the man. "I'll call the constables if you toss me from my own house!"

"By all means, do so." Edward shoved him through the door with a significant glance at his footman, lurking nearby, before closing and barring the door. Watts hammered on it for a moment, then fell silent.

Back in the hall, Georgina's sobs had quieted. "Mama, I don't want to live with Aunt Franny," she was pleading.

"I won't make you go," promised Mrs. Haywood as she dabbed a kerchief to the tears on Georgina's cheeks.

"Her father wished me to raise her." Francesca's voice was even, although Edward heard the thread of anguish in it. "I'm only doing as her parents wanted."

"Papa didn't say that, did he?" Georgina appealed to Mrs. Haywood.

The woman bit her lip. "Well—yes, Georgie, he did, but that was years ago."

"It was little more than one year ago," Francesca said quietly. "Ever since Giuliana died, John asked me to see that Georgina was raised as her mother would have done."

Mrs. Haywood's color faded. "He didn't know how I would come to care for her."

"Papa . . . Papa wanted me to live with Aunt Franny?" asked Georgina in a small, uncertain voice. Her tears had stopped.

"He wanted you to have a wonderful life, darling, filled with people who love you." Francesca made a helpless motion with one hand. "He wanted you to be happy."

"Yes, Georgie, he did." Mrs. Haywood's voice broke. "And if you should decide you would be happy living with your aunt . . ." She paused. "Do you wish to?"

Georgina cast a fearful glance at Francesca, who smiled tremulously. She had regained her poise, but Edward saw the tightness of her mouth and the rigidity of her shoulders. He felt a surge of bittersweet pride at her equanimity in the face of such crushing disappointment. "N-N-No," said Georgina, drawing the word out hesitantly. "But I have missed her. I would like to visit her, if I may."

For a moment all was silence. Francesca's knuckles

were white where she gripped the doorknob. "I would very much like you to visit me, Georgina," she finally replied, her voice a thin thread of sound. "Any time you wish."

Mrs. Haywood seemed to understand this was an olive branch. "Yes, Georgie, you may visit her."

"Did you not tell her where we lived now, Mama?" The tears were dry now, and Edward saw a trace of Francesca's spirit in the little girl as she backed out of Mrs. Haywood's arms. "She said you didn't."

Mrs. Haywood paled. "I was wrong not to," she whispered.

Georgina looked between the two women. "And did my papa truly wish Aunt Franny to take me to Italy when I am older?"

Mrs. Haywood looked wretched. "Yes, he did."

The girl nodded slowly. "I think I would like that. I will live here, with Mama and the babies, and visit Aunt Franny in London. And perhaps, when I am older, I might wish to visit Italy, too."

Mrs. Haywood glanced anxiously up at Francesca. "Is that acceptable, Lady Gordon?"

Pale and tense, her mouth strained, Francesca looked at Georgina with heartbreak in her eyes. She gave a brief nod.

Mrs. Haywood gave a great gasp of relief, pressing one hand to her throat. "Thank you. Thank you!"

Georgina smiled uncertainly at Francesca. "I'm sorry I shouted at you, Aunt Franny."

Francesca fluttered her fingers. "It's forgiven, darling." She held out her hand, and Georgina ran back to her, throwing her arms around Francesca's waist. Francesca embraced her in return, bending her head low to rest her cheek on the girl's head for a moment.

"Good! I did miss you so. Oh—Aunt Franny, you must meet Rotter!" she declared as happily as if the previous confrontation had never happened. A dog was barking furiously at the back door. "Did you see him when you arrived? Mama said Rotter is a terrible name for a dog, but Uncle Percy calls him that anyway. Rotter is a nice dog, except when he's bad. He likes to sleep under my bed at nights. Would you like to see him?"

At Francesca's nod, Georgina ran to the door and unbarred it, admitting Percival Watts along with the furiously barking black terrier, who proceeded to race through the narrow hall and then back out the door with Georgina in pursuit. Edward made his way to Francesca's side and put his arm around her. She was shaking, even though she held herself rigidly erect. He squeezed her hand, wishing intensely that he could make this easier for her somehow.

"Shall we go?" he murmured to her. She nodded slightly.

"So you'll just be taking Georgie for visits?" demanded Watts, who had been in feverish whispered conversation with his sister. "That's all?"

Francesca raised her chin and looked at him, her expression growing grim. "Yes, Mr. Watts. For now."

He smirked. Edward could see why Francesca disliked the man.

"Mr. Watts," Francesca went on coldly, "I do not like you much. I know you return my dislike in full. For Georgina's sake, I am willing to pretend politeness, but only if you do the same. Perhaps it would be best if we didn't see each other much."

"That's a splendid idea," said Mrs. Haywood quickly. "Percy, would you go to the boys for a minute?" He glowered and grumbled, but stalked back down the hall. Mrs. Haywood looked fearfully at Francesca. "You'll really leave her here, then? With me?"

"She wants to stay," Francesca replied. Her eyes were clear, her voice level. Only Edward felt the tremor in her body. "I never meant to drag her away if she was happy."

"Thank you, Lady Gordon," said Mrs. Haywood, tears filling her eyes again. "I—I love her. She's not my daughter, but I . . . Thank you. It will be different between us from now on."

Francesca inclined her head. "I hope so, very much."

They stepped outside just as Georgina returned, lugging the wriggling terrier in her arms. Francesca smiled and let the little dog lick her hand furiously. Her niece clapped her hands in delight, promising that when Francesca came next, Rotter would do his tricks.

"I am sure he's wonderful at tricks." Francesca's smile was growing strained. "But we must go now. Edward?"

"Of course." He motioned to the driver. His footmen had already returned to their posts and one held the carriage door.

"Good-bye! I cannot wait for you to come again." The girl threw her arms around Francesca once more. "Good-bye, sir," she said more bashfully to Edward.

"Good-bye to you, Miss Haywood. It has been a great pleasure to meet you," he said gravely, making her a formal bow. Georgina gave him a huge, surprised smile, and he winked at her before turning back to Francesca. "Are you well, dearest?" he asked quietly.

She nodded. "Until later," she said to Georgina with a forced smile. She kept it on her face as they climbed back into the carriage. She wore it as she leaned forward to wave to her niece until they rounded the bend in the road and the small cottage was lost to sight. Slowly it faded from her lips and she covered her face with her hands. Edward pulled her into his arms, and finally her heartbreak spilled out.

Chapter 24

E dward took her to his home. Francesca didn't say a word on the way back into town. Grief seemed to have sapped her considerable strength, and laid low even her irrepressible spirit. He wrapped his arms around her and wordlessly offered all the comfort he could. Nothing he could say would ease the sting of Georgiana's words. Nothing he could do would erase Francesca's feeling that she had failed. So he just held her and absorbed the silent flood of her tears when she finally shuddered and sobbed out her despair. And he felt her pain as if it were his own; her devastated expression cut him to the core, because he knew what it felt like to feel as though one had lost everything of value in life.

In Berkeley Square, Edward helped her from the carriage and into the house. He ignored the butler's startled look and led Francesca up the stairs, right into his own suite of rooms. It was where she belonged, really, where he wanted her to be—forever. The truth of that was becoming very clear to him.

She seemed to recover some of herself as he gave orders to the maid hovering at the door. "I should go home," she said, dashing away the last of her tears and trying to draw herself up.

"Stay," he said, drawing her close to him. He pressed his lips to her forehead, and her shoulders heaved in a silent sigh.

"She didn't want me," came her whisper. "She wanted to stay with Ellen and *Percival*—"

"She's just a child," Edward reminded her. "I know you hate the thought, but Ellen is the only mother she remembers. And, in truth, I cannot say she appears to be a cruel or indifferent mother."

"No," Francesca admitted in anguish. "But neither would *I* have been! If Georgina had lived with me this last year, she would have loved *me* just as much. I lost her because I was too cautious, too softhearted—I should have demanded Ellen give her to me when John died, I should have put a pistol to Mr. Kendall's cowardly head and forced him to exert his position, I should have—I should have just taken Georgina away, even if I had to shoot Percival to do it!" She tried to twist out of his grip. "I'm such a fool!"

He grasped her shoulders and held her in spite of her struggles. "Francesca, listen to me. Don't blame yourself for any of that. You offered to take her when Haywood died, and Ellen said no. Do you really think it would have improved things to go about waving a pistol at people?"

"I don't care!" she cried hysterically.

"You do," he countered. "You wouldn't want to live a life in hiding, or in exile, which you might have been forced to do if you'd acted so rashly. You would have had Georgina, but at what cost to you—and to her?

Would Georgina thank you for taking her far away from everything she's ever known? Would your sister want you to raise her child that way?"

"She wouldn't want her daughter to be nurse to Ellen's children!"

"To her half brothers, you mean?" He raised one eyebrow. "You must try to see the best in this. She's happy and well cared for. Ellen loves her and has promised you may visit at any time. In time, as she grows older, Georgina may even change her mind. It's not the worst thing for her to grow up unspoiled."

Francesca glared at him. Her eyes were red and her face was puffy, and she was the most beautiful woman he had ever seen. "I hate it when you are so reasonable and right, Edward."

"Do you really?" He grabbed her when she would have backed away, and swung her up into his arms. "Does it make you feel better that I would much rather be wrong in this case?"

"No." She put her arms around his neck and dropped her head against his shoulder. "Put me down."

"As you wish." He carried her across the room, deposited her on his bed, and stripped off his jacket. She rolled onto her side, away from him, as Edward stretched out beside her. He snaked one arm around her and pulled her back into him. Her body fit so perfectly against his. "I'm sorry, darling," he whispered.

Her hand slipped into his. He laced his fingers through hers and stroked his thumb over her knuckles. "Thank you," came her thin reply. "For everything."

"I wish I could have changed things."

She sighed. She felt so small and limp in his arms,

as if she'd been drained of everything vital. "Nobody could. I suppose I could have dragged her away, but I couldn't bear to hear her cry and beg to go back to Ellen."

"I know," he said, stroking one hand down her back. "I know."

"I couldn't bear to make her miserable—by taking her to stay with *me*," she went on. "I couldn't bear it if she hated me."

"She wouldn't hate you."

"She might have."

He held her for a long time, until he felt her muscles ease and her breathing deepen in sleep. Even then he didn't move, content to stay curled around her for the foreseeable future.

This was not at all how he had expected the day to go. Last night, lying sleepless in Francesca's bed, he'd thought long and hard about what he would say and do in Greenwich. He had asked her on impulse, but as soon as she said yes, of course, as if there had never been a doubt she would go with him, the thought popped into his head that he should propose. It made a great deal of sense at the time, when he'd expected Georgina to come live in Francesca's house soon, and it perfectly satisfied his craving to have her in his bed every night, at his table every morning, and in his arms whenever he wanted.

He was a little shocked by how quickly and easily the idea took root in his mind. His last marriage proposal, to Louisa, had been the result of discussion with his father and practical analysis of the Halston properties, the advantages of the match, and his compatibility with Louisa herself. It hadn't happened quickly, but only after prolonged thought and evaluation. In contrast, he barely thought about the disadvantages of wedding Francesca—his unsettled inheritance, the difference in their stations, the rather short duration of their acquaintance, their opposite natures—and instead was consumed by the advantages—namely, the intense happiness he felt in her presence, the way she made him laugh, the way he burned for her. He'd tried to tell himself once upon a time that it was just lust, potent but passing, but now he knew that wasn't true. Edward, who had thought love was something one cultivated and grew in the appropriate place, had discovered that love could also be a wild, fierce thing that grew where it should not and flourished when it should have died, even when he himself had tried to smother it.

As he lay listening again to the soft, even sound of Francesca's breathing, he knew that she was the one for him, whether society approved or not. Whether he was Lord Edward de Lacey, brother of the Duke of Durham, or just Edward de Lacey, with no property and virtually penniless. As long as she would have him, the rest of the world could go hang.

Francesca woke up several hours later. She hadn't known she was tired until Edward laid her down and held her, but once he did, exhaustion almost swallowed her whole.

It took her a few moments to realize where she was. The sky outside the windows was deep indigo, and the room was cloaked in shadows. She pushed herself up and took in the luxurious bed hangings, the finely

carved marble fireplace, the elegant furniture and ac-
coutrements. It was the largest bedchamber she had ever
seen. It was without question the home of an illustrious
person—of a duke, in fact—and suddenly she felt very
out of place.

As she slid off the thick, soft mattress, she saw
Edward. He sat at a wide desk on the other side of the
room, near the windows. He looked up when she stirred,
and put down the papers he'd been reading. "How are
you feeling?"

She smiled ruefully as she crossed the room to him.
"Better. And worse."

His face relaxed in understanding. He got to his feet
and took her hand. "No doubt."

Francesca bit her lip as an awkward silence descended. Awkward for her, at any rate. Edward was perfectly at home in his private rooms, where he belonged.
She was the one who didn't belong, with her wrinkled
riding habit and waterlogged eyes and hair that must
be absolutely frightful. "I should go," she said. "Mrs.
Hotchkiss will summon the Runners."

"I sent a man to tell her you were here."

"Thank you."

"Are you hungry?" he asked. "I can send for a tray."

She hadn't eaten since breakfast, but shook her head.
"No. I—I really should go home."

Edward put his finger under her chin and tipped up
her face. "Why?"

She knew it would hurt to go home, where there was
a room all prepared for Georgina that wouldn't be used.
"I've imposed on you enough for one day. I'm sure this
is not at all what you had planned . . ."

"I'm perfectly willing to make a new plan." He smoothed his hands over her jaw, around her neck, into the mass of her hair. Francesca swayed toward him at the seductive pull of his touch. "There is a large bath here," he said between light kisses on her forehead. His fingers were combing through her hair—picking out pins, she realized vaguely. "Bathe with me."

As always, she was helpless to resist when Edward set out to persuade her. The bath chamber was on the other side of his dressing room. He must have been plotting this bath before she awoke, for the deep copper tub was filled with hot water in no time. The servants slipped out the door, and they were alone.

"I've never bathed with a man before," she said as he unfastened her buttons. The steam in the air was turning her hair into curling tendrils, and she shed the wool bodice with a sigh of relief.

Edward's eyes were fixed on her as he pulled off his cravat and then his waistcoat. "I shall do my best to make it memorable."

She managed to smile. He wanted to help her banish the memory of Georgina's rejection. She was sure that was why he wanted her to stay, even though he was disrobing her with raw sexual hunger in his face. And really, she couldn't think of a better way to distract herself from melancholy thoughts than to lose herself in Edward's arms, and give herself over to the scorching passion that flared between them. For a while at least it would burn away the anguish that hovered just around her.

He made love to her in the bath, bringing her to climax twice before the water cooled. Then he carried her back to his bed and worshipped every inch of her with his mouth until she felt wrung out and exhausted, her mind happily blurred. But it didn't last forever. Reality slowly settled back over her, and Francesca sighed. "I really should go home, you know."

"By all the gods, why would you do that?" He trailed kisses down the side of her throat until she arched her neck.

"I don't belong here . . . even though you've been so good to me . . ."

Edward raised his head. "Why don't you think you belong here?"

Faint pink colored her face. "What would your brother say if he knew you brought your mistress to his house?"

Edward's mouth crooked at the thought of Charlie being offended by a mistress of any stripe—Charlie, who would likely as not have a Cyprian's ball in the house when he took possession. He shook his head. Then he laughed. "If only you knew," he said, still grinning. Francesca flushed darker and turned her head away. "It's just a house," he said, realizing that it *was* just a house: a fine, elegant house, but still merely a building of stone and wood. He wasn't even particularly fond of it, to be honest. He had thought he would fight to the death to keep this house, but now he thought he could be just as happy—happier, even—in Francesca's home, or any other building, really, as long as she was there with him. "It's just a house," he repeated. "And Charlie of all people won't turn you away. Once you meet him, you'll understand at once."

"Just because he might be understanding—"

"You most certainly do belong here." He ran his palm down the curve of her hip and leg. "Here with me." She stared at him for a long moment, her eyes shadowed. "Trust me," he added. "Don't go home tonight. I want you to stay."

There was too much at her home to remind her of Georgina and the plans she had made for the girl. He didn't see any reason for her to bear the full weight of her dashed hopes tonight.

"All right," she said after a moment. "Just tonight."

There was a light tap on the door. Edward ignored it, but it came again a few minutes later. He sighed, rolling off the bed and reaching for his trousers. "I'll be back in a moment."

"What is it?" he snapped at Blackbridge when he opened the door.

"Beg your pardon, sir," said the butler in a ponderous whisper. "But His Grace has arrived and is asking for you."

It took Edward a moment to realize Blackbridge meant his brother and not his father. Somehow the thought of Charlie as the duke—no matter how insecure his grip on the title—made him grin. "Very well, I shall meet him directly."

Blackbridge bowed as Edward closed the door. He went back to Francesca. "I should have a word with my brother. He'll only be more intolerable the longer I leave him waiting."

"Of course." She got up and wrapped his dressing gown around herself, her copper hair shining brightly against the dark blue velvet. "I should send Mrs. Hotchkiss a note. She'll be anxious to know what happened."

"By all means. There's paper in the second drawer."
He indicated the desk before pulling her close for another kiss. "This dressing gown suits you," he whispered, running his hands down her back to cup her
bottom.

"Your brother is waiting," she said even as she leaned
into him.

"Bugger him." Edward kissed her again, hungry and
deep. He almost asked her right then to marry him,
but reluctantly acknowledged that he wouldn't be any
more ready to leave after that, and it seemed rude to ask
and then leave to see his brother. "I'll return soon," he
promised, reaching for his shirt.

"I'll be here," she replied with a trace of a smile.

He found his brother in the library. Charlie was rum-
maging in the drawers of the chiffonier by the tall windows overlooking the garden. He barely looked up when
Edward came into the room. "Didn't Father keep the tobacco in here?" he grumbled. "I can't find his particular
blend anywhere, and it's damned smooth . . ."

"I've no idea. Father hadn't been here in three years."

Charlie blinked. "Really? So long? Well. I suppose it
would have gone off, then . . ." With visible reluctance,
he closed the drawers.

"What are you doing here?" Charlie hadn't called
once since Edward came to London, and now he was
prowling around the room looking cross and restless.

"How are we getting on with the solicitor?" Charlie
asked instead.

"We are stuck in a morass of parliamentary law,"
Edward replied with a mild spark of surprise. It was the
first sign of interest he'd seen from his brother. "Wittiers

has prepared a very solid case laying out our claims to legitimacy, and thus your right to the title. Your petition has been prepared and filed with the Home Office. He sent word all was completed yesterday."

"That's excellent." Charlie seemed genuinely relieved. He grinned and clapped Edward on the shoulder. "Good work. I knew there was nothing to worry about with you on the case."

"And it may all go for naught if Dorothy Cope turns up alive and well, or even dead and gone, if she's only been thirty years in her grave," Edward went on as if his brother hadn't spoken. "Wittiers cannot change anything in that event, although I did instruct him to fight tooth and nail to disprove it. He also cannot prevent Augustus from filing a petition for the title, and God alone knows what might happen then, even though I've already set Wittiers to undermining Augustus in any way possible."

Charlie's face darkened. "Then what the bloody hell are we to do? What have you *been* doing?"

"A damned sight more than you've been doing," Edward said. "And now I'm done."

"Done?" Charlie frowned in suspicion. "What do you mean, done?"

He was quiet for a moment. "This is your fight. Your title. Your estate. Your claim to stake. Not mine."

"Not yours," his brother repeated blankly. "You've lost your bloody mind. You've almost as much to lose as I have!"

"You don't care for something unless you fight for it," Edward said. "I'm not the duke, Charlie—you are, or should be. If you want Durham, fight for it yourself."

"We'll all be penniless nobodies," exclaimed Charlie. "You've gone mad—is it that woman?"

He grinned wryly. "Not for the reason you think. But yes, it's because of her that I'm done. And for you," he added as his brother opened his mouth again. "You don't need me to wage this battle for you. I'll help you in any way I can, but now I have something else that needs my attention."

Charlie still frowned peevishly. "Well, I suppose I'm the last person who ought to complain if you've decided to lose yourself in a woman's skirts for a few months. But it's not like you, Ned, not at all."

"I know." He couldn't stop grinning, which was also unlike him. "I'll send you copies of my correspondence with Wittiers in the morning, so you can proceed."

"What? Oh, bloody hell, no, you won't!" His brother looked thunderstruck. "Edward, be reasonable! I don't have the first idea what to do with correspondence and documents! At least say you'll keep on with that part!"

Edward made a show of looking around the room. "Then I suppose we'd better begin packing." Charlie began cursing, but Edward held up his hand. "Do you know Father thought you'd react this way? He was desperate to beg your pardon with his last breath because he expected you to crumble under the strain." His brother glared at him, but Edward just shrugged. "I, however, know better. You've spent most of your life trying to prove him wrong, or at least confound his expectations. Why should you stop now? I think you'll discover what to do once you make up your mind to solve this problem instead of hiding from it."

The murderous but thwarted expression on his

brother's face was priceless. Edward smiled, rather pleased with himself, and turned to go. When he reached the door, Charlie called out, "You're a heartless manipulator."

"I thought that was one of my finer qualities."

"It is," grumbled Charlie, stalking across the room and then out the door Edward held open. "I hope she's worth it."

"More than I could ever tell you," Edward replied.

Chapter 25

❧ ∞ ❧

Edward went back upstairs, his pulse quickening in anticipation. He should ask on one knee, so she would know he was serious. Out of instinct he began listing arguments in favor of their marriage, just in case she made any protest. He wasn't used to being refused, and in this particular circumstance would do anything to persuade her. He had never been more certain of his actions. Shedding the responsibility for the Durham title onto Charlie felt surprisingly right, and soon he would have Francesca.

He opened the door to see her standing at his desk, head bent. Firelight gleamed on her hair. She still wore his dressing gown, but Edward knew there was nothing beneath it. He closed the door and was halfway across the room when she turned.

He stopped in his tracks. Good God. Her expression was not what he had expected. A prickle of alarm ran up his spine as she just stared accusingly at him.

"What is this?" she asked when the silence had grown taut and sharp. She held up something . . . the report Jackson had first given him, the one about her.

Damn it all to bloody hell. He knew he should have burned that.

"This isn't about Georgina, or Ellen Haywood, or Percival Watts," she went on, her voice beginning to shake. "This is about *me*. You led me to believe the man you hired couldn't even write, and here are pages and pages about my parents, my marriage, my friends. Why do you have this?"

Edward was frozen. God, another lie he had forgotten, when he'd been trying to stifle his interest in her.

"Why?" she asked again. "I would have told you everything in here, if you'd only asked."

His throat seemed paralyzed. How could he say he had wanted to know long before she would have told him, when he had no excuse for asking her directly? How could he explain that he was captivated by her almost from the first moment he saw her, and that it had overridden his sense and judgment too many times to count? How could he admit he had been a damned fool, but was sorry now because he realized what an insult it was to her open, honest nature? How could he tell her now that he loved her, that he'd been about to fall to his knees and propose marriage?

When he said nothing, she flung the papers at him. Edward flinched. The pages uncurled as they hit him in the chest and then fluttered to the ground, like discarded feathers from a bird soaring away.

"I'm sorry," he said. "It was a mistake."

"A mistake?" She folded her arms and put up her chin, like the undaunted Francesca he knew so well. It only allowed him to see the tears glimmering at the corners of her eyes this time, though, and it made him feel filthy and craven.

He opened his mouth to explain, and the words scattered. "I cannot defend it," he said helplessly.

"I would believe almost anything you wanted to say in explanation," she whispered.

"I wanted to know." Each word was bitter, and difficult to form. "I should not have done it. I should have waited until you were willing to tell me what you wished me to know of you. I should have resisted the urge to control things . . ." He cleared his throat. "I'm sorry."

Her eyes closed for a moment, and Edward felt a surge of fear and hope. Hope that she would accept his apology, that she cared for him enough that this wouldn't divide them. Fear . . . that she did not. Fear that he had given his heart again to a woman who didn't love him back. Fear that he had made not the same mistake he'd made with Louisa, but a far worse one. Marrying Louisa had been the intelligent, rational thing to do. Pursuing Francesca had been against every sound reason he could think of—and yet he'd lost himself so completely to her, he didn't know how he could survive without her. When Louisa jilted him, he'd been angry. If Francesca left him, he would be broken.

"When?" she asked. "When did you ask Mr. Jackson for that?"

He couldn't make things worse by lying. "The day we interviewed solicitors here." Her eyes were shadowed as she stared stonily at him, no doubt reviewing the calendar in her mind. "I asked him primarily to find Mrs. Haywood and Georgina," he went on, feverishly hoping it would sway her. "I realized it would be difficult to find a solicitor to take your case—I had already begun thinking a private investigator was your best chance to recover Georgina. I acted without telling you, I admit, but I wanted a quick solution. And you did agree, when I laid out my reasoning to you."

Her brows drew together. "You wanted rid of me sooner?"

"Because I was so tempted," he admitted. "So desperately drawn to you, I thought it best. Yes."

She had started shaking her head as he spoke, a tiny movement at first that grew more emphatic. "You disliked me. I was a nuisance to you. I maneuvered you into helping me when you hadn't really done anything wrong, when you owed me nothing."

Edward cursed and ran his hands through his hair. "Yes! And still I couldn't stay away, even when you told me I had done enough and was welcome to go away. I *couldn't* go away, even when I told myself it was the wise thing to do."

"Then this was just an irresistible urge to you." Her gaze dropped to the hateful papers scattered on the floor. "And you made sure I was safe enough to have an affair with, before things even got that far."

Edward swallowed hard. Unconsciously he drew himself up straighter, taller, colder, bracing himself for the coming blow. "No. That wasn't it."

She raised her eyes to his. "That's what it looks like."

He said nothing. She was correct; that's what it did look like, now. He had known when he did it that he ought not to have instructed Jackson to report on her. He just hadn't expected it to haunt him so cruelly.

Francesca seemed to slump. Without another word

she turned and crossed the room, snatching up her clothing as she went. She left and closed the door behind her.

Edward felt the air leave the room with her. He made it to a chair before his knees gave out. His head fell into his hands and he squeezed his temples, frantically trying to think, and coming up with nothing but blank misery. He was not accustomed to having no idea what to do; the fact that his mind was utterly devoid of any plan at all, even a bad one, was debilitating.

He waited an hour, then sent her a note. Just a simple one, asking if he might call on her the next day. He told his servant to wait for an answer, even if he must stand outside her house all night, but the reply the man brought was almost worse than none at all. She asked him not to come. There was nothing more; no final farewell, no recriminations, not even another invitation to defend himself and have a blazing row about it, just . . . nothing.

Edward spent a sleepless night staring at the fire, drinking his father's best brandy, and wondering what he should do now. He finally came up with three choices, none of which were clear good ones.

First, he could wait until she agreed to see him again, hoping she *would* agree to see him again. He did not like this idea. Every day she refused him would be like pouring salt in a wound. He had prided himself his entire life on his patience and fortitude, but the prospect of waiting for a summons that might never come was enough to break his soul. Waiting was not an attractive option.

Second, he could force his way into her house and pour out his heart, explaining everything he'd done and his reasons, standing outside her windows and shouting it for all to hear if she tossed him out, and pray she could listen enough to forgive him. But this left open the real chance she would be even more appalled by such an out of character action, and never speak to him again. Edward had no experience in forcing his presence on a lady, and he wasn't sure he could do it. If she burst into tears and asked him to leave, he would probably go throw himself in the Thames.

That left the third option, which he didn't like any better than the others. He drank a lot more brandy trying to think of a fourth or fifth option, but in the end the dreaded third option was the only one that his conscience would allow.

He knocked several times before the door opened. The bleary-eyed servant staring at him was probably not reassured by his appearance, but Edward pushed past him. "Tell Lord Alconbury I wish to see him at once."

"His lordship is still abed," protested the servant. "Come back at a decent hour."

Edward fixed his iciest stare on the man. "Tell him," he said. "Immediately."

The footman scowled, but before he could argue further, a voice called from the top of the stairs, "This house had bloody well be on fire, for all the racket down there."

Edward looked up. "I'd like a word, Alconbury. About Lady Gordon."

The baron came slowly down the stairs. He had obviously come from his bed, a dressing gown pulled around him and his hair ruffled and unkempt. He waved his footman off, muttering to the man to go back to bed. The servant closed the front door and obediently slipped away. "I don't think I care to hear what you have to say about her."

"No," Edward said. "It isn't what you think."

Alconbury raised an eyebrow. "Are you journeying to China by some odd chance, never to return?"

Perhaps. "I've come to ask a service of you."

"Indeed," said Alconbury in a dry tone.

His hands ached to curl into fists. He had to clench his jaw to keep his composure. "For her, not for me. I fear . . ." He hesitated in spite of himself. "I fear she will need someone. I understand you were indispensible to her when her husband died."

The other man's suspicion melted away. However much Edward disliked him, he had to admit Alconbury's affection for Francesca was real—which only made this harder, to be honest. "What's happened to her?" he exclaimed. "By God, de Lacey, what's wrong?"

"She's neither wounded nor ill." Not even the cold, hard reserve he had cultivated for so long was making this more bearable. Edward had to look away from Alconbury's concerned face, knowing it would be the one to comfort the woman he loved—and had possibly lost, through his own stupidity. "She's merely learned some displeasing truths about me. I'm sure she would be glad of a friend."

Alconbury looked suspicious. "I warned her you would hurt her."

Edward inclined his head. "You were correct."

"I was." Alconbury studied him with a slight frown. "She said you were a true friend to her when her husband died," Edward went on, hating every word. "I trust you can be again."

"I will try to be," said Alconbury slowly. Edward jerked his head in a nod of thanks. He couldn't quite bring himself to say it aloud, not when he had just handed the baron another chance at Francesca's heart. Sooner or later she would decide it was better to fall in love with the man who was always there to support her when another man broke her heart. "I thank you for the visit," Alconbury added, puncturing his thoughts. "I'll go to her this morning."

Edward pictured Francesca smiling across her breakfast table at Alconbury, sharing champagne with him in a darkened theater, letting him run his hands through her bright, silky hair, and a dark curtain seemed to pass over his vision. He had done what he came to do. There was nothing to be gained by lingering another moment. "Good day," he muttered, and left, brushing past the baron, letting the door bang closed behind him.

Francesca spent a wretched night tossing and turning, until finally she gave up and rose in the first light of dawn. She still felt numbed with shock that Edward had done such a thing: having her investigated! What did he hope to gain by that? He said it was because he was so drawn to her that he couldn't restrain himself even when he knew he should. Well, perhaps that sounded a little like her own actions, when she kissed him . . . and again when she invited him in for the night, planning to seduce him . . . but she at least had acted openly and honestly!

And what would he have done differently, she wondered in renewed despair, if he'd learned something unpleasant about her from Mr. Jackson? Would he have turned her away, or gone on and bedded her anyway, knowing he could discard her at any time? If he had ever made any declaration of his feelings, she would have been able to cling to it and convince herself *that* was the truth between them, and whatever had motivated him to have Jackson look into her history and habits was an old impulse, fallen by the wayside and no longer valid.

But he had never said anything. Not even when she all but begged him to say it, even if it was a lie, he hadn't said it.

Desperate for something to take her mind off Edward, she decided to go see Georgina. Ellen had promised she could visit at any time, and Francesca wanted to take some of the gifts and clothing she had bought for her niece. She was upstairs choosing which items to take when Mrs. Hotchkiss came up the stairs to say Lord Alconbury was waiting in the drawing room.

She went down to meet him, glad he had come to her again. A corner of her heart was irrationally disappointed it wasn't Edward come to see her, determined to win her back by scooping her into his arms and making love to her until she forgot her own name, let alone that he had investigated her before bedding her . . . but she reminded herself she'd told him not to come. She could hardly blame him for acceding to her wishes. Just because it was what *she* would do, if their circumstances were reversed, was no reason to expect Edward to do it. She hoped Alconbury would take her mind off it, because she didn't know what else to do.

"Alconbury, how nice of you to come see me," she said, holding out her hands to him. "I've missed you."

"And I you." He kissed her cheek, then stepped back to inspect her. "You look haggard this morning."

Her laugh was despondent. "A charmer, through and through! You'll steal my heart, talking that way."

He reached out and brushed a wisp of hair back from her temple. "Is it still free for me to steal?"

No. She smiled again, a bit forced this time. "Shall you stay for breakfast? I haven't eaten yet, but I smelled coffee earlier. Mrs. Hotchkiss would be delighted to serve you a cup."

Alconbury looked at her for a long moment without answering. "I had an odd visitor this morning," he said. "He nearly broke down my door a few hours ago—I thought the house was being robbed, or set ablaze—but it was only de Lacey."

Francesca's heart gave an extra beat just at the sound of his name. "Good heavens. How rude of him."

"Very," Alconbury agreed. "He asked me to call on you. He thought you might need a friend this morning."

Somehow she twisted her lips into a wobbly smile. "I'm always glad to see you, Henry . . ."

"No," he said gently. "You aren't. That night at the theater, you told me not to come—because you hoped he would still be here in the morning."

She pulled her hands out of his grasp and walked out of the room, into the breakfast room where Mrs. Hotchkiss had already laid out the table. How cruel of Alconbury to jab her with that memory, when she'd been as giddy as any girl, entranced with everything about Edward and thrilled beyond measure that he had found her at the theater, daring any scandal. When she had been so wildly, blindly, in love with him.

Alconbury followed. "Francesca, what's he done?"

She poked around the dishes on the sideboard. "Nothing, really."

"Then what did you wish him to do?"

His perceptive question stung like nettles. She had to gulp in a few shallow breaths to keep from bursting into tears. "I told you: nothing," she said, her wretched voice just barely trembling. "He made me no promises, and I expect nothing from him."

"Expect," he echoed. She continued rattling the dishes, even though she had looked in every one already and seen nothing she wanted to eat. "Then what did you *want*?"

I want him to love me as much as I love him. Mutely she shook her head.

His hands were gentle as he took her by the shoulders and turned her to face him. "A week ago your face lit up when he walked into the room, no matter who was watching. Now you say you expect nothing from him, even though I can see the words make you sick. Do you think I can't recognize heartache, Francesca?"

The tears spilled down her cheeks. "He doesn't love me," she whispered. "I thought he did—or at least *might*—but he wouldn't say it."

"Ah." Alconbury drew her into his arms, letting her rest her wet face against his chest. "Not every man is as wonderful and honest as I am, my dear. Most fellows turn pale at the sound of that word, not fall to their knees and readily confess it." He nudged up her chin until she looked at him. "If you'd said yes to me a fortnight ago, you'd have heard it every morning since."

"I know," she said with a watery hiccup. "I should have said yes . . ."

He chuckled, then sighed. "Of course you should not have done that. I was a fool to ask. I knew you were in love with him, or at least not with me. And unless I miss my guess, he is very much in love with you."

She swiped at her wet eyes. "He had me investigated. *Before*."

"He's a controlling sort of bastard," Alconbury said. "I'm not surprised he did it."

"He should have just asked me, if he wanted to know who my parents were and what happened to Cecil," she added.

"Of course he should have. Your family secrets aren't written in the gossip papers, unlike his own."

She winced at the thought of Edward's family history being gleefully dissected and dirtied in every paper in town. It made him furious, but he never gave in to that anger. "He doesn't deserve it."

"None of us deserve it. Some merely bear it better than others."

"You're saying he did it because he was in such a foul mood about the gossip?" She regarded him with doubt.

Alconbury smiled sardonically. "I'm saying men are prone to moments of idiocy. If I found myself about to lose everything, with my entire family being mocked in every drawing room in London, and a troublesome red-haired wench forced her way into my life and demanded I drop everything to help her, I might commit some regrettable acts as well." He leaned toward her, his voice dropping. "Especially if I found her irresistible."

Francesca stepped out of his arms and away from him. Edward *had* said something like that, that he was just so drawn to her . . . "You're only trying to make me feel better."

"Of course I am. But it's probably true. And whatever his motives then, he's in earnest now. Did I mention he woke me before dawn to ask that I come comfort you?"

She lifted one shoulder. She would have preferred it if Edward had come to comfort her himself, which was irrational because she had told him not to come. She didn't want to face him yet, but talking about him with Alconbury was making her want to see him more than ever. Most of all she hated that he had made her feel this way, irrational and confused and so bitterly sorry that she had told him to stay away. "I already agreed that was very rude of him."

"Yes, and Edward de Lacey is so often rude," Alconbury replied. "A veritable heathen, in his manners." She glared at him. "What was he thinking, to show up on my doorstep before dawn, bleary-eyed with drink, looking as though he'd been dragged behind his horse to my house, and then all but order me to console the woman he happens to know I proposed marriage to? The woman he's been seen with all over town, I might add, leading more than one person—including myself—to believe his intentions would lead to the exact opposite of what he actually did. The man must be a lunatic. Or perhaps . . . just perhaps . . . he's only mad for you."

Francesca had had enough. Perhaps it was true. She certainly wanted to think it might be. "Thank you for coming, Alconbury," she said in a stronger voice. "Your advice is as always invaluable to me."

He smiled. "Let's hope it does you some good this time." He paused and sniffed. "And since I've done de Lacey a tremendous service this morning, might I enjoy a cup of his coffee before I go? I'm not sure how I can hate the man who persuaded you to have Mrs. Hotchkiss brew coffee for me."

Chapter 26

Francesca's stomach twisted as she rapped on Ellen Haywood's door. Today she was able to take in more details of Georgina's surroundings. The steps were neatly swept, and a small pot of bright flowers bloomed in the window beside the door. The garden beyond was large and well-tended. It looked as though the household was doing better, and Ellen had promised things would be different now, but she still held her breath as the door opened.

"Please come in, Aunt Franny," said Georgina, her eyes shining as she curtsied very politely.

Francesca's heart seized with relief as she returned the gesture. "Thank you, Miss Haywood. It is a pleasure to see you again."

Her niece laughed and launched herself at Francesca, wrapping her arms around her waist. "I'm so glad you came! It seems so long since you said you would!"

Francesca hugged the little girl tightly. "It does, doesn't it? But I've brought you some things, and it took me a while to pack them up."

"I'm just happy to see you," said Georgina shyly, but as Mr. Hotchkiss got out the large box, her eyes grew wide and round with delight. She looked behind her almost worriedly, but Ellen, who had appeared in the parlor door, simply nodded.

"Good morning," Francesca said to her.

Ellen bobbed her head. "Good morning, Lady Gordon. Won't you come in?"

Mr. Hotchkiss carried his burden to the parlor, where Francesca unpacked it. She had brought some dresses for Georgina, along with several books and a locket that Giuliana had given her years ago. Her niece looked more and more amazed as Francesca dug deeper into the box, as if Father Christmas had come early. With some difficulty Francesca banished the lingering resentment that Ellen had kept her from Georgina for six months. She tried to console herself with more comforting observations: Georgina was well cared for, her long dark hair brushed to a shine, her cheeks pink and her eyes shining. She wasn't spoiled, from the way she exclaimed over an illustrated copy of Aesop's fables and the simple but pretty dresses Francesca had brought.

"Oh, thank you, Aunt Franny!" cried the girl at last, looking up from her new treasures. "I didn't expect you to bring so many gifts!"

Francesca smiled. One of Ellen's sons toddled into the room, and Georgina immediately pulled him onto the chair beside her to show him the pictures in her book. Behind her, Ellen stirred as if she would take the child away, and Francesca reached into her box once more. "I've brought a few other things, if Mrs. Haywood permits," she said, looking at Ellen. "For the children."

The look of surprise on Ellen's face was priceless, mingled with a bit of wariness and puzzlement. It dissolved into pure blank shock when Francesca took out a set of carved wooden animals, just the right size for a toddler's hand. She handed one to Georgina, who turned to the little boy beside her and held it out to him. "Look, Billy," she said happily, "look what my Aunt Franny has brought for you. Wasn't that very kind of her?"

The boy stared at the wooden horse for a moment with wide blue eyes, then took it from Georgina's hand and put the tail in his mouth. Georgina laughed, Francesca smiled, and Ellen made a strangled gasping noise before leaping to her feet and running from the room.

Francesca gave Georgina a wooden dolphin, then followed Ellen. She found the other woman in the hall, huddled in a corner with her hands over her face. When Ellen looked up at her approach, Francesca saw she was weeping.

"You have my humblest apologies, madam," whispered Ellen. "I—I believe I misjudged you."

Francesca smiled faintly. "And I you. Perhaps we had both better be a little more honest with each other, and a little less inclined to lose our tempers." She put out her hand. "There is something very special that binds us together."

Through her tears, Ellen smiled as Georgina's high, sweet voice floated out of the parlor, reading the tale of the honest woodcutter to her little brother. Ellen laid her hand in Francesca's and gave a tiny squeeze. "Indeed it does. She's a wonderful girl. I love her as if she were my daughter in every way."

A bittersweet sigh slipped through Francesca's lips. "You do," she said quietly. "I see it now."

Ellen wet her lips. "I acted out of fear, earlier. I wasn't

in my right mind, and it was too easy to believe you would take her away from us. It was never about the money, although I admit her maintenance has been invaluable to us. But if it had only been the money, Lady Gordon, I swear on my husband's grave I would have let you take her and raise her, as he promised you. But to lose her, after losing her father so suddenly—" Ellen stopped, her throat working as grief twisted her face. "She is such a *dear* child. No one who knew her could not love her. But I acted badly, and I confess my brother did as well. Percy was so worried about providing for us, he wasn't himself when he ordered you away that time." Francesca still thought that was Percival's true nature, but she said nothing. "I'm very sorry," Ellen finished in a whisper. "You *do* love her."

"Very much," Francesca agreed.

Ellen nodded. "And I know what heartache it is to consider losing someone so beloved. I thought only of my own grief, if you should take Georgie, and I allowed panic to guide me."

Francesca turned toward the parlor doorway, where Georgina's voice had broken down into giggles at whatever the little boy was doing. "I admit in turn I lost my temper. I thought I would be doing you a favor, and when you didn't respond as expected, I grew upset. Then angry, and then suspicious. And after that I stopped considering your point of view at all." It wasn't entirely true; she had thought of Ellen's trials as a young widow, left pregnant and penniless with a dependent child not her own. But she underestimated the possibility that Ellen might grow to love Georgina as much as she herself did, and so she had never really looked on Ellen's actions as those of a mother protecting her children. In her place, faced with the chance of losing a beloved child and knowing her legal claim to the child was weak, she would probably have done the same thing. She would have taken Georgina and run to Italy or some other place far beyond the reach of any English court. Ellen had merely been constrained by two infants and a severe lack of funds.

"So," Francesca went on, "I hope we shall get on better now. Georgina is always welcome to visit me at any time. I'll do my best not to spoil her, but some excess must be allowed in a fond aunt." She glanced warily at Ellen, who responded with a shaky smile. "And if you ever have need of anything . . ."

"Oh." Ellen flushed. "We're doing much better. Percy's sold a few paintings, and hopes for more. Moving away from town has been a great inspiration to him."

Francesca said nothing. She didn't care two farthings about Percival's inspiration, but she did care that Georgina never felt poor or went hungry.

"You will always be welcome in my home, as long as Georgina lives here," Ellen said, confirming their tenuous peace. "I swear it to you."

Francesca just nodded. It wasn't what she had wanted, what she had worked so hard and so long to achieve, but it was a fair solution. Georgina had a family who loved her, with siblings and a mother she had known most of her life. And now she had her aunt back as well, to dote upon her and visit her and ensure that she never forgot her natural mother, who had loved her every bit as much as she and Ellen did. Francesca shoved the remaining bit of loneliness and heartbreak that Georgina hadn't wanted to live with her after all deep into the darkest corner of her heart. Hopefully in time it would wither and die, parched of the suspicion and enmity that had fed it.

She took her niece to Hyde Park, where they walked under the elms and along the Serpentine. Georgina chattered the whole while, entranced by a part of London she hadn't seen before, and Francesca felt happiness almost soaking into her skin, from the smiles of her niece and the warm sunlight of the afternoon. Georgina had the bright, outgoing personality of her mother, and Francesca was entranced. In just six months her niece had changed from a child into a growing young lady, with unexpected humor and keen observations. She still had a child's knack for touching on the one subject Francesca didn't want to contemplate, though.

"That gentleman who came with you," Georgina said abruptly. "Are you going to marry him?"

Francesca almost tripped and fell over her own feet. "Oh, dear," she said with a shaky laugh. "Why would you ask that?"

Georgina gave her a guileless look. "Because you're not married. And he called you 'dearest.'"

"Adults may call each other 'dearest' and not be married."

"I know, but he put his arm around you."

It took Francesca a moment to regain her voice. Here in the park, far away from Edward and basking in the delight of Georgina's company, she should have been able to keep her composure. Apparently not. Georgina's words brought back every moment of her last conversation with Edward, and even worse, all of Alconbury's

words this morning as well. She closed her eyes for
a second and could almost feel the solid, comforting
weight of Edward's arm around her, when she had suffered that cruelest shock in Ellen Haywood's house and
heard Georgina declare she didn't want to leave. And
then he had let her sob all over his shoulder as he took
her home, where he made love to her and told her she
belonged in his life and in his home. But he didn't love
her, at least not enough to say it aloud, not even when
she demanded to know why he'd had her investigated.
Surely if he loved her, he would have said it . . .

"He was being kind," she said to Georgina's question.
"It doesn't mean he wants to marry me."

She cocked her head and thought. "Might it? He
looked very concerned for you."

"It doesn't mean he wants to marry me, Georgina,"
Francesa repeated in a voice of warning.

"All right." The girl was quiet a moment, then blurted
out, "Do you want him to?"

Francesca stopped short. Perhaps it did come down
to that. Perhaps Alconbury was right. She of all people
knew Edward didn't wear his feelings on his sleeve,
as she did, or said what he thought, damn the consequences . . . as she did. She had fallen in love with him
as he was, and should have known better than to expect
him to change, let alone so abruptly. She'd been so
shocked and hurt, she left before he could explain, and
then told him not to come see her. Perhaps she should
have been more temperate. Perhaps her offended feelings were as much to blame as anything Edward had
done. "Perhaps," she said softly.

Georgina beamed. "I thought so!" Her mind was

now apparently at ease; she pointed across the green and squealed. "Look, Aunt Franny! May we go see the boats?"

Francesca smiled and nodded. Yes, they could go see the model boats being sailed along the canal. And while Georgina exclaimed in delight, Francesca thought about how she should make Edward see that not only were they perfect for each other, he definitely should marry her. Or at least want to.

Francesca rapped the knocker of Durham House and stepped back to wait, casting a surreptitious glance up at the dark windows. The house, like the rest of Berkeley Square, was quiet this evening. Most of her trips to this house hadn't ended well. Inside her gloves her palms were damp, and she gripped her reticule as if she would strangle it. If this visit didn't go better than the last one, it would probably be her last.

Blackbridge opened the door. "Come in, madam," he said, bowing as if she were still a welcome guest.

She stepped into the hall. There was only a pair of lamps lit, and it was almost as dark inside as it was outside. "Is Lord Edward in?" She wondered if he would tell her honestly, or if Edward had instructed his servants to turn her away with polite lies.

"He did not tell me, madam," said the butler, "but I expect you would not be deterred by it in any event."

She smiled. "No." Behind her back, she waved at Mr. Hotchkiss, sending him home. Not having a carriage waiting at the door could only cause her to stay longer, and with any luck, she might not need her carriage again tonight.

She followed Blackbridge through the silent, unfamiliar corridors. When the butler tapped at a door and a moment later opened it, light poured out. Waiting in the shadows behind the butler, Francesca almost held her breath as she waited for his voice.

"Yes, what is it?" He sounded weary, and her heart gave a little throb.

The butler filled the doorway. "Lady Gordon is here, my lord."

For a moment there was silence. Francesca was just steeling herself to push past Blackbridge into the room, determined to have her say whether Edward wanted to hear it or not, when the butler leaped aside and Edward himself strode into the hall, in such a rush he nearly ran right into her.

"Francesca." His eyes roamed worriedly over her face. "Are you well?"

She nodded. "May I come in?"

"Ah—of course. Please." He put out his hand and ushered her into the room, which turned out to be the study. Lamplight gleamed on mahogany furniture, especially the enormous carved desk covered with stacks of papers and books. The windows reflected the fire crackling in the hearth. Bookshelves held an impressive collection of handsomely bound volumes, and above the fireplace was mounted a collection of battered but polished armor. The room smelled of old leather and mellow pipe smoke and, very faintly, of Edward. Or perhaps he smelled of the room, the power and wealth and prestige held by the men who had worked here. Regardless, it was *his* scent, and she loved it.

The door clicked softly behind them as Blackbridge

pulled it, bowing discreetly out of the room. Francesca
wet her lips. "I apologize for calling so late."

"No—no, I am glad you came." He seemed about to
say something else, but caught himself. "Won't you sit
down?"

She sat on the sofa, and he pulled a leather armchair
around to face her. The whole time, he watched her
face keenly, as if wary of what she would say or do.
Wary, but perhaps hopeful. She straightened her spine
and looked away for a moment, gathering her thoughts
and trying not to react to his nearness as she always did.
Her gaze fell on a large satchel sitting open on the desk,
and she realized he was packing.

"Are you leaving?" she blurted out.

He blinked. "Ah—yes. I suppose I am." He hesitated,
and again she sensed he was waiting for her. "There's
nothing for me in London."

"Your brother's petition," she exclaimed in astonishment. How unlike Edward to abandon it now!

He lifted one shoulder. "Charlie should take responsibility for it. It's his title, not mine. I told him last night
he must exert himself or accept the loss."

"But you," she said in wonder. "You would also lose
all you hold dear . . ."

"I was at peace with the possibility of losing
Durham," he said softly. "When I lost you, I lost what
I hold most dear."

She had to pinch up her mouth. "Who told you I was
lost?"

His eyes brightened, but his grave expression didn't.
"You left. And you refused to see me."

"I said I wasn't ready to see you. I needed some time

to do my research." He looked at her blankly. Francesca opened her reticule and pulled out the papers folded within. "I wanted to know what I was getting into. It seemed wise, after all."

Edward looked faintly puzzled, but he sat back. Francesca cleared her throat and began to read the first page. " 'The late Duke of Durham was a wild young man who only settled down when he inherited the title at the age of forty and was suddenly pressed to have an heir.' " She looked up in expectation.

"True," said Edward slowly.

" 'He was known to be a hard, driven man, ruthless in pressing the advantages of his wealth and position. His duchess died after providing him with three sons, whom he raised to be just like him.' "

"None of us are just like him. And he was a kind and generous man to his family." Edward cleared his throat. "Otherwise it is true."

" 'Or rather, that was his bigamist second wife, rather than his duchess. The duke was secretly married in his wild youth, although no one has seen the woman in many years. Who is to say how the duke might have disposed of an inconvenient, unwanted first wife? And now his distant cousin Augustus stands on the precipice of inheriting the vast Durham estate and title, since the Durham sons are apparently only natural children with no claim at all to their father's properties.' "

"Embroidery and exaggeration," he said through thin lips.

" 'The eldest Durham son, Lord Gresham, is a rake of the lowest order. He has fought no less than eight duels, gambles constantly, drinks to excess, consorts with known reprobates and scoundrels, has cuckolded half of Parliament, is two hundred thousand pounds in debt, and broke his leg in a tavern brawl,' " she read on.

Edward's brows knit. "His debts aren't one tenth that size, to my knowledge. I believe he broke his leg falling down the stairs while drunk, and eight duels is rather more energetic than the brother I know. But the rest sounds like Charlie."

" 'The youngest son is a military officer who has been reprimanded for dangerous behavior as often as he's been commended for bravery. Just like his elder brother, he is known as a great favorite of the ladies, particularly his colonel's much younger wife.' "

"Gerard is too clever to have an affair with his superior officer's wife," Edward replied. "I hope." He leaned back in his chair and looked more at ease, as if he realized what she was up to.

Francesca turned the page and went on. " 'The middle brother is a cold and cunning man,' " she read, forcing her voice to remain steady. " 'He's ruthless in business and in love. It is rumored he broke off his engagement to Lady Louisa Halston upon discovering her father's desperate financial straits, abandoning the fair lady in her hour of need.' " Edward scowled and drew breath, but Francesca held up one finger. " 'It is also rumored Lady Louisa was instructed by her father to win Lord Edward's heart and thereby secure his family's fortune to her family's, and when the whispers of the Durham Dilemma reached town, she jilted him for the more financially sound Marquis of Calverton. Lord Edward has reputedly taken up with low class women as a result, but as he is about to lose his fortune and rank, this is

no doubt merely a portent of his future companions.' "
Edward muttered something under his breath, and again
Francesca motioned him to be silent. " 'It is also rumored that Lady Francesca Gordon schemed to disrupt
the engagement, and seized on the Durham rumors as
a chance to ply her wiles on Lord Edward, ruining the
Halstons' hopes and breaking Lady Louisa's heart, all
for the chance of winning herself a husband of higher
rank—' "

"Where the devil did you hear that rubbish?" Edward
snapped. His face had grown darker and darker as she
spoke.

"From Gregory Sloan's gossip rag," she said. "Some
from the *Register à la Mode*, and some from the *Scandalous Society* paper. I read them all."

"Lies."

She looked down at her papers. "Some of it's wildly
inconsistent as well. The stories about your brother are
incredible; he must be quite a man. It was far harder to
find anything about you."

"You wanted to know about me," he said slowly. He
had inched forward on his chair and was watching her
with an intensity that made her skin tighten and prickle.

"Yes," she said, holding her head high and meeting
his gaze directly. "I didn't have the time to hire an investigator, so made do."

His mouth twitched. "I would have told you anything
you wished to know."

"Would you have told me about . . ." She consulted
the paper again. "About the low class woman you are
seeing?"

"I'm not sure what I can say about her that you don't already know."

Francesca glanced at him warily. His expression was serene, but his eyes were glowing.

"In fact," he said, "there is only one vitally important thing you must know about her. She has been the salvation of me."

"Apparently she's the best you can hope for, in your new life as a penniless outcast."

His mouth curled. "She has always been the best I can hope for, since the moment I met her." Francesca raised her eyebrows in astonishment. Edward reached out and took her hand, gently and gingerly, as if afraid she would pull away. "I would rather lose everything associated with Durham, and have you, than keep Durham and never have you."

"You don't mean that," she said, though her heart almost burst to hear him say it.

He slid off his chair onto one knee. "For all my life, Durham was everything to me. Running it made my father proud of me, as his son and as a man. Neither of my brothers cared for it as I did. I never pursued the interests they did because I was consumed with crops and tenants and investments. My marriage to Louisa would have been the same; I was well aware that my family fortune would save the Halstons from any hardship and their properties from neglect and decay, and Louisa never would have distracted me from the ledgers."

"You loved her."

"Because I hadn't met you." He brushed his lips over her knuckles before pressing her wrist to his cheek, and a deep sigh shuddered through his body, as if a great tension had been released. Francesca felt it, too. Inside her shoes her toes uncurled, and when Edward turned her hand over to kiss the tender skin of her palm, she bit her lip to keep from throwing herself into his arms right then. "I never could have loved her the way I love you."

A loud sniffle escaped her. "You might have said that last night . . ."

"I had just been caught acting like an arrogant, over-bearing ass, and it looked very bad. I really had no idea what to say."

She laid her hand on his, loving the way his eyes half closed with pleasure at her touch. "In the future, there's no reason to wait to say it," she whispered. "For I love you too well to stay angry for long, especially when you kiss me."

He released her hand and cradled his fingers reverently around her head, stroking her jaw with his thumbs. "Then let me learn from my mistake." He kissed her, and Francesca almost swooned on the spot from the heady intoxication of it. He lifted his head and waited until she forced open her eyes. "I love you," he murmured. "Will you marry me?"

"Yes," she breathed, and leaned forward, pressing her lips to his again.

"Even if I'm to be a penniless outcast?" he asked between kisses.

"Especially if you're a penniless outcast." She wound her arms around his neck. "I shall support you as best I can."

"I am already anticipating it with pleasure." He

tugged her closer, pressing light, hot kisses down the slope of her throat.

Francesca let her head fall back as she sighed with pleasure, her body melting under his touch. "I wished you had come to me today . . ."

He paused. "You told me not to come."

"I know," she said, "but I wanted you anyway. I wished you had broken down my door and made love to me until I forgot I was angry with you."

A flicker of unease darkened his eyes. "I'm not that sort of man, Francesca."

"I know—that's why I came to you, because I *am* that sort of woman." She smiled coyly as desire flared in his face. "I've come to make love to you until you cannot keep from falling at my feet, and I forget we ever argued."

"I knew there were many reasons why I love you," he murmured. "So very, very many . . ."

"The only thing I must hold against you is sending Alconbury in your place." She put on a stern expression. "He was most put out with you for waking him so early."

"I knew his affection for you would outweigh any annoyance at me."

"What if he had begged me to marry him again?"

All expression vanished from his face. "Did he?"

"No, he told me you must be desperately in love with me to send him to comfort me."

"Well." Edward lowered his eyes and looked almost penitent for a moment. "I suppose it occurred to me that, seeing him, you might realize how much you preferred me to him . . ."

She threaded her fingers through his hair and

tugged. "As if I hadn't realized that some time ago!" He looked up from under his brows and flashed a hint of his wicked, sensual smile. Francesca laughed. "And where precisely were you going, that you must pack? Were you going to make me chase you all the way to Sussex?"

"Francesca, I was packing up everything about Durham that Charlie will need to pursue his claim. That satchel is going to him. I spoke in all honesty when I told him he must do it, or resign himself to losing the dukedom."

Her brow knit as he lowered his head to kiss her shoulder again. "You said you were leaving . . . there was nothing in London for you now . . ."

"Well . . . unless you had come to seduce me again . . ." He traced one finger over the swell of her bosom. "What should I have done?"

"This." Her body arched instinctively into his touch.

He surprised her by laying his head on her shoulder, his hands going still. "Thank you," he breathed.

She pressed her lips to his temple. "For what?"

"For coming back to me. For giving me another chance to explain." He sighed. "For forgiving me for being so bloody stupid."

"Then I must thank you for being so patient," she replied softly. "For keeping your temper when I lost mine." She craned her neck to see his face. "It's my greatest fault—I cannot promise it will never happen again."

"I love you, temper and all." He kissed her.

"And I love you, empty pockets and all."

"Well." Edward looked a little abashed. "I shan't be

utterly penniless. I do have a modest inheritance, some thirty thousand pounds—"

"Thirty thousand—" Francesca gaped at him. "It's a fortune! You made me think you wouldn't have two farthings!"

He laughed. "You would have taken me, even without two farthings?"

"Of course! But—you wretch!" She smacked his arm. "I thought we should have to give up the carriage, and economize on the housekeeping . . . burn tallow candles and dine on mutton . . ."

"I don't care for them, but since I shall be dependent on you, I must submit to your decision."

"Stop!" She laughed as he nestled his head on her shoulder again. "Dependent! You silly man; your income will still be three times mine, if you only put it all in the five percents."

"Francesca." Edward raised his head and gave her a look. "It's less than one year of Durham's income. It's one third of my mother's dower, divided among me and my brothers, as she wished and my father agreed."

"Well." She tried to look irked. "I shall be marrying very well indeed, although you must feel it a poor bargain."

"My darling," he said, "it is the very best bargain I have ever struck."

Chapter 27

It was a very small, quiet wedding. Georgina was there, bright-eyed and delighted to attend her aunt in a new pink dress. Ellen Haywood lingered at the back, as if uncertain of her welcome, but Francesca greeted her with a smile. It still hurt Francesca to see Georgina so affectionate with Ellen, but at least she was able to bask in her own share of Georgina's attention and love now.

Alconbury refused to come. He replied to her invitation that he had pressing family business; Francesca wasn't sure if it was true, and Sally Ludlow claimed ignorance of the matter. Sally was there with her husband, a bit awed by Durham House but increasingly cordial to Edward as he spoke with them at length. She whispered to Francesca later that he was indeed as charming as Francesca had always said, and if he loved her, who was she to protest?

Francesca also met some of Edward's family. She was utterly charmed by his uncle and aunt, the Earl and Countess of Dowling, a handsome elderly couple. Lady Dowling welcomed her very warmly to the family. She made Francesca promise to call on her for tea within the week, and scolded Edward for not bringing Francesca to her already.

"You and your brother," the countess said with a re- proving look at him. "I should box your ears for the way you've gone about marriage."

Edward smiled. "I've apologized twice, Aunt. But whatever Charlie's done, you cannot blame me."

"I didn't mean Charlie," murmured the countess.

"Gerard?" Edward frowned. "What's Gerard done about marriage? He left town weeks ago and hasn't sent so much as a word."

"His Grace, the Duke of Durham." Blackbridge's voice rang through the room before Lady Dowling could reply.

Everyone turned to look. The duke seemed to know it and paused in the doorway, looking rakish and elegant and very dangerous. Even Sally Ludlow, happily mar- ried to Mr. Ludlow for ten years, stopped and stared in admiration as His Grace prowled through the room like a panther, sleek and dark, despite the cane he leaned on.

Edward seemed to find him amusing. "How good of you to come, Charlie," he said to his brother. "This is my wife, Francesca. Darling, my elder brother."

"How good of you to invite me, Ned," drawled the duke. He fixed his dark gaze on Francesca and bowed over her hand. "I've waited far too long to make this lady's acquaintance."

"But I've heard so much about you, Your Grace," said Francesca as she sank into a curtsey.

Durham paused, his thumb stroking the back of her hand as he studied her through narrow eyes. "All of it wicked and scandalous, I hope."

She dipped her chin and smiled. "Very much so, Your Grace."

Slowly he smiled back. "Excellent. Welcome to the family, my dear. You must call me Durham."

"Ah," said Edward. "I'm glad to hear that at last."

The duke shot an annoyed glance at him. "Yes, damn it, you would be."

Edward just smiled and steered Francesca away. "It's about time he took an interest in the title."

"But you aren't planning to abandon it, either." She, too, kept her voice low. No matter what he said about being at peace with the prospect of losing Durham, Francesca knew he cared too deeply for his heritage to give it up without a fight.

"Of course not. But Charlie doesn't need to know that. It will do him good to work for it."

She choked back a laugh, and he winked at her. Francesca remembered how she had thought him cold and colorless, once upon a time, and shook her head. How utterly, wonderfully wrong she had been. He wasn't like her; rather, he complemented her in every way. His strengths supported her weaknesses, and—she hoped—her strengths would do the same for him. She certainly hadn't expected to find love with him, and was constantly being taken off-guard by how strong the feeling was.

Blackbridge approached, clearing his throat politely. He held out a rather battered letter. "A letter, sir, just arrived."

Edward raised one eyebrow as he took it and read the direction. Francesca saw the word *Imperative* scrawled on the front. He nodded in dismissal to the butler and broke the seal. For a moment he read in silence, then frowned.

"Good Lord," he said under his breath.

"What's wrong?" She laid her hand on his arm in concern.

"My brother Gerard," he said, still reading. He put his hand over hers, rubbing his thumb over the new ring on her finger. "He's gone and gotten himself into quite a mess, it seems."

"Do you have to go to him?" She shifted her weight, leaning lightly against his side.

Edward tensed, then relaxed. He glanced up and caught his brother's eye. "From Gerard," he said, holding up the letter.

The duke strolled back to them. "Have we a murderer in the family?"

Edward held it out. "It's for you."

Durham eyed it as if the letter were a dead fish. "Surely not."

"Read it."

Reluctantly, Durham took it. His bored, languid expression dropped away as he read, until he looked like quite a different person. "What the devil?"

"You should attend to it at once," Edward replied. "He needs help."

"Good God." His brother's eyes narrowed at him. "He wrote to you!"

"I can't go. I'm a newly married man." Edward smiled down at Francesca. "I have a wedding trip to plan." The duke seemed shocked speechless. "Godspeed, and good luck, Charlie," Edward told him gravely. Then he took his bride by the hand and led everyone into the dining room for the lavish wedding breakfast.

Avon Books is proud to support the Ovarian Cancer National Alliance.

September is National Ovarian Cancer Awareness month, and Avon Books is urging our authors and readers to learn about the symptoms of ovarian cancer, and to help spread the "**K.I.S.S. and Teal**" message to friends and family.

Ovarian cancer was long thought to be a silent killer, but now we know it isn't silent at all. The Ovarian Cancer National Alliance works to spread a life-affirming message that this disease doesn't have to be fatal if women **K**now the **I**mportant **S**igns and **S**ymptoms.

Avon Books has made an initial donation of $25,000 to the Alliance. And—with your help—Avon Books has also committed to donating 25¢ from the sale of each book, physical and e-book, in the "K.I.S.S. and Teal" promotion between 8/30/2011 and 2/28/2012, up to an additional $25,000 toward programs that support ovarian cancer patients and their families.

So, help us spread the word and reach our goal of **$50,000**, which will benefit all the women in our lives.

Log on to ***www.kissandteal.com*** to learn how you can further help the cause and donate.

KT1 0911

A portion of the sales from each of these September 2011 titles will be donated to the

Ovarian Cancer National Alliance:

Viscount Breckenridge to the Rescue
Stephanie Laurens

The Seduction of Scandal
Cathy Maxwell

The Deed
Lynsay Sands

A Night to Surrender
Tessa Dare

In the Arms of a Marquess
Katharine Ashe

One Night in London
Caroline Linden

Star Crossed Seduction
Jenny Brown

AVON

Ovarian Cancer
National Alliance
We work to save women's lives

An imprint of HarperCollins*Publishers*

www.avonromance.com   *www.ovariancancer.org*

KT2 0911

This September, the Ovarian Cancer National Alliance and Avon Books urge you to K.I.S.S. and Teal:

Know the Important Signs and Symptoms

Ovarian cancer is the deadliest gynecologic cancer and a leading cause of cancer deaths for women.

There is no early detection test, but women with the disease have the following symptoms:

- **Bloating**
- **Pelvic and abdominal pain**
- **Difficulty eating or feeling full quickly**
- **Urinary symptoms (urgency or frequency)**

Learn the symptoms and tell other women about them!

Log on to *www.kissandteal.com* for a downloadable teal ribbon—teal is the color for ovarian cancer awareness.

The Ovarian Cancer National Alliance is the foremost advocate for women with ovarian cancer in the United States.

Learn more at www.ovariancancer.org

KT3 0911

Next month, don't miss these exciting new love stories only from Avon Books

The Norse King's Daughter by Sandra Hill

When Princess Drifa discovers that the only reason Sidroc Guntersson has been giving her such lusty attention is because he needs a wife to win his inheritance, she hits him with a pot and leaves him for dead. Five years later, she needs his protection—but the handsome warrior finds erotic revenge more enticing. Will Drifa be able to shirk his temptations, or give in to his charms yet again?

In Total Surrender by Anne Mallory

Feared and revered by London society, Andreas Merrick is king of the city's underworld. Unintimidated by his reputation, the headstrong Phoebe Pace is only interested in his help to find her brother. But working so closely with Andreas has set off an intense and unexpected passion. Could falling in love with him cause her to risk it all?

Every Scandalous Secret by Gayle Callen

When Leo Wade, a rakish gamer, spots a woman he's certain was the model for a shockingly immodest painting, he's hell-bent on proving that it's her. Immune to his charms, however, Susanna Leland can't be bothered with this cat-and-mouse game. But when his temptation becomes too much to bear, Susanna learns that the price of trust could be worth every scandalous secret.

What a Duke Wants by Lavinia Kent

Trying to escape the secrets of her past, Isabella Masters is completely captivated when she finds herself in a passionate lip-lock with the handsome Mark Smythe—only to discover he's a Duke! When the two are caught together, scandal threatens to break them apart. Unable to walk away from love, only one possibility exists. Is it worth it?